"I really want to kiss you right now."

Her gaze dipped to his mouth. If he wanted to kiss her, she needed to kiss him. She slid her hand up his shoulder to the back of his neck and pulled him in. She stared into his eyes and saw a hunger there that matched her own. She'd never felt this overwhelming urge to be close to someone, let alone a man, but something about Rory drew her in and made her want to stay.

"Did you change your mind, or are you just trying to kill me?"

His deep voice resonated through her. She pressed her lips to his, thinking it just a test. A way to see if they fit, connected on a deeper level than the pull she already felt toward him.

The second her lips touched his, fire lit through her system. She pulled back surprised that a simple thing could spark such deep and overwhelming need. The same fire she felt flashed in his golden-green eyes.

"Once wasn't enough." This time, Rory pulled her back and kissed her, wrapping her in his strong arms.

By Jennifer Ryan

Montana Men Series
STONE COLD COWBOY
HER LUCKY COWBOY
WHEN IT'S RIGHT
AT WOLF RANCH

The McBride Series
DYLAN'S REDEMPTION
FALLING FOR OWEN
THE RETURN OF BRODY MCBRIDE

The Hunted Series
EVERYTHING SHE WANTED
CHASING MORGAN
THE RIGHT BRIDE
LUCKY LIKE US
SAVED BY THE RANCHER

Short Stories
CAN'T WAIT
(appears in ALL I WANT FOR CHRISTMAS IS A COWBOY)
WAITING FOR YOU
(appears in CONFESSIONS OF A SECRET ADMIRER)

STONE COLD COWBOY

A MONTANA MEN NOVEL

JENNIFER RYAN

AVONBOOKS

An Imprint of HarperCollins*Publishers*

AVON BOOKS
An Imprint of HarperCollins*Publishers*
195 Broadway
New York, New York 10007

First Avon Books mass market printing: March 2016

Avon Trademark Reg. U.S. Pat. Off. and in Other Countries, Marca Registrada, Hecho en U.S.A.
Avon, Avon Books, and the Avon logo are trademarks of HarperCollins Publishers.
HarperCollins® is a registered trademark of HarperCollins Publishers.

Printed in the U.S.A.

10 9 8 7 6 5 4 3 2 1

For the fans, especially Diana Davidson, Lori Perrone-Frazier, Ruth Becht, and Pamela Shagena.

For my family, who never waiver in their encouragement, enthusiasm, and happiness for me despite the long days I spend with my imaginary friends. As much as I adore them, I love you all more.

Sometimes you have to let go to find something worth holding on to.

STONE COLD COWBOY

CHAPTER 1

Sadie crested the rolling hill and spotted her target: her missing horses and a herd of cattle that didn't belong to her reckless brother. She didn't waste a hope he was saving them from some predator. Not with two of his miscreant cohorts right beside him pushing the mooing and bawling animals farther along the valley. Leave it to her brother to make trouble with no regard for the consequences. If he got caught rustling cattle, he'd expect her to get him out of it. She'd been saving his butt since he hit a rebellious stage at thirteen that turned into his way of life, escalating from pranks to petty theft and drug dealing. What happened to the sweet boy who loved to swing the highest at the playground? The one who cried at their mother's funeral and brushed his hand over Sadie's hair that same night while they cried themselves to sleep on their mother's side of the bed? At twenty-one Connor had changed from a sensitive boy into nothing short of a hoodlum numbed by drugs, with no regard for anyone else. One day she feared he'd end up in jail for the rest of his life . . . or dead.

If whoever owned those cattle didn't kill him, she might.

A soft pat on the neck and a nudge with her heels sent her horse Sugar down the hill in a trot. Sadie loved to ride, but chasing after her brother took the pleasure right out of it. The cold wind, scented with pine, grass, and rain from the storm last night that had left the ground muddy, whipped her hair out behind her and burned her cheeks. Her lips dried and cracked in the bitter cold.

Her horse's fast approach startled several cattle. They broke off from the herd and scattered. She rode straight up the middle and split the herd in two, hoping to discourage the animals from following the rider up front and the two flanking them. Her brother spotted her and reined his horse around to meet hers. She pulled up short and stopped beside him, glaring at his ruddy face, red from the cold. His intense gaze collided with hers. His pupils were the size of saucers. High. Irritated he'd been caught, he narrowed his eyes on her.

"What the hell do you think you're doing?"

Her lips drew into a grim line. "Saving your ass from making another mistake."

"Get out of here before you get hurt." Connor scanned the area, avoiding looking at the two guys with him, who closed in on them. "You have to go now."

Sadie sighed out her frustration. The cows had stopped walking down the valley and milled around them, chomping at the new grass just beginning to grow after the last of the snow melted. The cold temps remained even as spring pushed in to take winter's place. She stared at the poor, tired animals. Her brother and his buddies had pushed them hard and brought them a long way. One steer turned, and she caught a glimpse of the brand on his hide.

She sucked in a surprised breath. "These are Kendrick cattle. Are you crazy? Those guys will hunt you down and beat the living shit out of you. If Rory comes after you, you'll wish you were never born."

She'd gone to school with Colt Kendrick, but didn't really know him. The last time she saw him, he'd been sitting around a table with his two older brothers at the bar. She'd gone to drag her brother home after the bartender called to let her know Connor was playing pool and looking for a fight. He'd nearly gotten one when he stumbled into Colt and dumped beer down his front. Sadie stepped in just in time, blocking her brother from the punch Colt threw and almost landed straight in her face, until Rory grasped his brother's wrist and stopped his swing inches from her nose. When her brother tried to go after Colt, she'd tried to hold him off, but he got around her. Rory grabbed Connor by the shirt and held him off the ground in front of him like he didn't weigh more than a puppy. He'd looked her brother in the eyes and shook him hard to get his attention. He didn't speak. Didn't have to. The ominous look in his eyes made her brother quake in his boots. Rory set her brother down with a thud, and Connor ran for the door. Sadie chased after him, but not before she turned back and caught the feral look in Rory's eyes. The same kind of look she'd seen weeks earlier when she plowed into Rory's big, solid body in the feed store. The man was hard and unyielding, physically and mentally. You did not go up against a Kendrick, and especially him. Her stupid brother got off free and clear that time.

Connor scratched at a scab on his chin. "If you keep

your fucking mouth shut and get lost, they'll never know."

"You don't think they're going to know an entire herd of cattle is missing? You've lost your mind, little brother."

He puffed out his thin chest, his bony shoulders going back. "I'm not little. I can take care of myself," he whined like the child he acted like most of the time.

"You have yet to prove that in any capacity. If it weren't for me, you'd have been locked up in juvy at fourteen. All these years later, you're not proving to be any smarter than that punk kid who cried and begged me to save him. You promised me on our mother's grave you'd do better, you'd quit drinking and doing drugs. But you didn't keep that promise to me, or her."

"I warned you." The words belied the sad, resigned look that came into his eyes.

A split second later, she had the blink of an eye to understand what he meant. A fist slammed into her face, sending her off her horse and into the mud, grass, and darkness.

"Stop touching her. Let's just go and get the damn cattle to the trailers before we get caught." Connor stared down at her, lying on the ground practically naked.

What the hell? Her gaze locked on the man crouched beside her, his hand gripped around her upper arm, keeping her from scrambling away. Fear tore through her body. The cold bit into her skin and froze her bones. She clamped her aching jaw down tight to keep her teeth from chattering. She pushed up to sitting, her knees drawn up, and covered herself with her hands. Her cheeks heated with embarrassment. She scanned the area for her missing coat, jeans, and shirt. At least the asshole hadn't gotten her out of her panties and bra; still, it wasn't enough coverage to make her feel safe, or keep her warm.

"Give me back my clothes." Her sharp words didn't hide the fear shaking her voice.

"Shut up, or I'll clock you again."

Scott and Tony, Connor's so-called friends, stood over her smoking cigarettes. The three of them collectively added up to one brain. None of them came up with a good idea, but they sure could turn a bad one worse one-upping one another. Now that she was awake, their gazes shot from her breasts to her face, then off to the scattered clouds overhead.

Connor pushed away the guy beside her, someone she didn't know. "You don't need to strip her. You fucking lay another hand on her and I'll kill you."

She appreciated her brother's bravado, but the big dude with long, greasy dark hair; devil tat on his neck; and the wicked knife in his hand he whipped out from behind him could probably kill her brother with a look from his cold eyes. Her throbbing jaw attested to the guy's powerful right hook. If he'd hit a woman, no telling what he'd do to her brother.

The devil dude, as she immediately thought of him, stood and took a menacing step closer to her brother. "Your sister has one hot body. She'd look damn good in lace." He raked his gaze over her figure, grimacing at her cotton bra and panties. "I say we teach her a lesson about butting into my business." The devil dude smacked Scott on the shoulder, trying to get his agreement.

Scott and Tony continued to look uncomfortable, shaking their heads and toeing at the dirt, avoiding looking the devil dude right in the eye. They probably needed another hit of whatever they were on. Despite the cold, sweat broke out on their faces. Her brother didn't look much better.

"She's not going to say anything. The last thing she wants to do is get me in trouble." The assurance her brother tried to put into his words fell short, making him sound more like a sniveling child.

"You do that all on your own," she snapped, glaring at all of them. She stood up, realizing too late she didn't quite have her head on straight yet. Dizzy, she stumbled a step, then caught herself. She spotted her clothes tossed a few feet away and rushed toward them, hoping to grab them, run to her horse, and get the hell out of there before things got worse. She definitely didn't want to get hit again. The fear building in her gut that the devil dude might make good on his ominous threats, both spoken and unspoken, made bile rise to the back of her throat. She needed to get away now, before it was too late.

She wrapped her arms around herself, warding off another round of shivers, not all of which resulted from the cold, but the bone-deep fear they might not let her go.

"Where do you think you're going?" The devil dude grabbed her arm and spun her around. She took him by surprise, stepping in close and kneeing him in the nuts. He fell to his knees, his hands on his balls, the knife sticking out toward her.

"Sadie, no," her brother shouted.

"I'll make you regret that, bitch." The devil dude lunged for her.

She expected him to grab her, but she couldn't get out of the way fast enough. His hands clamped on to her shoulders. The knife handle dug into her arm, but fear for her life made her act. She brought her arms up and broke his hold. Surprise showed in his eyes, but they narrowed with determination. He grabbed her wrist and yanked her forward. She plowed into his chest with a thump. His cold leather jacket chilled her skin even more. He wrapped his arms around her back, squeezing her close. She head-butted him, hitting him more on the chin than nose than she'd like. He shoved her back to the ground and swiped the back of his hand over his face. Slumped in the dirt and grass, she stared up at him, trying to clear the haze from her aching head and vision, wishing she'd broken his nose.

She tried to think fast, but the guy came after her again, falling to his knees, straddling her hips. His heavy weight pushed her butt into the soft earth, and a jagged rock dug into her spine. He pressed the knife to her neck. The menacing smile on his face reinforced the dangerous look in his eyes. He'd do it. He'd kill her and not think twice about it.

Cold fear washed through her, stealing her every thought and breath. Her heart slammed into her ribs and stopped for a brief second. Her whole world halted as she stared up into eyes that held nothing but death.

"Kill her and I won't make any more meth," her brother yelled.

Startled by her brother's admission, Sadie glanced at Connor, caught the apologetic look, then stared back up into the devil dude's flat eyes.

"You'll cook, or you're dead. You owe me more than the price of those cattle."

"If I'm dead you get nothing. Don't kill her."

The devil dude smiled. It frightened her more than anything he'd done so far.

"Okay. I won't kill her."

The easy acquiescence didn't ease her mind.

"Grab that wire and rope from my saddle," he ordered Scott.

"We should get out of here. Those Kendricks come for their herd and we're dead." Scott tried to talk reason with the irrational devil dude.

"Get it now." The devil dude bit out the words. Scott jumped to do his bidding, beaten without ever really getting in the fight to save her.

The devil dude clamped his hand on her aching jaw and shook her face. "No one fucks with me. If they do, they get what's coming. You're going to get your due."

Sadie wanted to run, but he had her on the ground, that damn knife at her neck, pressed so hard to her skin she felt a trickle of blood run down her throat where he cut her. His gaze fell on the blood. The slow smile that spread across his face disturbed her, but not as much as the lust that filled his dark eyes.

Scott dropped the coiled barbed wire and rope next to her. Connor stood off to the side, pacing, biting at his thumb, his eyes filled with worry, but he didn't come to her rescue, just kept gnawing on his already raw skin.

"This is going to hurt, bitch." The menacing words held a note of anticipation and enthusiasm that soured her stomach.

He used his grip on her face to hold her down. He slid the knife into the sheath at his back, pulled a pair of wire cutters from his back pocket, and snipped a long length of wire from the coil. He held it up in front of her, set the tool down, took both her hands, and pulled them up in front of him. She bucked her hips and tried to pull free, but nothing worked to dislodge the big man from her body.

"Let me go, asshole." She tried to put as much bravado in her voice as she could conjure to hide her fear, but the tremble in her voice gave her away.

"You asked for it."

He wrapped the wire around her wrists and in between. The harder she tried to pull free, the tighter he wound.

Panic rose in her chest, making it difficult to take a deep breath. Her chest heaved in and out. In another minute, she'd be hyperventilating. "Stop. Please. You're hurting me."

"Ah, music to my ears." The amusement in his eyes told her how much he enjoyed her fear and pain.

"You sadistic son of a bitch."

"Yes, I am." His eyes went bright with delight.

The barbs bit into her skin. Blood trickled down her arms from multiple punctures.

"Go get the horses while I finish here," he ordered her brother.

Tony and Scott scurried away without a word. The dread in their eyes when they snuck quick glances back told her how much they feared this man.

"Leave her. You taught her a lesson. Let's go," Connor pleaded, pacing back and forth not even five feet away.

"I thought letting her walk home in her underwear in the cold would have taught her a lesson about sticking her nose into things that don't concern her. But your sister had to go and fuck with me." The devil dude leaned down close and stared her in the eyes. "You kick me in the balls, bitch, I'll make you bleed." The whispered threat didn't lessen the ominous reality that he meant it. He turned back to her brother and yelled, "Go get the horses. Hers too. We're leaving."

Connor backed up several steps, then turned and walked away without sparing her a single look, let alone an apology for his cowardice. She expected it, but it still hurt, leaving a pit in her stomach and an ache that squeezed her chest tight. Tears threatened to spill from her eyes, but she blinked them away. Her brother had proven more times than she could count that he'd cover his own ass over anyone else's, including his own sister's.

Her heart ached worse than her face, jaw, and bloody wrists combined. How could he just leave her here? How could he turn his back on her like this and live with himself?

A wave of terror overtook her. Against her will and knowing it wouldn't change her brother's mind, she gave in to her growing fear and screamed, "Connor, help me."

The devil dude laughed. "He owes too much money to go against me and help you. You've got some guts trying to fight me, but here's the thing—unlike your brother, I handle my business and any witnesses. Now, I said I wouldn't kill you, but I never said I wouldn't let the cold do that for me."

The tears she'd kept at bay filled her eyes and spilled down the side of her face into her hair. She lost all her bravado and begged, "Let me go. I won't say anything. I just wanted to keep him out of trouble. That's all. Please, let me go. I'll walk home like you said. I won't tell anyone about this."

He cocked his head to the side and smirked, though it wasn't reassuring. "Nice try. I might have believed you, but then you had to go and take a shot at my nuts. Now I'm going to teach you a lesson."

He pulled the rope close and tied one end to the wire around her wrists. She tried to pull free and scramble away, but she only ended up hurting worse when he wrestled her into submission, her hands crushed under his punishing grasp. Once the rope was secure, he finally rose up and took his weight off her middle. Finally, she could breathe easier, but her breath stopped when he walked right over her head, yanked the rope, and dragged her over the mud and grass. She rolled to her stomach, pulled back on the ropes, squealing out in pain when the wire dug into her skin, and rushed up to her feet. Better to trot after him like a dog on a leash than get dragged over the ground.

"Please, let me go."

He didn't respond, just walked right up to a big tree. She pulled back, not wanting to get tied to the trunk, but he had other ominous ideas. He held the rope close to her by one hand and used the other to toss the other end of the rope up and over a high, thick limb. He pulled the slack tight, then pulled again until her toes barely touched the ground. She wiggled to get free, but it only hurt her wrists more. Fresh blood trailed down her arms. She kicked out her feet, trying to get him to let loose the rope. He anticipated her move, drew his knife again, and slashed at her legs in a wide arc, catching her across her left thigh and right knee. She yelled in pain and stopped struggling, stunned he'd cut her. The sting burned like fire.

"Keep it up. I like it when you bleed." The menacing

note of truth in his words sent a bolt of fear through the denial in her mind that he couldn't be serious. But he was.

Afraid that all her fighting would only lead to more pain, she hung there, trying to think of anything she could say to change his mind about leaving her strung up in the biting cold. Even now, her skin felt like ice. She wiggled her numb toes, hoping to restore circulation. Thanks to the wire around her wrists, she couldn't feel her hands.

He came toward her again, this time with his eyes on her breasts that were now at his eye level. He reached out to touch her. She pulled her knees up to her belly, planted her feet on his chest, and shoved him away. "Don't you dare touch me." The order didn't hold as much weight when she ended up swinging back and forth from her hands, grunting in pain as each movement made the wire bite deeper into her skin.

He moved forward again. She kicked at him again and again, her body swinging and twisting from the rope. She ignored the excruciating pain. Too soon she tired and swung back and forth, unable to pick up her legs and strike out at him again. Defeat tasted vile. She swallowed the sour taste, hoping she didn't disgrace herself more and vomit.

He smiled and laughed, planting a hand on her belly and pushing, sending her swinging yet again. He'd been taunting her, tiring her out so she couldn't fight him off anymore. She'd played right into his hands. She needed to be smart, think, find a way out of this despite the reality staring her in the face—she was well and truly screwed.

"If I had more time, and those assholes weren't

so fucking stupid and could finish this job on their own . . ." He left the rest unsaid. He didn't need to finish. The leering gaze he swept over her body said everything. Her mind conjured one gruesome thing after the next; all of them made her stomach pitch, bile rising up her throat.

After so many minutes holding her up, he struggled to hold the rope and tied off the end around the trunk of the tree, leaving her dangling in the wind. The devil dude grabbed the bundle of barbed wire and brought it back. He wound one end around the wire at her wrists to anchor it, then wrapped the rest around both her arms, down over her shoulders. The sharp edges dug into her skin like little bites of pain.

She couldn't help the tears anymore, or the pleading in her voice she hated. "No, please don't do this."

"I like it when you beg, but seeing you bleed gets me off." He rubbed his hand over his crotch and leered at her again.

She met his lust-filled gaze, unable to watch him stroke the bulge in his jeans, knowing at any second he could change his mind, dump her back on the ground, and torture her a whole other way. "Please. The cold is enough. I can't get free. You don't have to do this."

He cocked his head and grinned. "I don't have to. I want to."

He put the truth in his words to work and pulled the wire around her back and across her chest, once, twice, and over her breasts. To punish her even more for getting in her licks earlier, he pulled the wire on both sides of her tight, making the barbs pierce her thin bra and skin.

"No." She bit back another yelp when he pulled the wire even tighter.

"Uh, the trucks will be at the meeting place in an hour. We need to go if we're going to make it in time and before it gets dark," Tony said from behind the devil dude.

"I'll be right there. Gather up any strays and start pushing the herd down the valley again."

Tony left without another word and without bringing his gaze up from his toes.

The devil dude glared at her. "You've cost me a lot of time." He wound the wire around her hips, then around one thigh several times and across to go around the other. The wire bit into the knife wound, making it bleed even more. Tighter and tighter he bound her legs until he had her feet wrapped so tight her ankle bones ground against each other.

He tossed the rest of the wire to the ground at her feet. He pulled the knife out again and held it up in front of her. The waning sunlight glinted off the already bloody blade. Her heart stopped. She didn't dare breathe or take her gaze from the deadly weapon and the man who liked to use it.

He jabbed her in the gut with his fist and the air whooshed out of her. She tried to suck in a breath, but ended up coughing before she could refill her lungs. She prayed he didn't hit her again.

"If you somehow manage to get out of this, you say one word to anyone, I'll hunt you down and make this"—he pointed the knife up and down her bloody body—"feel like a hug compared to what I'll do to you next time."

"Please, let me down. You can't leave me here."

The sharp point of the knife dug into her side between two ribs, piercing her skin, but not sinking deep.

Damn, those shallow punctures hurt like hell. Exactly his intention. He pushed, sending her swinging and the knife slipping free. Lucky for her, he didn't hold the knife there for her to swing back into.

"Pray the cold gets you before the wolves." The devil dude lived up to his wicked tat with that parting shot.

"You can't leave me here," she screamed at his retreating back. "Help me! Connor, you can't leave me here," she bellowed. "Connor!"

She waited, hoping he'd do the right thing for once. For her. She'd saved him so many times. This time, she needed him.

The wind whipped up again, pushing against her back. Not a sound reached her. From her place on the hill and behind the cover of trees, she couldn't see the valley, the cows, or even her brother.

No one came.

He didn't come.

Tears spilled down her cheeks. She shook with the sobs wracking her body.

I'm going to die here.

Not one to give in easily, she wiggled, trying desperately to get free. Her toes barely touched the dirt. The more she moved, the more dirt she displaced, until she hung with no purchase on the ground. If he wanted to torture her, he'd picked the perfect way to do it. The more she moved, the worse things got. The wires bit into her skin, sending fresh dribbles of blood down her body. The cut on her side bled freely down her stomach, soaking her panties. She couldn't hold up her weight, so her body dragged her down, making her wrists and shoulders ache.

A branch snapped. Her gaze shot up. The devil dude

stood ten yards away with her clothes tucked under his arm. He shook his head and smiled. He liked making her crazy, seeing her struggle, and knowing she didn't have a chance in hell of getting out of this alive.

She stared him down, not letting him see the fear growing inside her anymore. She used what little strength she had left to curse the bastard. "I hope those Kendricks find you. I hope Rory Kendrick finds you. Then you'll be sorry. You'll see. He'll make you pay."

Yeah, Rory would make him pay for the cows. Who would make him pay for what he'd done to her? No one. She'd die here abandoned by her brother and alone.

CHAPTER 2

Rory followed the tracks in the mud. After four hours in the saddle, his anger simmered. If he caught up to the men who'd stolen his cattle, he'd kill them just for making him chase them across his land and that of two neighbors. He'd noticed the thefts over the last three months. It started off slow. A couple cattle here. A few more there. At first he'd thought it nothing but strays working their way deep onto the property. He'd eventually find them. That all ended when, on a part of the property they rarely used, he spotted truck and trailer tire tracks on an old dirt fire road that wound its way out to the highway. If his guess was right, whoever stole his herd today was headed for another rarely used road and a bunch of cattle trucks. If he didn't catch up to them soon, they'd get away and he'd never find out who'd been stealing from him and his family.

The cold wind pushed him and his tired horse forward. He pulled his coat tighter around his chest, thankful he'd remembered his gloves and hat. When he started out looking for the cattle, he never expected to ride this far and long. He craved a hot cup of coffee and a bowl of chili. His empty stomach grumbled with the thought.

The wind shifted direction and blew down from the hills to his right. His horse slowed and shied, stepping back several steps and turning to face the hill. Rory searched for any sign of a predator that might have spooked the horse. He didn't see anything, but he did notice the muddled tracks in the dirt. Several horses had converged at this point. He spotted human tracks. Three men and either a younger teen or a woman, judging by the smaller shoe prints.

Why the hell did they stop here?

A fifth horse stopped a short distance away. Another set of large shoe prints walked toward the group. A crushed patch of grass indicated someone fell and rolled. He took it all in, including the drag marks leading up the hill and into the trees.

So, the would-be cattle rustlers got into an argument. Maybe someone came to his senses and tried to stop the others from doing something that could land them in jail for the next ten years.

Rory nudged his horse to follow the tracks leading into the trees. To avoid lopping off his head in the low branches, he dismounted and tied his horse to a thick branch. The horse still shied and spooked at some unseen threat. He wondered what the horse knew that he didn't.

Something didn't sit well with him. A strange shiver of awareness came over him, like someone had eyes on him. He pulled the rifle from his saddle, checked it to be sure all was as it should be, and headed up the hill to the rise. He stopped short near the top.

His eyes saw the gruesome image in front of him, but his mind refused to believe it.

The woman hung by her wrists from the tree. Dozens of punctures left ribbons of blood flowing over her body and limbs . . . everywhere. The majority of the blood came from a cut at her ribs and the slash marks across her thigh and other knee. Her head hung down with her chin resting against her chest. Her lips and skin were tinged blue from the bitter cold. He reached for her face, hoping, begging God, the universe, everything that was good and holy in this world to please let her be alive.

He pulled off his leather glove and touched her frozen cheek. Her head snapped up, her eyes flew open, she screamed and wiggled, trying to get away, but all she did was make things worse. The wire dug into her again. She went limp and moaned, and the sound settled heavy in his chest. Her eyes rolled back in her head and she passed out again.

"Oh God," he whispered like a prayer.

The sweet woman he'd seen around town, usually chasing after her delinquent brother. Sadie. Yeah, he'd asked around about her after she'd slammed into him coming around the corner in one of the aisles at the feed store. He'd felt a shock of heat slice through him, leaving behind a warmth he'd never felt. She'd backed up two steps, apologized, then stepped back another three steps when she looked up at him, and gasped. He scared her, but he didn't know why. Probably had something to do with that bar fight her brother tried to start with Colt and nearly got her punched in her pretty face. He'd saved her and that no-account brother of hers.

He scanned the wire up her arms to the way it was bound around her wrists, along with the rope holding her up and tied around the tree trunk. If he undid the rope, she'd fall to the ground and the barbs would drive into her body even deeper. He needed to cut the wire off her, then let her down.

"Sadie, it's Rory Kendrick. Do you remember me?"

Her eyes fluttered but never opened. "You're supposed to go after them."

"Who?"

Another soft moan escaped her blue, cracked lips.

"I'm going to cut you down. Hold on, Sadie. I'll be right back. I promise."

He ran down the hill to his horse. He shoved the useless rifle back in the scabbard, dug through the saddlebag, and found the wire cutters he kept there in case the cattle broke through a fence and got tangled. He pulled out the scarf he'd forgotten was in there and a knit cap. He'd drunk most of the water he brought along. The two inches of water in the bottle would have to do for now. He'd get Sadie to the hospital.

How? She was in bad shape. He couldn't ride the four hours back to the ranch with her in the saddle. She'd been tortured enough. He couldn't put her through a grueling ride, too.

Unsure how to take care of her, he ran up the hill to do what needed to be done immediately. He hated to hurt her, but getting her down meant cutting her free and pulling the wire out of her skin.

Seeing her strung up like that stunned him again. He feared he'd never get the gruesome image out of his mind. He skidded to a stop in front of her and fell to his knees. He started at her feet and snapped the wire around her ankles free. He unwound the wire up to her knees. Whoever had done this had made sure to inflict the maximum amount of pain. The barbs were spread out, but the way they wound around Sadie ensured nearly all of them bit into her pale skin. Some of the punctures would heal, but the deeper ones would leave lasting scars. Not as bad as the ones in her mind, he feared.

"Stop," Sadie whispered, her body shaking. She barely had the strength to wiggle to get away from him and make herself swing again.

Rory grabbed her thighs and held her still. She tried to kick him away, but he held her in place. One of the barbs sliced his palm. He pulled free, hissing at the sting it left behind. The thought of amplifying that pain more than a hundredfold over his body made his stomach tight and his heart sink. He tried not to imagine the agony Sadie felt, but he couldn't help himself.

Resolved to the task ahead, he used the cutters to snip the wires up the front of her, then he went to her back and did the same. Some fell to the ground, others remained stuck to her body. Those he gently pulled free at her sides, dropping the bloody mess to the ground. Once he had all the wire off up to her wrists, he scooped it all away from her feet and went to the tree. He untied the knot on the rope and gently lowered her down. With the slack let out, he walked back to her before she fell on her back. He held the rope in one hand and wrapped his other arm around her to hold her up. Once he had her secure against him, he let go of the rope. Her arms fell, her bound hands hitting the top of her head. She yelped in pain.

"I'm sorry. I should have thought about how much

your shoulders and hands must hurt from being pulled up like that." He held her with one arm and worked his jacket off with the other, switching hands to hold her to get the jacket free. He wrapped it around her back and gently laid her in the soft grass and mud. He pulled the jacket around her, hoping his warmth worked its way into her cold skin soon. The shearling lining would help hold in the heat.

At least the snow had thawed and the temps had risen above freezing. Otherwise, she'd be dead by now. She wasn't in great shape, but he thought she'd make it. If he got her the help she needed soon.

Her arms and wrists were sticky with blood. He cut the wires, but they'd dug into her deep. He peeled them away, his stomach souring at the sickening way the wire pulled out of her skin. He needed something to wrap the raw wounds and stop the bleeding. He pulled off his thermal and used the wire cutters to slit the material. He tore it into strips and used two to wrap around her wrists and hands. He used another thick swatch to press against the deep cut at her ribs.

"Hhmm. Stop. H-hurts."

"I know, I'm sorry." Rory pressed harder on the bleeding wound. "Are you cold?"

"N-no. Numb."

Fuck. A very bad sign. If she couldn't feel the cold anymore and didn't shiver, her body was shutting down. Hypothermia had set in. He needed to get her warm, and fast.

He shoved the rest of his shirt under her back and pulled it out the other side. He tied the ends off in front of her, tight around her middle to keep pressure on the small but deep wound at her side. He closed the coat around her, not caring that her arms weren't in the sleeves. He pulled the knit cap over her head and ears, hoping that helped keep what little body heat she had left from dissipating with the wind.

The cut on her thigh had stopped bleeding. The nick across her knee on her other leg didn't look bad on its own, but add it to the collection all over her body, and he cringed.

He wrapped the scarf around her feet and ankles, wishing he had something more to keep her warm. Short of stripping himself bare and freezing his ass off before he got her to the help she needed, he'd done all he could for her right now.

Dehydrated, she needed water, especially on her chapped lips. He unscrewed the lid on the water bottle, slipped one hand beneath her neck to hold her head up, and tilted the bottle to her lips, pouring the water in slowly. She sputtered, but then drank deep.

"That's it, sweetheart. Go slow." He wished he had more than a couple ounces to give her, but she drank what he had and settled again. He left the bottle on the ground, along with the wire cutter and bloody wire. He'd send the cops back here to investigate and clean up.

"I'm sorry to do this to you." He slid his hands underneath her and picked her up, pulling her close against his chest. She squeaked in pain as he settled her in his arms. That piercing sound tore his heart to shreds.

He'd never been sentimental. Not since his parents died in an avalanche when he was just a kid. He'd taken on his role as protector for his younger brothers and worked hard to raise them and keep his father's ranch above water. Hell, he'd put his whole self into being the head of the family. Yes, they had their grandfather to look out for them, but Rory had taken on the role of head of the family and business early on. Granddad was getting older, though that didn't tame his wild-at-heart ways and outrageous behavior. Rory had to be the serious one.

Still, this slip of a woman got to him on a deep level. One he didn't want to acknowledge or think about. So he tucked his emotions back in the box he kept them in, buried deep in his heart, and did what needed to be done.

He walked down the hill with her, trying not to jostle her too much. He approached his horse, wondering how to get in the saddle without draping her over his horse and hurting her more. He looked around, trying to find a way to make this easier. He spotted the boulders nearby, grabbed the reins, and led his horse over to the rocks.

Even as a kid he hadn't needed mounting steps, but with Sadie bundled in his arms, this would make things easier. He stopped the horse next to the rocks, climbed up on the boulder, turned to his side, put his left foot over the horse's back, and lowered himself into the saddle as slowly as he could so he didn't spook the horse. He fell harder than he'd like the last foot or so and the horse pranced, but didn't try to throw him and the extra weight he carried.

"That's it, boy." Rory settled Sadie against his chest and on his lap. He grabbed the reins and kicked the horse to move. They rode down the valley toward where he thought the cattle rustlers took his herd. Better to get to the road here than try to take Sadie all the way back to the ranch. He tried to picture where they were in relation to his place and the neighbors' houses. No matter which way he worked out the journey, they were all too far.

Rory pulled the reins right, leading his horse up a tall hill, hoping he'd get a cell signal way the hell out here. The chances were slim, but he had to try. The horse took the steep terrain at a lumbering lope, jostling Sadie against him. She twisted to get more comfortable and ended up with her face buried in his neck and her chest pressed to his. His coat kept her warm and helped to keep him warm, too, though his bare back froze. He held her close and tilted his head to press his cheek to her forehead and add what warmth he could to her.

The horse made it up to the rise and he scanned the area, making sure the bastards who took his cows and did this to Sadie weren't near. He pulled his cell from his back pocket and swiped his thumb across the screen. Great, not only was his battery at twenty-four percent, but he had only one bar. Even if the call went through, it would probably be dropped.

"Come on, give me one small break," he said to the sky, knowing his chances were slim.

He hit the speed dial for the ranch, hoping his grandfather or one of his brothers actually picked up.

"Yo, what's up?"

Rory had never been happier to hear Colt's voice. "Grab some blankets, the first aid kit, and hall ass down to Miner's Road where it cuts close to the creek. You know the place?"

"What the hell happened? Why are you way out there in the boondocks?"

"Don't ask questions, just get moving, or a woman is going to die." He hated to speak his worst fear. Her still body, shallow breathing, and utter quiet sent fear shivering through him that had nothing to do with the dropping temperature.

"On my way. Need anything else?"

"Water. Hurry the hell up. Break every speed law you ignore anyway." Giving in to the desperation gnawing at his insides, he begged, "Please, Colt. Hurry the hell up."

"On it." Colt hung up. Rory lit a fire under him. Rory hoped Colt got there before things got worse.

"Come on, Sadie, hold on. Help is coming."

He nudged his horse down the hill. Since Sadie passed out, which only made him worry more, he kicked the horse into a trot. He'd beat Colt to the meeting point, but he needed to get Sadie off his horse and check her wounds again. He glanced down at her bruised face. Whoever did this hit her. He didn't tolerate others who got off on teasing or hurting other people. It wasn't right to make others feel bad for any reason, but especially because you thought you could get away with it. This went beyond anything he'd ever seen or thought could happen to a person. To string her up like that, using the barbed wire they'd cut from his own fence lines. Bastards. He wanted to get his hands on them and make them pay.

Rory halted the horse by the road, noting the cow and horse tracks, along with the deep ruts from the trucks and trailers that hauled away his herd. He kind of wished the thieves were here so he could teach them a lesson about hurting innocent women. He'd like to show them how much the kind of torture they inflicted on her hurt. Whoever did this to her liked cruelty. Rory vowed to take him down, because no way in hell Rory let him get away with hurting Sadie, or anyone else.

He turned his focus back to the woman in his arms. He gave in to the strange need overtaking him and pressed his cheek to her head and hugged her close.

"Help will be here soon." *Hurry the hell up, Colt.*

Sadie's legs hung over his arm. Her feet remained bundled in his scarf, but her legs had to be cold. He swung his leg over the horse's neck and slid off the saddle, landing hard on the ground. It wasn't easy, but he managed to untie the saddlebags and toss them to the ground. He turned and pressed Sadie's legs to the horse's side, hoping the heat from the animal and him would warm her up even more. The cold breeze blew against his back. If he was this uncomfortable, he could only imagine how Sadie felt tied up and hanging in the biting wind, practically naked, for God knew how long.

Torn from his dark thoughts by the sound of an engine, he stared down the road as Colt skidded around the bend, driving way too fast. Thank God for little brothers who like to live on the edge because they haven't learned they aren't invincible. Colt made him worry far too often, but today he'd take his brother's devil-may-care attitude.

Colt hit the brakes, and the truck slid to a stop feet from him. Rory pulled Sadie close as his horse shied away. Rory rushed Sadie to the back of the truck. Colt let down the tailgate, spread one of the thick blankets, and Rory laid Sadie down, tucking her legs up on the bed of the truck.

"Open that medic kit. Pull out the bandages and gauze," he ordered his brother, who stared down at Sadie, not saying a word.

Rory slapped him on the shoulder. "Colt. Move."

Colt got busy, basically dumping the contents and

sorting through them. Rory pulled open the jacket, undid his tied shirt, and pulled the bloody swatch off her side. The ride had been hard on her, tearing open the cut and making it bleed freely again.

"Holy fucking shit, what the hell happened?" Colt asked, finally finding his tongue.

"Some twisted fuck hung her from a tree with barbed wire."

"Is that what all those holes and scratches in her are?"

"Yes," Rory bit out the single word, trying to hold on to his temper. Every time he saw the wounds, his fury surged, but with no outlet, it burned in his gut.

Rory took the thick gauze pad and pressed it to Sadie's side, staunching the blood.

"That's not from the wire," Colt said.

"No. I think they used a knife."

"Someone punched her in the face." Colt's words held a world of sympathy.

"Hand me that tape. Let's get her patched up and to the hospital."

They worked in silence, unwrapping and rewrapping her wrists with clean bandages. Colt took one foot; he took the other.

"This is inhumane." Colt shook his head, dabbing at the caked, dried blood on Sadie's thigh.

"Just do the best you can for now. They'll clean her up at the hospital."

"I called Ford, told him you needed help. Take the truck. I'll take your horse back to the ranch. Ford and I will meet you at the clinic."

"You don't need to come. I've got this."

"We'll meet you there."

Rory nodded. Since their parents died, even before

but especially since, they did everything together. None of them went through anything alone. He appreciated his brothers' support and understanding.

With Sadie tended to the best they could for now, he bundled her in the blanket and carried her to the passenger side of the truck. Colt opened the door and he stood on the running board and slid her in head-first. Colt pulled out the blanket from the floorboard and shook it out. Rory took it and tucked it over and around Sadie.

"She's out cold," Colt said.

"Exhaustion. She'll do better once she's had some rest." Rory spotted the bottles of water on the floorboards. He grabbed one, uncapped it, and held Sadie's head up again. "Drink some water, sweetheart." He tipped the bottle to her lips. Again, she sputtered, but drank a few ounces.

He laid her back down, drank the rest of the bottle himself, then jumped out of the truck and closed the door.

Colt peeled off his jacket and the thick flannel he wore underneath. He held the dark blue and white plaid out to Rory. "Take this. It'll be too small, but at least you'll have something to wear."

Rory stuffed his arms into the sleeves. If he flexed too much, he'd probably tear the material. He pulled the sides together and barely managed to button the thing at his sternum. No way he buttoned it across his chest.

"You look like the Hulk in that thing," Colt teased.

Rory couldn't even muster a smile at the stupid joke. "Take my horse back. It'll be a long ride, and I'm sorry for that."

"No worries. I got this."

"Swing by Sadie's place on your way to town. Tell her father what happened and where she is."

Rory ran around the truck, hopped into the driver's seat, started the engine, and turned the heat up to warm him and Sadie, though she was bundled well in the blankets. Rory turned the truck and headed down the road, Colt already in the saddle and riding back home.

Rory drove like the devil was after him. He sped past other vehicles, ignoring the honks when he cut things too close between a slow car and oncoming traffic. He didn't care if the cops came after him; he needed to get Sadie to the clinic. With that thought in mind, he pulled out his phone, scrolled through his contacts to his grandfather's favorite doctor, and hit the call button.

"Dr. Bowden."

"Bell, it's Rory."

"Hey, Rory, how is Sammy? Everything okay?"

"Granddad is fine. Ornery as ever. Are you at the clinic?"

"Yeah, I get off in an hour."

"I'm on my way. I need you to get ready for a woman I'm bringing in. She's suffering from hypothermia. She's got three deep cuts that will need stitching. She's covered head to toe with puncture wounds from being tied up with barbed wire. Her wrists and ankles are raw and bleeding badly. She was hung from her hands, so her wrists and shoulders are sore. Maybe she's got some pulled muscles and tendons, I don't know."

"Got it. Is she awake and lucid?"

"No. Not really. I've got her warm now, but I don't know how long she was hanging there."

"Oh God, Rory. Okay. I'll get everything ready for when you arrive. How far out are you?"

"Twenty minutes." A long fucking time in Sadie's case. She must be in so much pain. The thought drove him to push the gas pedal harder, drive faster, regardless of the danger. "They hit her, Bell. They cut her. She's in bad shape." The words came out softer than he intended since he could barely choke out the words past the lump in his throat, but Bell heard him.

"I'll take care of her, Rory." Bell's calm assurance bolstered his waning confidence that he'd gotten to her in time.

"Thanks, Bell. I'll be there soon." Choked up, he disconnected the call. He reached down to touch Sadie's shoulder to reassure her in some small way, but he pulled his hand back, afraid to touch her and disturb any of her wounds. In the end, his unusual need to comfort made him brush his fingers through her long blond hair. She stirred beside him, tilting her head into his soft touch. He did it more, hoping that small comfort gave her strength to get through this. Her small bloody hand reached out from the blanket and settled on his thigh. He pressed his hand over hers and swore he'd keep her safe from now on. No one would ever hurt her again.

CHAPTER 3

Rory paced outside the hospital room door Dr. Bell Bowden shoved him out of five minutes ago, trying to hold on to his sanity. She'd let him stay while they cleaned, dressed, and stitched Sadie's wounds, but not even his good friend's wife let him stay while they photographed Sadie's many injuries and examined her to see if she'd been sexually assaulted. He hadn't even considered it when he found her nearly naked. He didn't want to think about it now. The way he found her, the pain inflicted on her was enough for any one person to bear. To think whoever did that to her touched her, hurt her in that way made the rage roiling in his gut feel like a ticking time bomb about to go off.

He turned back toward the room on his journey back and forth down the short corridor just as Bell stepped out of the room with a nurse, carrying several metal instruments on a tray. The nurse walked away, but Bell stood staring at him, a serene look on her face and in her blue eyes.

He let loose his fisted hands and raked his fingers through his hair and held the back of his head. He stared at the floor, trying to pull himself together as the wave of relief washed through his system.

"The sheriff's deputy just walked in, Rory. I'll speak to him and give him the details. Because of doctor-patient confidentiality, I can't share the information with you."

"You don't have to. As I'm sure you planned, I can read it on your face. Whoever the fuck did this to her didn't rape her."

Bell didn't say a word to confirm it. Her eyes softened on him. "You can sit with her if you'd like. I gave her a sedative to keep her calm. She probably won't wake up for hours."

Rory walked right past the deputy and straight into Sadie's room. She lay in the bed, covered by a sheet and blanket up to her chest. Her hands lay at her sides. The bandages around her wrists hid the ominous cuts and bruises but not her swollen hands and fingers. The many red nicks and scratches all over her arms, chest, and shoulders made her look like a gruesome pincushion.

Afraid to touch her, he stood at the edge of the bed staring down at her.

"Hey Sadie, it's Rory. I'm back. You're not alone. I'll keep you safe." He didn't know why he spoke the words. She was passed out and probably couldn't hear him, but if she did, he wanted her to know. He meant it.

She flinched in her sleep, her eyes squinting and her lips drawing into a tight line. Caught in a nightmare, her eyes rolled beneath her closed lids.

Disturbed by her distress, he reached out and touched her hand. She flinched, then settled again. "Shh, you're okay. You're safe."

Rory didn't so much sit in the chair beside her as fall into it, exhausted in both body and mind. He scrubbed his hands over his face, scraping his palms on his rough jaw. He needed a shave, a shower, food, and for Sadie to wake up and be okay. He dropped his hands back to his thighs, hitting the sore spot on his palm. He held up his hand and stared at the deep gash. He'd washed his bloody hands in the restroom, but the cut still stung. He'd ask one of the nurses to bring him some antiseptic to clean it out.

Sadie got a tetanus shot to go along with her dozens of stitches. Bell did a fantastic job taking care of her. Seeing Sadie laid out on a hospital gurney came a close second to the worst thing he'd ever seen. Right behind her hanging from a tree. Thank God for the new private rooms at the recently opened clinic. He'd have hated to make her endure the long drive to the Bozeman hospital.

Rory answered the tap on the door. "Come in."

The sheriff's deputy stepped into the room, his gaze shooting from Rory to Sadie in the bed beside him.

"I'm Deputy Mark Foster. Rory Kendrick?"

Rory nodded.

"Dr. Bowden filled me in on Sadie Higgins's condition. I've been out to the site where you found her. Gathered all the evidence. Mind telling me what happened?"

Rory ran his free hand through the side of his hair. The other he kept on Sadie's swollen one on the bed.

"I understand it's difficult to talk about it." The deputy glanced at the marks marring every bit of skin not covered by the blankets or bandages and grimaced.

"You should see the rest of her."

"Unfortunately, I saw the pictures."

"I was out checking the cattle this afternoon. Just a normal day." Then it turned to shit. "The herd I had grazing in the south pasture was missing. One of the fence lines had been cut, not pushed down by the cows. I spotted the horse tracks and figured out what happened."

"They took the wire with them and used it on her," the deputy guessed.

"Yes," Rory bit out. "I followed the tracks that led across my land and two neighbors', straight for Miner's Road. I figured if I could catch up to them, maybe I'd find out who's been stealing cattle from me these last months."

"How many cattle did they steal?"

"They started off small, which is why I didn't really notice right away. They'd take three, four at a time. By the time I realized what was going on, twenty-two cattle were missing. Today, they took ninety-seven."

The deputy blew out a soft whistle. "That's brazen."

"Yes it is. Reckless, but well coordinated. They had the trucks ready to take the cattle away."

"Your brother Ford contacted the sheriff's office and reported the missing cattle. We're looking into it. How did you come to find Sadie?"

"A fucking miracle, really." The thought that he could have ridden right past her, left her hanging there . . . He couldn't bear the thought. "My horse shied at one point. I think he smelled the blood on the wind. Who knows? I noticed the disturbed ground and drag marks. Looked like a fight broke out among the assholes who took the cattle."

"I saw the spot. Judging by that nasty bruise on her face, I'd say one of them went after her for some reason."

"My guess is she tried to stop them."

"You don't think she's in on this?"

"No." Rory's gut said no way in hell. If she was, she'd paid a mighty high price. Still, it didn't feel right from what little he knew about her. "I tracked four horses from my place to that spot where a fifth horse showed up. I don't know why she was out there. Not exactly an easy or logical place to ride from her place."

"Could be this has to do with her brother, Connor. He's been in a lot of trouble over the years," the deputy pointed out.

Right. The guy who nearly got her clock reset in an almost bar fight. Would he leave his sister in the middle of nowhere tied up to freeze to death? Rory hoped not for Sadie's sake, but if he did, Rory wanted to get his hands on him . . . now.

"This isn't any small thing. If I hadn't found her when I did . . ." Rory hung his head, then turned and stared at Sadie. Every cut, nick, and bruise sliced a strip right off his heart.

He shouldn't feel this way. This deep. But he did. Something about her spoke to him since that day in the feed store. Her quiet intensity, contrasted with her soft, sweet smile, and the I've-seen-way-too-much-in-my-short-life look in her eyes.

"Mr. Kendrick." The deputy called him out of his dark thoughts.

"Sorry. It's been a long day."

The deputy pointed his pen at Sadie, then him. "So, you two together, or something?"

"No. We've never officially met." He went to the diner where she worked sometimes. He never sat in her section. Just watched her from across the room. He saw her at the feed store sometimes and the gas station where she worked, too. The woman worked her ass off.

"What are you still doing here then?"

"Her father hasn't shown up to take care of her. I can't just leave her here," he snapped.

"My partner went out to her place. Her father isn't well. He's unable to come in his condition."

That surprised Rory. He had no idea her dad was ill. Poor Sadie, two people she had to take care of and not one of them showed up for her. "I take it you didn't find her brother."

"Her dad said Connor hasn't been home in days."

That raised a red flag for Rory. Connor could definitely be involved then.

"Her father thought Sadie was at work. He didn't even know five of his horses were missing."

"So it was Connor."

The deputy nodded. "Evidence points that way. If there's nothing else you can tell me, I'll be on my way. I'll talk to her tomorrow morning, get her side of things." The deputy pulled out his handcuffs.

"What the hell are you doing with those?"

The deputy picked up Sadie's hand and carefully put the cuff on, avoiding hitting her bandaged wrist. Rory stood and leaned forward. The deputy eyed him, a warning to back off. He hooked the other side of the cuffs to the metal bed rail.

"If she is involved, I don't want her escaping before we can determine who else is a part of this."

"I'm telling you, she didn't do it. Take those off her."

"Mr. Kendrick, you said it yourself. You've never met her. I've dealt with her brother many times. Sadie isn't one to do anything wrong, except if you count the ways she covers for Connor. You don't know what really happened out there. I'll have a deputy stationed outside until she wakes up and answers our questions." He stared down at Sadie again. "I want to believe she isn't in on this. She's suffered enough, but I need to do this by the book and treat her like the suspect she is until I confirm otherwise."

Rory fell into his chair, defeated. Nothing he could do about the cuffs, or changing the deputy's mind. But he didn't like it, or this feeling that he'd failed to protect her.

"No matter how this turns out, she owes you a huge debt of gratitude. You saved her life."

She didn't owe him anything. But if her brother was involved, he sure as hell had to answer for what he'd done.

"If she wakes up, give me a call. We'll get this sorted out." The deputy handed over his card. Rory stuffed it into the front pocket of his too small shirt.

Rory sat with his feet propped on the cart beside Sadie's bed, his arm along the length of her leg, his hand over hers. He rolled his head to the side when someone entered the room. He expected the nurse to come back and check Sadie's vitals again, but Ford and Colt walked in and stopped short, both their gazes locked on his hand on Sadie's.

"What are you guys doing here?"

Ford held up the pizza and six-pack in his hands.

"I brought dinner and beer. Thought you might be hungry." He set both on the tray table at the end of the bed.

Colt held up a duffel bag and yanked the shirt down from over his shoulder and tossed it to Rory. "Brought you one of your shirts. Stopped by her place and talked to her dad. He's not well at all and scared for her. I told him we'd take care of her and see she gets home whenever they release her. I packed her some clothes." Colt dropped the bag at the end of the bed without hitting Sadie's tiny feet.

Rory pulled off Colt's flannel that had kept him warm but was damn uncomfortable when it pulled and pinched every time he moved. He tossed the flannel on Sadie's bag and pulled the dark gray thermal on. Comfortable and able to flex his arms and move his shoulders, he relaxed.

"Thanks, guys."

"There's something you should know." Colt unscrewed the cap on one of the beer bottles and took a long pull. "I found the Higginses' five horses, saddled and grazing in the back pasture outside their house."

"Based on the missing horses, the deputy thinks her brother is involved." Rory swore and shook his head.

Colt scrunched one side of his mouth into a lopsided frown. "Those damn fools just left them there. That or they turned them loose and the horses found their way home."

"They hurt her, left her and the horses, they don't give a shit about anyone or anything, just taking the cattle and running off with them." Ford clenched his hand tight on the end of the bed frame and stared down at Sadie.

Rory popped the top on his own beer and drank deeply, wishing it was something stronger. "I find her asshole brother, he's going to wish he never stepped foot on our land or left his sister for dead."

"Why the hell is she handcuffed to the bed?" Colt asked, shaking his head. "Even if she took the cattle with those guys, she's suffered enough."

"She didn't do it." The warning in Rory's voice made Colt narrow his eyes.

"I never said she did it. I'm just saying . . ."

"I know, I'm sorry. I'm pissed and tired and frustrated as hell."

"So, a normal day," Ford tried to tease him out of yet another of his black moods.

Sometimes Rory found the overwhelming responsibility to oversee the ranch and take care of his family wore on him. He spent too much time working, not enough time . . . doing anything else. He couldn't remember the last time he took a day off. He couldn't remember the last movie he went to see in the theater, let alone the last time he went out with a woman. He vaguely remembered sex involved more than a hot shower and his hand.

He felt Sadie's soft skin beneath his fingers. In the past, just the sight of her stirred something deep inside him that felt like the crack of a seed just beginning to sprout. But without any light inside him, it died each and every time he walked away from her without so much as a hello.

Now, sitting beside her, touching her skin after all he'd been through today, it felt like the newest seed to crack open inside him not only sprouted, but sprang a new leaf, trying to reach up and out of his chest and finally grow into something. What? He didn't quite know, but he was tired of everything he wanted and needed being smothered under responsibility.

"Rory, you stare at her any harder, you'll wear a hole in her." Ford handed him a paper plate with two slices of bacon and tomato pizza. His favorite. "Eat, man. We'll figure this out."

"Nothing to figure out. We need to find her brother and whoever else did this to her."

"The cops can't even find that fuck." Colt wiped his mouth with a paper napkin. "Asshole's been running around for years doing anything he damn well pleases."

"She always pays the price," Ford said.

"What do you mean?" Rory asked, eyeing his brother.

"It's no secret she's the one who cleans up that guy's messes. That fight with Colt isn't the only time he went into that bar and started some trouble. She's paid off bar tabs, gambling debts, lawyer bills when Connor actually got caught, and settled up with folks when her brother stole their shit."

"No way she can come up with the cash for the herd. Fuck. Those were some prime beef cattle." Colt might be the youngest and the most reckless of them, but he understood that he was just as responsible for the success of the ranch as any of them. Oh, he'd skipped out on work plenty of times, but when he was really needed and the chips were down, Colt came through.

"Since when did you two start keeping tabs on Sadie's family?" The last thing Rory wanted to find out was that either one of them was dating her, or had in the past. They were brothers. There was an unwritten, unspoken code to follow. Why Rory was even thinking about dating her, he didn't know. Nothing had changed.

Based on the few times they'd run into each other, she had no interest in him.

"If you spent any amount of time off the ranch, you'd know all this," Ford scolded. "Everyone in town knows that everything at the Higgins place went to shit when Sadie's mother died. She's been mother, maid, and caretaker of her brother and father since she was sixteen."

"She missed all the fun in high school," Colt added. "She kept her head in her books, after-school work at the diner and gas station, and tending to her daddy's ranch the best she could. Guys would hit on her in school, ask her to bonfires and dances, but she never accepted."

"Ah, little brother, is there a woman out there who actually turned you down?" Ford teased Colt.

"She was damn pretty then, even more beautiful now." His eyes held a gleam of sadness when he glanced at her and took in all her injuries. "I never asked her out, but I wanted to. She doesn't smile very much. I always thought she needed a break."

Rory understood exactly what Colt meant. Sadie had been running hard her whole life just to keep up, but no matter how hard she ran, she just kept falling behind, her brother putting one obstacle after another in her path, keeping her from getting ahead.

"Her daddy used to run some pretty nice horses," Colt went on. "The ones I saw today are the last of his stock. Looks like she's sold them off over the years."

"Yeah, to pay off her brother's debts."

"I wouldn't mind having a few of those horses to breed," Colt said. "Her place is falling into disrepair. Looks like her father's health is declining fast."

"Do you know what's wrong with him?" Rory asked.

"I didn't ask. He didn't say."

Sadie began to stir in the bed. Whether disturbed by their voices or another nightmare, she flinched and shook.

"What's wrong with her?" Colt asked.

"Bell said she'd probably do this off and on through the night due to the trauma she suffered." Rory slid his fingers up her arm and down, trying to soothe her.

"Rory," she whispered, tensing under his hand. "Dev-vil," she mumbled.

Ford and Colt both turned to him. Colt busted out laughing. "She thinks you're the devil, man." He tipped his head. "You two know each other? Did you actually leave your monastery and we don't know about it, monk?"

Rory hated that nickname. The glare he sent his brothers only made them smile more. "I don't know her."

"In the biblical sense," Colt prodded. He never knew when to quit.

Rory leaned forward in his chair and bit out, "You want to live, you'll shut the fuck up."

Ford planted his hand on Colt's chest to stop him from sputtering another smart-ass remark. "Let it go, little brother, or you'll be laid out on the floor."

"Rory. Devil," Sadie muttered again. "Get him." She thrashed about in the bed.

Rory stood and pressed lightly on her shoulders to hold her down so she didn't hurt herself more. "Shh. You're okay." He gently ran his fingers down her hair again and again. "Shh." She settled back into a deep sleep and his fisted gut let loose again, but the band around his chest remained tight. He didn't understand why she called his name and thought him some kind of devil. He'd helped her. He'd never done anything to her. So why did she fear him this way?

"Hey, man, I'm sorry. I didn't mean anything by it. The way you looked when I got to the two of you. I can't imagine what you saw and felt seeing her strung up like that." Colt hung his head and shook it. "I see you want to—"

"Doesn't matter what I want," Rory cut him off. "I found her. I'll see she gets home safe. That's all there is to this."

Ford laid a hand on Rory's shoulder. "If there's more—"

"There's nothing." Rory shook off his brother's hand, hoping those two didn't start spouting all kinds of assumption, thinking they knew anything. There would never be anything between him and Sadie. Right? What the hell would she want from a guy like him? A man who'd turned hard and shut off everything inside himself except his drive to get the job done, keep the ranch surviving and thriving, and see his brothers find their way out of their grief after losing their parents and become the men they were today. Happy. Making their own way in the world. Just what his parents would have wanted for them. Exactly what he'd promised them the day he put them in the ground. He'd take care of Ford and Colt. He'd make sure they always had a home and they stayed together. Granddad helped hold them together when they were kids, but as the oldest, Rory took on the responsibility of parent and big brother.

Rory fell back into his chair and avoided looking at his brothers, knowing the cold, hard truth. "I don't know her. She doesn't want to know me. You heard her. She thinks I'm the devil." Rory shook his head, trying to ignore the tightening of his gut and the hurt that settled in his heart that she'd think such a thing about him. Had he become so closed off from other people that they feared him because he'd never let anyone really get to know him?

Sadie twitched and moaned again, clamping her hand down on his arm and holding tight, her nails digging into his arm. "Rory. Get them."

"You might consider that she knew those cattle belonged to us and told her brother and his friends that you were going to go after them."

Rory wanted to believe Ford's words. He really did. He covered Sadie's hand with his and she relaxed. He tried to pull his arm free, but she clamped down tight again. For whatever reason, she didn't want to let him go. He didn't want to let go of her. He stared at her face, hoping for any sign that she knew it was him sitting beside her. When he turned back to tell his brothers to go on home, he found they'd already gathered the empty pizza box, plates, napkins, and empty beer bottles and left without so much as a goodbye. Not that he'd have heard them; he was so focused on Sadie and the colliding thoughts in his head.

One side of himself told him he was crazy for thinking she'd wake up and be happy to see him. The other side told him to walk away now before she woke up and called him the devil to his face and ordered him out.

Neither side won; they just kept up the verbal war in his head. He talked himself out of getting to know her better and into staying right here beside her. Funny, no one talked him into anything. He wanted to stay. He wanted to convince her she didn't know him, but he wanted her to. The why and how of it eluded him, but he didn't get up and walk out the door. This was where he wanted to be. Right beside her.

CHAPTER 4

Sadie felt the bite of the wire cinch around her wrists, ankles, and body like a vise. She screamed and fought to get free, but nothing worked and the cold froze her down to her bones. The devil dude came after her with the knife raised over his head, slashing it down. She screamed again and his image turned into a much larger, darker man, then shifted back to the devil dude again. "Rory. Devil," she gasped, thrashing to get away.

Someone grabbed her shoulders, shooting pain through her arms and up her neck. Her eyes flew open and she stared into a pair of golden-green hazel eyes. "Stop. You're hurting me."

Rory pulled his hands away from her and held them up in front of him like he was being stopped by the cops. "I'm trying to stop you from hurting yourself. Calm down. Take a breath."

For the first time she realized she was nearly hyperventilating. She tried to put her hand on her heaving chest, but something clanked and tugged sharply on her arm. She stared down at her aching hand and saw the handcuffs. She panicked, which didn't help her breathing situation.

"Hey, now. Look, this hand is free." Rory picked up her hand and held it softly in his big one, which set off a new round of fear. Why was he here? Where was here? Was she under arrest?

"I didn't steal them. I tried to stop them. You have to believe me. I'd n-n-never . . ." She couldn't get any air. Flashes of light sparkled in her vision.

"Sadie, damnit, breathe."

She couldn't. Everything went dark.

Rory wanted to shake her awake. Bell rushed into the room along with a nurse and a dark-haired woman. Luna, if he remembered her name right, who worked at the diner with Sadie. He stood over Sadie feeling like he'd just been kicked in the chest by a horse.

"Rory, what happened?" Bell asked.

"She was having another nightmare, thrashing around in the bed. I touched her shoulders to steady her and keep her from hurting herself. She woke up, saw me, and I don't know . . . She freaked out."

"What did you do to her?" Luna demanded.

"Nothing," Rory bit out.

"Panic attack." Bell tapped the monitor by the bed. "Her heart rate is coming down. She passed out. She'll wake up soon."

Sadie's heart rate might be slowing down, but his stopped when her eyes rolled back in her head and she went limp. He fell back into the chair he'd sat in all night and raked his hands through both sides of his hair and tried to hold it together. He'd barely slept. His back ached from the uncomfortable seat. He needed a huge dose of caffeine and a chance to set the record straight with Sadie. If she called him the devil one more time, he might lose it. He hated that she thought he'd hurt her.

Bell's hand settled on his shoulder. "Don't worry. She's okay."

"Do you think these nightmares and stuff will last long?"

"I don't know. It depends on her and how well she's able to cope with what happened."

"Sadie's tough." Luna touched her hand softly to Sadie's leg, staring down at her friend. "She'll get through this."

"She needs time to heal both her body and her mind. What she went through out there?" Bell frowned and her eyes went soft with sadness. "I can't imagine it, Rory."

"Me either. I just want this to be over for her."

Luna stared across Sadie at him. "Dr. Bowden told me you found her. Thank you for saving my friend." Tears welled in her eyes.

Rory nodded, unable to say or do anything else.

The nurse finished checking the IV line and monitors and slipped out the door.

"Do you need anything?" Bell asked.

"I'm good."

"You should go home and get some sleep."

"I can stay with her for a little while," Luna offered.

"Later. I need to talk to her."

"About the cattle?" Bell asked.

"Fuck the cattle," he spat out, then realized he'd let his anger override his good sense. "Sorry, Doc. I didn't mean to snap at you."

She smiled. "It's okay. I get it. You're worried about her."

"How long does she have to stay here?" Luna asked.

"Depends on how she feels when she wakes up. If the cops decide to take her in—"

"She didn't do anything," Rory snapped.

Bell's hand contracted on his shoulder. "If they don't see it your way, I'll make up an excuse to keep her here another day if you'd like."

"That might give me enough time to find her brother and make him answer for this instead of her."

"I hope you do. Someone needs to teach him a lesson." The determined look in Luna's eyes said she'd like to see Connor pay for hurting her friend.

"So you think he's involved with this, too?" Rory asked.

"Not think. Know. If Sadie is in the middle of it, it's because she rushed in to help him." Luna frowned down at Sadie. "In this case, it's probably more accurate to say she tried to stop him. I wish I'd known what happened yesterday. I didn't find out until I went in to work this morning. Everyone is talking about it."

"I'll see what I can do to keep her here if it comes to that. I'll keep the deputy waiting outside until she's up to talking to him. I have another patient to check on before Dane and I leave to go to breakfast. Your favorite girl is outside waiting to see you."

He smiled, thinking of the little blond angel who'd stolen his heart. "Send her in." He pressed his hands on the chair arms, making his hand sting again. He caught Bell before she walked out the door. "Hey, Doc, can I have some antiseptic and ointment for this?" He held up his hand, showing her the wound.

"Did the barbed wire get you?"

"Not nearly as bad as it got her."

"When's the last time you got a tetanus shot?"

"About four years ago. I'm good."

"Be right back."

Rory eyed Luna eyeing him. "What?"

"You've been here all night?"

"Yeah. So?"

"Because you want your cattle back or compensation for them? Or some other reason?"

"No. And yes."

"Always a man of few words. Wanna tell me why you're still here?"

"No." Truthfully, he had a hundred reasons and none. Nothing really made sense, except he couldn't leave her.

"Have anything to do with you staring at her at the diner all the time?"

He didn't answer, just stared at Sadie's face, waiting for her to wake up again.

"I guess that answers my question."

Rory glanced at Luna and followed her gaze to his hand over Sadie's. He hadn't realized he'd held hers again to keep her calm and reassure her she was safe.

Luna gave him a nod, pulled out her chirping cell phone, and checked her messages. Rory went back to his vigil, waiting for Sadie to wake up and talk to him. What he'd say to her, he didn't really know.

Sadie woke up to the chatter of a little girl and slowly opened her eyes. She stared through her lashes at the last image she ever thought she'd see. Rory sat in the chair beside her, a beautiful little blond girl in his lap.

"This not good. Mommy says clean first." The little

girl dabbed the cotton ball on the top of the bottle she held in her other hand, then pressed it in the middle of the big hand Rory held up for the little girl.

Rory hissed with the sting of the antiseptic. The little girl pulled the cotton ball away. "Blow make it butter." She blew on Rory's hand with short little puffs of air. Rory smiled at the top of the little girl's head as she bent over his hand. Everything about him changed. His face and eyes softened. His shoulders eased. She'd never seen the man look anything but intense. But when he smiled . . . Wow.

"Butter?" the little girl asked.

"All better. Thank you, angel baby. Now what?"

"Mommy says goo."

Rory's smile grew and he let out a soft chuckle that made Sadie's stomach flutter. The deep rich sound made her insides warm.

"That's right, the goo."

The little girl unscrewed the cap, pressed with both hands to push some of the ointment out of the tube, and then swiped her finger over the top to grab it. Rory held his hand open for her. She smeared it in place, a look of utter concentration on her sweet face.

"And aid." She looked around her, searching.

"Here it is." Rory held up the princess bandage. "You sure this is the one we want?"

"Oh yes."

"Okay," he conceded, letting the girl put the pink bandage on his hand. He held it up so she could see her handiwork. "Great job, baby. I'm all better."

"Not yet. Kiss make it butter." She leaned in and kissed Rory's hand. "Der. All butter."

"Yes, I am." Rory hugged the girl close, noticing Sadie staring at him for the first time. "Hi."

"Hi," she said back.

"You're awake." Her best friend, Luna, leaned over from her other side and hugged her close. Sadie let out a heavy sigh and leaned into her friend, trying not to move too much. Everything ached. But she needed the warmth and reassurance of a good friend.

Choked up Luna came, Sadie asked, "When did you get here?"

"About twenty minutes ago. I'm so sorry, Sadie, if I'd known what happened I'd have been here sooner."

"It's fine. I'm fine," she said automatically.

Luna released her far too soon and stood beside the bed. "You are, thanks to him." Luna cocked her head toward Rory.

Avoiding him and what his presence meant, she changed the subject. "Aren't you supposed to be at work?"

"I had to see you, but yes. They can't survive with both of us out."

"Go. I'm fine."

"Oh for God's sake, stop saying that. You're not fine. Look at you." The tremble in her friend's voice upset Sadie even more. She hated to make her friend sad.

Sadie tried to clear her fuzzy head, but couldn't bring herself to look at the damage. The images in her mind were enough to make her cringe. Luna's steady gaze grew even more worried, drawing lines across her friend's forehead.

"Please, go to work. I'll be okay. But come back and see me after your shift if I'm still here."

"Count on it. In the meantime, call me if you need anything." Luna leaned down and hugged her again, whispering in her ear, "I want to know what happened, and where I can find that brother of yours so I can kill him. Also, I want to know more about the hot and very intense cowboy." Luna stood and brushed Sadie's hair back from her face. "You need me to stay, I'll stay."

She eyed Rory still sitting quietly with the little girl, watching her. "I'm fine."

Unconvinced, Luna's mouth dipped down on one side. "I will call you later, unless you call me first." Luna eyed Rory. "I take it you're staying, making sure she gets what she needs."

"Count on it," Rory said.

Luna tilted her head in acknowledgment, patted Sadie's hand, then left, leaving Sadie wondering why her friend believed Rory meant those stern words and didn't mean to take out his anger on her over what her brother did.

She must have missed something. Right?

"Who's your friend?" Sadie asked, stalling as long as possible the confrontation about her brother that Rory no doubt wanted to have.

"Kaley," the girl announced. She turned back to Rory. "Uncle Rory, can I goo on her? She need lots."

"I don't know, she's hurt real bad."

Sadie couldn't resist the little girl. "Come here. I need some of your magic medicine."

Kaley beamed a smile at her. Rory held her close and stood, setting the little girl on the bed. "Be very careful not to bump her leg. She's got a bad cut," he warned.

"I see." Kaley tried to pull down the blanket.

Rory gently pulled her hand away. "No, you stick with the small cuts on her upper arm."

Kaley pointed to the handcuffs. "Bad guy."

Sadie sucked in a breath. She opened her mouth to explain, but Rory held her gaze and answered for her. "She's not a bad guy. Once the cops talk to her, they'll take them off." The reassurance was for the little girl, but also for Sadie.

"I can explain."

"He's the devil," Kaley announced, smudging more goo on her arm than needed.

Sadie's eyes went wide.

"You keep calling me that in your sleep," Rory explained.

"No I didn't."

"Did too." Kaley singsonged the words.

Heat rushed up her chest, neck, and face. "Rory, I didn't mean—"

Dane walked in the door and smiled at her. "This is a hell of a way to get some attention, honey."

"Dane." The sigh she let out wasn't enough to emphasize the relief she felt seeing her old friend. She'd known Dane since kindergarten.

Another reprieve from the confrontation Rory wanted. Damn her brother for getting mixed up with the likes of Rory Kendrick. She'd warned him. Since Connor wasn't here to answer for his misdeeds, it was left to her to answer to the big, forbidding man.

"Does it have to be every blonde in the state?" Rory snapped.

Dane's gaze shot from her to Rory. The mischievous grin reminded her so much of the boy she knew and the young man who'd loved, and never turned down, a good time, which accounted for his reputation with the ladies.

"What? Just because I've seen her naked—"

Yeah, when they were little kids, stripping down and jumping in a swimming hole.

"Excuse me," a woman in a white doctor's coat said from the door, glaring at Dane.

"Now, Bell, didn't you say something about getting pancakes?" Dane tried to weasel his way out of that loaded statement.

"I get to play the pregnancy craving card, not you."

"Um, so I see you've met Sadie." Dane tried to get things back on track. "Sadie, my wife, Dr. Bell Bowden. Most just call her Bell."

"Dr. Bowden, so nice to meet you. I heard this one got married." She turned to Dane. "You look so happy."

His smile kicked up another notch. "I am. I see you've met our little girl."

Kaley planted her hand on Sadie's thigh, jumped up on the bed, and ran for her dad. "Ancakes," she shouted.

Sadie tried to squelch the yelp of pain, barely. Her eyes rolled back and she pressed her hand to her throbbing leg.

Dane's hand settled on her calf. "Sadie, I'm sorry."

"It's okay." She hissed the words out, wishing the pain away.

Rory took a step toward Dane, glaring at him like he wanted to kill him. Sadie didn't know what was going on here, but she wanted to go home. She needed to find her brother. If the devil dude did this to her, no telling what he'd do to her brother if Connor didn't deliver on whatever drug deal they had going. She needed to stop

Connor and get him to turn himself in before it was too late.

"How did I get here?"

"Rory brought you in last night," Dr. Bowden said, pulling her chart from the end of the bed and reading over it.

Sadie turned to Rory. "It wasn't a dream."

Rory scrunched up one side of his mouth and shook his head. Weariness filled his eyes and the sigh he released from his wide chest. He'd been through a lot to save her.

Dane shook his head and pulled his wife into a hug. "I'll let you finish here, then we're going to breakfast. You need to eat." He kissed her on the forehead, then glanced at Rory. "It's not what you think." Dane released his wife and walked to the edge of the bed and laid his hand over her handcuffed one. "Did Connor steal those cattle?"

She stared at the handcuffs and sighed out the answer she didn't want to be true, "Yes."

Dane gave her hand a gentle squeeze. "Connor's the one who deserves to be in handcuffs. You've done all you can up to this point. You need to let him go before he really does get you killed."

She stared up at him, holding his beautiful daughter, a girl he'd taken in because she needed a family. Dane would do anything for family. "If it were one of your brothers, would you let them go?"

"He left you out there, didn't he?" Dane asked.

"You don't understand."

"You've been the cleanup crew since your mother died. You've held everything together. You've lived for them. When will you start living for yourself, Sadie? Do it now before it's too late."

He rattled the handcuffs to point out that she might end up in jail, an accessory for stealing Rory's cattle.

"Rory saved you last night. If he hadn't come along . . ." Dane left the rest unsaid.

She'd be dead right now.

Dane leaned down and kissed her on the forehead. He hovered over her and whispered, "Your life has been one hard choice after the next. This is something you have to do, Sadie. Save yourself."

Tears shimmered in her eyes. She knew he was right, but she couldn't bring herself to do it. Connor was her brother. He needed her. She'd get through to him, make him see reason. A small voice inside, the one she never listened to, whispered, *He'll never see reason. He'll never change.* She turned her face into the pillow and wept.

Dane brushed his hand over her hair. "You call me if you need me."

"I've got this," Rory said behind her.

Which could only mean that he meant to make her and her brother pay for what happened. That, or he really did believe she wasn't the bad guy and he pitied her for all her injuries and what happened. She didn't know which was worse.

Sadie wiped her eyes. She didn't have time for self-pity or crying over what couldn't be changed.

Dr. Bowden took Dane's place beside her after he walked out the door. Sadie stared up at the beautiful woman and sucked it up, mustering what little strength she had left.

"Congratulations on the wedding and the new baby.

Kaley is amazing. She got that one to smile." Sadie cocked her head in Rory's direction.

"He's a sucker for her."

"I see Dane is, too. So, Dane finally found you again. You're her, right?"

Dr. Bowden sucked in a surprised breath. "You know about our meeting by the river?"

"Though I haven't seen Dane in a good long while, since he ran off to ride the rodeo circuit, he and I have been *friends* forever. When I really needed one, he was there for me. I've been so busy lately, seems I keep up with my friends more through the town grapevine than in person."

"Life gets in the way sometimes." Dr. Bowden touched her arm, understanding in her eyes. "How are you feeling?"

"Sore. Everything aches. My wrists, shoulders, and ankles are the worst. I can feel the stitches at my side and on my legs."

"Yeah, sorry Kaley got you."

"She didn't mean it."

"Considering what you went through, your injuries aren't too bad. I'll take the stitches out in seven to ten days. The cuts were deep. Your wrists and ankles are cut, scraped, and raw. That will take the longest to heal. I'll prescribe some antibiotics to stave off infections. Right now, you're getting them through your IV."

"Did you call my dad?"

"A sheriff's deputy contacted him by phone, then Rory's brother went by to see him."

Rory stepped close. "My brother Colt stopped by your place last night. He packed you some clothes and talked to your dad. He found your horses saddled and in the pasture. He took care of them and put them back in their stalls, fed and watered all the horses."

"Damnit, Connor just left them like that."

"He left you hanging from a tree," Rory snapped out, his voice laced with pent-up rage.

"The deputy is waiting outside to speak to you," Dr. Bowden said. "I'll be back later to check on you."

"I want to go home."

Dr. Bowden's eyes went to the cuffs on her hand. "We'll see." She left the room.

Sadie rattled the cuffs, frustrated, pissed, and overwhelmed.

"Stop. You'll hurt yourself."

"I don't see how it can get any worse."

"It can always get worse," Rory said.

Deputy Foster stepped into the room.

"Hello, Mark."

"Sadie. We meet again."

"No offense, but I'm tired of seeing you."

"None taken. How about this time you give me some straight answers without trying in vain to make me believe your brother didn't mean for this to happen and isn't responsible for stealing nearly a hundred head of cattle."

Sadie stared up at the ceiling wishing she was anywhere else but here. How the hell could she protect her brother when everything led straight to him? Did he really think he'd get away with this, or that she could get him out of it? Why did she even bother to try anymore?

Because she couldn't live with herself if she didn't.

"So, what's it going to be? Straight up, or the merry-go-round ride we've been on these last ten years."

"You're the longest relationship I've ever had. I hate to end it now."

"Since I never get to see you naked, and I don't want to see you behind bars, let's play this straight. This is serious, Sadie. Your brother is going down for this. Nothing you say or do will get him out of it, but what you say may land you in a cell, so tell the truth for once, so I don't have to read you your rights and arrest you."

Everything he said was true, but she didn't want to face it. She didn't want to believe it had come to this.

Needing a minute to collect herself, she moved her hand. "Can you take these off so I can at least pee before we do this?"

Mark unhooked her and stepped back. Sadie sat up, pressing her hand to her side when the stitches pulled. Rory kept a close eye on her. She owed him an explanation and a huge sum of money for those damn cows. The thought of how she'd repay that debt weighed heavy in her heart.

She threw the covers off her legs and stared down at the bruises and cuts, the bandage wrapped around her thigh and ankles. The image of the devil dude wrapping the wire around her as tight as possible came back and stopped her breath. She couldn't take her eyes from the gruesome injuries marring both her legs.

The fear washed through her again. "He said, 'I like it when you bleed. It gets me off.'"

Rory swore beside her.

"Who, Sadie?" Mark asked, leaning forward, anxious to know who needed to be locked up.

"The devil." She finally broke from staring at her injuries and looked up at Rory. "I swore to him he'd be sorry. You'd find him and make him pay." She swung her sore legs out of bed, grabbed hold of the IV pole, used it to support herself on her aching feet, and hobbled the short distance to the restroom. She turned back to Rory. "For the cows," she clarified.

His intense gaze met hers. "For you, the devil will get his due."

Rory waited for her to close the bathroom door. He hated seeing the pain etched in her face and filling her eyes with each step she took. He breathed a sigh of relief that she really didn't think him the devil. He hated to think he'd been the torment of her nightmares all last night.

"Do you know who this fucking devil is?" Rory asked Mark, the deputy Sadie obviously knew well. First Dane, now this guy.

"Sounds like her brother's stepped up from small time to big time. If she's talking about Derek Pete, he's a known drug trafficker. Runs things out of Smithy's Bar. He's been busted for any number of things. Served time for assault a couple of times. Likes to use a knife and has a very distinct devil tattoo on his neck."

Rory nodded, finally understanding her reference and the fear in her voice last night when she mumbled about him.

Sadie stepped out of the bathroom. "You two compare notes and condemn me?"

"You didn't do anything wrong. Sticking up for your brother is admirable, but useless at this point." Rory shook his head when she stared at him, shock and fear in her eyes. "I know you didn't have anything to do with stealing the cattle. I tracked your brother and his three buddies from my place to where you showed up on a fifth horse."

"You could tell all that by the tracks."

"And where the fight broke out and Derek decked

you." He cocked his head, indicating the bruise on her jaw.

Sadie placed her hand over her swollen face. "It hurts like hell."

"I bet."

"Derek?" she asked, confused by his earlier statement.

"Derek Pete. Devil tattoo on his neck. Long, shaggy brown hair. Mean dude with a wicked sharp knife," Mark filled her in.

"I guess that's him. I didn't get his name." Sadie lowered herself into the bed like an eighty-year-old woman with arthritis. Every bit of pain that showed on her face tightened Rory's gut. He helped her with the covers and IV line.

"So, we've got the usual suspects. Connor, his two buddies Scott and Tony, and the newest and most lethal addition to his cohorts, Derek. Your brother's been dealing marijuana and prescription pills for years. What's he into now? Meth?"

Sadie didn't say anything, just stared down at her hands.

"Keeping what you know to yourself isn't going to help your brother," Mark pointed out. "Derek is the worst person your brother could have gotten mixed up with, Sadie. If he's in with Derek, the only way he's getting out is in a pine box."

Sadie flinched, but she still held her tongue.

"Where is he?" Mark demanded.

"I don't know. He hasn't been home in two weeks. When I discovered the horses missing, I went after him."

"Why? Because you knew he was going to steal the cattle?" Mark asked.

Rory hoped she didn't know ahead of time. If she did, she'd be charged with the crime.

"I wanted my horses back. I was afraid he'd sell them for quick cash, or worse, leave them somewhere to fend for themselves."

"How'd you know where to find him?"

"I didn't. Like Rory, I followed the tracks. When I saw where he was headed, I veered off for the hills that overlook the valley. I thought I could head him off. I was too late."

Too late to stop Connor and turn him back and return the cattle before the theft was discovered. Rory swore.

"I'm sorry. I tried to stop them. They wouldn't listen. Connor owes this guy money. Even the cattle weren't going to be enough. I don't know how much he owes or for what."

"Probably for the supplies to cook the meth, or a deal gone bad. Your brother thinks he can cash in on a big payday, but Derek is never going to let that happen until your brother proves himself a reliable cook and distributor." Mark jotted down notes like Sadie's world wasn't falling apart.

Rory saw it written all over her face. She'd tried for years to stop this from happening, stop her brother from taking things too far until there was no going back.

"You don't know that," she said to Mark, another effort to save her brother or just pure denial.

Rory wondered if she'd ever give up. Dane told her to save herself. She'd almost gotten killed trying to make her brother do the right thing. Would she stop before it really did cost her life?

Rory swore he'd never let that happen, but how could

he make good on that when she wasn't his to protect and probably wouldn't listen to him anyway?

"Where are they cooking, Sadie?" Mark demanded.

"I don't know."

"Look, he's already got you mixed up in cattle rustling, now he's associating with a known drug trafficker and got you covering for him. I can't keep protecting you. Tell me where he is."

"I don't know where he is."

"You do, you're just not saying. Look at you. You nearly died last night. What's it going to take for you to see he's no good, and he's going to take you down with him?"

Tears ran down her cheeks. Each one lashed at Rory's heart. He got that she didn't want to rat out her family, and this was tearing her apart, but she needed to speak up.

"Where is he?" Mark pushed.

"I don't know. He left me there. I begged him to help me, and he just left me there." The softly spoken words punched Rory right in the gut. She'd tried so hard over the years to help her brother, only to have him turn his back on her when she needed him to save her.

The deputy shook his head, as disgusted as Rory about this whole damn thing.

"You know the drill. If you hear from your brother, or find out where he's hiding, you need to call me. If you don't, if you give him money or any other kind of help, you'll be an accessory. Don't let that happen, Sadie. You can't help him this time. You've already found out the hard way that Derek Pete is not a man to be messed with. Unless Connor turns himself in, he's going to find the path he chose only leads to hell."

CHAPTER 5

Sadie woke up, staring at the window who knew how long after Mark left, leaving her with those ominous words about her brother heading straight for hell. Well, she felt like she'd been living there a long time, her brother's mistakes setting flames at her feet, making her dance to get out of them, and him out of whatever trouble he got into. This time, he'd tied her hands. Literally and figuratively. She tried to raise her hand to look at her swollen fingers and the bandages around her wrist to remind herself that he'd left her without even trying to help. Someone held her hand still. She glanced down and straight into a pair of bloodshot hazel eyes. Rory sat beside her bed, holding her hand, waiting for her to wake up and . . . what? What did the man want from her?

"You were having another nightmare."

"I don't think I'll ever sleep again without thinking of what happened," she admitted.

"Me either."

She eyed him, wondering what he meant by that.

"When I found you, I thought you were dead. I've

never seen anything so gruesome and cruel. I never got a chance to ask before . . . Are you okay?"

He'd seen her hanging from that tree, the damage inflicted to her body. He asked about something deeper. He wanted to know about her mind and heart. Her mind wanted to deny what happened. Her heart broke the minute she'd seen her brother stealing the cattle and shattered into a million pieces when he turned his back on her.

Tears welled in her eyes. She wondered if she'd ever think about what happened and not cry for all the reasons, all the wrongs.

"I will be fine," she vowed. "I always am." She'd held it together through all the tough times in her life. Losing her mother. Trying to raise her brother the best she could and feeling so inadequate for the task every time he chose to do the wrong thing. Begging her father to see a doctor when what seemed like nothing more than a bug and fatigue turned into a way of life that got progressively worse these last months. She barely recognized her father now. His mind and body deteriorated with each passing day.

"I know you will. To survive what you've been through . . . takes guts and determination."

"Thanks. What are you still doing here? You look wrecked. Go home and get some sleep."

"I'm not leaving without you."

"Look, if it's about the money I owe you, I'm good for it. I won't run off. I pay my debts."

"You don't owe me anything. It's not your debt to pay. I'm not worried about you running off, but I am concerned about how you'll get home."

"I'll give Luna a call and see if she can take me home."

"I'm here. I found you. I'll take you home."

"You found me, so you're keeping me?" She narrowed her eyes, trying to figure him out.

"Sounds good."

"But you don't even like me. Every time you see me, you glare a hole right through me."

"What? No I don't."

"Yes you do. You're doing it right now."

"I am not," he snapped.

"Are you always this grumpy?"

"No. I barely slept last night. I saved your ass, and now you're giving me grief." His deep frown and narrowed eyes showed his annoyance, but the way he held her hand, his fingers lightly tracing her palm, said something else entirely. Over the last few years, she'd caught him watching her on occasion. She always thought it had something to do with her brother. That Connor had pissed Rory off about something and he'd been looking for a way to get back at Connor, or for her to make things right. She'd left it alone, hoping to never have to confront this huge, kinda scary guy. But now, looking closer, he wasn't really scary at all. Just gruff, to the point, and, dare she say, shy. While he had no problem looking at her, he had a hard time holding eye contact. He groused at her instead of really talking. He seemed perpetually perturbed. But maybe she'd read him all wrong. After all, she didn't even know him.

Sadie grabbed his hand and gave it a firm shake, ignored the pain in her wrist, then held it. "We've never actually met. You graduated before I got to high school. I'm Sadie Higgins. I owe you my life. Thank you for finding me and getting me to the hospital. I owe you a debt of gratitude I can never repay, but I'll sure try."

"Uh, Rory Kendrick. I'm glad I found you when I did. You don't owe me anything."

"Yeah, I do." He opened his mouth to argue, but she squeezed his hand. "I'm just as stubborn as you, so don't try to convince me otherwise. It's useless and will only make you frown more."

His sour face deepened until a touch of temper showed through.

"We need to get Kaley back in here. Seems you only smile for her."

His mouth softened. He did not smile. "She's a sweet girl."

"Yeah, and I'm a pain in your ass because I can't tell you where my brother is, or what happened to your cattle."

The frown came back. "That's not why I'm here."

"No. You don't care where he is?"

His eyes narrowed with determination. "Oh, I will find him, but I'm here for you."

Surprised, she blurted out, "Why?"

He stared down at their joined hands. She had yet to pull hers free. She didn't really want to, because as long as he touched her and the buzz crept up her arm, she didn't have to think about anything but the warmth of his skin against hers.

"I want to help you," he whispered. "Your brother, I want to kill." He cocked up one side of his mouth, like, *Obviously*.

"Well, if you think he's coming here to check on me, you're wrong."

"Exactly the reason he should be shot. You don't turn your back on family."

"Another thing I've tried and failed to teach him."

"I'm happy to do so for you."

Sadie stared around the room. She hated hospitals. "I really need to get home to my father. He needs me."

"You're in no condition to go anywhere right now."

"Did Dr. Bowden say I had to stay?"

He frowned. "Bell stopped by while you slept. She'd like you to stay another day."

"I can't leave my dad for that long. He's sick. I'm fine. Nothing that won't heal on its own."

The deep frown came back. "Hang tight, let me go see what she says." Rory walked out of her room and returned a few minutes later, looking grim. "Bell said that since the cops aren't arresting you, I can take you home to finish recuperating, though I don't agree."

Sadie sat up, wincing when she hit a particularly bad cut, proving that Rory might be right about her staying at the clinic longer, but she needed to get home to her dad.

"You okay?" He squeezed her hand.

"I think it's going to be a few days until at least a few inches of me feel better. The rest will take time. Mind handing me my bag?"

Rory let go of her hand, but didn't move away. He stared down at her. She stared back, waiting to see if he'd speak his mind.

"You're beautiful." He reached out and traced a lock of her hair, tucking it behind her ear.

She didn't move, didn't breathe, didn't know what to say. His softly spoken words went in through her ears and dropped straight down into her heart. She held on to the warmth that settled there.

He turned to get her bag from the set of drawers across the room, but she snaked her hand out and grabbed his forearm. His very thick arm.

"Thank you."

He turned back and stared down at her, this time looking her right in the eye and holding it. She read so much in that look. A deep longing. A truth that went beyond words. Sincerity to match the depth of emotion he put in those simple words. She saw deeper to the part of him that wanted to say more, share more, but held back for whatever reason, so all he said was "I mean it."

His gaze went to her hand on him. She thought he might have growled under his breath, but let it go as just her imagination. He saved her. They shared a traumatic experience in different ways, but still the same. He felt something for her because he'd seen her vulnerable. He'd seen her injuries up close and personal. If what happened to her affected her this deeply, seeing her bloody had to touch something inside him to make him stay by her side this whole time. He had a ranch to run, a family of his own, he didn't need to be here with her, but he'd stayed anyway. It touched her deeply that this strong, stoic, keep-to-himself man cared enough not to leave her alone during the worst time of her life.

"Where'd you go?" His rich voice resonated through her and connected to something deep inside she couldn't name.

"You stayed." It hit her all at once. The fog from the pain meds cleared enough for her brain to start putting things together beyond the events that landed her in this hospital bed. Her brother left her to die, but this stranger, this man she didn't know at all, not only saved her but stayed. He held her hand through the night and today. He might not be the best communicator, but he'd comforted her to the point that up until this moment she didn't realize her own family hadn't come to be by her side.

She didn't blame her father. His health prevented him from doing what he wanted. The stress of what happened probably made him feel worse. Still, it would have been nice if for once he'd come to take care of her instead of it always being the other way around.

"I couldn't leave you," Rory whispered.

Sadie fell back onto the pillows and stared up at the ceiling. "Why not? Everyone else has."

Rory planted his hands on either side of her shoulders and leaned over her, staring down into her tear-filled eyes. "I'd never do that to you." He quickly pulled away and stood up. "Sorry."

For what? Pointing out that a near stranger would do something her own family wouldn't or couldn't? Or that he'd gotten too close? She actually wished he hadn't backed off, but wrapped her in his thick arms and held her. She'd like to be wrapped up in all that strength. Stupid. Silly. She didn't need a hug; she needed to figure out how to repay this man for all he'd lost and all he'd done for her.

"It's okay."

Rory handed her the bag his brother had packed for her.

She unzipped it and shook her head. "Does Colt think I've got a hot date, or something?"

"What? Why?"

Without thinking, she pulled out the black lace bra and panty set Luna had bought her for her last birthday, teasing her that maybe if she wore them she'd feel sexy and say yes to one of the many guys who came into the diner and hit on them. She'd never worn them and didn't have time for dating. The guys she met never really captured her interest. Well, one man had her full attention. He stood in front of her, his eyes wide and locked on the lingerie in her hands.

"Uh, I guess he grabbed whatever was there."

"Yeah, right. He had to dig deep to come up with these." She slid off the bed. "My feet are still swollen." She wiggled her sore toes. "I'll make whatever he brought work. Really, I'm grateful you guys thought to do this for me, otherwise I'd be wearing this ridiculous gown home."

"It's better than what you arrived in."

She laughed under her breath, not really feeling it at all. "I guess you know black lace isn't exactly my everyday thing." That's right, he'd seen her practically naked in her less than appealing cotton bra and panties. Great. Add humiliation and embarrassment to everything else that happened to her.

"There's nothing for you to be embarrassed about." Rory's gaze dipped down, scanning her body all the way down to her toes. She felt the heat wash over her skin even as the flush bloomed on her cheeks. The man barely said anything to her, but what he did say seemed to hit her hard and deep.

She ducked her head, slid off the bed onto her sore feet, and hobbled to the bathroom, carrying the duffel at her side, happy to be free of the IV line. It brushed the gash on her leg, and she hissed in a breath. Rory was beside her in the blink of an eye. Who knew the big guy could move that fast?

He held her arm to keep her steady and stared down at her. "Are you okay?"

"I just hit the cut on my leg."

"Do you need some help getting dressed?"

She put her hand over his on her arm. "I've got this. Really, I'm okay."

He pressed his lips together. Lips that looked soft, despite how they always seemed to be turned down into a frown. "You don't look fine at all."

"You don't look so hot yourself, cowboy. You need to get some sleep and eat a decent meal."

"You barely ate your breakfast. You refused lunch."

"Sorry, I guess I should have given it to you."

"I don't want to take you home," he said out of the blue.

"What? Why?"

"I can't be sure you'll be safe there."

"It's my home. Nothing is going to happen to me."

"I bet you thought that when you went after your brother. His friends are dangerous. Do you have somewhere else I can take you? How about to Luna's place?"

"No. My father needs me. I'm going home." She stepped away, pulling her arm free of his light grasp. She walked into the bathroom and closed the door. She needed the distance. Rory sitting beside her bed watching over her gave her comfort when it shouldn't. She could take care of herself. Okay, except when some nutcase strung her up in a tree to get his rocks off watching her bleed. Still, she didn't need Rory to worry about her. She didn't need him to act like he cared.

She didn't need him.

But God, wouldn't it be nice to have someone like him. Strong. Dependable. Someone who cared about family, the land, a way of life she used to have but lost these last years as her ranch turned to dust and the horses got sold off. Instead of working her ass off to keep her head above water and her brother out of jail, what would it be like to have a home, a husband, a life that included love and happiness and laughter? God, when was the last time she laughed? When was the last time she went on a date? Or felt the way Rory made her feel with one look? Although sometimes those looks could mean he'd like to kill her as much as they could mean he wanted her. There wouldn't be a whole lot of laughing with him. The man never smiled.

Except for one little girl he called angel. Kaley changed everything about him. He responded to the little girl and let down his guard. His very fortified guard. Why did he need it?

She didn't know, but it made him less than approachable. So how the hell was she going to make things right with him when she didn't have the money to pay him back for the cattle?

With her mind still cloudy from the pain meds, she pushed her worries aside and undid the gown strings at her back. It hurt like hell to move. Everything ached, but she got the job done and let the gown fall and pool at her feet.

The bandages around her ankles and wrists sent a bolt of fear rushing through her. The sense of being bound and hung by her hands made her skin break out in a fine sheen of sweat. Naked, she stared down at her body and every nick, scrape, puncture, and cut.

"Are you okay in there?"

"I'm fine." She couldn't hide the quiver in her voice.

"Sadie." Rory's deep, rich voice held so much concern. For her. The sister of the man who stole from him. Tears welled in her eyes, but she blinked them away. She'd held it together so far; she wouldn't break down now. Not with Rory standing right outside the door.

"I'm almost done."

She pulled the clothes out of the bag and set them on the sink. The panties were pretty. She should wear them more often. For whom? She had nothing but work and debt in her life.

The lace molded to her hips. She slid her hands over the soft material, taking in something soft and good when so much in her life was hard and went from bad to worse. She pulled the bra straps up her arms and adjusted the cups at her breasts, but when it came to trying to fasten it at her back, it hit a particularly nasty cut and stung. She tore the bra off and tossed it back in the bag, opting to put the black tank top on without it. She pulled the black leggings on, thankful Colt hadn't brought her a pair of jeans. The soft cotton was much better on her legs than denim. Because of where the elastic waistband hit around her waist, she pulled it lower to avoid a particularly sore line of gouges at her sides and across her belly. She looked and felt like some abused voodoo doll a witch doctor used to curse her.

She leaned down to pull on her sock, but lost her balance when the movement hurt her sore back and shoulders. She let herself fall to the floor. Bad idea. She put out her hand to catch herself, only to hurt her wrist even more.

She groaned and sucked in a deep breath to stave off the pain.

The door flew open and Rory rushed in, bending down beside her and brushing his hand over her hair. She stared up at him, lost in the depth of concern filling his eyes.

"Are you okay, sweetheart? Did you fall?"

Sweetheart? Did she fall? Damn if her heart didn't trip, then stutter back to some new beat. Yeah, maybe she was falling for this quiet giant, but it needed to stop. She was tired. Hurt. Looking for something good and decent to hold on to and here he was, but he wasn't for her.

"Sadie."

"When you say my name . . ." She shook her head and stared down at the floor.

"What?" he asked the top of her head.

If feels like you're calling me home. She couldn't say that to him. He'd think her mad. Or at least drugged out of her mind. Yes. That was it. Nothing but all the pain meds they'd given her. She'd be thinking straight and clear again tomorrow.

"Nothing. Never mind. I'm fine." *No you're not. You're losing it if you think Rory would ever be interested in you for anything other than finding your brother and killing him.*

"I tried to put on my socks." What else could she say?

Rory's gaze narrowed on her and focused on her moving her hands back and forth, stretching her wrists. He tucked one arm under her up-drawn knees and the other at her back, his hand dipping under her arm. He picked her right up off the floor like a feather and settled her against his chest. He carried her into the other room and set her gently on the bed. Without a word, he went back to the bathroom, grabbed the bag, came back, and set it at her feet. He picked up her hairbrush from inside and stepped close next to her and began running the brush over her tangled mess of hair. Everything in her stilled at his soft touch, the rhythmic sensation of the brush sliding through her hair. A tidal wave of memories flashed through her mind.

"My mother used to brush my hair at night." She'd tell Sadie how pretty she was, how much she loved her. Sadie didn't feel either of those things right now. "I miss her."

Rory didn't say anything for a long moment, just kept brushing her long hair down her back. "My mother used to let me stay up on snowy nights," he said at last. "She'd put all of us boys to bed, then come back and get me so my little brothers didn't know. She'd take me downstairs to the big window in the family room. She'd sit in the overstuffed chair with me in her lap and we'd drink hot chocolate and watch the snow, the house dark and quiet. Her presence used to fill the quiet. I miss her most when it's quiet."

"You lost both your parents, right?"

"Avalanche covered their car on a back road through some steep terrain. They froze to death before help arrived."

Sadie turned to face him. "Oh God, Rory, I'm so sorry. Then you found me out there nearly frozen to death." She closed her eyes for a moment, imagining what that must have done to him. "I can't imagine what went through your mind."

"Murder."

"You thought I was dead? Great. Add that to the list of things I have to make up to you."

Rory shook his head. "No. I wanted to murder whoever did those heinous things to you."

"Yeah, well, get in line behind me."

"You do realize it's only a matter of time before the cops find your brother and put him in jail."

"That doesn't mean I'm going to be the one who puts him there." She raised her shaking hand to her head and pressed on her forehead above her eye where the stress headache gathered strength.

Rory took her shaking hand in his and held it. "Are you afraid to go home?"

Yes. No. Yes. "I don't have a choice." She stood beside the bed, but didn't step away. She couldn't.

Rory held firm to her hand. He didn't hurt her, just gently tugged to get her attention. "He'd be stupid to come after you again, knowing I'm coming after him."

She met his steady gaze. "Don't you think that's a bit arrogant?"

"It's the truth. I won't let anything happen to you."

She cocked her head, wondering how he planned to do anything once she was back home, back to her mundane life.

"If you need me, I'm there."

CHAPTER 6

Rory stopped the truck outside Sadie's home. Once she got dressed—and put a light blue sweater over the black tank top that hugged her curves and drove him nuts—she dragged her feet getting ready to leave. He hated the way her hands trembled, the lost look in her eyes as they drove, the quiet that grew thick inside the truck, and most especially the unnatural distance she kept between them, her side pressed to the door.

"Do I make you nervous?"

Her head snapped toward him. "No. Why?"

"Do I scare you?"

"That's ridiculous."

The front door to her house opened, drawing her attention. He reached over to touch her shoulder just to see what she'd do. She jumped, turned, and smacked his hand away. He held his hand up to let her know he didn't mean to harm her. Something died inside him, knowing she really did fear him.

"Rory, I'm sorry. I don't know what's the matter with me." She raked both hands through her hair and held it at the back of her head, staring out the window at her home with the sagging steps, weathered white paint, and cracked front window.

"You're scared."

"I don't have time to be scared."

"You've got no cause to be scared of me."

"It's not you. It's me. I can't get what happened out of my head. What he did to me. Why?" She let out a heavy sigh. "I'm just sore and tired and . . ."

"And?"

"I don't know if I have it in me to keep doing this."

"You do."

"How do you know that? Up until you found me the other day, the only other time we met is when my brother was stupid enough to take a swing at Colt."

"Going up against one Kendrick is stupid. Taking on all three of us is suicide."

She smiled. Not a lot, just enough to tilt her pretty lips up at the corner and put a little spark back in her eyes. Those eyes swept over him.

"I see your point. The three of you together is a whole lot of muscle. I appreciate you letting him go that night."

"If you hadn't stepped in—"

"And nearly gotten decked myself."

"We'd have taught your brother a lesson about being stupid."

"You let him go for me?"

Rory pressed his lips together and nodded. "You've got guts to put yourself in front of your brother and in between us. You've been holding this place and your family together for years. You need some rest, time to let what happened settle, and you'll bounce back."

"Right. Back to work. See if I can dig myself out of this hole." Sadie pulled the handle on the truck door and pushed it open.

"Hold it. Let me help you out. You're still recovering."

She turned back and looked him right in the eye. "You've helped more than I deserve. Thank you, Rory. You don't know what it means to me that you not only saved my life, but stayed with me. I can promise you, I'll try my best to pay you back."

"Sadie . . ."

She slipped from the car with her bag slung over her shoulder and headed for her father up on the porch. He held his arms out to her and she walked right into them.

"Hey, Dad. How are you?"

"No use fussing over this old man." He held her softly, not wanting to hurt her, but then stepped back and held on to her shoulders. "Are you okay?"

"Right as rain."

"No use lying to me, girl. That Colt Kendrick came by to tend the horses and told me all about what happened."

"I'm fine, Dad. Come on, let's go in and get you settled. You must be hungry."

He looked past her shoulder. "Who's your friend?"

Sadie spun around to face him, her golden hair flying out behind her. "Rory, is there something you need?"

"Yeah, you to stop dismissing me."

"I . . ."

"Mr. Higgins, I'm Rory Kendrick. Have you seen your son, Connor?"

Her father stepped beside her and hooked his bony arm around her waist, holding her close. "He's not about to show his face here after what he's done."

"What's that smell?" Sadie raised her face and sniffed the smoke on the breeze. Without a thought to her injuries, she bolted past her father and ran into the house.

Rory followed Mr. Higgins in and found Sadie in the kitchen, flipping the stove handle off. She used the potholder to shove the smoking pot off the burner. She waved the pot holder to clear the smoke in the kitchen, then stepped back and opened the kitchen window. Rory opened the one in the living room, noting the piled-up papers, food wrappers, and remotes on the table next to the recliner.

"Did you burn something?" Mr. Higgins asked, looking genuinely confused.

Sadie stared at her father. The initial fear from the fire faded to concern and sadness. "Why don't you go watch your show, Dad. I'll clean up here and make you something to eat."

Mr. Higgins coughed from the smoke, but the rattle in his chest and the way his face turned a deep red disturbed Rory. He took a closer look at the man who couldn't be more than fifty-five. His pasty complexion, thinning hair, frail frame, and the dark circles under his eyes made him seem older and like a man who'd been sick a long time.

"Mr. Higgins, are you okay?"

"Fine. Just trying to catch my breath." Mr. Higgins coughed a couple more times.

Sadie stood beside her father, rubbing her hand over his back.

Her father looked up at her and reached to touch the nasty bruise on her face. Like he didn't see it at all, he said, "You look so much like your mother."

"Come, Dad, sit in your chair. You need to rest."

"Your mama used to make the best fried chicken and biscuits. Mmm, mmm, those biscuits melted in your mouth."

Sadie led her father to his chair. Mr. Higgins shuffled along beside her and literally fell into the seat. Sadie handed him the remote and bent next to him, though it cost her to do so thanks to her many injuries. She squinted her eyes in pain, but didn't let her father know how much she hurt. That hurt ran deeper for her father's deteriorating condition.

"I love you, Dad."

Her father ran his hand down her head and held a lock of her blond hair in his hand. "Now, what's all this?"

"I had a bad day. I wanted you to know. I love you. I'll take care of you."

"You always do. You're a good girl." Mr. Higgins looked around the open room. "Will Connor be home soon?"

"I'm sure he will. Can I get you something to drink while I make dinner?"

Mr. Higgins patted Sadie's hand on his leg. "I'd like that . . . you know the . . ." Mr. Higgins's eyes squinted as he tried to think of the right word. "You know what I like."

"Sure, Dad. I'll get it."

Mr. Higgins focused on the TV. His face went soft as he stared. Rory wasn't sure he was actually watching TV or lost inside his muddled mind.

Sadie stood and cocked her head, indicating for him to follow her to the door. She walked out and down the porch steps, standing between the house and his truck.

"Thank you for driving me home. I appreciate all you've done, but I need to take care of things here now."

"What's wrong with your dad?"

She stared off into the distance and sighed so heavily her breath blew harder than the wind ruffling her hair. "He's dying." She whispered the words like she couldn't bear to speak them out loud.

"Of what?" he asked gently, wanting to comfort, but not really knowing how.

Sadie wrapped her arms around her middle and stared up at the darkening sky. "I don't know. Not for sure. At my prodding, he saw a couple of doctors, but would never tell me exactly what they said. Just a bunch of 'They're doing tests. Everything is fine.' I can't say when he went last. He's trying to protect me, but all he does is make me worry more.

"He's lost about thirty pounds in the last three months. He smoked for nearly forty years of his life. He up and quit about two years ago, but his cough just keeps getting worse. Now his memory fades. Sometimes he's so confused he doesn't know where he is or what he's doing."

"Like forgetting he left a pot of chili on the stove."

"A couple of times he wandered off in the middle of the night. When I found him walking down the road, he said he was going courting my mother." She gave a soft chuckle that held little amusement. "His mind takes him back to her. Always her."

"He must have loved her a lot."

Again, another soft smile that didn't really hold any happiness. "They were great together. Always smiling and laughing. They'd share these looks . . . Like they had a secret."

"My mother would look at my dad sometimes when he'd come in from working all day. They said so much with that look."

"I guess if you love someone that much, words aren't needed. That feeling is just there between you and it's enough to fill up the silence." Sadie shook off the cold and her thoughts with a shiver. "Sorry. Lost myself in romantic fancy there for a minute. Must be the pretty sunset and the waning pain meds."

"That's how it should be between a man and a woman." Rory didn't know what else to say, because he didn't want to dismiss what she'd said.

Her gaze met his. She didn't say anything but must have read in him his understanding of how she felt.

She sucked in a bolstering breath. "Anyway, I suspect my father is suffering from lung cancer and it's spread to his brain. Probably his whole body by now. Whatever the doctors told him, he's decided to live out his remaining days here."

"You think he's only got days?" Rory stared back at the house, hoping she was wrong. For her sake. He hated the sadness in her eyes. He knew what it was like to lose a parent and although she'd already lost her mother, he didn't want to see her lose her father. Not now. Not this way. "You and Dane are friends. Bell's his wife. Call them. She'll come by and check on your dad. Maybe there's something she can do."

"I don't think anything or anyone can help him now. I want to believe that what I see plain as day in front of me isn't the truth. I want him to live a good long time and see these hard times turn into good ones."

Yes, she wanted her father to see Connor turn his life around. Maybe see his daughter get married and have a family of her own. His grandfather nagged Rory daily for a great-grandbaby before he died. If Mr. Higgins truly was dying this young, he'd never see his own grandchild, let alone his daughter happily married.

Rory's gut tied in knots thinking of her with some other guy. Like he wanted to be with her. He did, but it didn't seem possible. Rory wanted to get to know her better. He'd like to see her smile. But with this business with her brother and what she had to deal with here at home with her dad, the timing sucked. Not to mention the fact he hadn't dated a woman properly in years. His skills hadn't just grown rusty, they'd turned to dust.

"I'm sorry, Sadie. I wish there was something I could do for you."

"You've done so much already." She eyed him strangely, made some decision he couldn't guess at, then rushed to him and threw her arms around his middle, locking his arms at his sides.

Stunned by her show of affection, he stood there stone still and took in her sweet scent, the softness of her body against his, the way her head lay against his chest, tucked under his chin.

"Thank you for saving me." She hugged him tight, then let him loose all at once and rushed up the steps and into her house, leaving him standing there dumbfounded.

What did that hug mean? Certainly not what he wanted it to mean if she ran away from him.

He stared back at the house and the closed door and wondered. They'd shared some personal things over the last day or so, but he wanted more. Did she?

CHAPTER 7

Rory rode back into the barn and dismounted from his horse. He pulled the reins over the horse's head and tried to contain his fury. Another five head of cattle missing. The asshole was brazen enough to steal an entire herd a week ago, and now he'd come back and taken more. The horse shied and sidestepped, reading Rory's foul mood. He tried to suck in a soothing breath and calm himself down, but he'd barely slept these last days, thinking about Sadie, dreaming about her. He didn't mind the nice ones where he kissed her and made love to her all through the night. The ones that turned to nightmares, with her bloody and swinging from a tree, left him awake and staring at the ceiling in a cold sweat. All he did was worry about her. He wondered if her injuries were healing. Had her brother come back home and put her in more danger? Did that asshole who'd strung her up want to hurt her again because she could ID him and send him to jail for what he did to her and for stealing the cattle? Were the cops keeping up with the patrols by her house? Was it enough to keep her safe?

Not knowing what she was doing, how she was

doing, drove him to distraction. He couldn't think about anything else.

A soft, feminine voice drifted on the wind.

Great, now he was hearing her in the barn.

"You keep looking like that, people are going to start crossing the street when they see your sour face."

Rory sighed out his frustration and raised his gaze to the rafters. "Granddad, I don't have time to spar with you."

"I only stopped to see what put you in such a foul mood. Not that you've had any other mood these last days. I'm on my way to the corral. Looks like our Colt done found himself a pretty woman."

"What?" Rory turned and stared out the barn doors. He didn't quite believe his eyes at first, but it was really her.

"What's she doing here?"

"She rode up with all them horses about ten minutes ago. Colt's been charming her ever since. I hope he decides to keep this one instead of just tossing her in the hay and sending her on her way."

"Over my dead body." Rory stormed past his grandfather, headed straight for his dead little brother.

"Well, now. So it's like that, is it?"

"Don't start." Rory didn't want to talk about his grandfather's obsession with them getting married and having babies. Right now, he wanted to get his woman away from his horny little brother.

Colt reached out and took Sadie's hand, turning it to see the healing wounds around her wrists.

Rory saw red. "Let her go."

Colt held her hand, but turned his head to stare at Rory. His brother's cocky grin set off another wave of rage inside him.

"I said, let her go."

"These look better. When I saw you laid out in the back of the truck after Rory found you, man, that was a sight." Colt gave Rory a devilish look, baiting him.

The reminder that his brother saw Sadie nearly naked pissed Rory off even more. His brain registered that Colt wanted to mess with him, but another, deeper part of him wanted to crush him for daring to touch her, let alone look at her.

Sadie pulled her hand free and wrapped her fingers around her wrist. "They're getting better. I get my stitches out in a couple of days."

Colt smiled at Sadie the way he did every girl he flirted with. "You'll be back to your old self, ready to put this all behind you and have some fun."

The implied *with me* didn't escape Rory.

"What the hell are you doing here?" Rory didn't mean for the question to come out quite so harsh or accusing, but Colt got the better of him and Rory lost his temper. Normally, he was the one razzing his little brother, but this time Colt got him back. It didn't mean Rory calmed down. In fact, Sadie's wide eyes and the way she flinched and took a small step back set off a whole new round of angry. This time at himself for making her think she needed to fear him and put more space between them.

"Never you mind my grandson," Granddad said, stepping up beside Rory and smacking him on the shoulder. "I'm Sammy, these two yahoos' grandfather. You're the Higgins girl, right, pretty girl?"

"Uh." Sadie eyed Rory nervously. "Yes, I'm Sadie Higgins, sir. I've come to pay part of my debt and speak with you about settling up the rest."

"What's this about a debt?" Ford asked, stepping up beside Rory.

Great. His whole family was here to witness him losing his mind.

"There is no debt. You did not steal the cattle. You don't owe us anything." Rory tried to keep his voice neutral, but it came out harsher than he wanted. Damnit, why couldn't she see her brother was responsible? He'd pay. She'd suffered enough and he wouldn't have her losing something, anything else in her life.

Sadie ignored him and addressed his grandfather again. "Mr. Kendrick, my brother is the one who stole from you. He's my family. My responsibility. He's not going to pay you back, but I will. These horses don't cover the whole debt, but they are well trained and from great stock. You could breed them, or sell them for the money I owe you."

"Sadie." Rory said her name in warning to get her to stop this.

She pulled out the papers sticking out of her back pocket and handed them to his grandfather. "Everything you need for the horses. Their bloodlines, vet records, and ownership."

"These are some damn fine horses, Sadie." Colt knew what he was talking about. He loved the horses on the ranch. Preferred them over the cattle since he was a kid.

Colt pat the palomino beside him. The horse rubbed against Sadie's side. She reached up and held the horse by the neck close to her. Obviously, this one horse held a special place in Sadie's big heart.

"Since they don't cover the cost of the herd—"

"Or the five cattle *your brother* stole this morning," Rory pointed out.

"What?" Sadie, Colt, and Ford all said at the same time.

"There are five more cows missing."

Sadie's eyes remained wide with surprise. "Rory, I'm so sorry. Are you sure it was him?"

"They came in from the back of the property again with a truck and trailer. Your brother and his buddies have been picking off cows for months."

She huffed out a frustrated breath and raked her hand through her hair. "How stupid could he be to steal from you again? Why not target another ranch?"

"I have some ideas about that." He didn't share them, even though everyone stared at him, waiting.

Her hands went up, then slapped against her thighs in defeat. "Well, I guess the debt keeps mounting. So, you have the horses." She pulled an envelope from her other back pocket and handed it to his grandfather.

Granddad opened the envelope and showed them all the stack of cash.

"It's not enough, I know, but it's all I've got after I sold off the hay and grass and settled up my bill at the clinic."

"Sadie, I mean it. Take your horses and your money back."

"Rory, I need to do this. I need to know I've made it right with you and your family. You saved my life and I've made yours worse. I can't live with that. I won't. My brother may not be a good person, but I am. I was raised to do the right thing, and I will do it now."

Determination gleamed in her eyes. "My circumstances make it difficult to pay you the rest outright, so I'd like to offer to work off the rest."

Rory opened his mouth to protest, but his grandfather clamped his hand on Rory's forearm. "Hush, boy."

Rory glared at his grandfather, not understanding one bit why he let this go on.

"What is it you'd like to do here, pretty girl?"

"Well, I have two jobs in town. During the week I work the breakfast and lunch shift at the diner. On the weekends I work at Zac's Gas and Grocery. Some nights I cover the late shift at the diner. So I could come in the early morning, feed the horses, muck out stalls, that kind of thing. I could come back in the evening and, I don't know, clean house, cook, whatever you need me to do."

"You cook?" Colt, Ford, and his grandfather asked in unison. They all stared at her with baleful, hopeful eyes.

Jesus, this was really happening. She'd be here all the time. And that's when it hit him. His grandfather didn't want her to pay them back, he wanted her here. Right under Rory's nose, so he'd get his great-grandbaby.

"Granddad," Rory warned, not liking this setup at all. He didn't want her working here.

"Now, Rory, you know we all can cook one thing or another that passes as decent food, but if this here pretty girl can cook something worth coming to the table for, I'm all for it."

"Uh, my mother taught me to cook. I sometimes cover for the cook at the diner. I've never had an angry customer or a complaint, so that's something."

"You're hired." Granddad stuffed the envelope and papers in his back pocket. "It's been a long time since we had a woman on the ranch. I hate to tell you the house could use some work." His granddad nodded and cocked up one side of his mouth, the decision made. "Yes, sir, we should have thought to do this a long time ago. We accept the bargain, pretty girl."

His grandfather held out his hand to shake Sadie's. She placed her hand in his and accepted.

"I'll be here tomorrow morning to work in the stables. Then I'll come back after my shift at the diner. I'll make dinner, maybe prepare something for your breakfast or lunch the next day, and do some cleaning."

"Sounds good. We'll see you then."

"No," Rory said, drawing his brothers' and grandfather's gazes. "You can come after your shift at the diner, but you are not working in the stables. You're still hurt and need time to heal. You need your rest. I'm not having you wake up extra early to work here, then work an eight-hour shift in town and here in the evening, too. It's too much."

"But . . ."

"No buts. That's how it's going to be if you insist on doing this and my family goes against my wishes. Your father needs you, too." Something sad and resigned crossed her eyes. "Is he worse?"

A Jeep pulled up. The driver honked the horn twice to get their attention.

"Is that Luna?" Colt asked, holding his hand over his brow to shield his eyes from the sun as he squinted to see the woman behind the wheel.

"She's here to pick me up," Sadie said. "We have a shift at the diner together this morning. I'll be by later tonight to get started."

Colt bolted for the barn, avoiding a woman for the first time in his life. Must be a story there, but Rory had other things to think about right now. Like Sadie at his house every night.

Sadie walked past Ford and headed for her friend.

"Sadie, your dad?" Rory asked, concerned for her.

Sadie turned back, the look on her face all he needed to know. Things were getting worse.

"I'm sorry about the cows."

"You know I have to call the cops."

She pressed her lips together, then softly said, "I know."

She walked to the Jeep, climbed in, shut the door, and stared out the window at him. Luna, her friend, had opened her door and stood, staring over the top of the car, her gaze locked on Colt's retreating back.

"Wasn't she seeing Colt's buddy a while back?" Ford asked. "What happened between them?"

"I don't know," Rory answered, barely able to keep up with his brothers' lives, let alone those of their friends. "Whatever it was, Colt's not happy about it."

Ford slapped Rory on the back. "So, will you and Sadie be messing up the sheets before she washes them?"

Rory shoved Ford away and pointed a finger at him. "I don't give a shit what her brother did, you will treat her with respect."

Ford held his hands up in defense. "Never said I wouldn't, but it's obvious you've got a thing for her."

"If she insists on working here for us, I'll let her, but you and Colt will steer clear."

"Got it. She's yours. I hear you loud and clear."

"She's not my anything. She's had a rough life, complicated by her no-account brother. Her father is ill and dying slowly right before her eyes. The last thing she needs is more grief, or you and Colt flirting with her while she's trying to do the decent thing."

"I'm sorry, man. I had no idea."

"Well now you do. You'll relay it to Colt when he gets his head out of his ass. Right now, we need to get these horses sorted out." Rory stared at the twenty horses gathered together in the small pen. "How did she get them here?"

"Saw her ride up with all them trailing behind her," his grandfather said.

"She rode? In her condition?"

"She looks fine to me," Ford said.

Rory spun and grabbed him by the shirt.

Ford put his hands up to ward off Rory. "I meant she doesn't look like she's hurting any." Rory shoved Ford back again. "Man, get a grip. I'd never go after your girl. Especially when you finally like one. I mean, seriously, when's the last time you were with a woman?"

Rory stared at the empty driveway Sadie had disappeared down. "Too long."

"Yeah, I got that from the pissed-off way you've been walking around here for months." Ford planted his hands on his hips and gave Rory a you-know-it's-true look.

"You're like a raging bull kept in his pen and away from the herd too long," his grandfather added.

"Look who's talking. You two don't have the ladies lining up at the door."

"No, but your lady will be back tonight." His grandfather started back up to the house. "You're welcome." Tickled he'd gotten the better of Rory, his grandfather chuckled.

"**What's with the** death glare at Colt?" Sadie eyed Luna, then grabbed the dashboard as her friend backed up too fast, hit the brakes too hard, then sped down the driveway like she was making a speedy getaway from an armed robbery.

"It's not for him, but myself."

"What do you mean?"

"Nothing. I thought maybe when he saw me he might come up to talk."

Instead, Colt had turned and walked away and obviously upset Luna.

"Did you two have a fight?"

"No."

"But he's angry with you?"

"Yes. No. Yes. I don't know."

"Do you want to explain what happened?"

"Not really." Luna turned onto the main road to town and gunned it.

Sadie put her hand on Luna's arm. "Hey, slow down. He's not coming after us."

Luna let up on the gas pedal and sucked in a deep breath and sighed it out. "Sorry. How'd it go with Rory?"

"He's not happy about my plan to pay him back."

"Is the man ever happy?"

Rory's solemn face came to mind. "No." She remembered the way he smiled at Kaley and the way it changed his face, made him even more handsome and approachable. "Actually, I did see him smile."

Luna glanced over at her. "A real smile."

Sadie chuckled. "He doesn't talk much, but he's got this sincere, softer side that surprises me."

Luna turned and gaped at her. "You really like him."

"He thinks I'm beautiful." Shy about it, she couldn't believe she told Luna that.

"Of course he does. You are."

Sadie appreciated her friend's kindness. "He stayed. It meant so much to me that he saved me, but it goes so much deeper that he stayed."

Luna's hand settled over hers. "I would have come sooner if I'd known what happened."

"I know you would have. I'm glad you stopped by to check on me."

"When I saw the way he looked at you, the way he refused to let go of your hand, I knew there was something there, but I didn't know if you felt something for him. I left knowing he'd take care of you and get you home, but I thought maybe if you spent time with him you might like him. And you do, right?"

"I think I do. I mean, I only just met him, but there's something about him that makes me look deeper to figure him out."

"You'd have to look deep to get past his hard shell, that's for sure."

"That's just it, that's an illusion. I actually think he's kind and warm."

Luna squeezed her hand. "I'm happy for you."

"Why? He saved me. I like him. But there's nothing else going on."

Luna pulled into the diner parking lot and slipped into an empty space. She opened her door, but turned back before getting out, with a bright smile on her face. "Maybe there's nothing going on yet, but give it time. With you working there, right under his nose, something is bound to happen."

Exactly what Sadie thought when she came up with the plan to work at the Kendrick ranch. She had to repay the debt somehow, but deep down she wanted to see Rory again. She couldn't stop thinking about him. Was there something there? She wanted to find out.

CHAPTER 8

Sadie pulled up in front of her house and stared at the back end of her brother's old pickup sticking out of the empty corral behind the barn. Empty thanks to her brother's thieving. If he'd come home it meant he was in dire straits, probably trying to shake down their father for some quick cash.

She hopped out of the truck and headed inside. She'd meant to stop at home only long enough to check on her father, change out of her diner uniform into regular clothes, and head over to the Kendrick place to do her chores there, make them dinner and another of the breakfast casseroles they liked so much before she came home to try to sleep through her nightmares and do it all over again tomorrow. The weariness building inside her slowly chipped away at her resolve.

She stepped into the house, startling her brother. Connor picked up the gun sitting on the table at his arm and pointed it straight at her.

Pissed off and beyond reason, she shouted, "Go ahead."

He set the gun down and shoveled in another bite of the beef stew she'd made for her father last night. His favorite, but in his weak state he'd barely finished half a bowl.

"That's the first smart thing you've done in months."

"Why are you pissed at me?" he asked, oblivious to anyone's feelings.

The lack of empathy or regret set off an explosion of rage in her gut. "Are you seriously asking me that after what happened?"

"What? You look fine."

After a week and a half, yeah, the bruises had faded, the cuts healed to red marks, but the nightmare hadn't left her, or the sense of betrayal she felt from her brother.

She pulled up her Crystal Creek Diner T-shirt and showed him the scar on her ribs and the double lines of barbed wire cuts running across her middle.

Connor's eyes went wide with shock. "Holy shit, Sadie."

"This is only what you can see. These marks run across my back, arms, legs, everywhere."

"I had no idea." His head bent, and he couldn't look her in the eye. The same gesture she'd seen when he was a boy and did something wrong.

"You left me with that guy. The one who likes to watch people bleed. The one who left me strung up in a tree bleeding and freezing to death while you stole the Kendricks' cattle."

His head snapped up and he tried to talk his way out of trouble. Just like when he was young. But this was a lot more serious than him smashing bottles against the side of the barn, or stealing an extra dessert late at night. "You got away. That was one hell of a walk back home though."

"You aren't listening, dumbshit. I didn't get away. How could I when that asshole friend of yours strung me up with barbed wire?" She held up her hands to show him the scars and bruises still circling her wrists.

"Fuck me. He did that to you?"

His ignorance and the way he'd gone on about his life oblivious and uncaring to what happened to her after he left set off another wave of anger. "What did you think he was going to do to me? Smack me around. Rape me. Murder me. Which of those things was okay for you to live with, because you had no problem with him stripping me and punching me in the face," she shouted, letting her anger get the better of her.

"Sadie, honey, you're home." Her father walked out of his room, leaning heavily on a thick stick she'd never seen.

Sadie sucked in a breath, calmed herself, and tried her best to appear composed for her father's sake. "Dad, are you okay?"

He stared down at the stick. "My legs aren't working quite right. I stumbled earlier, so I thought I'd give this a try. What are you two fighting about now?" Her father glanced at Connor. "Did you miss school again today?"

Connor's gaze collided with hers, his confusion clear to see. "Uh, Dad, I haven't been in school for years."

"Why not? Does your sister have to ride you every day to get you to do what you're supposed to?"

Connor looked to her for an explanation.

"You only think about yourself. You never see what is right in front of you. You didn't see the threat that man posed to me. You don't see what is happening here." She held her hand out to indicate their father, a man who didn't look anything like he did just a few short months ago.

"Don't you see the truth that is right in front of you?" She didn't want to let their father know they were talking about the fact that he was dying right in front of them.

"Sadie, I can't get out of it. I'm in too deep. I didn't know . . ."

"You don't care." She spoke the sad truth. He only cared about himself.

"You don't understand . . . the people I'm involved with . . ."

"Nearly killed me. But you don't care about that, not really. You don't care about us, the things we've sacrificed for you. The love we pour out, trying to get you to see and do the right thing, but all you do is wreak havoc in our lives. Do you have any idea what you've cost us this time?"

"Sadie, if I didn't take the cattle and pay some of what I owe they were going to kill me."

Sadie shook her head. "But it would have been okay if they killed me, so long as you got the cattle. It's okay that I had to turn over all the horses to the Kendricks to put even a small dent in what we owe them. It's okay that I spend hours over there cooking and cleaning to repay the debt when I should be here with our father, spending what little time I have left with him. It's okay that I make things right when you're the one who's done them wrong."

"You don't owe them shit. They've got the money to buy more cattle."

"That is not the point. You stole from them." She fisted her hands at her side, trying not to stoop to the level of wrapping her hands around his neck and shaking some sense into him. "You steal from your own family. You treat us like what we want and need doesn't matter. You take and take and take and leave nothing but destruction in your path."

Connor slammed his hands on the table, making the bowl, glass, and silverware rattle. "They'll kill me if I don't do what they want." The glimpse of the boy she remembered disappeared behind his anger, justifications, and the drugs that even now muddled his mind.

"Sadie, honey, what is going on?" Her father looked back and forth from her to Connor. "I don't understand what is going on?" The confusion in her father's voice broke her heart.

"I'm sorry, Dad, but Connor has to go."

"It's time for school?"

"Yes, Dad. He needs to go and learn something."

"Okay." Her father walked into the other room, sat in his favorite chair, and turned on the TV.

"What the hell is wrong with him?" Connor whispered from the table. "He's wasting away to nothing, and this talk about school? I'm twenty-one, not twelve."

"Then act like it. If you'd been here these last months instead of crashing on your buddies' sofas and doing wrong at every turn, you'd know that he's been sick and getting worse."

"What can I do?" He didn't really mean he'd do anything at all. He always offered when things got tough. Maybe he'd help out by putting in a halfhearted effort, but he never saw anything through. He never put them first.

"End this now before you get yourself killed. Turn

yourself in and beg for leniency. Pray the Kendricks don't get their hands on you first."

"You know I can't do that."

"You won't do it. Instead you come here and risk me and Dad getting arrested for aiding and abetting? Get out now, or I will call the cops and tell them you're here."

"You wouldn't."

"Don't make me."

Connor picked up the gun, stood, and pushed the chair back with his legs. He tucked the gun in his jeans waistband.

"Do you really think that gun will solve anything? If you can't see that even having that in your possession is another nail in your coffin, then you are stupid and have a death wish."

"I need it."

"You need your head examined."

Maybe she did, too, because wasn't the definition of insanity doing the same thing over and over, expecting a different result? Well, she wanted off the Connor crazy train.

He left his dishes for her to clean up. Like always. He moved around the table and stared into the other room at their father glued to some old Western on TV. He'd become partial to the shows these last months. She wondered if he watched them to relive his days here on the ranch the only way he could now. He barely left the house anymore.

"I wonder if he'll still be here when I come back."

"Don't come back, Connor." The words stuck in her throat, but she pushed them out anyway. Watching Rory and his brothers with their grandfather this past week showed her what a real family should be like. They worked together, joked and teased one another, helped one another without complaint or even so much as having to ask in most cases. They shared their lives and did so with respect.

"You don't mean that."

"You've gone too far. I can't get you out of this. I can't help you anymore."

Connor's eyes narrowed with anger. He lashed out at her, yanking her purse off her shoulder and down her arm. He turned his back and dug through it.

She smacked him between the shoulder blades and on the back of his head. He shoved her back, found the cash in her purse, all her tips from work the last two days, and stuffed it in his front pocket.

"Give it back." She felt like they were ten and five and he'd stolen her favorite toy just to be a brat. This time, she couldn't let it go. She needed that money. She refused to let him take anything more from her.

Connor turned on her, grabbed her arm, twisting and yanking it up her back. He slammed her into the wall and held her there. "You want me out. You don't get to fucking tell me what to do anymore."

"Lot of good it did, you always do what you want to do anyway and blame others when it all goes to shit."

"You think you know everything. Well, smarty, if Derek finds out you ratted him out to the cops about the cattle and messing you up, then you better watch your back. He'll come after you and shut you up for good."

The threat sent a wave of panic through Sadie that made her gasp and stop breathing. She couldn't believe her brother would threaten her like this, but it didn't really surprise her. Still, the memory of what Derek did to her made her whole body tremble.

"Watch your back, sis. I'd hate for something to happen to you."

Connor shoved her hard into the wall, hurting her still healing shoulder, let her loose, and stormed out the door. She held her bruised arm to her chest and stared out the open door until he drove past in a cloud of dust. It made her feel guilty as hell, but she hoped the cops patrolling past the house every hour or so caught him.

CHAPTER 9

Rory stepped into the corral and latched the gate behind him. He'd kept Sadie's horses here the past week because, well, they refused to go anywhere else. Every time he tried to lead the stallion out so that his harem of fillies would follow, they all cowered in the back of the corral. Today he meant to get them moved out into one of the bigger pastures. Maybe he'd take a couple into the stables and get them settled with the other horses.

Ford let out a catcall whistle, which meant Sadie finally showed up to work. Both his brothers whistled at her like that to say hello and piss Rory off. He hated that they found it so easy to talk and joke with her. He wished she didn't tie his insides in knots and fry his brain every time she was in the same room.

Over an hour late, he wondered what kept her. He looked up and caught her staring at him. She raised her arm and waved. He waved back, feeling like a damn fool. He didn't want to wave at her. He wanted to go to her, take her in his arms, and kiss her. Maybe then the knot in his gut he carried around with him the last week like a lead weight would unwind and he'd be at ease. He rolled his eyes. Not likely. She avoided him.

He swung the rope and lassoed the stallion, pulling him out of the herd. The damn horse whinnied and stomped, letting Rory know he wasn't happy about this situation. Rory wasn't either. He'd like the animal to act like he should and lead his lovely ladies out of here.

"Hey, what are you doing?"

God, her voice would forever be imprinted in his mind.

"I'm trying to get your stubborn horses out of here."

"You won't do it that way."

Rory glanced over at her for the first time. His gut went tight seeing her in the white T-shirt tied into a knot at her belly, showing off just a hint of skin above her tight jeans. He swallowed and tried to focus on her face and not the swell of her breasts pressed against the T-shirt's thin fabric. "These guys are his. They should follow him."

Sadie shook her head. "Just like a man to think so. He's not the leader of this group."

"What? He's the only male."

She pressed her pretty lips together, walked to the gate, came through, and closed it behind her. "Mind if I show you a thing or two about women and horses?"

Rory eyed her. "I'm pretty sure I've got a handle on both."

"Says every guy until a woman proves him wrong."

He chuckled. "Show me what you've got."

Sadie stared at him. "Did you actually smile at me?"

He frowned. "What of it?"

"You should do it more often." She held her hand up to the horse he had on the rope. "Let him go."

"But . . ."

"Let. Him. Go."

He relented, letting her do her thing. He hadn't had any luck the last week; he doubted she'd do any better. He'd keep an eye on the dangerous stallion and make sure he didn't get any ideas about protecting his ladies and trampling Sadie.

The second the rope came off the big guy, the horse trotted back to the group, and the mares circled around him.

"Now, cowboy, you want to move this herd, you need the true leader to come forward." Sadie whistled like a bird and her palomino walked forward and nudged Sadie's hand as she held it up to the horse. Sadie rubbed her hand up the horse's long nose to scratch at the white patch on her forehead. "Hello, Sugar."

Sadie turned to him. "How about a leg up?" She moved to the horse's side and held up her leg. He grabbed hold and boosted her up. She sat atop the horse, then leaned down and gave her old friend a hug. "Hello, baby. I miss you."

"You're the one who left them here," Rory pointed out.

"I pay my debts."

Rory rolled his eyes. "I'm not doing this with you anymore. If you want to ride, you're welcome to do so any time you like."

"You mean it?"

"Why wouldn't I?"

"That's really nice. Thank you."

"Why do you think I'm not nice?"

"I don't. It's just . . . I don't know . . . You don't seem like you want me here."

"I don't want you paying off debts that aren't yours. Doesn't mean I don't like you here. I do."

"Yeah, your brothers can't stop talking about my cooking."

"Best food we've had in years around here."

Her eyebrows shot up. "You never say anything about my cooking."

"Who can get a word in with my brothers tripping over themselves to beg you to cook even more?"

"They've got some hearty appetites."

"Yeah, well, so do I."

She cocked her head to the side and stared down at him. Yeah, she got his meaning.

He let his gaze drop to her thigh in front of him and her hand resting over the place she'd been cut. He wanted to ask if she got her stitches out, but the red marks on her forearm caught his attention. He took her hand and held it in front of him, tracing the marks lightly with his fingertips. "What happened?"

She tried to pull free, but he held on. "It's nothing."

"This isn't nothing, sweetheart. Who did this?"

She put her free hand over his. "Rory, please, let it go."

It hit him all at once. "Your brother did this to you." He looked her up and down. "Are you hurt anywhere else?"

She squeezed his hand. "I'm fine. He was at my house when I got home."

"That's why you were late."

"Yeah, sorry about that."

"Fuck sorry. He hurt you. Where the hell were the cops? They're supposed to drive by your place several times a day."

"They can't watch me and my house every second of the day."

Rory brushed his fingers over her arm again, offering comfort, but noticing it made her tense, then settle again.

She didn't let go of his hand. "I made him leave."

"He didn't go willingly." Rory indicated the marks on her.

"Not without stealing the money out of my purse."

"What the hell?"

"I know. I begged him to turn himself in. He refused of course. When I told him to leave or I'd call the cops myself, he got a little physical. He won't be back."

"How do you know that?"

"He's not stupid when it comes to saving his own ass." She slipped her hand from his and set it on his shoulder. "Thanks for looking out for me."

"Seems to be my favorite thing."

"Why?" she asked, a shyness in her voice he'd never heard.

It took him a second to get the words out. "I like looking at you."

"It might help me to believe that if you smiled."

"You smile at me and I'll smile back."

Skeptical, one of her eyebrows went up. "Because you want to, or because I'm asking you to."

"Every time I think about or see you, I'm smiling on the inside." He set his hand on her thigh in front of him and squeezed softly. This time, he didn't look away, but stared into her pretty eyes. "Which means I'm smiling on the inside all the time, because I can't stop thinking about you." The gruffness in his voice probably told her that admission didn't come easy.

"Um, I don't know what to say. You barely speak to me, and when you do, you say that."

"Tell me it's just me and I won't say anything like it again."

Her hand contracted on his shoulder. He leaned in closer. She bit the inside of her bottom lip. The way it twisted her mouth made him want to kiss her even more.

"It's not just you." The shyness in her words didn't dim the reality of what she'd just admitted.

Those words hit him square in the chest. She liked him. She felt something for him. Taking a chance for once in his life, his next words tumbled out of his mouth quicker than he expected. "Would you like to go to a movie tonight?" He held his breath, hoping she said yes.

"A date?"

"Yeah, you know, one of those things where we go out, get to know each other better without being watched by my brothers and grandfather."

She looked past him. He had no doubt Ford and Colt had stopped unloading the feed to stare at them. His grandfather was probably staring out the top-floor window.

He didn't care. He was tired of looking at her from afar. Right now, he was a foot away. Still too far for his liking, but he'd take it over watching her in a store, from across the street, or from the booth at the back of the diner.

"I would love to see a movie with you, but . . ."

"Can we stop with the buts?"

She laughed and he smiled up at her. One of her eyebrows shot up. "There it is."

"What?"

"Your smile."

She did something completely unexpected and touched her fingertips to his cheek. "You're really handsome when you smile."

"And when I'm not smiling?"

"You're a whole lot of intimidating."

"I've perfected it over the years, I guess, trying to keep my brothers in line."

"I know how you feel. You've done a much better job than I ever did."

"That's because I'm bigger than you, little bit."

She laughed again and the knot in his stomach loosened up again.

"I noticed." Her gaze slid over him.

Heat spread through him like wildfire across a dry field, igniting something inside him he hadn't felt in a long time, if ever. God, how he wanted her.

"What is the but?" he asked, trying to keep things on track and get her to accept a date with him.

"I need to stop by my place after I finish up here and check on my father. I don't like to leave him these days. His confusion is getting worse."

"I'm sorry, sweetheart. If you want, go on home and watch over him. I'll pick you up later."

She shook her head. Stubborn woman.

"You're not going to give up paying me back, are you?"

"No. I owe you, plus . . . It gives me a reason to see you." She shrugged like that should be obvious to him. It hadn't occurred to him that she'd set this up to get to know him better. "I kind of got used to having you around at the hospital."

"I had a hard time leaving you at your place."

"Then stop trying to send me away all the time."

He smiled up at her. "Stay, but you don't have to work here."

"Here I thought you liked my cooking. I was going to make you some of those fried potatoes you liked so much the other day."

"Oh God, I will be your slave for more of those."

She laughed again and slid her hand from his shoulder up his neck to his hair. Her fingers toyed with the strands, sending a shiver of electricity down his spine. He stilled beside her; his hand on her thigh contracted.

She stopped her fiddling and pulled her hand back. "Sorry. I, uh . . ."

"It's fine, Sadie. Don't stop. More. All you want." He smiled to keep things light. He teased, but not really. If she saw that he could be fun and lighthearted, all the better. She made him want to be that way.

She let out a nervous laugh. "Um, where do you want these horses?"

"Running away?"

"Stopping the show." She tilted her head up toward the house. "I'd rather we keep this between us."

"Just so you know, Sadie, whatever happens between us is up to us. It has nothing to do with my family, or yours."

She nodded, but he didn't think she really believed him. This thing with her brother weighed heavily on her. She didn't like that her brother wronged Rory's family. She wanted to make things right. He got it. If it had been one of his brothers, he'd have done the same thing. He had to respect her for that.

"Take the horses past that first gate to the second one that's open." He pointed down the fence line for her to see where he meant her to go.

"Got it. Watch this, cowboy." Sadie gave her horse a soft kick and turned her back to the herd patiently waiting behind them.

Rory moved out of the way and went to open the gate for her to take the horses out. She circled around the corral once and picked up about five of the horses. They followed her around one more time, gathering another eight horses. The dust kicked up as Sadie and her followers passed him again. This time, she rode out of the corral with all the horses following, the stallion at the back, watching over his ladies. He had to hand it to her, she'd trained her horses well. She thought her palomino was the alpha in that group, but he saw deeper to the love the horses had for their mistress. They followed Sadie.

God, she was a sight, riding bareback along the dirt road and straight into the pasture he'd pointed her toward. Once all the horses ran through the gate, Ford closed and latched it. Sadie didn't quit; she ran the horses in a wide circle around the grass, letting them get their run on.

Rory stood beside Ford. Colt joined them a minute later. They stood side by side as Sadie passed them, a huge smile on her face, her blond hair flying on the wind just like the palomino's mane and tail.

"Damn, that's a pretty sight." Colt nudged Rory's arm. "She's beautiful."

"Did you finally ask her out?" Ford eyed him, one eyebrow cocked. "Because if you wait any longer, I'm going to."

"Not before me," Colt added.

Rory stood in the middle of them, planted one hand on each of their shoulders, and shoved them away.

They stumbled sideways, righted themselves, and came back to slam into his shoulders, squishing him between them. "Keep this up and someone's going to get punched."

His brothers laughed. All in good fun. This is how life had been since their parents died. He appreciated the normalcy of it all when his world felt like it was about to change, because of the woman on the back of a horse flying across the field.

"We're going out to a movie tonight. Please don't give her a hard time about this. It's new and could fall apart any second. We barely know each other. This thing with her brother is still between us."

Ford clamped a hand on Rory's shoulder. "Stop talking yourself out of this."

"Yeah, turn the grump down and the happy up and you'll be fine." Colt stared across the field as Sadie rode toward them. "Let her pick the movie and the snacks. Hold her hand during the movie. Kiss her good night."

Rory rolled his eyes. "I am not taking dating advice from my little brother."

"You should. The last date you went on was before the last Ice Age, which accounts for your sour moods." Colt took a step away, anticipating the swat Rory threw at him. Rory didn't miss, making Colt flinch. "Seriously, she's pretty, she can cook, she's nice, she can cook, and for God knows what reason she likes you. Don't fuck this up."

"You said the cooking thing twice," Rory pointed out.

"Yes, it's worth mentioning again. We haven't eaten this good since Mom was here." Ford sighed.

They all felt the impact of their parents' absence the same way and in their own way. After all these years living on the ranch, just them boys, it was nice to have a woman in the house, a reminder of their mother in some small way.

Sadie had already left her mark. The house smelled different, felt different, was different when she was in it.

"Don't you cowboys have anything better to do than stare at me," Sadie called from atop her horse.

"No," they said in unison.

Sadie laughed and so did all of them.

Rory climbed over the fence and dropped down on the other side. Sadie's gaze locked on him as he closed the distance between them. Her gaze dropped from his face, over his shoulders and chest. He had an overwhelming urge to flex, but didn't. Not with his brothers standing there taking in the show, watching every little nuance between him and Sadie.

Him and Sadie. He liked that. The idea. The reality. The possibilities of what they could share.

"Your horses are where you want them." She swung her leg over the horse's neck to slide down, but Rory caught her under the arms and lifted her off the horse and gently set her on the ground in front of him. "I can manage on my own."

"What fun would that be for me?"

She shyly ducked her head and stepped back, so she could look up at him without craning her neck. "I'm heading up to the house to make dinner." She turned to leave, but glanced over her shoulder. "See you later?"

"Nothing will keep me from you and dinner."

That made her smile at him again. She walked toward the house. Fifteen feet away, she turned back. "Are you staring at my ass?"

Yep, that sexy, sweet smile just might kill him.

"What else would I be doing?"

"Go feed the horses or mend a fence or something, anything else."

"If you're walking, sweetheart, I'm watching." He couldn't help the smile. He liked the feeling. He liked the way he was with her—somehow the weight he carried on his shoulders lessened when she was near.

She spun back around and continued on to the house, checking over her shoulder a couple times to see if he watched her. The smiles she sent his way, the little extra swing she put in her hips, cast a spell over him. He wanted her, no doubt, but he found he liked her more and more. Everything about her drew him in and made him wish for things he'd only ever thought of in the abstract but now wanted to make a reality.

CHAPTER 10

Headlights swept across the front windows. Sadie's stomach did a strange rise and fall like she'd raced down a huge dip on a roller coaster. Butterflies swarmed her belly. She tried to hold back a nervous smile, but failed. She couldn't help it. She'd been on other first dates—too many of which never turned into a second date—but this one with Rory felt different in a good way. In a way that she didn't quite get. Maybe because she didn't quite get Rory, but it still felt right. He felt right.

"There's your guy. You look real pretty, honey." Her father stared up at her from his favorite chair in the living room, a celebrity news program on the TV. "You look so much like your mother."

Sadie smiled, remembering her mother leaning over the counter toward the mirror, putting on lipstick to go out on a date with her father. She'd pressed her lips together and made a funny popping noise, then smiled down at Sadie. She'd kissed Sadie goodbye that night and Sadie made that same popping noise as her mother waved goodbye and left her and Connor with the sitter to go out with their dad. "I miss her so much."

"Me too. Go, sweetheart. Have fun tonight. Be young and happy. You deserve it."

"I love you, Dad. I'll be back in a couple of hours." She leaned over and kissed him on the cheek.

The smile he gave her was real. His eyes were clear. No sign of the confusion he suffered more and more lately.

She walked out her front door light of heart. It stuttered when Rory walked around the front of his truck and toward her wearing a navy blue thermal Henley, dark blue jeans, and black cowboy boots. The deep blue shirt made his golden hair brighter and his hazel eyes greener. He smiled at her, and her heart fluttered and lifted in her chest. She pressed a hand to her belly, but it didn't calm those swarming butterflies.

Rory's gaze scanned over her hair and face. She'd taken extra time to curl her long straight hair into chunky waves and added a touch of soft pink eye shadow to her usual eyeliner and mascara. She'd even dabbed on some tinted lip balm. His eyes stopped on her mouth, before his gaze swept over her rosy pink top down to the floral skirt that hugged her hips and flared out in a ruffle, ending several inches above her knees. She completed the outfit with her favorite pair of brown cowboy boots and executed a little shimmy, circling for him to see the whole outfit, hoping the cute clothes distracted him from the healing cuts across her thigh and knee, the nicks and scabs on her arms.

"You like?" The slight tremble in her words revealed her nerves and how self-conscious she felt about her scars and his approval.

"You're beautiful. Nice moves." His voice came out gruff.

"Maybe next time you'll take me dancing."

He shook his head. "Only if you want me to step on your feet."

She smiled and walked down the first step, but hesitated when all of a sudden his sheer size and narrowed gaze turned those nervous butterflies into a tremble of fear. Ridiculous. She set aside the nightmares that kept her up at night, and walked down the other three treads, standing close to him, but still up on the last stair so she could look him nearly in the eye. God, the man was tall. And built.

She covered her hesitation to approach him by saying, "I love to dance."

"I've got two left feet," he admitted with a self-deprecating grin.

"Are you really a bad dancer, or have you never been taught how to do it?"

"Both. About all I'm good for his holding you and swaying back and forth."

"Well, that's something."

He put his hands on her hips. She jumped, but settled quickly when his warmth seeped through her clothes and into her skin. He held her gently, sensing she needed a second, but he didn't ask about her odd reaction. To reassure him and steady herself, she swept her hands over the sides of his wide shoulders and set them on top.

"Maybe that's all I want," she admitted, liking having him close enough to smell his light, woodsy scent mixed with something uniquely him.

"We don't have to go dancing for you to get me to hold you." He reached up and traced a curl spiraling along her face. His gaze held hers.

Hers dipped to his mouth, the bottom lip just a touch fuller than the top. She slid her hand up his shoulder to the back of his neck and pulled him in for the kiss she didn't just want but needed. She hesitated a breath from his lips and stared into his eyes. The hunger there matched her own. She'd never felt this overwhelming urge to be close to someone, let alone a man, but something about Rory drew her in and made her want to stay.

"Did you change your mind, or are you just trying to kill me?"

His deep voice resonated through her. The slight tilt of humor in his lips made her smile softly. She pressed her lips to his, thinking it just a test. A way to see if they fit, connected on a deeper level than the pull she already felt toward him.

The second her lips touched his, fire lit through her system. She pulled back, surprised that such a simple thing could spark such deep and overwhelming need. The same fire she felt flashed in his golden-green eyes.

"Once wasn't enough." This time, Rory pulled her back in and kissed her, wrapping her in his strong arms. Cocooned in his warmth, she hooked her arms around his neck and pressed her body down the length of his. He engulfed her and she felt protected. Safe.

The fire sizzled through her when his tongue swept along hers in a soft sweep that was undemanding. The man knew how to take his time. She appreciated that he didn't rush, but let the intimate moment stretch.

He ended the kiss with a soft brush of his lips to hers. It took her a second to open her eyes and look up at him. God, the man was handsome at a distance. This close, he was so damn hot she wanted to lean in and kiss him again.

"Wc should go." He didn't move.

She didn't want to go anywhere. She'd like to stay right here with him in the bubble of closeness they'd created where nothing else mattered except the two of them.

She leaned back, putting some distance between them so she could cool her heels and take a breath without feeling him do the same, despite how much she enjoyed it. She got that whole magnetism thing now.

He let her go, sliding his hands down her back and taking her hands. He stepped back and pulled her off the step. "Come on. Let's go have some fun."

"I don't know about you, but I was having fun."

He opened the truck door. She hopped in and turned to face him. He leaned in the door. "You are trying to kill me." He kissed her again. Just a friendly, we're-not-done kind of thing. "I was right, once wasn't enough."

"I was wrong about you. You're nothing like what I thought."

"I'm sorry I gave you the wrong impression. I'm trying to show you who I really am."

"You're off to a really good start."

Rory kissed her again. Not just because he could, but because he needed to. She looked so lovely sitting in his truck, her hair falling in waves, framing her beautiful face, her eyes locked on him. Her soft lips melted below his. She tasted sweet and tempting. She truly was turning into an addiction. Now that he'd started kissing her, he never wanted to stop.

Her hand pressed to the side of his face. "We should go," she said against his lips.

He pulled back. She leaned forward, following his exit. The smile on her face, the laugh that bubbled up when he playfully shoved her back and closed the door between them made his gut tight and his own laugh burst free.

He pointed his finger at her. "You're dangerous."

She laughed again, covering her mouth with her fingers. He rounded the truck and slid in behind the wheel. He started the engine and pulled out of her drive, headed straight to town with Little Big Town's "Pain Killer" playing on the radio. Yeah, a little dose of Sadie sure did make everything all right.

He reached across the seat, took her hand, ignored the instinctive flinch, and linked his fingers with hers, trying not to think about the reasons why she shied away for those tiny moments before she overcame the jolt of fear that asshole Derek instilled in her. "What do you want to see tonight?" he asked to distract her and keep her focus on him.

"To tell you the truth, I'm not sure what's playing. I work so much, it's been about six months since I went to the movies."

"Really? You don't have a string of hot dates lined up behind you?" He was teasing, but he also wanted to know if he had some competition out there.

"You're the only hot date I've had in . . . If I can't think of how long it's been, then that should tell you it's been a long time. Luna and I caught that Leonardo DiCaprio movie a while back."

"What was up with that look she shot Colt when she came to pick you up at my place?"

"All I know is that she used to date Colt's friend. Then something happened with the guy and Colt."

"Do you know what?"

"No. She won't say. I guess you'll have to ask Colt."

"He's a vault. I asked him about it the night she came by. You'd have thought I asked him to relive his worst nightmare by the look on his face."

"I relive mine every night."

Rory squeezed her hand. "Having trouble sleeping?"

"It won't go away. Sometimes I find myself drifting off during the day. I get sucked back to that day, the fear, the knowing I'm going to die out there alone."

Rory felt the shiver from her body race up his arm. "I think about it, too. I dream about you hanging there. I know how it turns out. You're fine, but it still wakes me in the night and leaves me cold. I need to see you. I need to know you're all right." More than he wanted to admit, but there it was. He thought about her all the time.

He hated that she was still suffering, still fearful after what that asshole did to her.

"The cops still haven't found Derek. Aside from your brother stopping by your place today, no one has seen him."

"They've got to have a secret place where they're cooking the drugs."

"When did your brother get into drugs?"

"After my mother died. I found him stealing booze from the house, drinking in the barn. He started smoking pot, which led to him selling it, pills, mostly oxy and Ecstasy. Last year, he got busted for possession with the meth. I had no idea he was making it."

"That's some serious shit."

"Believe me, I know. I've seen him at his worst, but I still remember the scared little boy who ran into my room in the middle of the night afraid of monsters. The day they stole the cattle, I could tell he hadn't slept in a couple of days. He was going to crash hard. I've been thinking about it. If he's cooking and stealing the cattle, the two things have to be located close to each other."

Rory eyed her across the seat. "Why do you say that?"

"Because he's drugged-up stupid. He's not going to put himself out or work hard to do anything. He owes money, so the easy and convenient thing to do was steal your cows. He'd get between seven and ten grand for the small groups he took. The herd, I don't even want to think about what that cost you. Not just in the animals themselves, but the offspring you would have had from them."

Rory didn't want to think about it either. The theft put a dent in his family's business. It wasn't hard to remember it wasn't her fault, but the anger still rose up inside him. He tamped it down and focused on what she knew about her brother. Maybe they could put the pieces together to figure out where he was hiding and put an end to his drug manufacturing and distributing in and around their town. The growing problem needed to be nipped in the bud before they had a full-blown epidemic.

"So you think this place is near my land."

"It makes the most sense. From what you and your brothers told me, the smaller number of cattle he stole off the back road went on for quite some time. The larger theft only took them across all that land because they couldn't get the cattle trailers up that road."

A four-by-four and a small trailer could make it, but a huge tractor trailer, no way. Rory should have asked her about this sooner. It might have saved him losing the last five cattle taken. That road ran across the back side of his property. He thought about what else was back that way, anywhere that Connor and his buddies could set up a trailer, any abandoned cabins, sheds, or barns. Nothing came to mind, but he didn't use that part of the property often, so nothing struck him. He'd have to get Ford and Colt to ride out with him soon.

"I lost you." Sadie squeezed his hand to get his attention.

"Sorry." He pulled into the movie theater lot and parked. "I was thinking about where your brother might be hiding out. My brothers and I will check it out."

Sadie turned in her seat and gripped his hand tight. "Rory, let the cops check it out. Connor isn't dangerous, neither are his two friends, Dumb and Dumber, but Derek . . . You saw up close and personal what he's capable of."

Yeah, Derek still terrorizes her even when he isn't here.

Rory didn't want her to worry about him, but he appreciated it. He liked they could talk about everything, but right now, he just wanted to have a good time. "Let's leave this alone for now. We're supposed to have fun."

Rory opened the door and stepped out, pulling Sadie along the seat to follow him. When she reached the end of the seat, he let loose her hand, tucked his hands under her arms, and plucked her out of the truck, setting her down in front of him. Her hands rested on his biceps. She squeezed his muscles and smiled up at him, the light of appreciation sparkling in her eyes. She made him feel appealing. Women stared at him all the time. He got from the flirtatious smiles and suggestive glances that women liked the way he looked. Still, no one in recent memory made him feel like, while they appreciated the way he looked, it went a lot deeper.

Sadie pushed on his shoulders to make him turn away and gave him a push. "Come on, cowboy. You said we're going to have fun, so let's get to going." She closed the truck door behind him.

He hit the lock button on his key fob and took a few steps toward the theater. Just to tease and have some of that fun he talked about, he asked, "Are you staring at my ass?"

"If you're walking, I'm watching."

He'd said the same thing to her. He turned back to her laughing and smiling. He couldn't remember smiling this much or feeling this light in a long time.

"I need to send the Levi's company a thank-you letter."

"Who do I thank for that skirt?"

She executed another turn, smiled, and smoothed her hands over her hips. "What? This old thing?"

He held his hand out to her. "Come here."

She took his hand, and he pulled her in for a quick kiss.

He kept things light and walked beside her, holding her hand on the way to the ticket booth outside the theater. "There are three movies playing within twenty minutes of each other. Which one do you want to see?"

"I get to pick? This is setting a dangerous precedent, don't you think?"

"Only if you pick the chick flick."

"Which you'd sit through just to spend the evening with me." She batted her lashes at him, messing around.

"Yes. Of course I'd have to find something to do when I got bored. You'll probably miss most of the movie."

She laughed. "I wouldn't do that to you."

"You can do whatever you want to me."

She looked away, a pretty blush glowing on her cheeks.

He'd made her nervous. He didn't want to do that, so he dialed it back. "Really, whatever movie you want is fine with me."

"So we're down to the superhero action flick or the historical drama. It's really no choice at all."

She walked up to the ticket guy and asked for two tickets to the newest Avengers movie.

"Have I told you how much I like you?" He bumped her shoulder and handed the money over to pay for the tickets.

"How much?"

He leaned down and kissed her softly. "More than that."

She grabbed his hand and tugged him toward the door. "We need popcorn. No butter. Unless you like butter, then we have to get separate tubs."

"No butter." He liked it salty, not soggy.

"Great. My kind of guy."

"I guess I am." And that felt so right. Now if he could make her his woman.

"I don't drink soda, so I'll have an iced tea."

"Really? No soda?"

"Too sweet."

Rory ordered the tub of popcorn and two iced teas. They walked to the theater, and he handed over the tickets to the usher, whose eyes nearly popped out of his head when he caught sight of Sadie in that damn sexy skirt. He wasn't the only guy Rory ended up glaring at to keep their distance from his date.

He followed Sadie to their seats in the middle of the theater, several rows up past dead center. She liked to be up high, but not at the back. She knew what she liked and didn't mind letting him know or doing what she wanted. She didn't just go along. He appreciated a woman who knew her own mind.

They watched the opening trailers, laughing when they bumped hands reaching for the popcorn. So in sync it happened nearly every time. A quarter way through the movie, Sadie propped her feet on the empty seat in front of her, leaned into him, rested her head on his shoulder, and held his hand through the rest of the movie. He laughed when she jumped during a few of the more intense scenes. She punched him in the shoulder for spooking her as the background music intensified and the scene built for the bad guy to attack the good guys. She didn't settle back into him, so he reached over and pulled her close. She settled in with an "I'll get you for that."

The movie ended, but they didn't get up right away. Instead, they sat together, holding hands, watching everyone else file out.

Sadie sighed and leaned away from Rory. "I really enjoyed the movie, but it's late, and I'm sorry to say, I need to get home and check on my dad."

He kissed her forehead, completely understanding her worry. He stood and pulled her up beside him. He walked from the theater to his truck, holding her hand, thrilling at the heat still radiating inside him and the connection they kept building between them.

She climbed into the truck and pulled her legs in, smoothing her skirt down her thighs. He meant to close the door. He really did. Instead, he reached for her, gripping her thighs, turning her back toward him, and used his other hand to tilt her chin up so he could kiss her. He had to kiss her.

Her hand fisted in his shirt at his shoulder and she tugged him closer. He couldn't get close enough with her skirt keeping him from spreading her legs and pulling her hips to his. He gave in to his need to touch her, sliding his hand down from her jaw to her neck, tracing her throat with his fingertips and down over her chest. She changed the angle of her head and took the kiss deeper. He trailed his fingertips over the top of her breast, then laid his palm over the soft globe and squeezed.

She sighed and nearly undid him altogether.

So soft. So sweet. So his, but he reined it in, sweeping his thumb over her hard nipple, sliding his hand up over the soft mound, back up her chest and throat to her silky smooth cheek. He ended the kiss with a soft brush of his lips to hers, pressed his forehead to hers, and just breathed her in.

"Dangerously addictive," he whispered, trying to hold on to his control.

"Yes, you are." She smoothed her hands over his chest and up to his face. She held him away from her and looked up at him. "I'm glad you asked me out."

"So am I."

He stepped back, gently touched his hand to her legs to get her to turn back into the truck. This time, she didn't flinch even a little bit at his touch. Her hair fell down her back in waves. He reached for one of the wavy locks and let it slide through his hand over her chest. The back of his hand brushed softly over her breast a second before her hair fell free. Her breath caught and her eyes widened with surprise at his touch, then blazed with heat. He closed the door even though he wanted to have her right there on the front seat of his truck in the middle of the parking lot. He rounded the hood, taking a deep breath to cool off, and hopped into the truck beside her.

Sadie shimmied over to him. No hesitation, just the same need to be close that he felt for her. The quiet drive home never felt uncomfortable. In fact, she sat beside him, holding his hand in both of hers, tracing his fingers in an absent way that showed him she liked being with him. He really liked being with her. So much so that he was thinking up a thousand and one ways to see her again.

CHAPTER 11

Sadie sat bolt upright and squeezed Rory's hand. "Stop the truck." She turned to him and grabbed his shoulder. "Stop. Stop right now."

Rory slammed on the brakes and pulled off the road.

The lights from her home shone in the distance, but that's not what caught her attention. She'd been staring out the window, wishing on stars, high on the happiness she felt after such a great evening with Rory. Then she spotted a shadow in the field and panicked.

Sadie grabbed the handle, pushed the door open, jumped out, scrambled through the barbed wire fencing, and ran. She sprinted across the field as the shadow stumbled. It seemed to take forever to reach her father, but when she did, she held him by the shoulders and looked him over from head to toe.

"Dad, what are you doing out here?"

"I can't find her. She's not in the house. I thought she came out to see the stars. She loved looking at the stars."

Sadie let out a frustrated breath, the fear ebbing inside her. Rory ran up and immediately reached out to brush his hand down her hair. The relief in his eyes that she was okay touched her.

"Dad, Mom isn't here. Let's go back to the house."

"I have to find her."

Sadie took her father's too thin face in her shaking hands. "Dad, do you see me?"

The fog of uncertainty cleared from his eyes and turned to a fear she hated to see in their depths. "Sa-Sadie."

Tears clogged her throat, but she blinked them away from her eyes. "Yes, Dad. It's me. You've been wandering again."

Her father turned his head this way and that. "I . . . I got confused."

"It's all right. I'm here now."

"My feet hurt." Her father stared down at his bare feet.

Sadie knelt and looked more closely, unable to make much out in the dark night. "Rory, can you hold on to him, please. Dad, lift your foot for me." He'd walked quite a distance over the rough, rocky terrain. "You've got a couple small cuts and scrapes."

"I can carry him to the truck," Rory volunteered.

Sadie stared across the field. Quite a distance to the truck, but Rory was a big, strong cowboy more than capable of carrying her thinning father, who was a good six inches shorter than Rory's six-four frame.

Rory didn't wait for an answer, just dipped, put his arm at her father's back and knees, and picked him right up.

"Hey, I can walk."

"I got you, Mr. Higgins. You don't want to upset your daughter. Let's get you home."

"Sadie, honey, I'm sorry."

Sadie trotted after Rory, trying to keep up with his

long strides and still carry the heavy weight of guilt knotted in her gut. "It's okay, Dad."

Rory lifted her father over the wire fencing and set him on the grass on the other side without breaking a sweat or grunting with the effort. He ducked through the wire and held it open for her to climb through. He gave her a soft smile and rubbed her back as they stood outside his truck. Her father climbed up into the seat. The overhead light made it easier for her to see his poor feet.

"We'll clean your feet and put something on those cuts when we get home."

Her father stared past her at Rory with his hands on her shoulders. "I'm glad she's got you looking out for her."

"I won't let anything happen to her, sir." Promise filled his deep voice.

It touched Sadie. Her heart swelled, and all those thoughts about how much she liked him coalesced into one wondrous and yet not so surprising thought. This thing they shared was something more, deeper, special.

His hand brushed down her hair and closed around a chunk. "Come on, sweetheart, let's get you both home."

For the first time, she let her mind go to that dark place she'd avoided these last months. Soon, she'd be living in that house alone. Her father would be gone, her brother out of reach, and she'd be alone.

Overwhelmed with sadness, she turned to Rory and hugged him close, her face buried in his chest.

He leaned down and whispered in her ear, "I'm here," and held her close, his fingers rubbing back and forth on her back.

Yes, Rory was there for her. He saved her. He wanted to be with her. But for how long? Would it last? Was it real or just her need to find something good to hold on to when everything else in her life seemed to be slipping through her fingers, no matter how hard she held on?

His hands rubbed up and down her arms. "It's okay."

Lost in her own swirling thoughts about how not okay this situation with her father was, she released Rory and climbed into the truck beside her dad.

Rory closed the door and walked around the front of the truck.

"You two are right together," her father said, patting her leg as Rory climbed in and drove them to the house.

Were they? Did Rory think so, too? How could she ask him something like that? They'd only started seeing each other. Of course, she saw him every day.

Rory pulled up in her driveway. She got out, and Rory helped her father up the porch steps, his arm braced around her father's shoulders.

"Take him back to his room. I'll gather what I need to fix his feet."

Sadie grabbed a large metal bowl out of the cupboard and ran the water in the sink until it warmed. She filled the bowl, grabbed some paper towels, and took both down the hall to her father's room.

She stopped short and took in her father's soft words.

"She needs someone like you."

"I need someone like her, sir. Don't worry. I'll take care of her."

Sadie remained stuck in place outside the room out of their sight. She didn't know if Rory was only trying to appease her father, or if he meant those seemingly sincere words.

"It won't be long now," her father said, tearing another hole in her broken heart.

"She won't be alone."

As much as Sadie relished these moments when her father was lucid and alert, Sadie couldn't take much more. She stepped into the room, trying her best to put on a brave face and not cry out all her sorrow and anger that her father was dying, that he was going to leave her. Stupid. Unreasonable. But that's how she felt and it made her mad, because she didn't want to feel this way. She wanted her father to be okay, but it was long past wishing.

Rory sat beside her father, a look of sorrow drawing his features into lines on his forehead and around his mouth. The grim look made the smiles and laughs they shared earlier seem so far away.

Rory stood and came to her. He placed his hand on the side of her head and tilted it toward him. He kissed her on top of the head and left the room without a word.

Sadie mustered up her resolve and got down to business. She didn't want to dwell on their exchange or the rioting feelings inside her.

She set the bowl of warm water on the floor and placed one of her father's feet inside. She gently washed away the grime, then dried it with the paper towels. Rory walked back in with the first aid kit he must have found in the bathroom next to her bedroom.

"Thanks."

He left again in his quiet, intense way without saying anything. She washed and dried her father's other foot and helped him scoot back on the bed. She dropped a pillow behind his back at the headboard and set his feet on the mattress.

She stared into his familiar eyes, so filled with pain and regret now her heart ached. "Dad, what's really going on with you?"

"You know what's happening. Is the why and how so important when the outcome is still the same?"

"Maybe a doctor could . . ."

Her father shook his head, his eyes filled with a deep resignation that nothing could or would change the inevitable.

"I like Rory. He's a family man, the kind who works hard and sticks."

Knowing time was running out, she thought of all her father would miss in her life, and it made her heart ache even more. "He's a good man."

"Do you love him?"

"We've only just started seeing each other, but what I feel for him is so deep and overwhelming."

"I'm happy for you, Sadie. I'm glad I got to meet him."

"Dad . . ." She didn't know what to say.

"You can't change what is, honey. Not with me. Not with life. Not with love. Accept. It makes things a lot easier."

"Are you scared?" she asked, because her fear for him grew each and every time something like tonight happened.

"Sometimes. But not for you. I know you'll be okay. You're strong."

"I don't feel that way sometimes."

"But you always pull through. We can't always be at our best. Sometimes we need to lean on those closest to us. I lean on you. You lean on me. If you truly care about Rory, let him in. Lean on him when you need him. Relationships are built on the good times and the bad. Working through the bad draws you closer together and makes the good times you share so much richer and better."

If she and Rory could get through her brother stealing him blind, maybe they had a chance of having something more.

She quickly spread ointment on the small nicks and put bandages on the deeper cuts.

"My feet look a little like you did when you came home. We're a pair, aren't we, honey?"

Choked up, she whispered, "Yes, we are."

His mouth tipped down into a regretful frown. "Connor's in trouble, isn't he?"

"Yes. He stole from the Kendricks. He's working with some really bad people."

Her father laid his hand on her scarred wrist. "I'm sorry he hurt you."

"Dad, I'm okay."

"Unless Connor changes his ways, I fear his life will be fraught with pain and unhappiness. Don't let his life, his choices ruin yours. You are not responsible for his happiness. Don't give up what you want, trying to help him. You cannot make him see things your way because he doesn't have your kindness, your thoughtfulness, your heart." Her father placed his hand on her cheek. She leaned into his comfort and warmth. "Please, honey, promise me you'll choose happiness, you'll choose *you* before him. If you always put others first, you'll always come in last."

"Dad, Connor has lost his way, but I can't believe he's hopeless."

"No, Sadie, he chooses the wrong path even when he has other options available to him. If you have a chance for something more, something good, take it. Don't let him keep taking pieces of you and what is yours. Don't sacrifice what you have and what you want for someone who won't do the same for you." Her father's fingers traced the scars on her wrists again.

"Since your mother died, you've had to do what needs to be done. You got through school. You worked to earn money that we needed here, but mostly to keep your brother from spending the rest of his life in jail. There's little left here for you. I'm sorry about that. I wish these last years had been different for you, less struggle and more living your dreams. Everything I have will go to you, Sadie. Not because I don't want to leave your brother a piece of what I worked so hard to hold on to, but because I leave it to you to decide how best to help your brother.

"Maybe that means not helping him at all. Maybe instead of catching him, you need to let him fall. Maybe that's the only way he'll learn that it hurts and to make better decisions.

"You're a smart girl. You'll know what to do. You can't blame yourself for the things he's done. His happiness and life are not your responsibility. His shortcomings are not your failures.

"My grief over your mother's death made me too lenient with him. I regret that now. I should have been tougher. I shouldn't have let you pick up my slack and take the lead with him. I should have been a better parent. I taught you how to be strong and see things through, but I forgot to teach you that sometimes if you hold on too tight, all you get are rope burns."

"It's hard to let go." She sat beside him on the bed, leaned into him, and tilted her head to his.

Her father took her hand and squeezed it. "Yes, it is."

CHAPTER 12

Connor's back slammed into the stone wall. He barely had enough strength and presence of mind to keep his head from cracking against the jagged rocks. Derek's forearm pressed against his throat. The guy smelled like stale beer and sweat, making Connor want to gag. Scott and Tony tossed their cards on the folding table and scooted their chairs back enough to give them the ability to run for the cave entrance if things went to shit. Tony slowly reached for the glass pipe and the small baggy, fisting both in his hand and stuffing them into the pocket of his too-loose jeans. They'd been playing poker and riding their high. Scott and Tony hadn't shut up for hours, but Derek showed up and they had nothing to say.

"You fucking tell me where my drugs are or I'll kill you."

"They're safe, man. Swear."

"They're supposed to be in that shack you call a lab."

Connor hadn't slept in two days. He needed another hit and stared at Tony's hand pressed deep into his pocket. Connor wanted to tell him to fucking give his drugs back. He needed them. His skin crawled with the need. Even now, with death looking him in the eye, he scratched at his leg and wished for one more fix. The high wore off and he needed sleep, but all he could think about was sucking on that pipe and flying.

"You've been missing in action for days. We're out here day in and day out cooking that shit. We take all the risks. What the hell do you do?"

"I fucking get you what you need to make that shit you smoke day in and day out. I'm the one who sets up the buys. Where are my fucking drugs?" Derek's voice rose until the last was said in a barely controlled roar.

"We don't deliver for two more days."

"Fucking junkies." Derek shook his head. "I told you that three days ago. You dumbshits were supposed to be ready to move tonight."

Connor tried to think past the fear. His thrashing heart felt like a jackhammer in his chest. Sweat trickled down the side of his face and back, soaking his T-shirt. "Okay, I'll go get them. I can get them. I'll go. I'll bring them back."

"Where are they?" Derek shouted, spittle hitting Connor in the face.

"I hid them in the barn. They're there. I'll get them. I'll bring them back."

"Stop rambling, you stupid fuck. Are you telling me you hid them at your house?"

"Yes. Yeah. They're there."

"At your fucking place? Where that bitch of a sister lives? The one who's got the cops after us. The one who'd call the cops if she found those drugs."

"She won't find them. She's got no reason to go in the barn now that all the horses are gone. She won't find them. Swear."

"Yeah, you fucking swear all the time, but you fuck up more than you deliver. This is all I need, your fucking sister finding my shit and fucking my life again. I can't go back to my bar. The damn cops have it under surveillance. My house, too. I'm stuck sneaking around, and you three are here drinking, doing drugs, and not cooking my damn meth."

"We are. We did. We're out. Until you can get the guys to make another run. We cooked it all. It's done. Fine. Swear."

"You better be right about this." Derek finally backed off, shoving Connor aside. "Let's go."

Connor stumbled, but caught himself before he nosedived into his cot. "Go. No." Connor shook his head side to side. "We can't go. I'll go. You don't need to go."

"One sentence is enough. You really need to lay off the product."

"I'm fine. Totally fine. Swear."

"You're whacked out of your head. Let's move."

"If we all go, we'll get caught. I'll go, get the stuff, and meet you back here."

"No. We're meeting Trigger. Scott and Tony will take the bags from the sugar shack and drive down to Missoula."

Connor couldn't help the goofy smile. He'd named the shack just outside the cave the sugar shack. They used that term when talking or texting about the operation and how many bags of "sugar" they produced.

"I don't know what the fuck you're smiling about, man, this is serious shit. We don't deliver and someone's going to get their head blown off."

Connor hoped it wasn't him. He'd done his best to

keep up with Derek's demands, but all he wanted to do now was get out. Not going to happen. He'd screwed up the first few batches after he swore he could deliver. Instead of slicing his head off, Derek put him back to work to pay off his debt. At this point, Connor knew one thing for sure; the only way he was getting out was dead. No way he ended up in a cell detoxing and hurting with a need for the one thing he couldn't live without anymore. He'd gone down the rabbit hole and lost himself on the dark side.

"Do you hear me, man? We need to go. Now."

Scott and Tony rushed out to the sugar shack to pick up the duffel bags, then headed to Scott's car. Connor stared at Derek, wishing he could take the dude out. All he did was push, push, push. Connor just wanted to ride his high, forget about everything else, and feel that exhilaration. Derek's presence only made him angry. He hated when he lost control. It really killed his buzz, like when he thought about Sadie and what happened to her. So he smoked some more and let it all go.

"We go. We get it. We get out. You leave my sister alone."

"You do what you're told for once, and we won't have a problem."

"Right. I'm the problem."

Derek shoved him. "What does that mean?"

"Keep your hands off my sister. She's not a part of this." Connor pressed the heel of his hand to his eye, then up over his sweaty forehead. "All those fucking cuts on her."

Derek's eyes lit up with excitement. So much so that Connor might have thought he'd just used, but Connor knew better. Derek never touched the product. No, he liked something other than drugs. He liked to inflict pain. He'd caused Sadie plenty. So had Connor.

He hoped he got away tonight with the drugs from his house without Sadie finding out.

CHAPTER 13

Sadie walked into the kitchen and found Rory sitting at her breakfast table.

"How is your dad?"

"Sleeping." Sadie looked at the dark windows, then the clock. "It's late. You didn't have to stay."

"I wanted to." Rory held his hand out to her.

Sadie walked to him and took it. He gave her a soft tug. She sat on his lap, her legs between his, and leaned into him. He wrapped both arms around her. She leaned her head against his and sighed out her worry and frustration, feeling lighter just having someone here with her, having him here with her.

"No more working at my place. You need to be here with your dad from now on."

"I appreciate it, Rory, but I'm not going to change my mind about doing what is right."

"Sadie." He grumbled out her name like a warning.

She pressed her fingers over his tight lips.

Rory pulled them away and relented. "What can I do to make you feel better?" His deep, rich voice soothed her, but the sweet sentiment went right to her heart.

"You're doing it. I feel better already."

"I can do more than just sit here with you."

"You're here, Rory. That's all I need, just to be close to you."

His arms contracted around her. She settled into his big body, letting his warmth envelop her. The ripples of heat, the pulse of the pull between them, the way it felt right to sit in his arms resonated through her.

"I can't get much closer to you," she teased, trying to keep things light as nerves sent butterflies fluttering in her belly.

"You could." He slid his hand up her thigh and squeezed her hip. A deep groan rumbled in his chest. "It's never been easy for me to get to know people, especially women. Ford and Colt say I spend too much time alone on the ranch working. They're probably right."

"Don't worry, I won't tell them you said so." She loved the way the brothers teased one another. All in good fun. Rory had forgone a lot of the social aspects of life to fulfill his obligation to family and business. He knew what was important.

"Please don't. I'll never live it down." He kissed her on the side of the head. "What I'm trying to say is that everything seems easy with you."

She laughed under her breath. "You think finding me the way you did, staying up all night at the hospital, losing your cattle, what that means to your business and family, and my brother a sore spot between us is easy? If so, then the rest of our lives should be a piece of cake." She heard her words echo in her ears and backtracked. "What I meant was . . ."

He squeezed her thigh again. "Relax. I know what you mean. All that stuff is hard, but when it's just you and me"—he hugged her close—"like this, it's simple."

Someone hammered something heavy against metal outside. Rory stiffened against her. She tried not to think the worst, but had to face reality.

"Trouble just came home."

"Your brother?"

"Probably. It's coming from the barn."

"Stay here." Rory stood, pushing her off his lap and gently setting her away from him. "Is your brother armed?"

"With stupidity." She remembered the last time she saw him. "And yes, he had a handgun the last time he came home. I don't know where he got it. I'll be surprised if he hasn't shot himself in the foot yet."

That made him smile. He headed for the door, but she grabbed his arm and stopped him.

"I'm going with you. He'll listen to me."

Rory pressed his lips together and one eyebrow shot up. He eyed her, not believing a word she said. "Yeah, right."

"Rory, please, he's my brother."

He peeled her fingers from the grasp she held on his shirt. "I don't want you to get hurt again. If he brought his friends with him . . ."

"You'll be outnumbered."

"Trust me, sweetheart, that won't be a problem."

His assurance didn't help. Neither did the sheer size of him. All those muscles were impressive when combined with his height, but all she saw in her mind was that knife Derek liked to use. Her mind conjured one nightmare after the next, all of them filled with images of that knife plunging into Rory's chest.

Sadie let loose Rory's shirt and went to the cabinet near the front door. She opened the door and pulled out the rifle she'd cleaned, loaded, and tucked away just in case something like this happened.

"What are you doing with that?"

"Protecting what's mine."

Rory eyed her. "I am going out there."

"I'm not stopping you, but I'm not going out there without this gun. If Derek is with my brother, I'm not letting him get a piece of me. Or you."

"Do you know how to use that thing?"

"Yes. I do. Very well."

The banging stopped. The ensuing quiet turned to an eerie silence that thickened the tension between her and Rory.

"Let me go in first. If it's just your brother, we'll talk to him, see if we can get him to turn himself in." Rory pulled out his cell phone, scrolled through his contact list, and hit dial.

"Who are you calling?"

"Deputy Foster—"

"Mark? You're calling the cops." She shook her head and pinched back one side of her mouth in a half frown that didn't even faze him.

"It's Rory Kendrick. I'm at the Higgins place. Connor and maybe some of his friends are out in the barn. I'll try to detain him until you get here," Rory told Mark.

Sadie sighed, opened the front door, and walked away from Rory. He had every right to call the deputy sheriff and let him know her brother was here, but she didn't have to like it. She wanted to protect the little boy she held on to in her mind, but she knew she could no longer help the man who'd chosen a life that led to nothing but ruin. Connor needed to face reality. If she could get him to see reason and turn himself in to Mark, he might have a decent shot at making a deal to turn Derek over to the authorities. After all, Derek was the one forcing her brother to cook meth and sell it.

There you go again, making excuses for him.

She'd been doing it all her life. Hard to stop now, but like her father said, sometimes you have to let go of the rope, or you'll get burned. She needed to let go of the hope that the sweet little boy Connor had once been, before the drugs had erased him a little at a time, would somehow magically reappear. Not going to happen so long as Connor went headlong down the road to destruction.

Letting go wasn't as easy as it sounded.

"Sadie, hold up," Rory called in an angry whisper. "If he's in there, he's going to answer to me first. Then you can turn him over to the cops."

Rory's dark gaze and frown reminded her of the man she used to see in him. Now she knew he wasn't that guy, and the ominous look in his eyes was because he didn't want her to get hurt again.

They made their way across the grass and weeds, drawing closer to the barn.

"The stupid thing is stuck." Her brother's muffled voice carried out to them through one of the open barn doors leading out to a paddock.

"Bang it again. Get that damn barrel open. We don't have all night."

Sadie stopped in her tracks at the sound of that familiar voice. It followed her into her nightmares each night. *I like to watch you bleed.*

Rory stumbled into the back of her and grabbed her shoulders. He rubbed his hands up her trembling arms.

He leaned in close to her ear and whispered, "What's wrong?"

She turned her face toward him and whispered back, "That's Derek." The quake in her voice made Rory squeeze her shoulders.

"Give me the rifle and go back to the house. I'll take care of this."

"Hurry the fuck up," Derek ordered.

A shiver rocked her whole body, vibrating up her spine. Rory wrapped his arms around her from behind and kissed the top of her head. "You're okay, sweetheart. I won't let anything happen to you."

Sadie stiffened her spine and shook off her fear and Rory's embrace. She stood on her own and turned to face him. "You go that way around the back. They probably have a truck or something parked behind the barn. If they came in the back way, that's why we didn't hear them drive up. I'll go in through the front. I'll keep them focused on me and you make sure they don't leave before the sheriff's guys get here."

"Scott and Tony took the smaller stashes out to Butte and Missoula. We need to get this to my guy tonight, or it'll be my ass, which means it will be yours, too," Derek warned.

"This is a bad idea," Rory said.

He was probably right. She tried to think of a better plan than facing off with a knife-wielding drug dealer.

She wrapped her fingers around Rory's arm. "I just thought of something. If my brother drove, he left the keys in the ignition. He always does. No one would steal his piece of crap truck. Get the keys, then they can't leave."

"Cover the front, but do not go inside." Rory touched

her chin, tilting her face up to his. He leaned down and planted a soft but quick kiss on her lips. He gave her one last resigned look and took off around the paddock to the back of the barn.

She hoped he found the keys in the truck and that stopped her brother and Derek from leaving long enough for the cops to arrive.

"Got it," her brother said, drawing her closer to the front barn doors to get a better look and keep an eye on them. If they tried to go out the back before Rory had a chance to get the keys, she'd stop them.

"Fuck yeah. Pull it out and load up the bags," Derek said.

Sadie snuck around the barn doors and slid along the aisle, her back against the stall wall. She stopped at one of the open gates and hid in the darkness. Her brother and Derek stood at the other end in a pool of weak light cast by a single bulb burning just outside the workroom door.

Connor pulled out several bags of packaged drugs from a fifty-five-gallon barrel and stuffed them into the duffel bag at his feet like stacked bricks. She'd never really noticed the barrels. They'd always been there, long ago used and left to rust as her father grew frail and the business dissipated along with his health.

"Hurry the fuck up," Derek ordered.

"I'm going as fast as I can. Once we deliver this, I'm out. I don't owe you anything more." Her brother's voice held little conviction. Too weak to stand up for himself, he'd keep going along so long as Derek threatened him. So long as Connor got the drugs he craved more than a life with his family.

"You're out when I say you're out." Derek picked

up one of the drug bricks and tossed it on top of the others.

Sadie worried about Rory, moving around the back of the barn and approaching the truck. He wouldn't have much cover. If he got into the truck, Derek and Connor might spot him. Sweat broke out on her brow. She kept to the shadows, barely breathing, hoping they stalled these two losers long enough for the cops to arrive.

Connor leaned over and zipped the first duffel bag closed, grabbed the handles, stood up, and tossed it straight into Derek's chest. "Take that to the truck. I'll pack up the last of this, then we're out of here."

Fear tore through Sadie's guts. She couldn't let Derek catch Rory.

"What the hell do you think you're doing?" Sadie stepped out of the shadows, the rifle butt tucked up against her shoulder, the barrel aimed right at Derek's chest.

Derek dropped the bag and walked back into the dim light, smiling in a way that sent a shiver of fear dancing up her spine. "You came back for more." The glint of excitement in his eyes shone brighter than the light gleaming on the knife he pulled from his back.

"Take one step and I'll shoot you dead."

"Yeah, right. You can barely hold that gun, let alone hit the side of this barn."

Sadie kept her gaze locked on Derek but addressed her brother. "Who taught you how to shoot, Connor?"

"You did."

"Who never misses?"

"You." Connor tugged at his hair and swore under his breath. He scratched at his leg, then his arm, and wiped the sweat from his face. Dark circles marred the undersides of his eyes. His pale skin made him look sickly, but it was nothing more than the drugs he kept pumping into his system. Just looking at him made her sad.

"Seriously, Derek, don't fuck with her. You got away with it once, doesn't look like she'll let you do it again."

"That's right." Sadie sent Derek the same menacing smile he'd given her.

Derek took a step toward her, testing her. She fired, missing his head by a good six inches and blasting a chunk of wood out of the workroom wall next to him. Splinters sprayed his hair and shoulder.

"I said don't fucking move."

"Don't *you* fucking move."

The deep voice startled her, but the hand that gripped her hair and the gun barrel pressed to the underside of her chin stunned her. Her breath caught in her throat, her heart stopped, and her mind went blank except for one thought. *I'm dead.*

The man holding the gun moved from the side to stand in front of her, just off to the side of the rifle she still held pointed at Derek.

"You just had to come out of the shadows," he whispered for only her to hear. "I hoped it wouldn't come to this."

She eyed him wondering what he meant. Wasn't he with Derek and Connor? He looked like a thug. Shaggy dark hair brushed his shoulders and tattoos wove up his arms—an intricate tribal pattern overlaid with a twisting vine of wicked blades for leaves, an open rose in full bloom, and an ominous skull in the center of his forearm. But his softly spoken words and the resignation and regret she caught in his eyes said there was more to him than the tough exterior.

He nudged the rifle with his shoulder. "Toss that to your brother." His deep voice demanded one thing, but the hand softly holding her hair at the back of her neck said something else altogether.

She slowly lowered the rifle from her shoulder, held it by the barrel and stock, and tossed it to Connor.

"Put that thing in your truck bed, then come back," the man ordered her brother.

Connor rushed to do his bidding.

"You're going to get it now," Derek mocked. "Shoot that bitch, Trigger."

Sadie swallowed hard at the menacing nickname.

Trigger cocked up one side of his mouth. He glanced over his shoulder. "Get that shit packed up." His gaze locked on hers again. He pulled her close and barely spoke above a whisper. "Reach into my jacket. Find the inside pocket and pull out the slip of paper inside."

She glanced over Trigger's shoulder. With him standing in front of her, Derek and Connor couldn't see what she was doing. The gun still touched her chin, but barely pressed against her skin. She reached inside his jacket, traced her fingers over the lining, and felt the outline of a folded piece of paper. She reached up and into the pocket to pull it free. She crushed it in her hand and let her arm fall to her side again. "Good girl. Contact DEA Special Agent Cooke. Give him that paper. You can't save your brother from what's coming, but you can save yourself."

"Who are you?" she whispered.

"Do what I say. I'll get you out of this barn without that fuck hurting you again."

"We've got it all. Connor, stash it in the truck, I'm going to play with your sister."

"Leave her the fuck alone. We got what we came for, now let's go."

Derek grabbed Connor by the front of his jacket and hauled him close, holding the knife up to intimidate him.

"No," Sadie yelled.

"Shut up, bitch." Derek got in Connor's face. "Your brother needs to remember his place."

"You touch my sister again, and I'll take off with these bags and dump them, then we'll see if the boss wants to play with you."

Derek shoved Connor away. Connor stumbled back a few steps, then rushed forward and grabbed the two bags from the floor. He turned his back on the knife-wielding hothead and stormed off to the truck.

Sadie shifted her gaze to Derek, who slowly walked forward, the knife in his right hand, his left index finger poised on the wicked-sharp tip of the blade.

"I'm going to make you bleed, bitch." He slashed the knife through the air across his body.

Trigger shoved her back two steps, putting distance between them and Derek. "You're not slicing her up. We have business, and we're late."

"Come on, man, it'll only take a minute."

"Touch her and you're dead." Rory held the rifle pointed directly at Derek's head.

Connor rushed back into the barn. "Where the hell did you come from?"

"Get over there," Rory ordered.

"Take him down," Derek called, moving forward to help Connor.

Rory anticipated Connor's rushed move, side-stepped, and cracked Connor in the ribs with the rifle stock. Connor pressed his hand to his side and fell to his knees, trying to catch his breath.

Trigger glanced past Sadie and out the other side of the barn. Sirens sounded in the distance. "Cops are coming. We need to get out of here."

"Not without the drugs." Derek ground the words out, crouching, ready to go up against Rory.

Trigger grabbed her arm and hauled her to the side and shoved her into an empty stall. "Stay put," he demanded under his breath. He held the gun up trained just over Rory's shoulder. "Don't be stupid, man. You don't want to start something I'll have to finish."

Trigger ran to Derek and grabbed him by the arm. "We have to go now. They'll be here any second, and we'll be screwed."

Rory kept the gun trained on all three men.

Connor made it to his feet, his arms banded around his middle. Trigger tugged Derek backward to the other side of the barn. After several stumbling steps, Derek finally turned and ran with Trigger and Connor out the doors and off into the night.

Rory ran to Sadie just as she walked out of the stall. He grabbed her and held her close. "Are you okay? Did that guy hurt you?" Rory rubbed his hand over her hair and neck and looked her up and down.

"No. I'm fine. He didn't hurt me at all."

"He pulled your hair." Rory tipped her chin up to look at her skin where Trigger pressed the gun. "There's no mark."

Sadie wrapped her arms around Rory's neck and held him tight. "He barely touched me. He didn't want to hurt me. In fact, he whispered that he'd make sure nothing happened to me."

"He did?"

"Yes. It was strange. He gave me this." Sadie held up the slip of paper.

"What's in it?"

She opened it up and stared at the strange arrangement of letters that didn't spell anything. "A code?" she asked.

"Could be. Stay put. I'll catch up to them."

She held tight to him. "No. Let the cops handle it."

"But . . ."

"Rory, let it go."

"You can't keep protecting him."

"I'm not. I'm protecting you. One's got a gun, the other likes to play with knives. If something happened to you . . ."

He crushed her against his chest and kissed the top of her head. "I'm just glad nothing happened to you. When I saw that guy with his hands on you and that gun pointed at you . . . I told you to stay outside."

"I thought they might see you by the truck."

Cop cars pulled into her driveway, their headlights blinding Rory and Sadie. The blue and red lights swirled around the inside of the barn.

Sadie dipped her hand in her blouse and tucked the paper into her bra. Rory's gaze followed her hand's progress. She gave him a shy smile and shrugged. "He told me to give it to a DEA agent. It seemed important that only he get it."

"I don't like this," Rory said.

Mark cautiously entered the barn, gun in hand and pointed at the ground. "You guys okay?"

"Fine," Rory answered. "They're on the run. I think they had another vehicle nearby. The drugs are in the back of Connor's truck." Rory turned to face the other end of the barn. A car engine roared to life up the road. Tires squealed on pavement and the car took off at high speed, the rev of the engine fading into the night.

Mark listened to his radio as other sheriff's deputies relayed information about the suspects speeding away in a black Mustang.

"What happened?" Mark asked.

Rory ran down the events for the deputy.

"Was this Trigger guy one of the men present when Derek attacked you?" Mark asked.

"No. I've never seen him before. I don't know if he's working for Derek. It seemed that Derek and Connor were nervous about him," Sadie said.

"Trigger seemed to be here to make sure they got the drugs and delivered," Rory added.

"Okay, we'll check out the truck. Head on up to the house. I'll take your statement before I leave."

Rory took Sadie's hand and carried the rifle in the other as he led her up to the house. Her father missed all the action and remained asleep in his room. Sadie sat beside Rory at the breakfast table, holding his hand.

"You're too quiet." Rory traced his fingers up and down her arm.

"Did you see all those bags of drugs?"

"Yeah. Why?"

"How many people do you think would take those drugs, get addicted, maybe die? How many lives would be ruined?"

"I don't know, sweetheart."

"He made them. He barely got through chemistry

class, yet he can mix up those chemicals and create something that kills like it's no big deal."

"Sadie . . ."

"Did you see him? He looks like a walking zombie. He doesn't even sound the same. It's bad enough I have to watch the cancer take pieces of my father, weakening his body and stealing his mind, killing him a little more each day, but do I have to watch my brother do the same by his own hand?"

"Sadie, sweetheart."

She squeezed his hand and shook her head. "Don't. I know there's nothing to say. Who can make sense out of that?" She let go of Rory and reluctantly stood and went to her purse on the table by the door, and found her phone. She swiped her finger across the screen and Googled up the number for the DEA and dialed the Billings division office.

"Who are you calling?" Rory asked.

Someone answered. "Yes, I'm calling to speak with Special Agent Cooke."

"Who's calling?"

"Sadie Higgins from Crystal Creek. I have a message from Trigger."

"Please hold."

Sadie waited, surprised when the deep voice that came on the line sounded very close to that of the man who'd given her the slip of paper. "Cooke."

"Agent Cooke, my name is Sadie Higgins. I have a message for you from Trigger."

"What's the message?"

"I don't know."

"Look, I don't have time to play games, either give me the message, or . . ."

"I can't read the message," she admitted.

The silence stretched for a good ten seconds. "Read me the letters and tell me where the breaks are."

She read off the letters and spaces.

"Who are you?"

"I told you, my name is . . ."

"No. How do you know Trigger?"

"Oh, well, he held a gun to my head and saved me from a knife-wielding maniac who likes to watch me bleed."

"Uh, when did this happen?"

"Twenty minutes ago."

"Where is Trigger now?"

"On the run from the sheriff's department after he, my brother, and Derek Pete ran away."

"I see. Anything else I should know."

"He's not what he seems." She didn't know why she said it, but it seemed important.

"Do not ever say that to anyone else. Are you safe where you are?"

"Yes. The deputies are outside investigating the scene and sorting out the bags of drugs."

"They didn't get away with the drugs?"

"No. My boyfriend stopped them." She turned and stared at Rory, still sitting at the table watching her talk on the phone. His eyes narrowed on her, but one side of his mouth cocked up in a half grin.

"Burn that paper he gave you. Do not tell anyone about it."

"Well, I kind of told my boyfriend about it."

"Can he be trusted to keep it a secret?"

"I'd trust him with my life." He'd already saved it twice.

"How did Trigger look?" The softness in his voice surprised Sadie.

"He looked okay. Kind of tired and at the same time resigned, like he didn't really want to be there. I can't explain it better than that."

"I'll be in touch." Agent Cooke hung up on her.

Sadie stared at her phone and frowned. "You're welcome."

Rory held out his hand to Sadie. She walked to him and took it, falling into his lap when he pulled her down. He wrapped his strong arms around her and kissed the side of her head. "You're a good woman, Sadie."

"Why do you say that?"

"All I saw was some thug. You saw a guy who didn't want to be doing what he was doing. You looked past the guy holding the gun to the man who wanted to help you get out of there unharmed."

"I think he's working for that Agent Cooke."

"Maybe. Might explain why Cooke cared to ask about his welfare."

"I think it's something more."

"Like what?"

"I'm not sure." She leaned her head to his and sighed. "I know how that guy felt. I'm so tired of all of this."

"Hopefully they'll run them down, arrest them, and this will all be over."

Sadie didn't think so, but she appreciated his optimism. It didn't make the fear in her heart and gut dissipate. Instead, a sense of dread settled over her.

CHAPTER 14

Connor sat in the backseat of Trigger's car, his hands clasped together, sandwiched between his thighs. His sister nearly got herself killed again tonight, and she royally fucked him. He'd be lucky to make it out of this car alive, let alone live another day when Derek's short fuse went off. Fuck, he needed to get amped. Instead he picked at the Crank Crater on his face, making the sore bleed once again. He attacked one on his arm, waiting for the inevitable explosion to happen.

Derek raked his hand through his hair, then punched the dashboard. "We're screwed."

And there it went. Connor sank deeper into his seat, trying to hide, knowing he had no place to run.

Trigger drove the car down the dirt road, one hand on the wheel, his other arm propped on the door. He stared straight ahead, acting like he hadn't heard a word Derek spoke.

"What the hell are we going to do now?"

Trigger still didn't speak. Derek smacked him on the shoulder to get his attention. Trigger reacted with lightning-quick speed, reaching over and grabbing Derek's hair, squeezing tight, and pulling the strands.

Fucking stupid to go after Trigger. That dude scared Connor even more than Derek did.

"Reach for that knife and I'll slam your head straight through the windshield."

Trigger always seemed pissed off and ready to kill, but the way he threatened Derek made Connor think the dude might actually lose his shit this time for real.

"Be cool, man." Derek held perfectly still. Even he didn't want to fuck with Trigger.

"You really know how to fuck up a good thing, you know that?" Trigger shook his head, watching the road ahead. "All you had to do was pick up the drugs and get the hell out of there."

"That bitch got in the way."

Trigger scrunched up his face. "Yeah, that tiny little woman is the reason you two fuckups botched an entire batch of meth. She's the reason you borrowed money you can't pay back. She's the reason you stole some rancher's cattle and have the law after you. It's her fault."

"Yes, it is," Derek replied.

"She didn't do shit," Connor said under his breath in the backseat, realizing too late he should have kept his mouth shut.

"That's right. She didn't do shit, but you two sure fucked up good." Trigger released Derek, shoving him away.

Derek rubbed at his scalp, then glared over his shoulder. Connor stared out the driver's side window, keeping his peripheral vision on Derek. He wasn't stupid enough to look away and get caught off guard.

"That cattle thing turned out in the end. We'd have gotten the drugs tonight if she and that damn cowboy hadn't interfered."

"Why the hell did you stash the drugs there in the first place?" Trigger asked.

"No one would look for them there," Connor answered.

"What are you going to do now?" Trigger asked Derek.

"Me? I'm not the one who fucked up tonight."

"Is that what Torres is going to say?"

"Don't worry about Torres. I'll take care of it."

Yeah, right. Torres matched Trigger's lethal look and vibe. It wasn't just the threat they posed, but knowing they'd sure as hell kill you. Derek fucked up a lot of people. He liked to fight. He liked to use that damn knife. Torres and Trigger didn't need to put on a show. They'd just shoot you dead and be done with it.

"Seems to me you're going to owe some big money to cover this loss," Trigger said.

"Connor and his two buddies are going to get their asses moving to replace what his sister cost us."

"I told you I'm out." Connor needed to get out before it was too late. Maybe it already was. Maybe he was already dead and reality just hadn't caught up. He scratched at his arm again, watching it bleed, wondering when he'd run out of blood.

"You keep saying it, but you wanted in and now you're in. You don't get out when you owe."

"Fuck you," Connor spat out. "You keep telling me I owe, but you're the one who keeps fucking up. You and this damn obsession with my sister. I told you I'd go alone. She'd have let me go if it was just me."

"Even you don't believe that anymore. If you do, you're stupider than you look. The next time I get my hands on her . . ."

"What? You're going to lose another shipment because you're so focused on her, you can't see that we're fucked. We don't deliver, we get killed," Connor yelled.

Derek pulled the knife, twisted in his seat, and swung, slicing Connor's cheek. Connor pushed back into the seat, but with nowhere to go, no way to get out the single door on Trigger's side of the car, he was as good as dead. He slapped his hand over his bloody cheek. Derek pulled his hand back to stab him, but Trigger pressed the barrel of his gun into Derek's temple.

"Move, fucker, and I will blow your head off."

I'm surrounded by fucking madmen.

The car rolled to a stop and they all sat in the tense quiet.

"Get that fucking gun away from my head."

"Screw your head on straight. We don't need this fucking bickering. You're supposed to deliver at midnight. Where?"

"I'm not fucking telling you."

Derek refused to introduce Trigger to the head guy. Probably because Torres would choose to work with Trigger over Derek. At this point, so would Connor. The dude might be lethal, but he kept things straight and focused on the job. Derek needed that because he tended to work on Tweak Time, setting out to do something, getting distracted, and finding that what should have taken him an hour took four.

They probably would be better off with Trigger in charge. He wouldn't be bleeding. No, if he pissed Trigger off he'd be dead. Probably the only way he'd get out of this shit pile that kept getting deeper.

"Man, I have been in this shit with you for months.

I stopped that bitch from blowing off your head tonight and you still can't trust me to come through for you."

Trigger narrowed his eyes. Something dark and deadly lurked in the depths. Even Connor could see it in the dark car interior. It didn't help that he still held the gun to Derek's head.

"I need to make a call."

"Put the knife away and make your call." Trigger didn't move the gun.

Derek carefully sheathed the knife and held his hands up in front of him as he turned and sat back in his seat.

Connor let out a sigh that sounded pathetic to his own ears. He gritted his teeth against the pain in his cheek.

"You okay, man?" Trigger tucked the gun back in his belt.

"He sliced my face."

"Next time it will be your throat," Derek said through tight lips.

Trigger glared. "Don't you have a call to make?"

Derek pulled the door handle, shimmied out of the car, and slammed the door. He stood outside in the cold a few feet away and glanced over his shoulder and directly at Trigger. The intense stare-down turned the air thick and heavy in the car. Trigger watched from the front seat, his eyes narrowed and ever watchful of Derek, waiting for the guy to either make his move or get on with his call.

Connor had a bad feeling, like Derek still had a gun to his head. With Connor trapped in the backseat, maybe he did too.

CHAPTER 15

Rory walked into the house through the back door. He pried off his dirty boots and set them on the metal tray Sadie had found and put down to help keep the laundry room clean. He and his brothers tended to track in the yard. She got tired of cleaning up the dirt, dust, and field debris every day. He looked around the small room, taking in the piles of clean clothes she left for each of them on the table by the window. The washer and dryer gleamed white when it, too, had been covered in dust from them traipsing in and out through this room. The tile floor was scrubbed clean; a new multitoned brown rug she made Ford buy covered the floor.

He made his way into the kitchen, hoping for a cup of coffee to ward off the cold day and warm his bones. He expected to find Sadie at the stove, cooking dinner or some other meal she'd leave in the fridge for them to heat and eat whenever they got hungry. He'd gotten so used to having her in the house, the emptiness of the kitchen unsettled him. His spirits sank. He stood in the quiet room and stared at the spotless counter-tops and cooktop. Only a few dishes sat in the sink to be washed, whereas before they'd piled high until he or one of his brothers decided to finally fill the dishwasher. The basket of mail sat on the countertop by the phone. No messages. Sadie hadn't brought the mail in like she did each day when she arrived and picked it up from the box up on the road.

"Sadie," he called through the house, hoping she was upstairs, cleaning one of the rooms.

"Rory," his grandfather called back from the office off the living room.

"Yeah, Granddad, it's me." Rory made his way out of the kitchen and through the living room, which had been touched by Sadie, too. Not a single speck of dust or fingerprint marred any surface. The pillows were neatly tucked into the corners of the couch. A cream-colored blanket draped over the brown leather sofa.

In the five nights since his first date with Sadie and the incident with her brother and his friends and the cops showing up, he'd barely seen Sadie outside this house. She came each and every day, did her work, and left to be with her father. He didn't know how she did it. He'd lost his parents in a cruel and unusual way, but at least he hadn't had to sit there and watch them die before his eyes.

"She's not here," his grandfather said.

"I see that. Where is she?"

"Don't know. Maybe you should call and check on her. It's not like her to be late, let alone not show up."

Granddad's concern infused with Rory's. He pulled his cell phone from his pocket and hit the speed dial for Sadie. She didn't answer. Voice mail picked up, and although he loved hearing her sweet voice, a sense of dread came over him.

"Hey, sweetheart, it's me. Where are you? Call me as soon as you get this."

"You really are sweet on her."

Rory tucked his phone back in his pocket. "Don't start, Granddad."

"I'm not starting. I'm happy. Can't I be happy for my grandson, especially you?"

Rory narrowed his gaze, not understanding his grandfather's meaning. "Why especially me?"

"Don't get me wrong, your brothers deserve every happiness, but they aren't like you."

"What the hell does that mean?"

"You're so serious all the time. You work hard, but you don't take time for yourself."

"I haven't exactly been living as a monk these last years."

"Might as well have been. There's no wife sleeping in your bed. No kids running around this place."

"Granddad, enough with all this talk about babies."

"Hasn't this thing with Sadie's father taught you anything? Time is precious and passes far too fast. He's more than twenty years younger than me, and I will outlive him. Is it so much to ask that before I die I get to see my boys happily married and raising families?"

"Who says I even want to get married?"

"Now you're just lying or fooling yourself. I saw the way you looked around the house. She's made her mark here and in your life. You miss her when she's gone."

"She's not gone. She's just not here."

"And how much does that bother you? How much do you want her here?"

Too much to admit outright to his grandfather, who'd

be calling the preacher and buying a cradle before the day was out.

"Love is one of those things you just know, like the sun will rise again tomorrow."

"We've had one date that ended in a raid by the cops. She cooks and cleans here because her brother stole our cattle."

"What does any of that have to do with how you feel about her?"

Nothing. Everything. The date might have ended badly, but he'd enjoyed every second he spent with her. He admired her strength and resiliency. The way she cared for her father and tried to help her brother told him how important family was to her. The same way it was important to him.

"Don't make things harder than they have to be." His grandfather had been saying that since he was a kid.

"I'm not making them hard. Things are complicated right now. I've barely seen her these last few days."

"And you miss her. Tell her that. She'll like it. Send her some flowers. Better yet, pick her some and take them to her. Tell her in person how you feel."

"She knows I like being with her. She even called me her boyfriend."

When she called him her boyfriend, he had to admit his heart leaped in his chest. He'd liked the idea that she belonged to him and he belonged to her. He liked the connection they shared, the way she made him feel, and the way she'd gotten him out of his tired routine. He really did look forward to seeing her smiling face when he came in from work.

And she wasn't here today and the disappointment still lingered in his mind and heart.

Damn, he really did like her, but did he love her?

Maybe. When he saw that guy with a gun to her head, his heart stopped. The thought of her dead . . . The rest of his lonely life spread out ahead of him; it seemed so bleak.

He should do more to show her how much he wanted to be with her. He didn't really know what to do. No one would say he was a romantic. A job needed doing, he got it done. He wished he knew what to do to win Sadie's heart and affection.

"I don't know why she's not here. Maybe something happened with her father. I'm heading over to her place to find out." He had to go and see for himself, because staying here another minute would only mean an evening spent worrying, which would drive him crazier than he felt right now.

Rory went back through the kitchen and into the laundry room to stuff his feet back in his boots. Ready to leave, he held the door handle, but stopped at his grandfather's words.

"It's okay to love her, Rory. She won't leave you like your parents did."

This certainly had nothing to do with his parents. He didn't think she'd leave him. Certainly not without cause. But did he give her enough reason to stay? He feared he'd held back too much of himself from Sadie.

His mind spun. He didn't share his thoughts or feelings with his grandfather. He didn't share them with anyone most of the time.

"That's not what this is about," he denied, hoping his grandfather would drop all this so he could figure out what to do about Sadie on his own.

"Isn't it? Isn't that the reason you hold on to Ford

and Colt and me and this ranch so tight? Isn't that the reason you've never let anyone close to you, because you're afraid they'll leave?"

Rory walked out and closed the door between him and his grandfather. He closed the door on the conversation. Rory wasn't afraid of being left alone. But the thought of his future on this ranch without a wife and children made his future seem empty and lonely.

If he missed Sadie the way he did now, what would it be like if she was there every day, in his bed, in his life? He didn't want to think of having all that happiness and the possibility he could lose it if she left him. But, he realized now he'd risk the hurt to have at least a little bit of happiness—for however long it lasted.

Rory pulled up in front of Sadie's house and slammed on the brakes. A sense of dread washed through his system, knotting his gut at the sight of the front door left wide open. Sadie's truck wasn't here. Where was she? The possible answers to that question rolled through his mind and unsettled him even more.

He jumped out of the truck and scanned the surrounding yard, paying particular attention to the open barn doors. Nothing moved in the dark interior. No sound that someone lurked nearby. Nothing but the empty yard and whispering wind.

He rushed to the house and leaped the porch steps. The quiet disturbed him, but the trail of blood leading back into the house stopped his heart, constricted his chest, and made it impossible to breathe.

He sidestepped the drops of blood and smeared drag marks and followed the trail back to Mr. Higgins's room. He stood in the doorway, his mind rebelling against the bloody scene in front of him. The bedcovers draped over the side of the bed and pooled on the floor. A smashed lamp lay on its side, the dented shade tilted, the bright bulb a blinding light, highlighting the blood splattered on the floor and walls. The right side of the night table beside the bed had been jarred and shoved into the wall, leaving a hole where the corner went through the sheetrock. A bloody shirt lay balled and crumpled on the mattress, like someone had used it as a compress against a terrible wound.

"What the fuck?"

Lost in his dark thoughts, Rory hadn't heard anyone come in. He spun toward the shocked voice and spotted the last person he expected to see. He reacted without thinking. Rory grabbed Connor and shoved him back through the bedroom door and slammed him into the hallway wall. Pictures of him and Sadie growing up through the years rattled against the wall along with Connor's bones. Rory held him off the ground, his forearm pressed to Connor's throat. The nasty gash across his cheek had scabbed over, but the angry red splotch along the edges indicated it had become infected. Rory didn't care about that; he only wanted to know one thing. "Where is she?"

Connor gasped and tried to speak, but Rory had cut off his air. Rory adjusted his arm across Connor's collarbones, but didn't let him go.

"Tell me where she is." The dead calm in his voice didn't reveal the chaos of fear and desperation eating away at Rory's insides.

"I don't know."

"If you hurt her, if that asshole you call a friend laid one finger on her, I swear to God . . ."

"I didn't. He's not here. Swear. I came back to tell her I'm sorry about . . . about everything."

"You're sorry," Rory roared. "Do you have any idea what you've put your sister through?"

"I . . . I never meant for any of this to happen."

"And yet you did let it happen. You let that bastard string her up with barbed wire in a tree and slice her up with a knife." Rory ignored the shame and regret in Connor's eyes. He didn't believe it. At least not enough to think Connor had any intention of making things right and making better choices in his life. "You let that asshole convince you that making and dealing drugs is a great way to earn a living. You stole my fucking cattle."

"You don't understand . . ."

"Save your excuses for your sister. She's the only one who will listen to that shit, because she still believes that you will eventually do the right thing. I know better. You only look out for yourself."

"That's not true."

"Isn't it? Aren't you really here to convince her to get me to forget about the cattle you've stolen?"

Connor's eyes went wide with surprise that he'd guessed right.

"You think just because I'm with your sister I'm going to let you get away with anything. No way in hell, not after what you let happen to her."

"I didn't do it."

"That's not fucking good enough. You left her there. You didn't do a damn thing to save her. Did you even think to call anyone to go and find her? Did you wonder at all what happened to her?"

"I—"

"Shut the fuck up." Rory saw it in his eyes. He'd left her there, so focused on saving his own ass, he hadn't thought to do anything to save his sister. The drugs had stolen all his empathy and compassion for others, until all he thought about was himself and his next fix. Probably in the exact opposite order. "What you've done is unforgivable and it's time you paid."

Rory pulled out his phone, but before he called the cops, it rang.

Bell's picture popped up on his screen and Rory closed his eyes for a moment, bracing for the worst.

"Bell, please tell me Sadie is okay."

"She's fine."

"You swear."

"Yes, Rory, she wasn't hurt."

Rory forgot himself, leaned back, and exhaled. Connor took advantage and shoved him back. Rory stumbled, but made a grab for Connor. He dodged and evaded, running down the hall and out the door. Frustrated, pissed, too worried about Sadie to care what happened to Connor, he let the punk go.

"What happened? Where is she?"

"Her father fell and hit his head. He's got major head trauma and lost quite a bit of blood."

Rory glanced back at the bloody room and shook off the dread he'd carried, thinking someone died in that room.

"I stabilized him, but had to send him to the hospital in Bozeman. He and Sadie left in the ambulance a few minutes ago."

"I tried to call her, but got her voice mail."

"She's barely left her father's side. Rory, the prognosis . . ."

"It's not good, I take it."

"She's beside herself. I thought you might like to know since the two of you seemed close after you brought her in."

"We're seeing each other. I'll head to the hospital now."

"If you can, bring her something to wear. She found her father and she's kind of a mess."

"I'm on it. Thanks, Bell."

"You're welcome. I'll see you soon."

Rory tucked his phone back in his pocket, kept his back to the mess in Mr. Higgins's room, and walked down the hall to Sadie's room. He stood in the doorway, staring at her double bed covered in a navy and white floral-patterned quilt. A hairbrush sat on her dark wood dresser next to a picture of her as a little girl up on horseback, with her mother standing beside her holding the reins. A second picture sat next to her bed. Sadie and Connor as children sitting on the porch, Connor on a lower step, Sadie above with her arms wrapped around her little brother.

"You've been keeping him safe for a long time, sweetheart. Holding on to him. But who holds on to you?"

If her father didn't make it, and Bell had hinted that he wouldn't, who would look out for Sadie? Certainly not her brother. Rory would make sure no one hurt her, especially not her self-centered kid brother who'd never grown up and still left all the hard work to his big sister.

Rory went to the closet door, opened it, and pawed

through Sadie's things and came up with a purple tote bag. He went back to her bed and the basket of laundry beside it. He pulled out a couple of clean T-shirts, a pair of jeans, dark blue leggings and another pair of black leggings, and some bundled socks. Just in case, he picked out a white tank top–style nightgown that flared out at the bottom. Enough clothes to get her cleaned up tonight, but also in case she needed to stay at the hospital or a motel nearby a few days. He'd try to get her to come home, but knew she wouldn't want to leave her father.

Rory left her room, knowing he'd picture her there whenever they weren't together. He'd see her in that bed and dream about being there with her. Right now, he needed to find her and give her the support and comfort she needed to get through this tough time.

He closed up the front door, but didn't lock it, walked to his truck, and opened the cab door. He tossed Sadie's bag on the passenger side, climbed in, started the engine, but didn't pull out of the drive. Instead, he pulled out his cell and tried Sadie again. He got her voice mail.

"Hey sweetheart, it's me. I'm headed your way. Be there soon."

He hung up and called the ranch.

"What happened?" his grandfather asked.

"Her father took a bad spill and split open his skull. Bell sent him to the hospital in Bozeman. Beyond that, I don't know anything more. I'm headed there now." Rory put action to his words, driving down the driveway to the main road.

"What can we do to help?" his grandfather asked.

"Call that cleaning service we use a few times a

year. Send them to Sadie's place. It'll probably cost extra, I don't care, but tell them there's a lot of blood in Mr. Higgins's room. It'll need to be scrubbed and disinfected. I don't want Sadie coming home to that."

"I'll have the whole place cleaned. Anything else?"

"I'll let you know. Tell Ford and Colt to hold down the fort. I'm not sure when I'll be back. I'm staying with her as long as she needs me."

"That's exactly where you should be. Don't worry about things here. We've got it covered."

"Thanks. I'll be in touch."

"Take care of your girl."

"I will." He'd always take care of her. It finally sank in that he not only wanted to take care of her, he needed to do it because she meant so much to him.

It was a long drive into Bozeman. By the time he got there, he was desperate to see her and make sure she was okay. He missed her so damn much these last few days. The few minutes they shared before she dashed off to see her father weren't enough, but he understood. She needed to be with her dad. He hoped Mr. Higgins's accident was just a setback and not the end, for both his and Sadie's sakes.

CHAPTER 16

Sadie sat in the chair by her father's hospital bed and stared at his bruised and swollen face. As best she could tell, he'd tried to get out of bed, got dizzy, and face-planted into the dresser, bouncing off the wall and landing on the floor. His left eye was black and swollen shut. The splotchy bruising went down his cheek and across his nose. Bandages wrapped around his head, covering the deep four-inch gash across his head and into his hairline. She'd never seen anything so ominous. Blood had poured down his face and neck. He'd tried to get up and help himself, but only ended up passed out on the floor. If she hadn't stopped at the house on the way to Rory's place . . . Well, she didn't want to think what might have happened to her father.

"Miss Higgins?"

Sadie glanced over at the doctor standing at the end of the bed with a thick folder in his hands. She'd met several since she arrived, but couldn't remember their names or faces really. She didn't think she'd met this guy.

"Yes, I'm Sadie."

"Sadie, I'm Dr. Bird. I saw your father about five months ago."

"You did?"

"He was referred to me after he saw another doctor about having some shortness of breath and chest pain."

"What kind of doctor are you?"

"An oncologist."

"My dad has cancer." Deep inside she'd known, but saying it out loud made it all the more real. That dreaded thing no one wanted to say, let alone have. Her gut soured and the sense of dread she'd lived with these last months and had grown over the last weeks intensified.

"Stage four lung cancer."

Even that didn't stun her. Forty years of smoking, killing himself a little bit with every puff. Connor was doing the same, only he'd chosen a much more expeditious form of death.

"I see. So was he undergoing some kind of treatment? Do we need to start something now?"

"I'm sorry to say that your father refused chemotherapy and radiation."

"What?"

"As I explained to him, it may have prolonged his life, but not saved it. By the time I saw your father, the cancer had already spread to his liver and other vital organs. Your father understood it wasn't if he'd die from cancer, but when. He didn't want to spend his final months in and out of the hospital for treatments that would prolong his days, but steal his quality of life. That was his sentiment. And though I wished he'd given us a chance to help, he wanted to be home with you."

She believed her father chose his quality of life over the side effects of aggressive treatments, but she also knew her father chose to be home with her and spare her the cost of those treatments. They had insurance, but it didn't cover even half of everything, based on how much Connor's hospital visits cost them. She'd spent the last years trying to keep their heads above water with the bills and Connor's added debts. Her father didn't want to saddle her with more burdens. She understood his way of thinking, but she didn't like it. She wanted him to fight to live. Not give up because of the financial and emotional cost. Her father had always been practical, straightforward, and had always done what had to be done. Like her.

"What do we need to do for him now?"

"I've compared his new MRI, X-rays, and blood work. I'm sorry to say his condition is worse and deteriorating quickly."

"What does that mean?" She couldn't help the catch in her voice or the tears gathering in her eyes. She didn't want to hear the dire news, but had to face the reality staring her in the face.

"Have you noticed a change in your father recently? Has he had trouble with his motor skills and memory?"

"Yes. He tells stories over and over. He forgets words. I think reading has become difficult. His balance seems off." She stared down at her father's battered face. "I've found him wandering outside, looking for my mother, or just simply lost."

"The cancer has spread to his brain." The doctor said the words she didn't want to hear and tried to deny.

Tears streamed down her face. She swiped them away, but more fell.

"How long?" She choked out the words, but didn't want to hear the answer.

"It's hard to say for sure, but with the brain injury your father suffered during the fall, not long."

"He's not leaving this hospital, is he?"

"No. I'm sorry. He signed a Do Not Resuscitate order. We will keep him comfortable."

"Do you think he'll wake up again before . . ."

"It's not likely. I suggest you talk to him. One never knows how much a patient hears while in a coma." The doctor glanced at her shirt and hands. "I'll ask a nurse to find you something to change into. You should wash up. You'll be more comfortable."

Sadie held up her hands and stared at the dried blood smeared over her skin. Her shirt had mostly dried into an ugly brownish-red splatter.

"Is there someone I can call for you?"

She thought of Rory. She should have called him to let him know she wouldn't be coming to his house today. She wished he was here. She needed to feel his strong arms around her. She needed his strength and understanding and comfort. She needed him to tell her everything would be all right.

Unbidden tears kept coming, trailing down her cheeks. She didn't wipe them away, but stood like a statue unsure what to do.

"Miss Higgins?"

She turned to face the doctor and spotted Rory walking down the corridor from the elevator behind him. She didn't think, didn't say a word, just went with instinct and ran to him.

Rory caught her when she leaped into his arms and slammed into his chest. She wrapped her arms around him and buried her wet face in his neck. He held her close, her legs dangling against his shins. The wracking sobs she let loose made him think the worst happened, but he spotted the doctor standing in the doorway of the room she'd come out of and headed in his direction, carrying Sadie down the corridor.

"I got you, sweetheart. Everything is going to be all right."

"It is now that you're here."

Those words went straight to his heart. He held her tighter and kissed her on the head. He stopped in front of the doctor.

"I'll leave you two alone with Mr. Higgins. If you have any questions, Sadie, or need anything, please ask the nurse to call me. I'll be back later to check on your father."

The doctor nodded at Rory, then walked down the hall. Rory took Sadie into the room. He dropped the bag he'd brought on the floor and sat in the chair beside her father's bed. He cradled Sadie in his lap and let her cry.

Rory rubbed Sadie's back. "It's okay, sweetheart, let it all out."

A nurse came in with a box of tissues and set it on the bed within reach. "Can I get you anything?"

"If you don't mind, a glass of water, please." Rory hugged Sadie closer as her tears faded, but her grief kept her clinging to him. He didn't mind. In fact, her need for his comfort, the way she'd flown into his arms, relieved to see him, spoke to how close they'd become in such a short time.

The nurse handed him the glass of water. "I'll be back to check on Mr. Higgins in just a little while. Uh, there's a bathroom two doors down if she'd like to get cleaned up."

"Thanks, I'll take care of her."

Rory waited for the nurse to leave. He held Sadie close, his cheek pressed to her head. Her breath washed over his neck in uneven gasps and hiccups. She lay curled into his chest on his lap. He rubbed her back in soft circles until her breathing evened out and she rested quietly against him.

"Sadie, sweetheart, drink some of this water. You'll feel better."

She sat up on his lap and took the plastic cup. She sipped the water, then set it on the nearby table. The sigh she let loose reverberated through him.

"Better?"

"Not really, and yes." She finally looked him in the eye. Hers filled with unshed tears again. "I'm so glad you're here."

He leaned in and kissed her softly.

She leaned back. "I'm sorry I cried all over you." She wiped his shoulder, over his wet T-shirt.

He took her hand to keep her from fussing for no reason. "I don't mind. I'm sorry about what's happened and that you're sad. It kills me when you cry."

Rory gently pushed her forward to stand as he rose from the chair. He took her hand and led her to the door.

"Where are we going?"

He held her hand up for her to see. "You need to get cleaned up. We'll only be a few minutes," he added when she stared back at her father. He picked up the bag he'd dropped on the floor.

"Where did that come from?"

"Your closet." He led her down the hall to the bathroom door. He knocked once to make sure it was empty, opened the door, and pulled her inside behind him.

"You went to my house and packed my clothes?"

Rory turned the water on in the sink and adjusted the hot and cold to make the water warm. "When you didn't show up at my place, I went hunting for you. I saw your father's room. Man, Sadie, that scared me to death."

"I'm sorry I didn't call you."

"You were taking care of your father. Now, let me take care of you. Come here." He took Sadie's hands and held them under the water.

"I forgot." She held her hands up, staring at the red water running over her hands.

"I'm here to think about the mundane. You've got far more important things to think about right now."

"My heart is in that room with him, but all I can think about right now is how lucky I am to have you here with me."

Rory stopped in the process of scrubbing soap over Sadie's hands and forearms. He rubbed his thumbs over the scars on her wrists. "I almost lost my chance with you, and now all I think about is being with you. You're kind of driving me crazy."

That earned him a small smile.

"I am, huh. Well, I'll try to stop."

He shut the water off and pulled two paper towels from the dispenser. He patted her hands dry. "It really is your fault I get nothing done anymore. I find myself wondering what you're doing. I lose all track of time daydreaming about you."

"What am I doing in all these daydreams?" Her

husky voice and the way her eyebrow cocked up made him grin.

"You don't want to know what I picture you doing," he teased. To keep things light, he distracted himself from looking at her by picking up the duffel bag and setting it on the lip of the sink.

"Maybe I do. How else am I going to fulfill your every fantasy?"

He groaned, reached out for her neck, and drew her in for a soft kiss. He lingered over the task. His pleasure to take his time and taste her sweetness. He brushed his lips to hers, then pressed his forehead to hers. He didn't open his eyes, but held the image of her and him in bed together in his mind. "You win. I'll stop."

"Please don't. Not on my account." She pressed her lips to his, sliding her tongue along his, tempting him to take more. He did, taking command of her mouth and holding her close, her breasts pressed to his chest. Mindful of where they were and why, he didn't mind distracting her from reality, but he wouldn't give in to her temptation here. He wanted her with a desperation that went beyond a simple hunger that could be slaked with a quick romp. When he made love to her, he wanted to take his time, explore all the wonderful things about Sadie, and tap into this sultry, seductive side she hinted at with her bold statement about fulfilling his every fantasy.

Just the thought made him ache, but he kept the kiss tame with a hint of the heat they could share.

She pulled away and pressed her rosy lips together, her eyes still closed. "Rory." His name on her lips sounded so sweet. Like a siren's song. But he didn't answer it. He reined in his baser needs and brushed his hands down both sides of her long blond hair, remembering his true reason for being here. To comfort her.

"Take your clothes off."

Her eyes flew open and went wide. Her fingers dug into his shoulders. "What? Here?"

"Yes." He loved teasing her, but had to put a stop to this before he couldn't stop. "You're covered in blood. You need to change out of those dirty things and put on the clean clothes I brought you."

"Oh." She released him and stared into the bag he'd packed.

"When I finally get you naked, we will be somewhere private. We will have all the time in the world to be alone and together."

She stared up at him. "I wish that's where we were now instead of here."

He leaned down and kissed her. "Me too." He held her gaze, letting her see in him how much he wanted her. How much being with her mattered to him.

She sorted through the clothes he'd packed, looked up, and smiled. "So your brother prefers lace panties, but you'd rather I wear none."

"Um, I guess I wasn't thinking when I packed."

Her mouth turned down into a fake frown. "Perhaps your subconscious made the slip on purpose."

"I'll be sure to thank it later."

Sadie smiled, gathered her stack of clothes in her hands, sidestepped around him, and set the clothes on the toilet tank. He turned away, giving her space to get dressed. Didn't mean he didn't sneak a peek at the back of her in the mirror. She pulled her soiled T-shirt over her head and dropped it to the tile floor. Ruined, better to just throw it away than try to clean it. She probably didn't want to wear it again and remember today.

She shimmied out of her jeans, giving him a nice view of her round bottom encased in pink cotton panties with white lace trim. He gulped and averted his gaze.

"The blood soaked through everything." The tremble in her voice made his chest tight.

"Take it all off. There's no one here you need to impress or be embarrassed in front of."

"Can you pull out the dark purple shirt you brought? I don't want to wear the white without a bra. Don't want to give the whole hospital a show."

Rory wet some paper towels for her to clean up. He handed them back to her and she cleaned the blood from her body and tossed the mess in the trash. He pulled the shirt out of the bag and held it out behind him without turning around. She took it from his grasp, and he caught a glimpse of the side of her breast and her bare bottom in the mirror. Not even the faint puncture scars dotted all over her took away from her beauty.

"Are you peeking?" The teasing lilt in her voice made his immediate fear she'd be pissed at him turn to embarrassment.

"Uh, I'm a guy. Of course I peeked."

"See anything you like?" This time her voice held a hint of shyness.

"I like everything about you, sweetheart."

She pulled the leggings up over her hips. He had to admit, the disappointment hit him hard. She had a really great ass.

She glanced over her shoulder and met his gaze in

the mirror. "What would you do if I turned around right now?"

He swallowed, knowing exactly what he'd see. Her bare breasts. His mouth watered just thinking about putting his lips on her skin and sliding his tongue over her nipples.

"Have mercy."

Her eyes narrowed and her lips hinted at a wicked smile. She turned just slightly. He held his breath, his gaze dipping to her bare shoulder, anticipating what he'd see. At the last second, she turned back, grabbed the shirt, and pulled it over her head, giving him another glimpse of the curve of her side and full breast.

"You're killing me."

Her soft laugh didn't hold much humor.

"Sweetheart?" He hoped he hadn't made her uncomfortable.

She quickly pulled on her socks and stuffed her feet back into the pair of tennis shoes she'd slid off earlier.

"I'm fine."

Rory turned to her as she bent to pick up her discarded clothes and rolled them into her jeans.

"I'll ask the nurse if she's got a bag to put these in."

"I'm sure we can find something."

"Okay." She turned and headed for the door. With her hand on the knob, she stopped and hung her head.

"Sweetheart, what is it?"

"In here, it's you and me talking, teasing, being together, and experiencing this thing between us that seems so new but is as comfortable as a favorite blanket. Out there, my father is dying."

Rory closed the distance between them, letting her feel his body pressed to the back of hers. He kissed the top of her head. "As much as I like being in here with you, I'll still be out there with you, too. You're not alone, sweetheart, but you are strong enough to face this."

She leaned back into him. He wrapped his arm around her middle and pressed his hand to her stomach, holding her close.

"Promise me when this is over, we'll make more moments like this."

"Count on it."

They walked back to the room. Sadie stood at the end of the bed, staring at her father's still form. "He liked you."

"What's not to like," he teased, hoping to keep her spirits up. "I like him, too. I wish I'd gotten to know him better. He loves you."

"Yes, he does. I miss him already." She placed her hand on her father's foot and rubbed softly. "I'm here, Dad."

Mr. Higgins didn't acknowledge her. Rory felt her disappointment.

Sadie tossed her bundle of clothes on the floor next to her purse. Rory set the bag next to both. Sadie squatted and dug through her purse, pulling out her phone.

"You called me."

"Twice."

She listened to her message and smiled softly at him. "You're sweet."

"On you, yes."

That earned him another soft smile. "Did you threaten to kill my brother?"

"Several times," he admitted.

"And you tried to strangle him?"

"I thought some of the blood in your father's room might be yours, so yeah, when he showed up and I couldn't find you, I demanded to know if he had something to do with your disappearance. You'll remember how I found you the first time we met."

Sadie put her hand on Rory's chest. She needed that connection. "I'm sorry. That must have been scary to see all that blood and not know what happened."

"I thought you were dead. That's twice now. I can't do that again, Sadie." Rory pulled her into his arms and held her close, his cheek pressed to the top of her head.

"Let's hope there won't be a next time."

"There better not be, or I won't be so nice to your brother."

"You choked him."

"I didn't kill him. In fact, I let him go."

"He wants to talk to me."

"I thought he shut his phone off or tossed it so the cops can't track him."

"He gave me a number to call."

"Call him. He's probably worried about your dad."

Sadie stepped back just enough to look up at him and see the sincerity in his eyes. "You mean that. You're not going to demand I call the police and give them this number?"

"If it was me, I'd want to know about my dad, no matter the circumstances. He'll probably ditch the phone as soon as he speaks to you anyway."

"So we'll get him another day, is that it?"

"Today is about what you need, Sadie. This is about your dad and family. We'll deal with everything else your brother has done another day."

She pressed her hand to the side of his face. His

beard stubble scraped her palm. "You're a really good man."

"Doesn't mean I still don't want to kill him for what he did to you."

"And for stealing your cattle."

"I can live without the cattle."

Sadie held her breath. Difficult to do with her heart growing ten sizes in her chest with his unsaid *I can't live without you.* Maybe he didn't speak the words, but she knew he meant them. The intense way he stared at her implied how much he wanted her to hear what he couldn't quite bring himself to say.

"Call Connor. Tell him what's happened with your father."

"I wish he could come here and . . ." *Say goodbye.* She couldn't speak the words, because she didn't want to say them herself.

"Maybe this will make him realize there is nothing more important than family. This is where he belongs."

"You think that. I think that. Connor only ever thinks about himself."

"Remember that the next time you try to help him and it turns out you're the one who really needs the help. He's proven he'll save his ass over yours. I have two brothers of my own. I'd do anything for them, just like you've tried to do for Connor."

"But."

"But I know sometimes the best thing I can do for them is knock their heads together and shake some sense into them."

"Your brothers can be reasoned with. Mine's got a brain addled by drugs. He doesn't see reason, or even right from wrong anymore. He only sees what he wants and does things without thought to consequences or how it affects others. He's got a false sense of being invincible."

"Unfortunately, he'll learn he's not the hard way, because talking to him does no good."

Mr. Higgins gasped for breath behind the oxygen mask covering his nose and mouth. He struggled, inhaling and exhaling in uneven gasps. Sadie took his hand and placed her other hand on her father's heaving chest. His breaths evened out but remained labored. His heart rate skipped across the monitor, erratic even to her untrained eyes.

The ICU nurse rushed in, checked the monitors and her father's vitals. "Looks like he's in need of some more pain meds. It's rather soon, so I'll have to consult the doctor. I'll be back shortly."

"Call your brother," Rory coaxed, placing his hands on her shoulders.

She dialed quickly, pinching her lip with her fingers, waiting for her brother to answer, but he never did. Of course she couldn't get ahold of him when she needed him.

"Either he dumped his burner phone for a new one, the phone is off, or he's not picking up."

"Try him again later."

She raked her fingers through her hair and admitted, "Actually, I'm kind of glad he didn't pick up. I've got more than I can deal with right now. I'm happy to forgo the Connor drama until later when I'll have to tell him . . ." She couldn't bring herself to talk out loud about her father dying.

She leaned down and kissed her dad's cheek. "I love you, Dad." His hand contracted in hers. Just for a second and barely more than a twitch, but she felt it and it eased her heart.

Sadie turned and stared down at the man sitting behind her, waiting for her to come to him, knowing that she needed him. He held his hand out to her. She took it and he tugged her down into his lap. He didn't say anything, just held her knowing there was nothing left to say. She didn't need the words. She knew how he felt and what he'd say.

The heaviness in her heart eased just being close to him, feeling his strength and kindness surround her.

Rory stayed by her side through the difficult night. They barely slept, watching her father struggle to breathe, his erratic heartbeat sounding alarms nearly every other hour.

The calmer morning gave way to an afternoon filled with denying the end was near and Rory coaxing her to drink or eat something she didn't want. Not when her heart had dropped into her stomach like a stone that weighed half as much as her grief.

Sunset brought another round of her father struggling to breathe and Sadie holding her breath as she waited to see if the long seconds he didn't take a breath meant he was finally gone. She hated to see him struggle and suffer. As shadows filled the room, she stood by her father's bed, held his hand, leaned down and rested her chest against his, and whispered into his ear, "Let go, Daddy. I will be all right. Mom's waiting for you. Go to her. I love you."

The wracking breath her father sucked in let out on a long sigh. She kissed his cheek, knowing he'd finally gone. The nurse turned off the machines and patted Sadie's shoulder as she lay over her father's lifeless body, her heart pressed to his. Rory's hands settled on her back and rubbed softly up and down.

"I'll leave you two," the nurse said. "Take all the time you need."

Sadie needed another thirty years. She needed a thousand more hugs. Hundreds of more conversations. More memories to tuck away and cherish.

She told him to go, but she wanted him to stay. She didn't want to be all alone. Connor was still here, but not with her, not on her side. He wasn't likely to come running if she was sick or in trouble. He'd likely run the other way.

She had Rory in her life. But after all that happened, would she prove to be more trouble than she was worth? Or worse, would he find her boring without all these distractions keeping him from getting to know the real her.

"Sadie, sweetheart, come here."

She kissed her father's cheek for the last time, stood, and turned into Rory's open arms. She buried her face in his chest. He sidestepped around her, sitting back against her father's bed, and held her close between his legs. Her tears came all at once. She pressed her face into his shoulder, soaking his shirt again.

She leaned back and wiped her hand over his shirt. "Seems all I do lately is cry all over you."

"Sadie, sweetheart, your dad died. You can cry all you want."

"I don't know what to do now."

"We'll figure it out together. I'll take you home."

CHAPTER 17

Rory pulled up in the drive and parked behind his brothers' trucks. Sadie leaned against his side. Not asleep, but not really aware of where they were or the long drive home. He'd left her long enough to make a phone call to his family to let them know what happened and that they were coming. Sadie took care of the paperwork at the hospital and made arrangements for her father's burial.

The headlights cut out when he shut off the engine. He didn't move, but waited for Sadie to come back to herself. He stared at his home. The lights in the windows welcoming him, letting him know his grandfather and brothers were there waiting. He didn't want to take Sadie back to her empty, dark place. Too many memories for her right now. Besides, this was where he wanted her to want to be.

"I thought you said you were taking me home."

"I did." He didn't say whether he meant that's what he'd said, or that's where he'd brought her. He wondered which one she thought he meant.

"I like it here. I like seeing you with your family. You're so close to all of them."

"They like having you here. And so do I." Rory opened the truck door and slid out. He held his hand out to her. "Come inside with me." Sadie took his hand. "Bring your purse and bag."

"You're not taking me home later."

"Stay here with me."

Their gazes held for a breath, then Sadie grabbed her stuff and slid out of the truck, her fingers linked with his as they walked up to the house. Rory opened the front door and greeted his brothers and grandfather with a nod.

"Come here." His grandfather held his arms open. Sadie let Rory's hand go and walked right into them. She held tight to his grandfather. "I'm sorry for you loss, pretty girl."

"Thank you." Sadie choked out the words and gave his grandfather a squeeze.

Granddad released her and Ford stepped in to hug her, too. "My condolences."

Ford released Sadie into Colt's embrace. His little brother kissed her on the head and held her close. Rory wanted to smack him, but refrained because Colt only meant to comfort her. "Sorry about your dad. I don't really remember mine and the loss is a pain that aches. I can't imagine how it feels for you when you've had him so long and it's still not long enough."

Rory thought about his parents all the time. He tried to keep his memories fresh, but they faded over time and he had to work to bring them into focus. He'd often wondered if Colt's few memories stayed clear, or if he remembered them at all now. The sadness he felt for Sadie's loss intensified with his brother's poignant words.

"Thank you, Colt. That's exactly how it feels." Sadie stepped back and kept coming until she ran into him. He wrapped his hand around her middle and hugged her close. She pressed her hands to his arm at her stomach and held him tight. He kissed her head and glanced at Colt, seeing the same hurt he saw in Sadie in his brother's eyes. He glanced at Ford and Granddad and saw it there, too. If he looked in the mirror, maybe he'd see it in himself, though he tried to hold it together and not make Sadie's loss about his. Still, when someone died, you remembered those you'd lost, too.

To help keep her from falling into her sorrowful thoughts, he nudged her to walk toward the dining area off the kitchen. "Something smells good."

"Tonight, we cooked for you, pretty girl," his grandfather said, leading the way into the other room.

Sadie stopped in front of Rory. He put his hand on her shoulder and stared over her at the table his family set for her. Chicken pot pie casserole. A bouquet of wild daisies and white candles, their flames dancing and making the wineglasses sparkle. His grandmother's dishes were set out with the silver. A table set for family and a special occasion.

"It's beautiful," she whispered.

"You must be hungry," Ford said taking his place at the table.

"Rory said you've barely slept or eaten," Colt added.

Sadie turned and stared up at Rory. "You called them and set this up."

"I made the call. They did all this for you."

She went up on tiptoe and wrapped her arms around his neck. She hugged him tight, kissed his neck, and whispered in his ear, "Thank you."

His family watched them. Each of them gave him a nod. They approved of her. Not that he needed their approval, but he appreciated that they gave it. Sadie saw and understood they'd done this because they cared, and because they thought of her as part of the family. They accepted her.

"Let's eat, sweetheart. You're wiped out. You need to take care of yourself now."

Rory held the chair out next to his grandfather's place at the head of the table. Sadie sat. He took the seat next to her. Colt poured the wine, something special for Sadie. They usually drank iced tea or beer with their meal, but thought she might prefer this.

Once all the glasses were filled, his grandfather raised his glass. "A toast." His grandfather took Sadie's hand into his and held tight.

Everyone else raised their glasses, their gazes locked on his grandfather.

"To Mr. Higgins. You raised an exceptional daughter. I know you are watching over her. We'll do the same. Rest in peace." His grandfather tapped his glass to Sadie's, kissed her hand, and sipped his drink.

Tears gathered in Sadie's eyes as she tapped everyone else's glasses. She took a sip and set her glass down with an unsteady hand.

Rory reached for her, rubbing her back and brushing his fingers through her long hair. "How's that pack of ornery horses doing?" Rory wanted to get everyone talking about something to get Sadie's mind off her dad, at least long enough to get her to eat something. Her pale skin and the dark circles beneath her eyes made him want to take her upstairs and tuck her in bed, but she needed some food and time to settle her mind and heart.

"They miss you, Sadie," Ford said.

"You and Rory should go for a ride tomorrow," Colt suggested.

Sadie swallowed the small bite she took. "It's been a while since I got a ride in. I'd love to go."

"Anything you want, sweetheart." Rory squeezed her hand on the table.

"I hate to take you away from your work longer."

"These guys can cover for me."

"Lord knows Rory works harder than all of us. He deserves to take whatever time he wants. Being with you is a good reason to set work aside for a few days and enjoy your company," Granddad said, stuffing another bite of pot pie into his mouth like he wasn't playing matchmaker.

Rory didn't need the help. Didn't want it, but he appreciated that his family didn't mind his taking some time off to be with her.

Sadie mindlessly ate her food, surprised she could swallow past the lump she couldn't dislodge for the building emotions roiling inside her. She missed her father, felt overwhelmed by what she needed to do next and the life she had to face without the support, understanding, and love from her dad.

Rory caught up on the ranch business with his brothers. Grandpa Sammy interjected his thoughts, orders, and niggling comments, all laced with a touch of humor, to the boys he so openly adored. They had such an easy way with one another. In addition to the love they showed each other, respect shone through in the way they interacted. Although Rory oversaw the ranch, it was clear he valued his brother's opinions and contributions. She'd never felt the camaraderie she witnessed among the brothers. Their parents' death had brought them together and bonded them as more than family. They were friends. They were brothers in the deepest sense of the word.

"Pretty girl, do you want some more?" Grandpa Sammy asked.

She stared down at her empty plate. "Uh, no thank you. It was very good. I don't know why you guys wanted me to cook."

"It was my late wife's best dish," Grandpa Sammy said, pride and sorrow laced in his words.

"I'd love the recipe."

"I'll teach you how to make it one day soon."

"It's the one thing he insisted all us boys learn to cook," Rory added.

"It's nice that you all switch off cooking each day."

"Let's face it, Sadie, we're all happier and eat better when you're doing the cooking. We get by, but you outdo us every time," Ford said.

Sadie gave Ford a halfhearted smile, unable to keep up the pretense that she wasn't falling apart on the inside.

"Oh God." She smacked the back of her hand to her forehead. "I totally forgot to call work and let them know I wouldn't be in today. They probably left me a dozen messages."

Rory touched her shoulder. The comfort and warmth that simple touch evoked in her made her heart soar despite the weight of grief dragging it down.

"Sweetheart, I called work for you. Luna took your

shift. She said she'd give you the tips because you need them for school."

Colt pressed his lips together and turned his head to hide the glimpse of regret she saw in his eyes when Rory mentioned Luna's name.

"Thank you for doing that. I seem to have lost my mind yesterday. I still don't quite have it back."

"It's fine. I took care of it. Luna said she'd call you tomorrow. If there's anyone else you'd like me to call, I'm happy to do it for you."

It was hard to believe she once thought this sweet man forbidding or scary.

"I've got a few distant relatives to contact, but I'll wait and do that when I have the funeral details."

"What's this about school?" Grandpa Sammy asked.

"Um, I take online college courses. I'm working on my English degree. By that I mean I've been taking classes for the last eight years, trying to finish it."

"Do you want to be a teacher?" Rory shifted in his seat, turning his big body and all his attention to her.

"Well, that would pay the bills and be a hell of a lot better than waitressing, but ultimately I'd like to be a writer." The last words came out on a whisper. Her dream put into words she could barely speak because she'd never told anyone but Luna. Her father had caught her scribbling and typing away on her ancient laptop. When he asked, she'd passed it off as nothing more than fooling around. But now, with him gone, her degree only months away from becoming reality, and her life her own to live, she needed to make some real decisions about what she wanted to do.

"What do you like to write?" Rory asked.

She glanced over at him, waiting for some sign that

he thought her crazy for wanting to do something so fanciful. Nothing but interest showed in his eyes. She glanced at the other men at the table. They all looked back at her, eager to hear what she had to say.

"Um, well, I like to write fiction."

"That's kind of broad. Come on, tell us about one of your stories," Rory coaxed.

"Are you writing one of those *Fifty Shades* type books?" Colt teased.

"Actually, yes." She held the straight face when all their eyes went wide.

"Seriously?" Rory asked.

"No." She laughed and pressed her lips together to fight the smile spreading across her face. "Mysteries."

"Really?" Grandpa Sammy asked. "I love a good mystery. It's fun to try to figure out who done it."

"Yes. Exactly. I like the intricacy of the plots, laying out the clues and red herrings, tricking the reader into thinking they know who did it until the end when you discover it's someone else entirely. At least, I hope I do that. My professors seem to think I've got a talent for it." She glanced at Rory again, wondering if he thought her nuts.

"Sounds like you've got quite an imagination. I'd love to read something of yours."

She cocked up one eyebrow. "Seriously?"

"Hey, I like to read. When I have time. For you, I'll make time."

"Okay. Maybe. Right now the only people who have read anything are my teachers."

"Have you tried to get anything published?" Ford asked.

"No. It's hard enough to turn in my work and have

my teachers grade and critique it. I haven't gotten up the courage to send it to any of the publishers."

"What kind of grades do you get in school?" Colt asked.

The blush rose up from her neck to her face. "Um, mostly A's."

"Mostly?" Rory eyed her with a skeptical look.

"I have a 4.0 GPA."

"You're a brainy nerd," Colt teased. His head cocked to the side. "Wait. Didn't you win some writing contest in high school?"

She nodded, uncomfortable tooting her own horn. "And a ten-thousand-dollar scholarship. That's how I started attending classes. It's been a lot harder to finish with my limited resources."

"You mean with your brother sucking up every last dime you have for lawyers and repaying his debts." The anger in Rory's voice was warranted.

Out of habit, she was about to defend her brother, tell him that Connor never got over their mother's death, and acted out to get the attention he wanted. But she'd suffered the same loss and found a way to go on without all the self-destructive drama, breaking the law, or hurting people.

Rory frowned, pulled her close, and kissed the side of her head. "Sorry. You're tired. Come on, I'll take you upstairs. You can take a shower and get some rest."

She'd been in the same clothes for two days. She desperately wanted a shower, a soft bed, sleep, but she had one thing left to do that she dreaded. "I need to let Connor know about our father."

"You know where he is?" Ford asked.

"No. I'll try him at the last number I have, but he

didn't pick up earlier. I have to try. He needs to know what happened."

She wished Connor to be a different kind of man. A man with principles and honor. A man like the ones she sat with at this table. A man like Rory, who knew how to take care of the people he loved. Which she just realized included her.

Grandpa Sammy stood and picked up her dish and his. "Take her up and get her settled. We'll clean up down here."

Rory stood, held out his hand, and pulled her up out of her seat when she automatically took it. He led her out of the dining area to the stairs.

"They're good together," Grandpa Sammy said, thinking she and Rory were out of earshot. Or maybe not.

"At least one of us won't be sleeping alone tonight," Colt grumbled.

Halfway up the stairs, Rory casually said, "Don't worry, you can take my bed. I'll sleep on the couch."

"I don't want to kick you out of your bed."

They entered Rory's massive bedroom and stood in front of the king-size bed. She wanted to ask him to stay, but didn't know quite what to say. She didn't want to be alone.

Rory cupped her face in his big calloused hands and stared down at her. "As much as I want that to be *our* bed, this isn't how I want our first time to be. I won't take advantage of you or the situation. You're sad and don't want to be alone. I get that, but that's not a reason for us to make love tonight for the first time. It should be you and me in that bed because we want to be with each other, not because you need a distraction. I'm not saying that's all it is, I'm saying I want it to be only that you want me."

She slid her hands up his chest over tight muscles and sighed because she wanted to yank his shirt off, feel his skin against hers, and lose herself in his arms. But he was right. She couldn't say that wanting him, taking that next step in their relationship, wasn't prompted more out of her grief and need to connect with him than it was the overwhelming urge she always felt in his presence and when she thought about him to be closer to him. She'd never felt this kind of deep attraction to someone. He wanted that attraction to be more than a physical release or consoling her. He wanted a commitment and a promise of a future built on trust. He didn't want to be used even in the smallest way.

They hadn't talked about sleeping together, though everything was leading them in that direction. He'd given her the truth about how he felt, so she found the bravery to give him back the truth and do so bluntly.

She met his intense gaze and held it. His heart thundered under her palm. "I want you. More than I've ever wanted a man in my life. Not because you're gorgeous and kind and sexy as hell." That earned her a cocked-up eyebrow and a surprised grin. "I want you because you're Rory. The way you make me feel when I think about you, when I see you, when you hold me, when I hear your voice, when I see you on a horse and in your truck." The last made him chuckle and shake his head. "I can't explain why all the simple little things you do drive me crazy to want to touch you, but they do. But when you smile at me, I'm lost. I want you. What we have is something deeper than finding distraction and relief in sex."

"I'm not really against either of those things. But the first time should be—"

She pressed her fingertips to his lips, cutting off his words. "More." She sighed out the weariness building inside her. "It's not fair."

"What?" He rubbed his hands up and down her back, relaxing her against his big body.

"My family keeps getting in the way of what I want."

"Sadie," Ford called from the bedroom door. Her phone chirped with a text message. "I'm sorry to interrupt. Here's your stuff. Your phone hasn't stopped in the last few minutes. Someone is desperate to hear from you."

Sadie fisted her hands in Rory's shirt at his sides, groaned out her frustration, leaned back, and stared up at him. "See. How much do you want to bet that is my brother?"

"I don't make ridiculous bets."

Sadie let go of Rory and reluctantly stepped out of his arms and took her things from Ford's outstretched hands. She dropped her tote bag on the bed and dug through her purse for her phone to stop the annoying noise it made because she'd missed several calls, and her brother now sent text after text.

UNKNOWN: Where are you?
UNKNOWN: What happened to Dad?
UNKNOWN: Talk to me!!!
UNKNOWN: Tell me what's going on!!!!!!!!!

Tired beyond words all of a sudden, she sat on the edge of the bed and raked her fingers through her long hair.

Rory waved Ford off. He left them alone. Rory sat beside her and wrapped his arm around her shoulders.

"You need to get some sleep."

"I will."

"I'm going to take a quick shower, unless you want me to stay."

"I got this."

Rory kissed her softly and brushed his fingertips across her cheek. The compassion and warmth in his eyes eased her heart and the rising tide of nerves in her belly. She hated to deliver such sad news to her brother because there was no telling how he'd take it. If he was sober and levelheaded, he'd probably be okay. If he was high and aggravated, no telling what he'd do.

Rory walked over to the open bathroom area, reached over his head to the back of his neck, grabbed his shirt, and yanked it over his head. The full display of his eight-pack abs and massive shoulders reflected in the mirror.

She shook her head, unable to keep from staring. "See, now that's just not fair."

Rory tossed his shirt in the hamper next to him and gave her a wicked grin in the mirror. His hand went to the button on his jeans and flicked it open. She groaned.

Sadie pointed to the door leading into the bathroom, silently ordering Rory out of her sight.

"You're so pretty when you blush."

She appreciated that he was teasing her out of her funk, but the man was temptation times infinity and she needed to talk to her brother, not drool over the hot cowboy who could be in this bed with her right now if not for the drama and baggage in her life.

She sucked in a bolstering breath and called the new number Connor used to text her.

"Where the hell have you been? I've been trying to contact you for hours," he snapped.

She wanted to hang up again, walk into the bathroom, join Rory in the shower, and wash away this day with his arms wrapped around her. But no, she needed to deal with her brother.

"I was at the hospital with Dad. He's gone, Connor."

"He's not dead. He's fine. You're lying."

Leave it to her brother to deny the cold, hard truth.

"He had cancer. It spread to his brain."

"He's really dead?" Connor's voice cracked, driving her sympathy to new heights.

"Yes," she whispered, holding back another round of tears as grief swept her anger away. "He died a few hours ago."

"Why didn't you call me?"

"I tried, but obviously you've changed phones again."

"You were with that Kendrick fuck."

"Yes. I was with Rory, who stayed by my side for nearly two days, holding me and consoling me as Dad died right before my eyes." She choked back her tears.

His heavy breath whooshed through the phone. "I should have been there."

He said the words. Probably meant them, but that didn't change the reasons why he wasn't there.

"What did Dad leave us? How long until I can get my hands on the money?"

"What? Are you fucking kidding me right now?" Stupid question. Of course Connor only thought of himself and what he needed.

"The drugs we left behind the other night were worth a lot of money. You and your boyfriend fucked everything up. You owe me. I'm in deep shit."

"You're not getting any money."

"Fuck, do you want to see me shot dead over this?"

She let her head fall back and stared up at the ceiling. "I want you to turn yourself in to the police. Get the help you need."

"I don't need fucking therapy or rehab. Going to jail won't solve anything. These guys have people in prison. People who will kill me for what I've done. Dad had to have left something behind."

"He left you and me behind. We should be planning his funeral and grieving our loss, talking about all the good times we shared, but all you're interested in doing is saving your ass and taking what little is left of the ranch Dad built with his two hands and more hard work than you'll ever do in your lifetime," she snapped.

"Why are you being such a bitch?" The fury in his voice matched her own.

"Because I'm angry and upset and sad and devastated that we lost our father in such a terrible way and far too soon and all you do is think of yourself."

"Sadie, please, I need your help." Deep fear underlay the angry words he bit out.

"You do need help, but I can't do this anymore. I love you, Connor, but you're on your own. I won't put my life on hold anymore because I'm too busy cleaning up yours. I found someone I love." The admission startled her, because she hadn't intended to say it, but it was true. Real and scary, what she'd found with Rory she didn't ever want to lose.

To hold on to Rory, she let go of Connor.

"I won't let your life destroy the happiness I've found in mine." The ache in her chest grew so heavy she bowed over and wrapped her arm around her waist.

"If you show up at the house, I will call the cops. Please don't contact me again."

"Sadie . . ."

"I'm sorry, Connor." She hung up as her brother let loose a string of curses and threats that wouldn't sway her. Not this time.

She meant what she said. She couldn't do this anymore despite her assurances to her mother that she'd always look out for her little brother. Her brother's life had taken over hers for far too long.

She tossed her phone on the bed. It rang immediately. She ignored it and pulled out the clean nightgown Rory had packed for her. She walked out of his room down the hall to Ford and Colt's shared bathroom, her back to the ringing phone and a past she needed to leave behind. Her father told her she'd have to make the hard choices where Connor was concerned. She never thought it would hurt this much.

She closed herself into the bathroom, turned on the shower, stripped, and stepped into the hot spray, letting the water wash away two days of hospital smells and the tears of grief she shed over losing her father and brother all in one day.

CHAPTER 18

Rory walked out of the bathroom with a towel wrapped around his waist and his hair dripping down his back. He hated to tempt fate, but had planned poorly and forgotten to grab a pair of sweats to wear after his shower. He wondered what Sadie would say to him walking back in nearly naked. He stood in the wide opening and stared at his empty bed, her cell phone sitting in the middle of the mattress, buzzing and chirping every ten seconds.

With Sadie gone, he quickly went to his dresser, found a pair of comfortable black sweatpants, and dragged them on. Tired of the incessant noise coming from her phone, he grabbed it off the bed. The screen lit up with three missed calls from an unknown number and a dozen texts.

The last one chilled his skin and froze his heart.

UNKNOWN: I'll fucking kill you for this.

"Rory?" Sadie's soft voice called to him from the doorway. "What are you doing?"

He faced her with the phone in his hand. "He's

threatening you. What did he say to you when you spoke?"

"The people he's working with are going to kill him unless he comes up with the cash for the drugs they lost. Same shit, different day." She walked to him with her hand out. He dropped the phone in her palm just as it chirped again.

"What's it say this time?"

"Nothing." She scrolled the messages, a frown on her pretty lips. The single tear that rolled down her soft cheek pissed him off.

"Don't shut me out. I hate it when you cry."

"I'm not shutting you out. He doesn't mean any of this. At least he won't when he comes down off the high he's riding."

"That's just it. You're trying to reason with a junkie."

"I know what he is. I know who he is. I told him tonight that I can't help him. I'm done. I'm out. He's on his own. Happy?"

"Do I look happy?"

"No, you're back to scowling at me. And put on a shirt. I can't fight with you when you're naked."

That made him smile and laugh. "If I was naked, we'd be in that bed and you wouldn't be fighting with me."

"I don't want to fight with you. I'm sorry. I'm tired and angry and overwhelmed with you, my father, and my damn brother."

"All right, sweetheart, I'm sorry, too. I shouldn't have said anything. You've had two days of pure hell and I'm not helping."

"Believe it or not, you are. You brought me here because you knew I couldn't stay at my house alone. Your brothers and grandpa fed me and treated me like part of the family. The toast . . . was really sweet."

Rory reached for her, sliding his hand along her cheek and around her head to the back of her neck. He pulled her close. Not that she needed much coaxing to come into his arms. She laid her cheek on his chest and sighed.

"Oh God, do you have to smell so good and feel so warm?"

"I could say the same about you, sweetheart." As much as he loved her close, her hands rubbing softly up and down his bare back, her deep sigh and huge yawn made him gently set her away. "It's late. You barely slept an hour last night. Get in bed."

Her eyebrow shot up and a sexy smile tilted her lips. "Oh yeah?"

"Stop. You're killing me." Rory leaned down and pulled back the covers.

Sadie sat on the edge of the bed and stared up at him. "Thank you for understanding, taking care of me, and, well, everything."

He cupped her face, leaned down, and kissed her softly on the lips. With her here in his room, he wanted to take the kiss deep and lose himself in her, but this wasn't the right time. "No thanks necessary. I'm leaving before I can't stop myself from finding out what you've got on under that nightgown."

Sadie lay down on her side, her damp hair spread on his pillow. "You know exactly what I don't have on under the nightgown because you didn't pack me anything to wear under it. Either it's your diabolical plan to torture both of us, or you're just planning ahead for later and saving yourself time getting to me."

If she wanted to tease him, he was up for the game. He sat beside her on the edge of the bed and stared down at her beautiful, clean face. Without makeup, she appeared younger, more fragile. "It's both actually. Which is why I haven't put on a shirt either. To drive you crazy and you'll have less to take off."

"I appreciate it. You're so thoughtful. Are you wearing anything under those sweats?"

"Nothing but skin."

"Tease."

Ford and Colt pounded up the stairs and hit the landing, calling, "Night, Sadie and Rory," as they went down the hall to their bedrooms.

"I'm never going to hear the end of you being here with me."

Tears gathered in her eyes. She buried her face in his pillow and let the grief she'd held valiantly at bay take her.

Rory brushed his hand over her hair again and again. He soothed her with soft words and promises that everything would be all right while she cried out her grief until she fell asleep, exhausted after all she'd been through the last two days. He pulled the covers up and tucked them around her shoulders. He held her head, leaned down, and kissed her cheek. With his lips a breath away from her ear he whispered the one thing he didn't have the courage to say to her when she was awake. "I love you."

He pressed his forehead against her soft skin, inhaled her sweet spring scent, and made himself get up and leave her.

Rory grabbed a shirt from his dresser. He pulled it on over his head on the way downstairs and fell onto his back on the leather sofa, covering his face with both hands and letting out a ragged breath. The last two days weighed on him. He worried about Sadie, her brother, and what came next. One thought refused to leave his overtired mind. Sadie asleep in his bed, ready and willing to take their relationship to the next level. He wanted to take it all the way. Seeing her lying there, so sweet, asleep in his bed, made him want to beg her to stay there for the rest of their lives. She'd think him crazy if he asked her to stay, marry him, build a life with him here on the ranch so soon after they started dating. He'd have to convince her. Actually, he'd have to give her a reason to want to stay.

She definitely felt the connection between them. Did she love him, too?

CHAPTER 19

Sadie ran through the storm across a field, fear driving her to sprint harder. Her breath sawed in and out until she could barely breathe past the tightening band around her chest. Her heart pounded against her ribs until she felt like the bones would snap. The icy rain pelted her bare skin like razor blades. Lightning flashed, revealing the crimson blood running over her skin. Thunder boomed through the night as she ran for the man standing at the other end of the green field. Her father stood with his arms open, ready to take her away from the raging storm. And her life here. She screamed and sat bolt upright in bed, holding her arms up but seeing nothing except her pale skin with the red ring of scars around her wrists.

She sucked in a deep breath, trying to calm her heart, and raked her fingers through her still damp hair, pulling it away from her sweaty face. As the fine sheen of sweat covering her body dried, a chill raced over her skin.

She stared around the unfamiliar room, trying to orient herself. Rory's room. She was safe. No one lurked in the dark corners. No one was after her. No one screamed for her to help, but only ended up hurting her in the end.

She understood the dark nightmare. Her mind telling her to leave this thing with Connor alone. She couldn't fix it. If she continued to try, she'd only put herself in harm's way again. She'd end up dead and reunited with her father. The fear coursed through her, but she still faltered on whether she could turn her back on Connor and live with herself.

Sleep eluded her and offered little distraction for her overactive mind that used sleep to make her face things she didn't want to think about anymore. She threw off the covers and rolled out of bed. The house stood quiet around her. No lights hinted that someone might still be awake as the night neared two in the morning. She padded down the stairs and headed for the kitchen for a glass of water. Luckily a soft night light cast a warm glow over the countertops by the sink. She pulled a glass from the strainer and filled it at the tap.

Drawn into the living room where Rory slept soundlessly on the couch, she stared down at him, smiling to herself that his big frame didn't quite fit on the sofa. His huge feet sat propped on the armrest. He'd put on a shirt. Too bad. She liked looking at all those muscles. The man was built. Tall and lean. She ached to touch him. She wanted to run her fingers through his thick blond hair.

Moonlight streamed through the window and glinted off his golden beard. He hadn't shaved in a couple of days. She liked the scruff. It made him look dangerous, especially when he didn't smile. Which was less often now when she was with him. He smiled at her all the time. The first time she heard him laugh, her stomach knotted with nerves because she'd wanted to kiss him so bad for looking so good. He'd been sitting at the table with his brothers, talking about their day. Colt told them about how he'd been cleaning out horse stalls. One of the most ornery horses graciously made a fresh mess for him. When Colt cussed, the horse shifted and dumped Colt right on his ass in the pile of horseshit.

Grandpa Sammy nearly choked, coughing and sputtering his favored beer, but Rory tilted his head back and let out a huge belly laugh, the smile on his face making his eyes sparkle with mirth. In that moment, she'd seen the man he was meant to be, not the one he'd grown into as the head of the family and ranch, so filled with responsibility and duty.

She'd remember his laugh for the rest of her life. She hoped to find hers again someday. Right now, her feelings were all mixed up. Grief for her father. Anger for her brother. Fear Derek would find and use her again as leverage against her brother—or worse, as some sick and twisted payment for the debt her brother owed.

A chill went up her spine, shivering through her whole body, making her drop the glass of water. It thudded on the rug, but luckily didn't break.

"Sadie." Rory's deep, sleepy voice rasped.

"Uh, sorry. Let me get a towel to mop that up," she whispered. She dashed into the kitchen and pulled a clean dishtowel from the drawer beside the dishwasher. She ran back into the living room just as Rory set the glass on the table. He sat on the sofa and scrubbed his hands over his face, yawning.

"What are you doing up, sweetheart?"

Sadie mopped up the water, pressing the towel hard

against the carpet to soak up all the liquid. "I couldn't sleep. Nightmare."

"You look like you just had another one. Come here." Rory reached for her hand and gently tugged.

She stepped up off her knees and landed on the sofa next to him. She went willingly, feeling like a complete idiot for letting her ghosts spook her.

Rory turned toward her and reached for her face, his warm palm cupping her cheek. "You're so pale. What's wrong?"

She shook her head and sighed. "Nothing. Everything. I'm so tired, but I can't sleep."

"You're not used to being here. A strange place, it's hard to relax. After all you've been through lately, you're bound to have a few nightmares. What can I do?"

"Nothing. I'm sorry I woke you. I didn't want to be alone, so I came down for some water and . . ."

"And?"

"To look at you."

"Like what you see?"

She bumped her shoulder into his, smiling. She reached up, touched his face with her hand, and swept her thumb over the grin on his lips. "I really love it when you smile." She laid her head on his shoulder, sagging against him.

Rory slid behind her, settling back on the couch, and pulled her down with him. "Stay with me. I'll keep the nightmares away."

"Because you're a dream come true?"

He chuckled, tucking the blanket around her as she cuddled into his warmth. "If you say so."

"I'm totally losing it if I'm saying mushy things like that to you. Forget I ever said it. Please."

"No way. You said it. I'm your dream guy."

She couldn't believe the man she once thought cold grinned and teased with her in the dark, all to take her mind off her troubles and make her smile. Light, fun, the way he acted with his family, he now showed her so easily.

Rory's hand settled on her hip and squeezed. She snuggled closer, her bottom tucked up against his groin. Totally intimate. The chill that raced through her earlier was long forgotten under the wave of heat that spread through her system now with Rory's body cradling hers.

With his massive shoulders taking up all the space, she couldn't find a comfortable spot on his arm that he left out straight for her to lie on. In another ten minutes, he'd lose all circulation and she'd have a stiff neck.

"This couch isn't big enough for the two of us," she complained. "Make room for me." She flipped over, pulled on his middle for him to flatten out, then lay on her side, her leg over his, and laid her head on his shoulder, her cheek pressed to his chest. His arm was still out straight, so she shifted again. "Put your arm down my back and make sure I don't fall off."

"You asked for it." Rory draped his arm down her back and planted his hand right on her ass. "Better?" The laugh in his voice only set the butterflies in her belly to flight again.

"Yes." She rocked her hips against his thigh. "And no."

His hand tightened on her bottom. His other hand clamped on to her bare thigh. "Stop moving, or I won't be held responsible for what happens." He shifted uncomfortably below her, but only managed to rub

against her center with his thigh more. With no underwear and only the soft cotton nightgown between them,
she moaned.

"God, don't do that," he grumbled.

He smelled clean, like soap and a spring day. She
tilted her head and inhaled his scent. Restless, she
leaned up and stared down at him.

"What are you doing now?" His gruff, pained voice
made her smile.

"Kissing you good night."

He tried to say something, but she pressed her
thumb to his lips and trailed it down to his scruffy chin.
"Shh." Her lips met his in a soft kiss that lingered a few
seconds so he could settle in. Once he did, she swept
her tongue along his bottom lip, then kissed just that
one lip, sucking gently. His hands contracted on her
thigh and bottom. She kissed him again, sliding her
tongue past his lips to taste the need building inside
both of them. He pulled her thigh up his body and over
the rigid length of his erection, then back down again.

"You're playing a dangerous game, little one."

Inches from his face, she stared into his hungry eyes.
"It's no game, Rory. I just want to be close to you. You
make me feel, and right now, I want to feel all the good
until it fills me up."

This time she rubbed her thigh up his legs and over
his hard length, pressing her body against his as she
lowered her mouth to his again.

Rory groaned, giving in to her sweet temptation.
The woman meant to drive him mad, but if she wanted
to feel good, he'd make her feel damn good.

She slid her leg up and over his dick again. He slid
his hand down her thigh, under her nightgown, and

over her bare bottom. The woman had skin like silk. Everywhere he touched she was soft and supple. Her curves were sexy as hell. He tried not to think about the way she caressed him, the press of her breasts against his side, or the sensual way her tongue slid along his, slow and easy like a ballad, like she had all the time in the world to love him.

He dipped his hand over her bottom to her soft folds. Her leg stilled over his length and pressed down on him. She rocked against him to ease the ache, but it only made it worse, so he concentrated on his task— making her feel good.

He'd let her control the kissing, the timing, hell, him, but now he took the kiss deeper, letting her know he could command her just as she had him. He rubbed his hand back down her thigh. She breathed out her regret that he'd left the one place she really wanted him to touch her. He circled his fingers over her skin until her body softened against his. He swept his hand slowly back up her thigh, over her nicely rounded bottom, to her wet center. He rubbed the pads of his fingers ever so gently over her soft folds, teasing her with a light touch when what she really wanted was something much more intimate and urgent.

Her soft moan drove him on. He smoothed his fingers up, then down softly over her folds, driving one finger deep into her hot core. Her hips rocked back, and she took his finger deep. She broke the kiss, tilted her head back, closed her eyes, and sighed out her pleasure.

"God, you're so damn beautiful." He thrust his finger deep again just to hear her make those erotic sounds that echoed through his mind and heart like a beacon calling him home.

She slid one hand down his chest and stomach, then back up under his shirt. Her warm hand pressed to his pecs, her fingers squeezed his muscles, and she rocked back and forth into his hand.

He used his free hand to push her hips on top of his. His aching cock pressed to her soft belly. He took her mouth in a deep kiss, trying to hold off his own release as her body moved over his. It took everything he had not to free his swollen flesh and bury himself deep inside her slick heat.

"Rory."

His name on her lips sounded like the sweetest song.

He kneaded her bottom, pushing her down on top of him. He'd found his own soft rhythm, rocking his cock against her. She shifted again, rocked her clit against his dick as his finger sank deep again. She sucked his bottom lip, then kissed him hard.

"Rory, I want you inside of me when I come."

He thrust two fingers deep this time and she groaned, rocking harder against him. "Condoms are upstairs. This one is for you."

He spread his fingers wide over her ass and pressed her down on top of him, thrusting his fingers deep as she rocked back into his hand. She tightened around him and moaned, her forehead pressed to his chin. She rode out the aftershocks as he gently withdrew, pulsing his fingers in and out of her slick core until he was finally free. She stretched like a contented cat over him, rocking her pelvis over his aching flesh. He pressed both hands to her perfect ass and held her still.

"Stop. I'm riding the edge." His words were as rough and urgent as his need for her.

Without warning, she slid down his chest, grabbed

the elastic on his sweats, dragged them over his hard dick, and her mouth slid down his length before he had a coherent thought about her intentions. Seeing her come apart nearly did him in. Her mouth on him set fire to the fuse and sent him skyrocketing. She took him deep, wrapping her fingers around the base of his dick. She squeezed gently as her mouth rose up his flesh.

"Sadie, I . . ." He reached for her, thinking to pull her off before he lost control, but his hands smoothed over her head and shoulders as she sank back down and took him deep again. He let go. She moved up an inch, he rocked forward, and let loose the reins on the last of his control. His dick pulsed in her mouth. She rose up, her tongue sliding up his whole length. She pulled his sweats back into place and collapsed on top of him, her head on his heaving chest.

"That one was to thank you for the one you gave to me," she whispered.

"You didn't have to do that."

"Wild horses couldn't have stopped me."

"How the hell did I get this lucky?"

"You save her, you get to keep her." Sadie's groggy voice held a lilt of humor.

"Only if she's you. You I want to keep forever."

"Promise." The word came out on a soft exhale, like she hadn't meant to say it at all.

"Promise." He wrapped his arms around her as she lay down his entire body. He kissed the top of her head, knowing he held the center of his world.

Her hands gripped his sides. "Don't let go."

"Never."

He held her close, falling into sleep happier than he'd ever been in his life, and woke up alone, pissed and desperate to find the woman who righted his tilted world, brightening every dark corner of his heart, and made him love her.

CHAPTER 20

Rory sat up and swung his legs off the couch. He planted his feet on the floor and raked his fingers through his hair, remembering that he needed to get a haircut. Though maybe he'd leave it alone. Sadie sure did like running her fingers through it.

Sadie. Where the hell was she? After what they shared last night, he couldn't believe she'd leave without a word.

"Hey, man, you're up," Colt said, walking in from the kitchen.

"Where is she?"

"When I came down this morning, she was sleeping on top of you. I hated to wake her. Looks like she didn't get much sleep last night." Colt wiggled his eyebrows, suggesting without words that Rory had kept her up late last night. He had, but he wasn't about to give Colt the details, or let on that he was right.

"We had coffee together, then she went out for a ride."

He imagined Sadie sitting at the breakfast table across from Colt wearing nothing but her thin white tank nightgown and nothing on under it. "And did you get an eyeful of her in her nightgown this morning?"

Colt held up his hands. "No. She ran upstairs, showered and changed, and came back down fully dressed and covered while I made the coffee. Chill, okay."

"Sorry."

"She's like my sister, man. Get a grip."

Rory stood and stared at his brother. "You mean that? You think of her like a sister?"

"She's your girl. It's not hard to see how much you love her. I figure it's only a matter of time before you make her a part of the family officially and all."

"Did you finally ask Sadie to marry you?" Ford asked, coming down the stairs.

"Finally?" Rory couldn't believe his brothers' acceptance of his relationship with Sadie, though why he was surprised, he didn't know. They'd given him grief about other women he'd dated. Women they didn't particularly like. They seemed to take to Sadie right away.

"You've been staring at that girl from a distance for years," Ford said, like it was common knowledge.

"How the hell do you know that?"

"Every time we go to the diner we sit across the room from her section. You sit with your back to the windows so the only view you see is her. The question is, why did you wait so long to ask her out?"

"She's a lot younger than me," he pointed out the obvious.

Colt and Ford stared at him with nothing to say.

"Colt went to school with her. I didn't know her at all."

"I never dated her, man. I hardly spoke to her at school growing up. She took care of her family, worked, and kept her head down in class. She was brainy, not exactly the party girl I went for back then."

"Back then," Rory and Ford said in unison.

"Shut up."

"So let me get this straight, you two are fine with me asking her to marry me after only the short time we've been seeing each other."

"Intense situations lead to intense relationships," Ford said. "You love her. She makes you happy. That's good enough for me."

"That's all we want for you," Colt added. "You smile when she's around. You laugh."

"You're like the guy you used to be before Mom and Dad died," Ford added.

"Did you get her pregnant?" Grandpa Sammy asked, standing in the open office doorway.

"No." Rory let his outrage show and scowled at his granddad. "But that would probably please you to no end. All you talk about is getting a great-grandbaby from all of us."

"I want you settled with loving wives and kids, but you better do it right. You marry her, then have a family. When she's ready," he added. "Women choose those things. You get all the fun, but they do all the work."

"Trust me, she'll have fun, too," Rory said, in a rare show of humor. His brothers were right; he did let loose more since he'd met her.

"What will I have fun doing?" Sadie walked in behind Colt and stared at Rory.

Rory, along with his brothers and granddad, startled.

"Are you blushing?" Sadie asked him, scanning him and the others, her eyes narrowing. "What are you guys talking about?"

"Nothing." Maybe he said that too quickly.

She frowned and pressed her lips together, a blush blooming on her already rosy cheeks from her ride in the cool morning air.

"How are you this morning, pretty girl?" His grand-dad drew her attention.

Sadie's sharp gaze hadn't left Rory's. "I'm fine, thank you. The ride was exactly what I needed."

Colt coughed to cover a laugh. Ford turned his head to hide a smile. After all, they had been talking about him riding Sadie and getting her pregnant.

"I have stalls to clean." Colt bolted for the back door.

"I'll help." Ford followed Colt out.

"If there's anything you need, pretty girl, just let us know. We're here to help."

"Thank you, Sammy. I appreciate it." The words she spoke didn't match the angry look in her eyes she cast Rory's way.

"I've got business in town." Granddad walked away to get his keys from the hook in the kitchen.

Sadie waited for the back door to close before she said anything. "Did you tell them we slept together?"

"We didn't sleep together."

"That's not what I asked."

"Why the hell would I tell them anything about what you and I do together in private?"

"It seems to me that when I walked in you were discussing sleeping with me."

"We were, but not in the way you think." He couldn't tell her they were talking about him marrying her, that his brothers and granddad expected and accepted it. Those two things meant the world to him, but he and Sadie weren't there yet. He wanted them to be, but rushing her could backfire. He needed more time to forge a stronger bond. He needed to know that she wanted a life with him. Forever.

She folded her arms across her chest, pushing her breasts up. "Rory, what is going on?"

"I'm sorry. I'm not explaining well enough."

"You haven't explained anything. Why would you talk to them about sleeping with me?"

"I wasn't. I didn't. My grandfather reminded us, me, that I need to be responsible and do the right thing always for you."

Her gaze softened, but not by much. "Don't you think you guys are a little old to be getting the talk?"

Rory shook his head, smiling at how ridiculous this conversation had become when all he wanted to do was kiss her good morning and savor his memories of what they shared last night. "Trust me, we got it a long time ago. Granddad has been harping on us for the past year to settle down and start a family before he dies."

Her hands fell back to her sides and alarm replaced the perturbed look in her eyes. "Is he not well?" The concern in her voice touched him.

"He's fine. But he's getting older and wants to see his boys happy and not alone like he's been these last thirty years."

"That's a long time."

"I'm not saying he didn't step out with a lady now and again. Always discreetly, you see, because he had three boys to raise."

"So he wants you married with babies."

"Yeah."

"That's kind of sweet. He loves you and wants you to be happy."

"What about you?" he asked, hoping to somehow feel her out about marriage and children.

"I want those things, too. With the right person, because when I make a promise like that, it will be forever."

Her gaze never left his.

"Anyone in particular you see yourself with forever?" he asked boldly.

She closed the distance between them, wrapped her arms around his neck, and went up on tiptoe. "Except for the whole you-and-your-family-talking-about-me-behind-my-back, you're looking real good this morning." Her lips brushed his in a soft kiss. She smelled of horses and grass from her ride.

"I hated waking up without you this morning." He traced his finger over her soft cheek and kissed the tip of her nose.

"I hated to leave you. You are so sexy when you're asleep, but your brother caught us and I didn't want the rest of your family seeing me lying on top of you."

"Why? They don't seem to care. In fact, they really like you. They actually expect you to stay here with me."

"Well, I like them, too. It's nice here. It feels like a family." The kind of family she'd had a long time ago, too many years and bad days ago to remember if it was real or imagined now.

Rory wanted to give her the family she hoped for and wanted, the happy life she deserved. "You're a part of it now, you know?"

"I want to be."

Not a definite *Yes, I am.* So, maybe she was still on the fence. He'd give her time. She'd settle her father's affairs and he'd keep her close and show her that he meant to remain by her side. Forever, like she wanted.

"So what's with your brothers?" she asked.

"What do you mean?"

"Well, if your grandfather wants you all happily married, why does Colt act like he murdered someone every time Luna's name comes up? I asked her about it, but she's uncharacteristically close-lipped about him."

"You said Colt used to be friends with Luna's ex. Whatever happened between them, it wasn't good."

"And Ford. He watches the TV news about the war like he's missing something and will only find it in those bombed-out towns."

"The girl he dated after high school joined the army and left him. I never thought about it, or saw what you see, but maybe he's looking for her."

"Those two may not admit it, especially to your grandfather, but they want something lasting and permanent."

"Maybe seeing me with you has made them look back at their lives and the women they've known and wonder what might have been."

"Or what could be," she suggested. "Maybe we should set up a double date with me and you, and Colt and Luna."

"I don't want them interfering in our relationship, so I'm not getting involved in Colt's life. They can get their own girls. After all we've been through, I'm ready to focus on you and me and some normal, drama-free days together."

"Is that right?"

"Yes."

"Well okay then."

"Good, now come here and kiss me good morning."
She looked behind her.

"We're alone. All they want is you and me together."
She walked into his arms and smiled up at him. "Is that right?"

"Yes. Now about last night."

"What about it?"

"That thing you did . . ."

She flushed pink to the roots of her hair.

"You are so pretty when you blush."

"You didn't like that thing I did. It was too much. Too soon. I didn't do it the way you liked—"

He cut her off with a long deep kiss that took her breath away. His tongue slid along hers in an urgent sweep. She went up on tiptoe and pressed her body against his, her softness crushed against all those hard muscles as his arms contracted around her. He broke the kiss, sucking in a deep breath, and pressing his forehead to hers. His hazel eyes held a depth of need that matched her own.

"I've never done that thing, so if I did it wrong—"

He cut her off with another kiss, this time softer, more coaxing. She settled into him again, trying to relax and let her nerves go. She didn't have a lot of experience with other guys. She hated to think she'd done something he didn't like, or that he thought was too forward. The last thing she wanted to do was give him the wrong idea about her. Rory had a deep sense of family, responsibility, duty, and honor. She loved those things about him and didn't want to do or say anything that made him think less of her.

Rory pressed another soft kiss to her lips. His hand came up, his fingers softly brushing against her cheek. He leaned back just enough to look down into her eyes.

"Damn, sweetheart, I really can't get enough of you." He brushed his fingers through her hair. "You are and were perfect. Have mercy on me if you decide you want to practice and repeat what we did last night."

The blush intensified, heating her cheeks and ears. "Rory . . ."

His finger settled beneath her chin to prevent her from looking away. "What we share in private is just that, Sadie. Private. You never have to be embarrassed or nervous or hold back. I don't want you to. I want exactly what we had last night. You and me completely lost in each other and the way we make each other feel."

"I'm sorry. I thought you thought I was—"

"Kind. Generous. Unbelievably amazing." Rory slid his hands down her back and over her round bottom, pulling her snug against him. He held her there, trapped in his embrace, a soft smile on his lips. "What I was trying to tell you before you went off on that tangent is that I want more of last night and more of you. Not on the couch, but in our bed upstairs. Stay with me tonight. For a few days at least. I don't want you to be alone at your place, because you miss your father, but also because the police haven't caught your brother and his friends."

Disappointment made her heart sink. "So, you want me to stay here because you're afraid they'll come back to my house and maybe hurt me?"

"If giving you a reason to stay here makes you want to stay, then yes, stay so I can protect you."

Despite the hold he had on her, she backed out of his arms, ready to say yes, but wishing for so much more.

Rory reached out and pulled her back before she got more than a step away. His eyes grew dark with worry. "Stay because I want you here with me. Please." That vulnerable "please" melted her heart. This wasn't easy for a man like Rory to ask because it meant something deep to him. As much as it did to her. "I don't want to lose what we shared last night. I don't want to see it fade when all I want to do is keep that fire burning."

She wanted the same. But she didn't want there to be any reason for her to stay except the one that mattered most. She wanted to be here. With Rory.

Fires burned out. You have to feed them, let them live and breathe.

Yes, sometimes they'd fade to glowing embers, but only if the fire was stoked enough to burn hot enough to create those coals. She didn't want their relationship to be something that flashed and burned out quickly. She wanted it to be a living thing they worked to keep alive. That was fire, life, a relationship, marriage, love.

"I need to go home and take care of a few things." The disappointment in his eyes warmed her heart and solidified her decision. "I'll pack up more clothes. Underwear."

The light in his eyes sparked. "You don't need those."

She laughed. "Maybe not, but they do make things more comfortable."

"Whatever. I'm glad you decided to stay."

"Yeah, well, at least until those guys are caught, right?"

"We'll see."

He may have said the words, but something told her he didn't mean them. Did he truly want her to move in with him? She didn't dare ask. It was too soon. Right?

And yet she planned to go home, pack a bag, and stay here for some undetermined amount of time. A flutter of anticipation shivered in her belly. Mostly because she thought of where she'd be sleeping tonight. In his bed. In his arms. After thinking her life was over hanging in that tree, her father dying so young, she didn't want to waste a single day she had left on this earth. She wanted to live and do the things she wanted to do. The things that made her happy. Not for anyone else, but for herself. She wanted to be with Rory, so she would be with Rory. She didn't care what anyone thought about them getting together so fast. It didn't seem fast to her. It seemed right. No, it was right.

"What is that face you're making? Are you angry?"

"No. Determined."

"Uh, about what?"

"Doing what I want for a change."

"Okay. What do you want to do?"

"Stop doing what others want me to do or think I should do. I want to be here with you, so I'm not going to worry about what other people think."

"Who the fuck cares what they think?"

"Exactly. You want me here. I want to be here. So I'm sleeping with you tonight."

"I'm all for that," Rory teased.

"I didn't mean it like that."

"Oh, I hope you did," he teased again.

She smacked him on the arm and tried to hold back the laugh she let loose anyway. "Stop. You know what I mean."

"I know, but I love it when you smile, even more when you laugh."

"You know what I like about you?"

"What?"

"The way you make me feel when you kiss me."

"Well, sweetheart, lucky for you, that's my favorite thing to do." He drew her close, dipped his head, and kissed her softly, his gaze locked with hers, a light of mischief brightening the hazel depths. He made her smile and forget all her troubles, if only for a little while. When she was with him, she didn't think about anything. Her worries went away.

She closed her eyes, sank into the kiss he masterfully laid on her, and let everything else go, hoping she could get through the next few days and settle her father's affairs. Then she could begin the next chapter of her life. Something she now looked forward to because she wouldn't be alone. No, that new life included being Rory Kendrick's live-in girlfriend and lover.

CHAPTER 21

Sadie held Rory's hand in the front seat of the truck. She'd gone quiet on him. Worried about her, every few minutes he cast his glance her way. She didn't meet his gaze; instead she stayed inside her head and the dark thoughts that intruded when she grew tired of trying to keep them at bay. Her father lying bloody on the floor moaning and holding his head, disoriented and in so much pain. The depth of agony in his dark eyes so different from the love she always saw there when he looked at her. That evening all she'd seen was his fear that he'd come to the end of his life and he wasn't ready to go. She didn't know how long he'd been on the floor. She'd done what she had to do.

Exactly what she needed to do now. Get the job done.

Which meant going back into the house, cleaning up the mess, sorting through her father's papers and things, and making the tough decisions about the house, her life, and her future.

"Sadie, sweetheart, we're here."

She stared at the house like she was seeing it for the first time. The four-bedroom, three-bath, ranch-style home needed a new coat of white paint. The gray

stone pillars that held up the wraparound porch over-
hang were covered in mostly dead vines that needed
to be cut down. A few rugged bushes and wild roses
flourished despite her neglect. The porch steps needed
to be repaired, along with several other things in the
house, including a few holes in the walls, thanks to her
brother. His bedroom needed the most work.

Yep, nothing much had changed in the last handful
of years. Except one thing. Her. She'd changed when
her father died. Maybe before that, when she met Rory.
The dreams she'd once held close, then buried in the
deepest part of her heart, sprang free and illuminated
a brighter future than the past she'd been living day
in and day out, never getting anywhere, always stuck
exactly where she was in life.

Not anymore.

"Sadie?" Rory's deep voice held a wealth of concern
about her continued silence.

"There's no one home."

The house stood as empty as her heart. The depth of
sadness washed over her for the loss of her family. The
loss of the dream of what she hoped that family could
have been, but never was. She'd had her mother for too
short a time, her father to see her through the tough
teenage years and the years trying to keep Connor on
the right path, but now she was as alone as her weathered old house looked without a family living in it.

She didn't know if she could live in it alone. The
loneliness of it just might kill her.

"Sadie, sweetheart, I am so sorry for your loss."
Rory kissed the back of her hand. So kind. So understanding.

"I tuck it away for a while, but then it hits me all at

once. This pain. He's gone. They're all gone. Connor may still be here, but I've lost him, too. He's not the little brother I remember. He's turned into a man I don't know, or understand, or even like."

She didn't have to stay in that lonely house. Tonight, for as long as he wanted her to stay at his place, she'd be with Rory. "I'm so glad you're here."

"You're everything to me."

Stunned by the softly spoken words, she let them sink into her heart, easing the pain and sorrow she carried with her. He meant those simple words, and they lit her up with love.

Rory leaned over and kissed her softly.

The connection, the love, the understanding they shared flared.

She pressed her hand to his smooth cheek and held the kiss for a couple extra seconds. As much as she loved his scruffy-beard look, the man was even more handsome clean-shaven. She slid her hand along his face and into his damp hair, holding the dark golden locks and him to her.

She leaned back, breaking the kiss, but not her hold on him. "I'm glad you're here." She meant more than just beside her in the truck, seeing her through this ordeal. She meant in her life.

"There's nowhere I'd rather be."

"Good, because I really don't think I can let you go." She gripped his hair a bit tighter, careful not to actually hurt him.

"Then hold on, because I don't want you to let go."

"Okay."

"Okay."

It seemed everything had been settled with those

simple words. An understanding they'd both reached separately, acknowledged and accepted out loud without spelling it out with words that didn't explain it accurately or completely. "Okay" explained it all.

"Do you want me to go in and pack some things for you? You can wait out here if you want."

"That's sweet, but I need to do it. I'm just stalling."

"You've got a dozen reasons for not wanting to go in there. Any one reason in particular holding you back?"

"I see him lying there in my head. Seeing the mess again . . . It's hard."

"Sadie, sweetheart, I should have told you. I had a cleaning crew come and clean the house."

She cocked her head and stared at him, surprised. "You did?"

"The day your father went to the hospital. I came here looking for you, saw the blood and thought the worst. After Bell called to tell me where you were, I called my house and asked my grandfather to send the cleaning crew here. I didn't want you to come home to that."

"I . . ." *Love you* stuck on the tip of her tongue. She couldn't just blurt that out because he'd done something so thoughtful and kind and sweet and just for her. "I don't know what to say."

"Thank you," he suggested. "It's nothing, sweetheart. The smallest thing I could do to make this easier for you."

"That's just it, isn't it? The small things people do to show they care. Those are the things that mean so much. So thank you. You're sweet." She kissed him softly. A small display of the depth of her feelings for him, but again, something simple that meant so much.

"Whatever you do, don't tell my brothers, or anyone

else, you think I'm sweet." He scrunched up his mouth into a sour face, but the light in his eyes told her he was kidding.

"Your secret is safe with me."

"There's a hint of the smile I've missed since we headed over here." He brushed his fingers over her lips, making her want to stay in the truck and kiss him the rest of the day and get another taste of the fire they'd started last night. "Don't look at me like that, we'll never get out of this truck."

"Would that be so bad?" She cocked up one eyebrow and smiled softly.

He pointed his finger at her. "Stop procrastinating and driving me crazy." The finger pointed at her shifted to point out the truck window. "Out."

"You're no fun." She pouted.

"That's not what you thought last night." With that parting shot, he opened his door and got out. She caught the hint of a smile on his lips when he turned back and held his hand out for her to take so he could help her out of the truck.

"I'm happy to let you change my mind back to what I thought last night."

Rory tugged her into his chest. His mouth crashed into hers for a hungry kiss. His tongue slid along hers, tasting and tempting her to ride the wave of pure lust he unleashed inside her. His hands slid down her back and over her bottom. He pulled her close, snug against his hard length. She rocked her hips against him. The low growl he let loose reverberated through her chest and straight down to her belly.

As fast as the kiss started, he ended it, holding her away by her hips. "No."

"No?" He'd scrambled her brain. She truly had no idea what he meant.

His soft chuckle made her focus on his smile, the gold and green in his eyes, the way his long hair swept back away from his too handsome face. "God, you're gorgeous."

"Are you drunk?" he teased.

"On you."

Rory took her hand and tugged her toward the house. "Come on, crazy girl. Let's get this done. I'll take you riding later."

"Really?"

"Sure. Why?"

"Don't you have work to do? I've kept you from it for days."

"My brothers and the ranch hands have it covered."

"You really don't mind spending all this time with me, doing all this depressing stuff."

"The circumstances may be hard, but spending time with you isn't." Rory took her keys and opened the front door. The fresh scent of pine and flowers the cleaning crew left behind wafted out on the soft breeze.

Rory took a step away, but she held him back, her hand locked in his, their fingers laced together.

"What is it, sweetheart?"

"Thank you." She walked right into him, wrapped her arms around his neck, and hugged him tight, taking in his now familiar scent. Horses, grass, leather, and him. The man she loved more and more. So much so that soon it would be too hard to hold back telling him. Showing him.

Why was she waiting?

He'd shown her time and again how much he cared

about her. Maybe he didn't love her, but he definitely wanted a relationship with her, but did he want forever, or just right now?

If she told him, would he back away? Would he tell her he loved her, too? If he did, would it just be because she'd said it and he thought she expected him to say it? No. Rory wasn't the kind of guy who said something without meaning it.

Still, she held back, but hugged him tighter, hoping he understood everything in her heart that she couldn't find the courage to say out loud. Not yet. But she would soon, because she didn't want to risk not telling him and him not knowing if something happened to her.

A chill ran up her spine. She wished she could shake the feeling that after all the bad she'd suffered, there was still more pain to come.

"Hey now, sweetheart, what's all this? Everything is fine." Rory rubbed his hands up and down her back, soothing her.

"It's nothing. I'm just so lucky to have you, is all."

"I'm pretty sure all the luck is on my side. Let's hope it doesn't run out. I'd hate for you to figure out you can do a hell of a lot better."

He teased, but under the joking she sensed a trace of unease in him. Maybe they both needed to be reassured everything was fine between the both of them. They were both dealing with uncertainty and the newness of their relationship. Not to mention the overwhelming connection and pull between them. Something she'd never experienced and didn't want to lose.

"I can't do better." She leaned back and looked him in the eye. "I already have the best."

His hands contracted on her hips. He held her tight,

staring down at her. The intensity in his eyes stunned her, but she fell into the depths and saw that her words touched him deeply.

Rory didn't speak. He didn't have the words to tell her what she'd said meant everything to him. He never needed anyone in his life to make him feel whole. He missed his parents. The knot of pain lived inside him. He'd gotten used to it. He felt their absence all the time. Somehow Sadie had become such a part of him that if he lost her, he'd spend the rest of his life feeling like a piece of him was missing or dead. Even the thought made his gut tighten and his heart squeeze painfully. Without her, it might stop altogether.

He bent his knees, drew his hands up her back, wrapped his arms around her, hugged her close, and picked her right up off her feet. Her toes banged against his shins. Her arms wrapped tight around his head. He buried his face in her neck and inhaled, filling himself up with her sweet scent and the way she made him feel.

"Rory, someone is coming down the driveway."

He gently set her back on her feet, cupped her face, and stared down into her worried blue eyes. "I'll never let anything bad happen to you again." He pressed his forehead to hers, then gave her a quick kiss to seal that promise.

"Miss Higgins?" the man asked, stepping out of his white Ford truck.

"Need to change that soon," Rory said under his breath.

"What?" Sadie asked, turning back from walking down the steps to greet the stranger walking their way.

"Nothing," Rory mumbled, waiting for the nerves to hit. Nothing. Not even a second thought. Just a sense that everything was right. The same feeling he got every time he looked at her.

He didn't like the look of the man approaching her. In a few long strides, Rory was off the porch and at her side, his arm banded around her back, his hand firm on her hip. He'd never been a possessive man, but with her, all bets were off.

"Who are you?" Rory hadn't meant the question to sound so much like a demand.

Sadie's head snapped toward him. The guy caught Rory's eye, then dipped his gaze to Rory's hand on Sadie's hip. Good. He got the message. *Mine. Hands off.*

"Agent Cooke." Sadie somehow knew the guy's name. Did she know him?

Cooke's eyes narrowed on Sadie. "How did you know?"

"You look just like your brother Trigger."

"Either he told you, or you're more observant than the average person."

"Observant. Especially when someone puts a gun to my head and goes by Trigger."

"Most people would freak out and blunder all the details."

"I'm not most people. Your brother made it clear in his own way he had no intention of hurting me despite how he made it look."

"Is that so?"

"Yes, so tell me why he'd do that when you're both after my brother."

"Observant and smart." Cooke shook his head, looked off in the distance, lost in thought.

"What do you want?" Rory asked, hoping to get

some information and some good news—like Connor and his cohorts would be behind bars immediately.

"The same thing you want. This to be over."

"Trigger needs to get out from under cover," Sadie said, her words soft and full of understanding. "You're worried about him."

"Let's hope you're not too damn smart for your own good."

"Watch it," Rory warned, stepping in front of Sadie and staring down the asshole.

"She figured everything out. She says one word to her brother and mine is dead."

"I won't do that."

"She wouldn't do that," Rory said over Sadie's words.

"If you do, I'll see you go down for aiding and abetting your brother. I will find every speck of dirt on you and use it against you both personally and legally."

Sadie stepped around Rory. "Hey. You don't need to threaten me. I'd never do anything to jeopardize your brother's life."

"Not even to save Connor?"

"As your brother already pointed out, nothing will save Connor from what he's done. I am not helping him anymore."

"Is that right?" Cooke eyed Sadie.

"That's right. You want to nail Connor, I won't be the hammer that strikes the blow, and I won't stand in the way."

"So after all these years of you saving his ass, you're out?"

Sadie held up her hands, showing the agent the scars around her wrists and on her arms. She pulled the hem of her shirt up and showed him the marks across her torso and the scar on her ribs.

Stunned she'd do such a thing, Rory stared at her, shocked. "Sadie." He tugged her shirt down for her.

"I've learned my lesson."

"Well, if it's any consolation, the charges against your brother are far less severe than the charges against Derek for what he did to you."

"That doesn't really ease the fact that I have to live with knowing my brother turned his back on me when I needed him the most."

"Then you understand why I'm here. I would never turn my back on Beck."

"Beck?"

"Trigger. If he trusted you with that message, despite not knowing if you'd betray him for your brother, then he's desperate to get out."

"Why doesn't he just come in?" Rory asked.

"He'd never jeopardize a case we've been working on for over a year. People are depending on him finishing this job. The lives he'll save if we get this crap off the streets and put these people behind bars . . ."

Sadie got it. "You're not worried about those lives, you're worried about his."

"I'm always worried about his, but what he did, giving you that message . . . it was reckless."

"No, it wasn't. He saw in me exactly what I saw in him. Resignation. Those guys are not going to stop, or think about what they're doing. They're reckless. That's what makes Trig . . . Beck nervous. That's why he wants out.

"I've watched my brother this past year, and especially these last weeks spiral downward into desperation. For his next fix, to make the big score, and to save his life. I'm sure Derek's experience tells him exactly what I know and have seen, desperate people do stupid things. Add in a sick sadist and it's a recipe for disaster. There's something about Derek that's just pure evil. I don't know how else to say it. He likes hurting people. Even when there's every reason to walk away—like you're stealing a herd of cattle and the owner is coming after you—he doesn't care and has to feed that need to hurt someone. He could have just left me out there in the middle of nowhere without my clothes or my horse, but instead he indulged that dark side. It's not the first time either. No telling what Beck has witnessed and stood by helpless to do anything or be caught out for who he really is."

Cooke shook his head and stared off in the distance again. "You said he didn't look good."

"Physically he seemed fine. You guys have an uncanny resemblance. He's leaner than you, but it's what I saw in his eyes—that's not quite right, it's what he let me see, so he could determine I was on his side. He's tired of the game. Tired in a way that goes so deep he's having trouble believing and living the lies."

"Which is why I need your help to end this. Beck won't come in until he finishes this case."

"I told you—"

"I don't give a fuck that you want to keep your hands clean." Cooke took a menacing step forward, then caught himself when Rory glared. "If you truly believe Beck can't live the lies, then he's dead. Dead. Do you get it?"

"I understand you're upset, Agent Cooke."

"Caden," he bit out, trying to rein in his temper and be civil.

"Caden, there's nothing I can do. I don't know where my brother is. He's not answering my calls."

"You've got a number for him?"

"He swaps out his burner phone every couple of days. They're not as stupid as you think. They know the cops are after them and using traceable phones will only get them caught. "

"You must know something."

"I know my brother and Derek owe someone a lot of money. That person is going to collect one way or the other and that scares me more than I can explain because my brother is all I have left of my immediate family. I know it will take a miracle for my brother to change his ways. He won't turn himself in no matter how many times I beg him to do so. He's a follower, looking for the big score that will set him up for life. He doesn't see that he will always be the little fish swimming with sharks who will turn on him to save themselves.

"I know he doesn't trust me anymore."

"Is there someplace he goes when he needs to hide? A friend or a girl who will help him out?"

"Caden, you're grasping at straws. The cops know all those things. Everything. This isn't my brother's first time hiding from the police. They've checked out every known haunt, friends, enemies, and girlfriends. If he's cooking up meth, he's doing it somewhere isolated. Not in town, but out in the country. Doesn't Beck know where?"

"No. For all their stupidity in other things they've kept their operation a secret."

"If Beck can't give you the information, then why do you think I can?"

"Because you know your brother. You know his habits."

"I used to, but he's been more out of my life than in it the last couple of years. I'm his go-to girl for bailout. I can't help you."

"It better be can't, because if it's won't, you'll go down with him."

Sadie threw up her hands and let them fall in frustration. "What do you want me to say? He's probably in some abandoned shack on someone's property. There'll have to be at least an old dirt road for them to get their supplies in and out. At the bare minimum, they'll need water, but even that they can bring with them. Since he's been stealing Kendrick cattle, my guess is that he's close to the Kendrick land. He didn't pick the Kendrick cattle for any other reason than he's lazy as hell when it comes to actual work."

"The sheriff's people have been all over that place and found nothing."

"Well, if Connor made it easy we'd all be doing better things right now. It's probably some trailer they're able to move, or a shack they've camouflaged. I don't know, but it's there. If I hear from him again, I'll let you know. I'll even try to convince him, again, to turn himself in."

Sadie turned her back and walked away, straight up the steps and into the house.

Rory hung back, eyeing the agent. "She really doesn't know anything."

"How is she? Those marks on her . . ." Caden shook his head, his mouth pulled into a tight line of disapproval and sadness.

"She's had it rough since Derek strung her up. Now

her father is dead and her brother is in dire need of money or he's going to end up dead, too. He's desperate. She hasn't said it outright, but she knows he'll use her to get that money if he has to."

"Does she have the kind of money he needs?"

"No. Her brother has sucked every last dime she's got. Hell, he still owes me. She's tried to pay off his debt." Rory read the disapproval in Caden's eyes. "Hey, I didn't ask her to or want her to. She has a deep sense of justice and right and wrong. She's not in this with those guys. I don't know if her father left any money for her. This property is worth quite a bit thanks to the rich folks moving in and driving up land prices, but she can't pull any money from the property on a dime. She'd have to get a loan from the bank and I don't think she'd do that for him. Not now. She's set on letting him go down for what he's done."

"I need more than her trying to convince Connor to turn himself in. I need her to actively try to make him do it. If I can get my hands on him, I can turn him against the others and pull Beck out."

"I won't let you use her as bait. Derek has a real thing for her. The way he looks at her, it's like a mountain lion hunting down prey. I won't let you put her in harm's way for a bunch of drug dealers."

"I can protect her."

"Bullshit. Your priority is your brother. She's mine. I'll keep tabs on anything she finds out—if her brother contacts her again—and I'll let you know. That's the best I can do."

Caden handed over his card with his information. "I need a location. If Beck finds it at the very last second, and I don't have eyes on it ahead of time, it may be too late."

"Understood. There's a lot of wild land out there to cover. I'd suggest you try a helicopter, or one of those drones everyone is arguing about on the news. You might have better luck that way than trying to cover all that territory on the ground."

"Are you willing to go for a ride to take a look? You know your land better than anyone, I presume."

"Sure. Set it up. I wouldn't mind getting some aerial shots for my own use."

"I'll be in contact." Caden held out his hand.

Rory took it and held tight. "You do anything that puts her in danger, and I'll take off your head."

"Understood. But she finds out anything, I want to know."

"Understood." Rory shook, then released Caden's hand. He waited for the guy to climb in his truck and drive away. When he turned around, he spotted Sadie standing in the open doorway staring back at him. If anything happened to her, he'd never forgive himself. He couldn't live without her. He didn't want to. But how to make her a permanent part of his life with all this turmoil mucking up their lives? He didn't know, but he'd find a way, because her happiness meant everything to him, and she meant everything to his future happiness.

CHAPTER 22

Sadie turned from the front door and walked down the hall toward her room. She stopped outside her father's bedroom door and stared at the stripped bare mattress. The cleaning crew had done a great job. Not a single drop or splatter of blood remained, but she still saw it clear as day in her mind. She closed her eyes and breathed in and out, trying to erase the image and the echo of fear running through her system.

Strong hands clamped on to her shoulders and rubbed her tight muscles. She exhaled and relaxed into Rory's touch. She'd become so used to him touching her in such a short time. "Used to" didn't quite cover it; she craved his touch. It always calmed and excited her all at once.

"What does he want from me? I can't tell him anything the cops don't already know. My brother is pissed at me, you, the world. What am I supposed to do?"

"Breathe, sweetheart."

She sucked in a ragged breath, turned, and pressed her forehead to his chest. His hands slid around her waist, and he held her gently. That was Rory, a steady presence. One who never pushed her, never asked for more than she was willing to give, and always stood with her.

She gripped his sides, pushed back, and stared up at him. Before she said a word, he leaned down and kissed her softly.

"What was that for?"

"You looked like you needed it."

She squished up one side of her mouth and nodded. "I always seem to need a kiss from you."

"Happy to supply as many as you need."

"One more, then it's time to get down to business."

Rory's smile just might do her in. He leaned down and pressed his mouth to hers, then brushed his lips over hers and sank in. She opened to him, savoring the glide of his tongue over hers. His hands slid up her sides a second before his thumbs swept along the outside of her breasts. She pressed close to him and his hands rubbed down her back and over her bottom. His fingers sank into her ass and pulled her up and closer, her belly rubbing against his hard length. She wanted to get her hands on him, but not here. Not now. He must have felt the same way, because the minute her hands touched his bare back under his shirt, he pulled away, breathing hard. His intense gaze met hers as he licked his bottom lip in a move so sexy she wanted to bite his lip and taste him again.

"Honey, you keep kissing and touching me that way, we're not going to get anything done."

She cocked up one eyebrow and gave him a half smile. "We'll get one thing done."

He planted one hand on her bottom and pushed her down the hall toward her room. "Pack."

"Spoilsport."

"You're asking for trouble, woman."

"I've got my hands full of it, I might as well have some fun."

"You like living dangerously."

"Nothing seems dangerous when I'm with you." She walked past her brother's room and stopped short. She went through the door and stared at the broken dresser drawer and the hole it made in the wall when her brother must have thrown it. "Connor's been here."

Rory bent and picked up an empty bottle of whiskey. The brown dregs settled in the corner of the bottle. "Looks like he might have slept here last night and drank away his sorrows."

"Probably waiting for me to come home. Even though we spoke last night, I didn't tell him where I stayed. Damn. He must be really hurting. I can't imagine how he feels. He missed being there in my father's final hours. He never got the chance to make things right."

"Maybe someday he'll remember he still has a sister and will want to make things right with you."

"Right now, I'd be happy if he made even one right decision." She backed out of her brother's room and walked into hers across the hall. She went to her desk by the window and used her keys to open her desk drawer.

"You need a key for your own desk?"

"If I want to keep my laptop from getting stolen, yes."

Rory frowned. "Your brother is an asshole, and I think cavemen might have used that same laptop."

"Yep. Will you grab my denim jacket out of the closet and my boots? I'm looking forward to going for that ride."

Rory did as she asked. She packed up her laptop in her backpack and made sure she had her books and homework assignment for her next class.

"When do you have school?"

"I have a class Tuesday and Thursday and another on Monday and Wednesday."

"How many more classes do you have to take before you graduate?"

"After eight years, these are the last. Finally."

"You're graduating?"

"In May. My father would have been so proud. I'm the first of the family to earn a college degree."

"Your father was proud. He knew you'd finish. It's not in you to quit."

"Yeah, well, I've got an assignment I need to finish and plan a funeral."

"About that, what do you want to do?"

"I need to look at my father's papers. He planned everything when my mother died. He'll be buried next to her. Everything else I need to know should be in his hiding spot."

"I can't believe you two had to hide and lock away everything."

"Life with a drug addict who will do anything, including sell anything he can get his hands on for his next fix." She cocked her head toward the door. "Come with me. I need your muscles."

"They're all yours."

She slid her hands up his arm and over his biceps. He raised his hand and flexed, breaking the hold she had on him with ease. "Oh God."

"That's what you'll be saying later." He hooked his arm around her back and pushed her forward, and grabbed her hips when she stood in front of him. He walked her forward, keeping in step with her, his mouth at her neck, kissing a trail up to her ear. "Stay focused, or we will never get this done."

"Hey, you're the one who flexed and made my insides quake."

His deep chuckle at her ear sent a shiver down her spine, but he was right; she needed to focus on the task and stop distracting herself from reality with the hot guy who went out of his way to make her smile and forget the reason she was here.

She walked out of his light grasp and stood next to her father's desk in the small office off the living room. She pointed to the fake ficus tree in the corner. "Pull the tree up when I release the bolts."

She squatted next to the small oak barrel planter and pulled out the black wrought-iron handle with the pin her father had rigged to hold the fake top and tree in place.

"Clever." Rory held the tree aloft like it was nothing more than a feather. She'd have had to struggle to pull the eight-foot top-heavy tree out and set it in the corner. Moss fell free and landed on the hardwood floor. She'd clean it up and spread it over the base again when they reset the tree.

"What's inside?" Rory asked, kneeling beside her.

Sadie stared into the barrel amazed by how much her father had stuffed into the small space. Her mother's jewelry box. She opened it and stared at the few but treasured pieces her mother loved. Her and her father's wedding rings. A pair of tiny diamond stud earrings. A couple of gold necklaces. One had two gold hearts dangling from the bottom. One with an S for Sadie, the other with a C for Connor engraved on it. Tears filled her eyes.

Rory's big hand settled on her back. "It's strange the things that remind me of my mother. The coffee cup I made her in fourth grade is still in the cupboard. Every morning when I grab a mug, there it is. Some days, I barely notice it. Others, it hits me so hard my heart feels like it's shattered all over again."

Sadie tapped the charms with her finger. "I remember every time she bent over to kiss me, this would dangle from her neck. I can still remember the smell of her hair, the way she smiled, the sound of her laugh, but my memories are fading into the realm of dreams. The further I get from those moments we shared, the less real she seems."

"That's life, sweetheart. You will never forget her, but you have to live your life. If Connor was here, you'd share your memories and stories. I used to with Ford and Colt all the time when we were young. We don't do it as much now, but maybe we should."

Rory took the necklace from her fingers, unclasped it, draped it around her neck, and fastened it. He pulled her hair free and brushed his fingers through the long strands.

Sadie pressed her hand over the two hearts that rested over her own heart. She felt closer to her mother, and even Connor, for having it.

"Let's sort through these papers," Rory suggested. He picked up the thick envelope and handed it to her, sucking in a surprised gasp. "Uh, that's a lot of money."

Sadie stared into the barrel at the bundles of cash

stacked at the bottom. "What the . . ." She reached in and pulled several out. "There's got to be at least ten thousand dollars here."

Rory pulled out the papers from the envelope. She counted the money.

"Look at this." Rory set one paper after another on the floor beside them. "He has a life insurance policy for one hundred thousand dollars. This is the deed to the ranch. And this is his will. Everything goes to you, Sadie."

"The night of our first, and only, date he told me that he trusted me to do the right thing where Connor is concerned, even if that meant doing the hard thing and walking away. Tough love. I'm trying to do that, even though it breaks my heart. Old habits die hard, I guess."

"This money, the house and land, he left it to you to make the life you wanted. He left a note." Rory held up the paper with only a few lines written on it. "'Buy something you've always wanted just because you like it. Pay off your student loans. Write what is in your heart. Live with no regrets. Love with your whole heart the way you've always done and find someone who will love you the same way.'" Rory's head came up and his gaze met and held hers. "I think you get your writing talent from your dad. As last words go, that's pretty damn good."

Tears spilled over her lashes and trailed down her cheeks. "Yes. It is."

"You took care of him and your brother for a long time, sweetheart. Now he wants you to take care of you. You feel guilty doing that, but you've got to ask yourself, when is it your turn? The answer is now."

"It's hard."

"I know. But you can't keep living for everyone else. Trust me, the only thing that gets you is lonely."

"Have you been lonely?"

"Until I met you," he admitted, his eyes soft on her.

"I didn't realize I was missing you until I found you. You weren't here and now you are and everything is different and better and complicated and simple. Does that even make sense?"

"You and me make sense. Everything else we'll deal with and get through together."

Sadie leaned forward on her hands and knees and kissed him softly. "That's the best thing you've ever said to me."

Rory slid his hand along her face and smoothed his thumb over her cheek. "You're the most beautiful woman I've ever seen or known. That beauty comes from your heart, Sadie." He kissed her this time. A soft touch of his mouth to hers that lasted seconds but held a depth of meaning that flowed through her whole body. She leaned into him and savored his touch and the warm, calm, loved way he made her feel. Yes, she felt loved. He didn't have to say it. She'd like the words, but somehow they'd seem flat compared to the simple, elegant, emotion-filled way he kissed her.

"You've got to stop being this fantastic. You make all other men look bad."

"Good. Then you'll never want anyone but me."

"Already done." She pressed her hand to his handsome face. "Still, you can't be this great all the time. I must do something that irritates you."

"I didn't want to say anything. I mean, you've got so much going on already, but seriously, what is with you putting ketchup on your tacos?"

The laugh and smile came out of nowhere. She tried to stop both, but couldn't. The disgruntled and disgusted look on his face only made her smile and laugh more.

"That's just not right. Guacamole, salsa. These are condiments for tacos. Ketchup is for hot dogs and hamburgers."

She playfully shoved his shoulder. "Stop."

"Never. Not when it makes you smile like that."

Sadie sat back and stared at him, then at all the papers they'd spread out. "Even during all of this, you find a way to make me happy again."

"That's my job."

"It's in the boyfriend job description?"

He stared at her a moment, letting that "boyfriend" hang between them. She'd said that once before, but this seemed more definite. They hadn't really defined this thing they shared so intensely. Saying it out loud made it all the more real.

"Something like that."

"Let's hope I live up to the girlfriend expectations."

"You're better than anything I ever expected."

"I'm not fishing for more compliments."

"I never thought you were. What I said is true."

"This from the man who never dates, according to his brothers."

"Not never. I just don't see the point in running through a string of women who aren't the right woman."

"How do you know they weren't the right woman if you didn't take the time to get to know them?"

"I don't know. How is it that the moment I met you I knew it was right? You felt it, too."

She nodded. "Still, you never really dated?"

"Just because my brothers didn't know about it, doesn't mean it didn't happen. I'm a guy. I like women. What about you?"

"I dated a few guys off and on over the years. Nothing serious."

"Until now?"

The bold question should have made her nervous, but she answered without a single flutter of nerves. "Yes. Until you."

"Good. Then let's finish this and go for our ride."

"That sounds a lot better than doing this. You take the cash. I'll put these papers together and make a couple of calls."

"Don't you want to deposit this money in your bank account to pay bills and stuff?"

"No. That's for you. I know it doesn't cover everything—"

Rory placed his finger over her lips, cutting off her words. "Stop. I am so damn tired of this."

She didn't move from his touch, but cocked up one eyebrow.

"You didn't need to give me your horses, the money, and clean my house. Yes, the cattle theft set me back, but it didn't ruin me. I don't want any more money. I don't want you working at my place. I just want you. Don't you get that yet?"

She nodded because he still held his finger against her lips

"Good. Now pack your stuff and let's go home."

He took his hand away, but she still didn't say anything. Did he hear what he just said to her? Let's go home. She was home. This was her house, but it didn't feel the same. She didn't really want to live here alone.

In fact, she wanted to be with him. Always. He hadn't asked her to move in. Not in so many words, so what did he expect going forward?

She didn't know, but tonight she'd be sleeping in his bed, and she didn't intend to be there alone.

"I'll be ready in a few minutes." It surprised her—in a good way—that she was ready to move on with her life with him. Yes, she grieved for her father. The ache sat heavy in her chest even now, but over time it would lessen. She'd learn to smile without having to try. She'd be happy again without feeling guilty.

CHAPTER 23

Rory put the last sandwich in the insulated bag and zipped it shut. He stared out the window at Sadie in her tight jeans, brown boots, and pink long-sleeved shirt with her hair blowing in the wind. She stood next to the corral watching her herd of horses romping around, showing off for her. Lost in her thoughts, she tilted her face to the wind and sun.

"She looks a little sad," Colt commented, coming to stand beside him. "Did everything go all right at her place?"

"Collecting her things and getting her father's paperwork was the easy part. Watching her struggle with her emotions, not so much. The DEA agent riding her for answers didn't help."

"DEA. Do they think she's involved with her brother?"

"No. They want her help to bring him in."

"If he won't listen to her, what can she really do?"

"Exactly. It's inevitable he'll get caught or killed. She'd rather have him behind bars than dead, of course, but he doesn't trust her anymore. Unless he calls her again, she can't do anything, including wasting her breath trying to find out where he is and convince him to turn himself in."

"Where are you two off to?"

"Listen, man, I know I've been absent a lot and you and Ford have been carrying the load around here."

"Hey, I don't mind. Neither does Ford. You want to spend time with your girl, be my guest. You've covered for us, hell you've toed the line and sacrificed a hell of a lot more than we have. If this is your chance for something with her, take it."

"You really like her?"

"She makes you happy, I'm happy."

"Thanks, man."

"Do you have everything you need?" Colt's gaze settled on the old quilt Rory had rolled up to take along.

"I thought I'd take her on a picnic to cheer her up."

"Is that what they call it now?"

"Shut up." Rory shoved Colt away. "You're just jealous."

"Uh, yeah."

"You ever going to tell me what the deal is with you and Luna? She is Sadie's best friend, you know?"

"Did Luna say something to Sadie and she told you?" The fear that Rory would disapprove of whatever it was showed in Colt's eyes.

"No."

"Well, that's something."

"What would she say?"

Colt shrugged. "Right now, I don't know. Something happened. Something I didn't mean to happen, something that shouldn't have happened, but it did, and now I'm not sure if it really was a bad thing."

"If you feel this bad about it, maybe you should apologize. Maybe she'll change her mind about you."

"You think she would?"

"Give her a reason to change her mind."

Colt walked out without another word, but the thoughtful look in his eyes said Rory might have gotten through to him.

While Colt needed to change a woman's mind, Rory hoped his woman didn't change hers about staying here. Right now, she had clothes hanging in his closet and filling two of his drawers. He didn't mind making room for her. In fact, his room felt different now. He used to go up there and dread sleeping alone. Now he couldn't wait for night to come so he could hold her, make love to her, and wake up to her beautiful face each morning.

He might have lost his mind taking things this fast, but he didn't care. He wanted her. He needed her. Being without her anymore just wasn't an option.

"Heading out?" his grandfather asked. He went to the coffeepot and poured himself a mug.

"Yeah. We'll be back in a couple of hours."

"Have fun. Looks like she needs some."

"Granddad, I didn't ask . . . I just moved her in here, and . . ."

"Hey, this is your house, son. I just live here. You don't need my permission to do anything that makes you happy. I'm glad to see things are changing in this house and in your lives."

"Yeah, maybe all your pushing and prodding for us to settle down had some merit. Don't tell Ford and Colt I said that."

"Never. And Rory, it's not about settling down, it's

about being with someone who makes you the best you. I think she does that for you. If you think so, too, then hold on to her."

"I'm trying." Rory tucked the quilt under his arm and picked up their lunch bag.

"Take one of the walkies. With all the trouble that's gone on, you can't be too careful."

"We're not going that far, but you're right. I'll grab one on my way out."

Sadie rode beside Rory down the long trail. She had no idea where he planned to stop for their picnic. She didn't really care. She loved being out on the land on horseback, nothing but wind, trees, and sunshine. She stared up at the sparse white fluffy clouds overhead. A beautiful day. The perfect afternoon for a picnic with a gorgeous cowboy.

"Are you falling asleep back there?"

Sadie brought her face back down and stared at Rory in front of her. "Just enjoying the day and the sights."

"See anything you like?"

"Every time I look at you, cowboy."

Rory tipped his finger to his Stetson. The man looked even more handsome and dangerous in the black hat.

"Ready to eat?"

"I'm starving." She looked around the area. "Hey, didn't we pass this spot about twenty minutes ago?"

"Yep."

"Why are we going in circles if this is where you were headed all along?"

"Because you needed time to relax and get out of your head."

She had to admit he was ri̇g— utes ago, she'd spent most of their hour— ing about everything that happened still had to do. She thought about her cl̇o room, her hairbrush next to his in the bathrȯȯ the fact she planned to sleep in his bed with him to. git.

The flutter of anticipation in her belly excited her. The eagerness and growing need to be with him zipped through her system and made her body hum. This wasn't just the natural progression in their relationship. It was a step toward their future.

She thought about that, too. Where they were headed. What the rest of their lives would be like now. She had a hard time picturing it clearly with everything from her past still so present now. She'd get through this rough time, sort out everything she felt was holding her back, and move forward with Rory. He was the one thing she felt certain about always.

"Do we need to take another circle, or are you going to come back from wherever you went in your head?"

She smiled down at him, surprised to discover they'd stopped and he'd already dismounted. "Sorry."

He took her by the hips and lifted her right off her horse.

"God, you're strong."

"You hardly weigh a thing, little one."

His hands slid down her hips to cup her bottom. She went up on tiptoe, her hands braced on his shoulders. He pulled her close and kissed her.

"Did you like the ride?"

"Yes. Very much. I'm sorry I wasn't great company. You wanted to show me your land and I barely paid attention."

not important."

Yes, it is. This is your home. Your work. It's what I've worked so hard to hold on to since your parents died."

"We'll ride as often as you like and you'll see it all then. Today, you needed the peace and quiet."

"You always seem to know just what I need."

He cupped her face and brushed his thumbs under her eyes and over her cheeks. "You need to rest. You barely slept last night."

"You had something to do with that," she teased.

He leaned down and kissed her again. "My pleasure. But you need to eat and get some rest. Come on." He took her hand and tugged her toward his horse. He released her long enough to unstrap the blanket and their lunch bag. He took her hand again and walked her up toward the cluster of trees with the soft grass and dappled light.

Another man had walked her into the trees once. It seemed a long time ago, yet fresh as if it were happening right now. She stopped midstride. Rory kept walking another step, tugging on her hand, but she didn't budge. Her mind took her back to the terror she felt that day and the bite of the wire pinching and poking into her skin.

"Sadie," Rory yelled, like he'd said her name more than once.

"Huh. What?"

"You're white as a sheet. What happened?"

"Nothing. Sorry. I got lost in thought." She stared up the sprawling tree branches.

Rory dropped their stuff and cupped her face, making her focus on him. "You're safe here with me."

She clamped her shaking hands over his wrists. "I know that. I'm fine."

"Then breathe."

She sucked in a ragged breath and tried to smile to wipe the concern from his narrowed eyes. She reached for him, pulling him close and pressing her body to his. "Did I thank you for saving me?"

"A dozen times, sweetheart. It's over. Soon that asshole will be behind bars where he belongs."

She pressed her hands to his chest and leaned back in his arms. "You're right. I'm sorry. It hit me all at once, seeing the trees, feeling the cool wind, and being out here again. I'm fine. Let's eat."

"I'm sorry, I should have thought before bringing you out into the woods."

"No. I love that you wanted to take me on a picnic. I don't want what happened to become so big in my life that I stop doing the things I love, like going for a ride and being out here with you."

Rory didn't look quite convinced, but he released her, picked up the blanket, shook it out, and spread it over the soft grass under the largest tree. Shaded from the afternoon sun, Sadie sat on the soft blanket and pulled off her boots, getting comfortable. She wanted Rory to see she had every intention of kicking back, relaxing, and enjoying their time together.

Rory set the lunch bag on the blanket. She pulled out the paper plates, wrapped sandwiches, and plastic containers. She found the two cans of PBR and bottles of water on the bottom, including her prize, a bag of her favorite chocolate chunk brownie cookies.

"How did you know these are my favorite?"

"I see you eating them all the time."

She held up the can of beer. "Planning on getting me drunk?"

"Sweetheart, if one can of beer gets you drunk I'm not letting you drink at all." The silly grin he gave her settled the last of the fear she'd felt reliving her nightmare.

She popped the top on the beer and took a deep sip. She swallowed and sighed. "That's good."

"Hand me the other. Let's eat."

The chicken, ranch, lettuce, and red onion on sourdough sandwich was also her favorite. One of the plastic containers had sliced apples. The other a pasta, broccoli, zucchini salad. "It's kind of creepy that you know all the things I like."

"I've been stalking you for years."

The teasing tone said one thing, but he'd been watching her for a long time.

"Why didn't you ever ask me out if you were so interested?"

Rory didn't look at her for a long while. He chewed his roast beef sandwich and stared off into the distance. "I intimidated you."

"You scared me. You take up the space around you like no one else I know. It's not just your size, but your presence. You never smiled at me to let me know you wanted to even say hi. Whenever I caught you looking at me, you walked away. I thought maybe I'd done something to piss you off. Or at least my brother had."

"It's no secret to anyone around town you watch over him like a hawk and he treats you like crap for all your trouble. That's what I didn't like. But that wasn't why I never said anything."

"Then what was it, because you don't seem to have a problem with me now."

"I never had a problem with you. I liked you. A lot. But you're Colt's age."

"So."

"So I didn't think you'd be interested in someone six years older than you."

"Age doesn't really matter. Not when you're headed toward your thirties."

"You've got a few years to go yet."

She shrugged. "Maybe, but it's coming quicker than I thought. So that's it, the age thing is why you never said anything, why you always sat across the restaurant. I thought maybe I smelled bad, or always had something stuck in my teeth."

Rory laughed at that and set his empty plate aside. He took a sip of his beer, then looked at her again. "I didn't know what to say, and it seemed too important to mess it up, especially when you didn't seem interested in me."

She went still, understanding the real reason he'd held back. The shyness most people didn't see. The depth of emotion Rory felt but never let show. He'd opened up to her and showed her who he really was these last weeks. The age thing was an excuse for him to cover how much he really liked her but feared doing something, saying something that ruined his chances with her, especially when she'd kept her distance.

His fault for always being cold and remote, never letting anyone in, until he'd saved her and they'd found each other.

"Besides that, I've been too consumed with raising my brothers and keeping this ranch. It's an all-day, every-day kind of thing."

"Yet you've barely worked since I met you." Because being with her had become more important. Like her, he found something he wanted and didn't want to waste this opportunity and good fortune.

"I've turned into a real slacker."

"After all these years, you don't even care."

"When I found you . . ."

He left off the part about how he found her and she appreciated it.

"I realized that I might lose you before I ever got the chance to see if what I felt for you was real or just some made-up thing in my head. I didn't want to lose it then, I certainly don't want to lose it now that I know how real and deep it is."

Sadie set her plate aside, finished off her beer, and lay back on the blanket, staring up at the branches and the blue sky peeking through the leaves.

"I'm kind of glad my brother stole your cattle."

Rory fell back onto the blanket beside her with a soft chuckle. "Don't tell my brothers I said this, but so am I. I'm not going to thank him for it, though, especially after that asshole left you out there . . ." Again, he couldn't bring himself to talk about it. He didn't have to. She got it, felt it, shivered with the gruesome memory.

"I never thought you would or expected it."

They shared the silence below the trees for several minutes, settling into the quiet and each other's company. It never grew awkward. In fact, the longer it went on, the more comfortable she felt in his presence.

Rory rolled to his side, propped himself up on his

elbow, and stared down at Sadie. Her pretty blue eyes were cast up to the trees. "I really want to kiss you right now."

"You should stop stopping yourself from doing what you want where I'm concerned."

He actually followed that convoluted sentence and went with his urge to kiss her, bending down and kissing her softly on the cheek.

She smiled and shook her head. "All that buildup for such a chaste kiss."

This time he reached over with his free hand, placed it on her hip, and pulled her across the blanket to lie down his length. He dipped his head and took her mouth in a searing kiss that was so far from chaste that he had her panting for breath when he finally eased back and kissed his way down her neck to her collarbone.

Her fingers slid through his hair. His hand on her hip slid up her side under her shirt and cupped her full breast. He swept his thumb over her hard nipple, tucked his fingers into the bra cup, and yanked it down. His palm settled over the mound, her nipple pressed against his palm, and he squeezed her flesh into his hand, molding it to his grip. She sighed, arching her back and pressing her breast into his hand even more. He reached around her back and undid the clasp on her bra.

He kissed his way back up her neck to her ear and whispered, "If you're not ready for this, say so now."

"Don't stop, Rory."

He slid his hand back around her side to her breast and rubbed his palm over her.

"I want you." She sighed.

That was all he needed to hear. He pulled his hand

free of her shirt, grabbed the hem, and dragged it up and over her head, catching her bra on the way up and pulling it off, too. He stared down at her creamy skin and pink-tipped breasts, her nipples hard and begging for his mouth, and thought his heart stopped along with his breath. "Damn, you're beautiful."

Her hand settled on his face. "Love me."

He already did, but right now he needed to show her more than he needed to say it. His mouth crushed hers. He needed that taste of her to settle his heart and give him a chance to hold on to his control before he tore the rest of her clothes off and drove his aching cock inside her sweet body.

Her hands smoothed over his back, grabbed hold of his shirt, and dragged it up and over his head. He broke the kiss long enough to let her do it, but quickly took her mouth again in a deep kiss. Her bare skin touched his, her hard-tipped breasts pressed to his chest, and she moaned into his mouth with the sheer pleasure she couldn't contain and he needed more of right now.

He kissed his way down her neck again. This time, he didn't stop at her shoulder, but trailed kisses over her chest and straight to one of her peaked nipples. He took the tight bead into his mouth and sucked softly, his hand sliding up her ribs to cup her breast. He licked the tip, circled his tongue around the tight bud, then took it into his mouth again, sucking harder.

Her fingers raked through his hair and gripped it tight. "Oh God, Rory."

Exactly. God sent him this gift and he meant to show his appreciation and love her the way she asked.

He took her breast in his hand, her nipple caught between his index and middle fingers. He squeezed and kneaded, kissing his way to her other breast and taking that nipple into his mouth. Her hands never stopped moving over him. She brushed them over his head, down his neck, and over his shoulders, arching her back and offering up the bounty he couldn't get enough of for more attention. He gave it to her, but he wanted so much more.

The little moans and sighs she made drove him crazy wild. He slid his hand down her taut belly to the button on her jeans. He pulled it loose, then unzipped the denim, sliding his hand inside and over her panties to cup her in his hand. She rocked her hips into his palm and he rubbed back and forth, hindered by the tight material. Frustrated he couldn't touch her the way he wanted, he leaned back, sat up, and hooked his fingers in the top of her jeans and pink lace panties.

"You're killing me, you know that."

She planted her heels on the blanket, lifted her hips, and he dragged the denim and lace down her legs. It didn't take but a second to pull her socks off her feet. With Sadie naked to the sky and his wandering gaze, he stared down at her and took her all in, from the fall of her blond hair over the blanket and her shoulders, to her softly rounded breasts, slender belly, slightly flared hips, and long toned legs. She had pretty feet and toes. It made him smile.

"What?" She covered the scar on her side and across her belly with her hands, which only made him stare at the scars around her wrists. The many other small marks all over her barely registered. All he saw was the beauty laid out before him.

"I am so damn lucky."

She leaned up, hooked her hand around the back of

his neck, and pulled him in for another kiss. He followed her back down to the blanket and started the dance all over again, because now that he had her naked, he wanted to touch every inch of her again and again, but his restraint waned until he smoothed his hand down her thigh, back up the toned muscles, and found her hot, wet center with his roaming fingers. He slid his fingers over her soft folds and sent one deep into her warmth. She rocked her hips into his hand and moaned out his name.

Her hand mapped his chest and down his taut stomach. He ached to be inside her, but settled for her hand sliding over his swollen flesh over his jeans. She wasn't satisfied at all and made quick work of undoing the button and zipper and dipping her hand down the front of his boxer briefs and along his aching cock. Her fingers wrapped around his length and squeezed. He rocked into her hand and groaned, sending his finger deep into her core. He pressed his thumb to her clit as she circled her hips and rubbed against him. Her hand sank deeper down his length, her fingers gripped his balls, and he sucked in a ragged breath and tried to hold on to his sanity.

He broke the kiss they shared and replaced her lips on his with her breast. God, the way she tasted. The way she felt. The way she tempted him.

Her hands rubbed up his stomach, around his sides, and down over his ass as she turned into him.

He licked the underside of her breast, took her tight nipple softly between his teeth, and licked the tip with a sweep of his tongue.

"Oh God, Rory, now." She pulled him close, both hands on his ass, squeezing.

He left her long enough to kick off his jeans and boxers. Her hands smoothed over his back. She rose behind him, kissed her way along his shoulder to his neck, her hand rubbing up his spine until her fingers dug through his hair. He could barely get his socks and jeans untangled from his feet for all the kissing and mapping his body she did with her mouth and hands.

At the last second, he remembered the condom in his pocket. He made a grab for his jeans again just as her hand came around his side and her fingers wrapped around his hard dick again. She worked her hand up and down his flesh, stroking and teasing, her cheek pressed to his shoulder, her lips softly kissing his neck. Frozen by her erotic attention, he completely forgot what he needed to do.

She shifted before he totally comprehended her intention and landed on his lap, her thighs straddling his hips. Her soft heat pressed against his shaft. She rocked and rubbed against him, her breasts right in front of his face. He cupped one and took it into his mouth, lost in her movements over him and the sweet floral scent of her.

Her arms banded around his head and held him close as she rocked and rubbed herself against him. He wanted to drive his aching cock into her right now, but kept his head, reached for his jeans behind her without leaving her sweet breast. He fumbled for the condom, found it, and tore his mouth free from her creamy skin so he could tear the package open with his teeth.

Rory sheathed himself, grabbed hold of her bottom, held her close, and rolled her over onto her back. He lay between her thighs, the head of his dick pressed to her entrance. He held himself above her on his elbows and stared down into her brilliant blue eyes so filled with love and lust he got drunk on her. The buzz raced through his veins, joined by the need gnawing at him to make her his. He slid into her slow and easy all the way to the hilt and watched the heat in her eyes flare when he joined their bodies.

He swept his thumb over her temple. "My Sadie."

She reached for him, bringing him down for a soft kiss. She pulled her knees up and out, planted her heels, and rocked her hips against his, taking him deep. "Love me," she said against his lips.

Her eyes fell closed and she let herself go in a way he'd never felt from any woman. She gave herself over to him and he lost himself in making love to her. His body pressed down on her. Hers rose up to meet him. Every soft kiss, tempting touch, soothing sigh, and moan fanned the flames and stoked the fire building inside him. Her hands smoothed down his back and over his ass again. This time when he sank into her, she pulled him closer. The feel of her body against his drove him on. He needed more. He needed all of her. She gave it, rotating her hips against his when he thrust deep again and again. Her body tightened around his and he pumped harder and faster until she threw her head back and her body fisted around his cock, sending him over the edge with her.

Rory rode out her release, then collapsed on top of her, his head in her soft hair, his breath sawing in and out at her neck.

Her arms clasped his shoulders. Her hands rested on his back, her fingers softly caressing his skin.

"Now I know why people become sex addicts," she whispered with a smile in her voice.

"I am completely addicted to you, sweetheart."

"Oh good, then we get to do this again."

He pressed up on his forearms and stared down at her smiling face. "All you want, sweetheart, but you've got to give me, I don't know, half an hour to reload."

Her giggle went straight to his gut. "Sure thing, honey." She snuggled against him, her hands sweeping up and down his sides. "Uh, why are you staring at me like that? Is there a spider in my hair?" She raked her fingers through the long strands, which only made her look more beautiful.

He stilled her hands with his and shook his head. "No spiders. You called me honey."

She bit her bottom lip, the plump flesh sliding free from her teeth. "You don't like it?"

"I do. You just caught me off guard. You've never said anything like that."

"You call me sweetheart all the time. I like it. It makes me feel closer to you. I want you to feel that way about me."

He pressed his hips to hers again. "I can't get much closer to you."

"I like this, Rory. Us, here, together, nothing else in the world intruding. Just you and me."

He leaned down and pressed his forehead to hers. "You and me." He kissed her, long and slow, like he had all the time in the world, because out here, right now, it seemed they did. He broke the soft kiss and planted one on her nose, each cheek, and her forehead.

"Honey, you're crushing me." She tapped her hands against his shoulders.

He chuckled, taking more of his weight on his arms than on her. "Sorry."

"Believe me, I love having you pressed against me, but I need to breathe."

He pulled free and rolled off her. He sat beside her, his knees drawn up, so he could take care of business. He stared down at the torn condom and everything inside him went cold. "Fuck."

Sadie rolled to her side and laid her hand on his arm. He raked his fingers through the side of his hair and held tight, trying to figure out a way to tell her that didn't make her panic the way he felt inside.

"Rory, honey, what is it?"

He stared straight ahead, but closed his eyes, savoring that sweet honey on her lips. "I don't know how to say this."

"You're scaring me. What's wrong?"

"Uh, the condom broke. I don't know what happened." He covered his face with both hands and scrubbed them up and down over his eyes. "Fuck. I'm sorry, Sadie." He wanted her for the rest of his life, but he didn't want to trap her into spending the rest of hers with him. This wasn't supposed to happen. Not this way.

Her hand contracted on his arm. He met her steady gaze. "Honey, it was an accident. A fluke. It happens." She sat up next to him, her hand still on his arm. "It wasn't in my immediate plans, but if I am pregnant, I won't be upset about it. I've lost so much lately, but I found something amazing with you."

"I don't know what to say, except I will take care of you and our child. I promise."

"If it happened."

He nodded, but still felt he'd failed to protect her. After all she'd been through with her father and brother, she deserved a chance to do whatever she wanted. Not be tied down without choice. The weight of responsibility settled on his shoulders.

Sadie gave him a quick kiss, hoping to erase the last of the concern from his hazel eyes. She didn't know what else to say to ease his mind. This could be huge—for both of them. A life with him and a baby would be such a joy.

Rory tugged on his clothes, pulled on his socks, and stuffed his feet in his boots. He'd settled back into his quiet intensity. She'd give him time to let things settle in his mind. He needed to mull things over, think things through, plan every possible scenario. He took responsibility seriously. One of the many reasons she loved him.

She dressed quickly, sat on the blanket, and put her own socks and boots back on while he cleaned up the food wrappers and packed up the containers. He tapped her in the shoulder with a water bottle. She took it, noting he didn't really look her in the eye. She hoped by the time they got back to the ranch he'd have it all worked out in his head.

Rory packed up the rest of their supplies and readied the horses. It gave her a minute to think about being a mother. She'd thought about it in the abstract. She loved kids, and babies especially. She placed her hands over her lower belly and smiled, the image of a tiny blond-haired hazel-green-eyed bundle in her arms who looked just like his daddy filled her mind. The spark that image flared to life in her heart grew until her chest ached with wanting it.

She turned to Rory, spotted him staring at her. He held the reins to both horses. God, the man couldn't look more gorgeous in jeans, boots, and that black Stetson. His eyes narrowed on her and she smiled, because deep inside she was happy. Under all the grief about her father's passing, the worry she always carried for Connor, and the uncertainty about her future, she couldn't deny the well of happiness building as dreams of her life with Rory and their child sprouted and bloomed in her heart and mind.

She closed the distance between her and Rory.

"You okay?" he asked, his voice soft with concern.

"Honey, I'm fine. You brought the condom. You used it. What happened isn't your fault. Until we know for sure, don't dwell on what was nothing more than an accident, or fate."

He gave her another of those silent nods that said nothing, but spoke volumes. She took her reins, planted her foot in the stirrup, and raised herself up into the saddle. Her horse danced sideways.

"Careful," Rory warned, his grip tight on the horse's bridal, steadying the horse.

By the time they rode into the ranch driveway, the silence between them had grown deafening. Rory dismounted and walked to her. He grasped her hips and pulled her from the horse, setting her gently on the ground. The muscle in his jaw ticked as he stared down at her for a long minute, then turned and pulled the blanket and lunch sack from his horse.

"You two have a good time?" Ford asked.

"Great," she said.

"Sure," Rory said, still stuck in his head. Rory handed her the supplies and turned to walk the horses into the stables. "Take that up to the house. I've got work to do. I'll be in later."

"Uh, did you two have a fight, or something?" Ford asked. "I haven't seen him like this in a while."

"No, something else," she said, her gaze locked on Rory's retreating back. "Hey," she called out to him. "Come back here."

Rory stopped in his tracks and looked at her over his shoulder. She dropped the blanket and bag on the ground and planted her hands on her hips, staring him down.

Ford ran forward to take the horses' reins Rory held up to him. Rory walked back to her and stopped three feet in front of her. "What?"

"Is that how you say goodbye to me now? No kiss. No 'See you soon, sweetheart.'"

"Sadie, I have to get the horses settled. We'll talk more later."

She swept her hands out, indicating the ground in front of her. "Do you feel the bricks you're laying between us? I can barely breathe for the suffocating silence. Don't do this. Don't be the quiet, distant guy I thought you were. Be my Rory." She couldn't hide the tremble in her voice or the sheen in her eyes.

He rushed her, wrapping his arms around her waist, lifting her right off her feet, and kissing her like he did when he made love to her, like she was his everything. His mouth softened over hers and he took the kiss deeper, sliding his tongue along hers. He tilted his head, melded his mouth to hers and held her tight with his arms banded around her back. He kissed her again and again until she placed her hands on his cheeks and pressed her forehead to his.

"It's all right, honey. Everything is fine. Make me a promise. Until I tell you one way or the other, let's go back to the way things were. No worrying about what might be. Please."

"I'll try, but I want to know as soon as you know."

"I'd never keep something like that from you."

"I know."

"For now let's do the same thing we've been doing. We stick together. We keep working on us."

"Us."

"Yes. Us. You and me."

"I like that."

"Good. I'm starting to like you again."

That made him smile. "You like ordering me around."

"It worked. I got my kiss."

"All you had to do was ask."

She eyed him. "Right. Go do your work. I've got to finish an assignment for school. I'll see you at dinner."

Rory kissed her softly on the lips, lingering for a long moment, hoping that extra time he took showed her how much he loved her because even now he struggled to find a way to actually tell her.

He kissed her one last time, set her back on her feet, handed her the things she'd dropped, and watched her walk away. He hoped she didn't ever leave for good.

Rory walked into the stables. Ford stood just down the aisle brushing down Sadie's horse.

"What did you do to upset her?"

Rory rubbed his fingers over his lips, remembering their kiss and all they shared this afternoon. He hadn't meant to upset her. "Nothing. Something happened. It was no one's fault." He believed that, but still the consequences weighed on him. "I went quiet on her, and she didn't like it."

"She's the best thing that ever happened to you. Don't fuck this up."

"Thanks. I'll take that under advisement."

"Seriously, she's perfect for you. She told *you* to come back to her." Ford's broad smile made Rory smile back. "That chick's got balls."

"No, well yes, but mostly she knows I'm at her beck and call."

"Then why the tension?"

"Leave it alone for now. We'll work it out."

"Do it fast. With everything going on with her family, she needs to know she can count on you when things get crazy again."

"Did something happen?"

"No, but I'm sure it will with her brother on the loose."

Ford was probably right. Sadie had just lost her father. Her brother was wanted by the cops. The DEA was breathing down her neck. He'd overreacted about something they'd tried to do right, but went wrong. Or maybe it didn't. She might not be pregnant at all. But the thought of having a baby with her didn't scare him. It didn't faze him in the least. In fact, as much as he'd fought the idea because of his granddad's prodding, the thought of a beautiful blond-haired, blue-eyed little girl made him unexpectedly thrilled.

"There's something wrong with your face."

"What?" Rory cocked his head at Ford.

"You're smiling. What are you thinking about?"

A wife. Not any wife, Sadie. Babies. A life here on the ranch that was more than hard work, but raising a family. He and his brothers used to run wild on this land. He'd love to see his kids, Ford's, and Colt's running around, riding the horses, playing and having fun.

"Sometimes, things happen that you want but didn't plan on happening right now. It's all good. At least, I hope it will be."

He'd wanted more time with Sadie, to grow closer to her, solidify their relationship and let it build into something lasting. Now, the stone in his gut felt as if everything was on a nine-month timetable. Sooner than that really. If she was pregnant, he needed to put a ring on her finger, marry her, and prepare for their child to arrive.

"She's really nice and thoughtful. She believes in doing the right thing. I'm sure you two can work it out."

Ford's words hit home. Would she marry him and be his wife and a mother to their child because it was the right thing to do, or because she loved him and wanted to make a life with him?

The question ate at him for the next couple hours while he caught up on work with Ford.

Rory walked into the house and smelled the chili Sadie had cooking on the stove. She took such good care of them, the house, her father and brother. Him. And he might have just given her someone else to take care of, too, just when her life was her own now, and she only had to look out for herself. Great. After the day he'd had, he hit the landing, worked up into a mass of tight muscles and a pounding headache.

Sadie set her laptop on the bedside table, stuffed her papers in a folder, stacked it on her textbook, and set them aside, too, just as Rory walked in the bedroom door.

"Hey, honey, all done working?"

"Yeah. You?"

"For now. I have some work to do on one of my papers, but it can wait until tomorrow."

Nothing. Not a word. He stood there staring at her, his face a mask, hiding his thoughts and feelings. He'd fortified those walls she broke down earlier when he went quiet on her the first time. She loved him. She thought maybe he loved her, too. She hated to see him retreat on her again.

"Rory, honey, why are you looking at me so hard?"

He started and finally focused on reality and not the deep thoughts that stopped his tongue and made him so distant. "Sorry. Uh, I need to shower. I'll be down for dinner in a few."

She tipped her head and studied him. From the set of his mouth, the tic in his jaw, and the slouch to his shoulders, she thought he carried the weight of the world, planning all he needed to do if she was pregnant. The last thing she wanted was to build a relationship on responsibility. Oh, he'd do the right thing, no doubt. But she wanted something solid, built on love, understanding, and an openness with each other that she didn't have to fight for every time things got tough.

Making love, the kiss they'd shared when they returned, well, she'd felt the depth of feelings Rory had such a hard time putting into words. He might have a hard time sharing his emotions, but he had no problem showing her how he felt. Rory spoke through action. She'd let their bodies do the talking for now to keep him close and break down those walls again. If she showed him how much she wanted him, loved him, maybe he'd open up and drop his guard for good because she couldn't live being kept at an emotional arm's length.

She put thought into action and grabbed the hem of her shirt and pulled it up and over her head.

Struck by her audacity, his eyes went wide. His gaze swept down her face to her lace-covered breasts.

Oh yes, she had his attention now.

She pulled the button on her jeans free, then ever so slowly pulled the zipper down. She reached behind her to unclasp the lace bra. He didn't say a word, but his hot gaze roamed over her, heating her bare skin.

He stood mesmerized, then caught himself. He kicked his leg out, catching the bedroom door, and pushed it closed. "What are you doing?"

She dropped the bra at her feet on top of her shirt, looked him right in the eye, and walked toward him half naked. She went up on tiptoe, locked her arms around his neck, and kissed him. Not a soft, gentle coaxing, but a full-on, mind-blowing, take-what-she-wanted kiss. Sparked by her need, he dove in for more, taking over the kiss. He wrapped his arms around her and held her close. She rocked her hips into his, grinding on him until he was hard against her belly. She broke the searing kiss, grabbed his shoulders, and jumped up, locking her legs around his waist.

"Take me to bed, cowboy."

"I'm all sweaty and dirty. I need a shower."

"I need you." She crushed her mouth down on his for another all-consuming kiss. She smoothed her hands down his back, grabbed hold of his shirt, and yanked it up. He let go of her ass long enough to hold his arms up so she could pull off his shirt. She stared down between them at his chest. "Now that is what I'm talking about." She rubbed her hands over his shoulders and down his chest over his tight pecs. "You are so gorgeous and strong." She scanned up his body and locked her gaze on his. "Make love to me the way we did under the trees. Let everything else go, and let it be you and me again."

The tension left his big body and his hands softened on her hips. This time, he kissed her. Soft. Slow. Sweet. Like he had all the time in the world to be with her. She wasn't going anywhere. She didn't want to. She wanted to be with him. He finally got it.

He walked toward the bed, his lips brushing hers. His legs hit the mattress and he climbed up and gently lowered her onto the bed, his body covering hers. He stared down at her, his eyes filled with tenderness.

She cupped his face, her fingers gently brushing his skin. "You and me," she whispered.

Nothing else mattered right now.

He dipped his head, kissed her lips softly, then trailed kisses down her neck and chest to her pink-tipped breast. He took the hard bud into his mouth, sucked softly, then hard. She sighed out his name and her fingers slid through his hair and held him to her breasts, feeling everything he put into touching her, loving her.

Too many barriers in the way. He kissed a trail down her belly to the lace edge of her panties peeking out the top of her open jeans. He leaned back, hooked his fingers in the lace and denim, and tugged.

She smiled. "Now I've got your attention."

He pulled her boots off, then her clothes. His gaze

swept up her legs, over her curves, to her face, his eyes glowing with appreciation and a greedy hunger that matched her own.

"You've got my undivided attention."

"But not those big hands on me."

He placed his hand on her knee, then slid it up her thigh and back down. Her body relaxed under his palm, but she wanted so much more.

"Better?"

"No. Not until every inch of you is touching every inch of me."

He leaned over her, holding himself above her on his hands and knees. He pressed down and kissed her, still not touching her with his body. He pushed back up and stared down at her, thinking he had the upper hand. Not so. She nimbly unbuttoned and unzipped his jeans, sinking one hand into his boxer briefs. She had him well in hand then. Her fingers circled and squeezed his swollen flesh. His eyes went wide, then softened as pleasure replaced surprise and she worked her hand up and down his hard length.

"You're overdressed. Get naked with me."

"You're beautiful and demanding in the sweetest way."

She cocked up one eyebrow. "You think I'm sweet?" She rubbed her hand up his hard length and back down again.

"Maybe a little wicked."

One side of her mouth tilted up into a half grin. Feeling saucy, she said, "Come and get it."

He squeezed her thigh. "You're nothing like I thought."

She slipped her hand free and slid it up his stomach

and rested it over his heart. Everything in him stilled at
the simple touch.

"It's you, Rory. I just want to be with you."

No words came to mind to respond to such an honest
sentiment.

If he didn't have the words, Rory could certainly
show her how much she meant to him. He stripped off
the rest of his clothes, letting the quiet settle around
them. He didn't rush, but let the moment stretch because it wasn't awkward, but comfortable. He had no
qualms about her seeing him. They'd already made
love once, but more than that, the way she looked at
him, devoured every inch of his skin with her gaze,
made him all the more anxious to be close to her. To
love her with his body the way his heart so easily let go
and did so without a hitch in its beat. It knew without
all the cluttered thoughts, reservations, and uncertain-
ties his mind conjured. What his brain made complicated, his heart simplified.

This time when he went to her, he did cover her, his
body pressed to every inch of hers. He stared down into
her eyes, still unable to come up with something to say
that conveyed the deep feelings filling him up.

His lips touched hers, but it was altogether different.
He poured everything inside him into the kiss. In her
unique way of reading him, she changed the kiss for a
moment, taking over and giving him back all he shared
with her. The silent conversation tore him down and
built him back up all at the same time into the man he
wanted to be for her.

He kissed his way down her throat to her breast,

took her hard nipple into his mouth, and licked the tight peak in a long, slow stroke that made her sigh. Her legs cradled his waist as he lay between her thighs, her knees up-drawn to accommodate his large body. He shifted his weight back, slid his hand down her soft skin, over her belly, side, and hip around to her smooth inner thigh. Her hips rocked forward seeking his touch even as her hand slid down over his head and shoulders. He circled his tongue around her hard nipple, took the bead into his mouth, and sucked hard, sliding his finger into her slick warmth at the same time.

The moan she let loose drove him on, his need for her a heat building inside him until the taste and touch of her wasn't enough. He needed to be inside her. Her nails dug into his back and raked up over his shoulders. The bite set off a wave of electricity through him. He thrust his finger deep, her hips rocking into his hand. She lost herself in his touch, and he became a slave to her every need. He circled her clit with his thumb, softly rubbing until she panted, her fingers digging into his back muscles. She pulled at him to come to her. Happy to do so, he slid his fingers up over her soft folds, over her belly and around her hip. He squeezed tight, slid up her body, and took her mouth in a searing kiss. With his weight balanced on one arm, he reached for the condom in the bedside drawer. He broke the kiss to lean further and snag his prize.

She planted soft kisses along his rough jaw to his ear. Her tongue skimmed the edge, her teeth clamped on to the lobe without hurting him, her lips closed over the soft flesh, and she sucked softly.

He tore the foil packet with his teeth.

"Love me, Rory," she whispered in his ear. The

same thing she said to him out in the grass below the trees. It was a request he was happy to fulfill again, now, whenever she wanted him to until the day he died.

Sheathed and ready for her, he pressed the head of his hard dick to her slick entrance and kissed her, sliding home in one long glide until he filled her.

"Oh yes." She sighed, igniting the fuse on his restraint.

He pulled out and thrust back home, loving the way her body rose to meet his. He didn't think anything could feel better than loving her the first time. He'd been wrong. Her arms wrapped around his back. She pressed her breasts to his chest. With her knees pulled up, her thighs cradled his hips. Her feet hooked over the back of his knees. She literally wrapped around him. She pressed a warm kiss to his throat and the underside of his chin. He thrust deep again and she sighed. Her rushed, heated breath washed over his skin.

Her body tightened around his. Her head went back into the pillow, eyes closed, her mouth slightly parted on a moan as her body quaked below him. The lit fuse she ignited detonated his desire and he rocked back into her, circled his hips, setting off another round of aftershocks deep in her core. He pulled back and drove home in an explosive release that had flashing lights spark against the backs of his eyelids.

Spent, satiated, he dropped on top of her, savoring the feel of her hands resting on the base of his spine, her fingers lightly caressing his ass. Her feet slid down his calves and fell back onto the mattress. Her erratic breath whispered through his hair as he lay on top of her, his face buried in her hair at the side of her head. His sawing pants came out warm against her ear, the heat washing over his face, too, but he couldn't move. Not yet. He wanted to lie here in her arms, feeling just like this. Happy. One with her.

She shifted beneath him. Her lips pressed to his head in a quick kiss. "Roll, big guy."

He managed to get his forearms beneath him and press up, taking some of his much heavier weight off her. He stared down into her beautiful face and bright blue eyes. "I think you're trying to kill me."

"Never. I just really like having your undivided attention."

The smile came easy, because she made everything easy. He shifted to her side, rolling to his back, and bringing her with him. She lay on her side, one leg draped over his, her cheek pressed to his chest with her hand resting over his thumping heart.

He lifted his head, stared down his body, verified the condom was still intact—thank God—and settled back into the bed.

"It's fine. Nothing to worry about, because I'm with you, and I know you're with me." Her hand slid over his ribs to his side and she hugged him close. "As long as we stick together, everything is fine."

He kissed her on top of the head and held her close, letting her words sink into his heart. *I'm with you.* Her way of telling him baby or no baby, she intended to stay with him.

The possibility of a baby changed things. He had so much more to protect. Her. The baby. And if there wasn't a baby now, he needed to keep her safe so one day the dream growing in his mind and heart became a reality.

CHAPTER 24

Sadie hugged Colt at her front door. "Thanks for coming." Her father's funeral took everything out of her today. Having everyone to the house after the short graveside ceremony fried her last nerve. She didn't want to answer any more questions about her brother's absence and anticipated arrest, or talk about her father's illness and his last days. She didn't want any more advice about what she should do with the ranch, or hear one more order that she better not sell it to some rich actor or businessman who wanted to pretend to play cowboy out here in the country only to drive up land prices.

"It was a nice service," Colt said, releasing her. "See you back home, sis." Colt walked out the door and joined Ford and Sammy at their truck.

Luna stared after Colt, trying not to make it look like she watched him. They'd done this same strange dance the whole day. They didn't talk to each other, but the awkward way they avoided each other grew thick with tension until they were both quiet, tense, and scowling at each other.

Luna wrapped Sadie in a tight hug. "I love you, lady."

"I love you, too. Thanks for helping out today. I needed you here."

"What are friends for? But you don't really need me, you've got a sexy, hot boyfriend," Luna whispered in her ear. "I'm so happy for you. You two are really great together."

"Thanks." Sadie squeezed Luna close, then let her go.

"I'd say I'll stay the night and we'll have one of our legendary ice cream–movie–girl talk sleepovers, but you've got all you need." Luna eyed Rory. "Take care of her."

"Always."

"I'll see you soon." With that, Luna walked out the door, leaving her and Rory alone together again.

Grateful for the quiet and Rory's comforting presence, she sighed and tried to let the stress of the day go.

She and Rory had spent the last three days and nights together and settled into a strange routine. She worked with her father's lawyer in town to settle the estate and file for the life insurance. She turned in her schoolwork, took a test, and studied. While Rory worked the ranch, she took a few hours each day to work on her novel.

Rory fell back into work with his brothers and came up to the house for lunch and dinner, and to spend his evening with her. It seemed she fit into his family. In fact, they sat around the dinner table chatting about their day and watching TV in the evening like they'd done so for years. The men included her in their discussions, asked her opinion, and generally treated her like she belonged. She loved it.

So much so that she looked around her family home feeling like it didn't quite fit her anymore.

"Where'd you go, sweetheart?"

She shook off her tumultuous thoughts and focused on him and the question in his eyes. "Sorry. I guess I'm tired." She stared into the kitchen and at the mountain of food platters, casseroles, and desserts. "We should have sent some of this home with your brothers."

"Granddad and my brothers took a bunch of stuff out to the truck to take back to our place."

Was that *our* place, as in hers and Rory's? Or his and his family's? She let it go for now.

"I go back to work tomorrow. Poor Luna can't keep covering all my shifts."

"Are you sure that's what you want to do?"

"Why wouldn't I go back to work?"

His gaze dipped to her stomach for a split second, then shot back to her eyes. "With the money your father left you, you could stay home, finish school."

"Rory, I'm nearly done with school." Instead of talking about the baby and her being a stay-at-home mom or a working mom, she changed the subject because she was too exhausted after her father's funeral to talk in circles about something they weren't even sure about yet.

"If I cleaned all the personal items out of this place, maybe I could rent it out furnished." She left off the part about how she'd be living with him.

"That's a great idea. If you rented it to someone who wanted to use the land, you could take part of the profits from that, too. Ford would probably love something like this."

"He doesn't want to stay on your ranch and work with you and Colt?"

"I imagine that's fine with him, but to have his own place, something of his own, he might like that a hell of a lot more. We could work both ranches together. Plus it'd still be in the family, right?

See, right there was where it got complicated. He said things like that, exactly what she wanted to hear. She was a part of his family, but still, his gaze dropped to her belly and made the elation she felt being included and an intricate part of his life deflate, because it now felt conditional on her being pregnant. Like would he be saying that if they were just together and nothing happened the first time they made love.

"Sadie, what is it?"

Drawn to the sincerity in his voice, she walked into his chest and wrapped her arms around his neck. He didn't hesitate to pull her close. She rested her chin on his shoulder and sighed. "My dad died." Today she'd laid him to rest in peace beside her mother. Somehow that changed everything, despite the fact it had been several days since he'd passed. All the overwhelming feelings and tasks that needed to be done stemmed from the simple fact that her father had died and it was left to her to carry on. She didn't exactly know how to do that right this minute. Not when her life had seemed to be going in one direction, but hit a fork in the road and sent her down another path and straight into Rory's arms. Now, she felt as if finding out if she was pregnant would be another fork in the road. She was staying at Rory's, but she didn't actually live there. She had a house and ranch and her father's things to settle. And her future hinged on one yes or no answer to a question they couldn't answer right now, but could change everything about her future.

"I have so many things to do, I'm not sure what to do first."

"First and always, you take care of you. Sit down and eat something. You've been on your feet and going all day without stopping. I'll make you a cup of tea."

"Hot chocolate."

He kissed the side of her head. "You got it." His arms contracted around her. "We'll figure it out, Sadie. All of it. Together."

She leaned back and stared up at him. "Do you mean that?"

He laid his hand on her cheek. "Yes." The honesty and intensity in his eyes told her he truly meant it. "You're feeling a little lost without your dad. I get it. But you have me, Sadie. I'm not going anywhere."

She laid her forehead on his chest and breathed him in. His hand slid through her hair and held her head; his strong fingers massaged her sore neck.

"I need you," she whispered, holding him close, her fingers digging into his back muscles.

"You have me."

She appreciated it so much that he understood her saying she needed him didn't translate to she wanted to have sex with him, but that she needed him in her life for so much more. She loved him. She wanted to spend the rest of her life with him. He seemed to want the same. That gave her a sense of security. Right now, she needed it. She let everything else go and held on to the hope that the bond and connection they shared would see them through, that she and Rory would have what their parents had strived for but never got—a long and lasting marriage filled with love and family and memories that stretched decades.

Rory backed her up into the kitchen and one of the chairs at the table. He gently pushed her to sit. She did and stared up at him. He squatted in front of her and laid his hands over hers on her thighs.

"I know it feels like it, but nothing has to be decided immediately. We can take our time."

"I feel like if I don't do something I'll be stuck in this strange uncertainty forever. I don't like feeling this way. I want things to go back to the way they used to be."

"We'll clean up here, then go home. Tomorrow, when you've had some rest and are ready to face the tasks ahead, we'll plan what to do about everything else. Okay?"

"Okay."

Rory made her hot chocolate and a plate of fresh fruit and banana nut bread someone had baked and dropped off after the service when everyone paid their respects. She ate at the table, watching Rory methodically put food into the fridge for later, or store it in the cupboards. He cleaned the kitchen, took out the trash, and kept a close eye on her. By the time they left, her home looked like no one had been there since she'd last sat with her father watching TV the evening before she found him bloody in his room. It was almost as if he'd be right back. The thought made the ache inside her throb and beat with her broken heart.

They drove back to the Kendrick ranch in silence, but Rory held her hand, his thumb gently rubbing against hers. They walked into the quiet house together and went up the dark stairs and into their room. Rory didn't say a word then either, just slowly undressed her and tucked her into bed. He undressed and joined her, pulling her backside against his front, his big hand settled over her stomach as he held her in the dark.

She stared at the wall, feeling his warmth behind her and his soft breath whispering through her hair. The numbness spread through her like a virus eating up all the happiness she'd ever felt. It left her raw and aching so bad, she pressed her hand over Rory's on her belly and slid her fingers into his.

His lips settled softly on her bare shoulder for a tender kiss. The simple touch eased the ache for a split second. A second she wanted back and to build on until she felt herself again.

She glanced over her shoulder. Rory opened his eyes and stared back at her.

"Make me feel something other than this aching emptiness."

Rory's hand smoothed over her belly, down between her legs. His knee pushed between her thighs, giving him enough room to slide his fingers over her soft folds. His lips settled on her shoulder again, planting soft, wet kisses up to her neck and ear. "Stop thinking. Just feel."

She reached over her head and slid her fingers through his hair as his lips pressed another soft kiss behind her ear. "Now I'm only thinking about you."

"What do you think about this?" He slid one finger into her slick center, filling her, but not enough.

"I want more. I want you." She rocked her hips into his hand, rubbing her bottom against his growing erection. She pressed back into his hard length, making him groan.

She closed her eyes and rode the ripples of pleasure Rory's hand and mouth evoked. She let go of everything but this moment with him. Her body softened and responded to his deep, intimate touch. Pleasure gathered like a storm in her belly.

She rocked back against Rory's hard cock, seeking more of his touch. Wanting him inside her, a part of her.

"Rory," she called out into the night.

He answered, slowly pulling his hand free, rubbing it up and over her thigh. His body shifted away behind her as he reached for the condom in the drawer. She smoothed her hand down his thigh, up, and over his hard length, stroking and teasing while he tore open the condom. He sighed behind her, then nudged her hand away with the back of his and sheathed himself. His big hand settled on her hip and pulled her back to him as he thrust into her. Filled, complete, she moaned. His mouth skimmed over her shoulder, his tongue sliding against her heated skin, sending a shiver down her back. His hips moved away, then he thrust back into her hard and deep.

What started slow and sweet turned urgent. She liked it, a lot, and rocked back into him when he plunged into her again. His grip on her hip intensified. She wanted to feel his strength and lose herself in the intensity.

He thrust into her again. The hair on his thighs tickled the backs of her smooth ones. She loved the roughness of him against her softness. He slid his free arm under her arm, wrapped it around her ribs, and rolled to his back, holding on to her upper body and hip. She lay down his length, her head on his chest. His hand smoothed over her breasts, his finger plucking at her tight nipple before he palmed her whole breast and squeezed. He moved his hips below her, sliding in and out of her in a soft, smooth rhythm she matched with her up and down movements. The hand on her hip slid across her belly and down to where they were joined. His fingers skimmed over her folds as he thrust into her again, then came up, and the pad of his finger stroked her clit, sending a shockwave of heat through her system. She rolled her hips, taking him in deeper, and increasing the pressure of his finger on her clit. Wrapped in his arms, his big body moving beneath hers and in hers, she let the wave of pleasure wash through her as her body tightened around his. She rode that wave as Rory thrust into her hard and deep until his body tensed below her and he let go and joined her in the heaven they created.

Sadie lay on top of him, his arm across her ribs, his big hand over her breast. The other hand rested over her belly, his fingers splayed wide.

He adjusted below her, sending an aftershock of pleasure through her system. He kissed the side of her head and hugged her close. "Are you okay?"

"Mmm, perfect." She snuggled against him, lingering in that space between utter bliss and blissful sleep. She didn't want to move. She wanted to stay right here, close to Rory, in this lovely paradise in the dark where time seemed to halt just for them.

In life, there are moments like this you wished you could hold on to. She hoped they'd share many more just like it, but an ominous vibe shivered up her spine like someone walked over her grave. She hoped it was only her grief and uncertainty about her future intruding on this precious moment, not a forewarning of more hurt and tragedy to come.

CHAPTER 25

Sadie walked out of the bathroom after throwing up, with a cold, wet washcloth pressed to her cheek. Rory stared at her from the bed, his chest bare, his eyes filled with a mixture of concern and surprise. She wished for some happiness mixed in, but didn't see it.

"Uh, so that just happened."

His gaze dipped to her belly and back to her face. She waited for him to ask if she was sure she was pregnant or if she just had the flu. Of course he didn't ask. The silent conversations they had every time he looked at her too long, every time they made love and fell asleep with his hand over her stomach, every time she showed even the smallest sign that she was tired or not feeling well in even the slightest way turned into this festering thing between them. He blamed himself for something he couldn't have prevented. Accidents happen. This one resulted in a baby.

She'd known a week ago when she was late—she was never late—but didn't say anything to Rory. She couldn't stand to see what she saw in him right now. The inevitability of what happened next. He'd do the right thing. Marry her. They'd continue on as they had these last weeks, ignoring the fact that this happened way too fast.

She didn't say anything these last days because she'd needed time to sort out her own mind and heart. Funny, where Rory worried, she felt at peace. Happy. Even elated by the news. Her father's death had renewed her sense of living life to the fullest. Watching him deteriorate had made her want to hold on to everything she had and strive for more. She'd opened herself to Rory and love. That love turned into something wonderful they shared each and every day. Everything would be perfect if not for this black cloud hanging over them. Not the baby, but Rory's strange and confusing feelings about it. He'd be such a great father. He wanted to be a father, but the way this happened bothered him on a deep level. She wished she knew what to say to make him believe her that she didn't blame him. She wanted him and their baby and the happiness they'd share for the rest of their lives.

"Uh, do you have anything to say?"

He continued to stare at her, his face a blank mask, except for the shifting emotions in his eyes.

"How are you feeling?"

"Better than you look."

Rory sat on the edge of the bed, planted his forearms on his thighs, and hung his head.

"Right, well, I've got some things to do at my place before I head into work." She'd been working her way through the house, sorting through years of accumulated family stuff that needed to be tossed, sold, or donated to the local thrift shop. While she prepared for the future she wanted with Rory, he brooded about it.

She shrugged off her short robe and pulled out one

of the two drawers Rory gave her when she essentially moved in. Soon, she'd need more space for her things. She wanted to put her mark on their room. She didn't want to keep going back and forth between here and her place, living in this limbo.

"Sadie."

She turned and stood before Rory in nothing but her panties, her hair tied up in a messy knot she'd hastily done before she yacked in the toilet.

"What?" She let her exasperation show in the heavy sigh she let out.

Rory's gaze finally met hers. "We need to make some plans for you moving in here permanently. We'll get married."

Sadie held up her hand. "Wait. What?" Married? Just like that. She didn't want to be an obligation, she wanted . . . more . . . everything. She wanted him to love her the way she loved him.

"You're mad."

"A little bit." And a lot disappointed he didn't show an ounce of excitement or joy for their baby, or about planning a life with her.

"I'm sorry."

"That, right there." She pointed a finger at him. "You think I'm mad about the baby. Well, you're wrong. I'm happy. I'm excited. I've already started thinking of names and buying a crib and seeing *our* child in your arms.

"I don't care how it happened. I am so thrilled to be pregnant with your child. Do you get that? You're going to be an amazing father. I can't wait to be a mother. But you are taking something that is an amazing gift in our lives and are turning it into something unwelcome."

"No, sweetheart, I want this child more than I can say."

She held her hands out and let them fall back to her thighs. "Then act like it. You finally have confirmation this morning, but you don't smile or hug me or . . . anything to back that up. You look like your world just ended."

"That's not it at all."

"What am I supposed to think with the way you've been acting lately? When I come home at the end of the day, you look at me like it's been forever since you laid eyes on me and you can't wait another second to be with me. You make love to me and everything feels so right. But then there are those times when you look at me and think about the baby and the look on your face is like I did something wrong."

The phone beside the bed rang. Rory ignored it. "No, Sadie, I swear to you I . . ."

"Rory, Agent Cooke is on the phone," Ford said, standing outside their closed door.

"I'll call him back."

"He needs to talk to you now."

Sadie shook her head. "Take it. I need to get dressed and get out of here."

"Sweetheart, please listen to me."

"Agent Cooke is waiting. Why is he calling anyway?"

"Your brother stole a dozen more cattle. At this rate, I'll run out of them before he's caught."

Sadie flinched, gasped, and pressed her fingertips to her lips. "Oh my God. Again. I'm so sorry." Light-headed, she swayed and reached out to the wall to steady herself.

Rory launched himself off the bed and grabbed hold

of her shoulders to steady her. "Are you okay? You're so pale."

"I'm fine. A touch of morning sickness. That's all. I need something to eat."

Rory pulled her to the bed, turned her, and made her sit down. "I'll get something for you. Stay here."

She clasped her hand over his forearm and stopped him from leaving. "I'll get something after I get dressed. Hurry up, take your call."

"Sadie . . ."

She squeezed his hand and kissed the back of it. "It's fine. I'm fine. Go."

He leaned down and kissed her forehead. "Please let me take care of you."

"You do. You are. I'm a little off after waking up the way I did. I'm sorry I'm all over the place. It's my fault."

"Nothing is your fault. Sweetheart, I . . ."

"Rory, man, are you taking this call or what?" Ford asked, tired of waiting outside their door.

Rory huffed out a frustrated breath. "We're not done talking about this." He snagged his jeans off the chair by the window, dragged them on, along with a T-shirt he took from the dresser, opened the door, and took the phone Ford handed him. "Hello." He looked back at her one last time, his eyes filled with regret they'd left too much unsaid, then closed the door and left.

She followed him down twenty minutes later, dressed and ready to get through this day so they could talk again tonight. His muffled voice came from the office to her right at the bottom of the stairs. She went left and headed for the kitchen and something to settle her queasy stomach. She found a sleeve of crackers and made herself a mug of herbal tea. She sipped at the tea and walked into the office just as Rory hung up the phone. He stood behind the desk, staring down at the huge aerial photographs he'd taken when Agent Cooke took him up in the DEA helicopter to scout the property, looking for her brother and where he was cooking up the drugs. They'd found nothing specific and had spent the last weeks checking out one lead after another, always ending up empty-handed. One part of her was grateful they hadn't found her brother. The other part wished they would find Connor and his friends, put them out of business, and end this thing once and for all before Connor got killed. For Rory's sake, and that of his family's business, she hoped they found Connor soon.

"Hey," she said from the doorway, popping another cracker into her mouth, trying not to think about the fact he'd announced they'd get married, but had never actually asked her.

Rory's head shot up and he stared at her for a long moment. "You look better."

"Thanks. You're gorgeous as always." That earned her a kind of smile. She missed the ones he used to give her so easily when things were simple between them and all they had to worry about was the asshole who liked to watch her bleed who was still out there.

Oh, the good ol' days.

She took another sip of tea, pulled another cracker from the sleeve tucked under her arm, and popped it into her mouth.

"Can I do something for you?" The concern in his voice touched her.

She walked forward and set her tea and crackers on

the desk. She looked him in the eye and said simply, "I could use a hug."

This time the smile was genuine and filled with relief that she'd asked for something he could give her and they both needed. She didn't want to fight with him. She wanted to revel in what they'd found together. They'd find their way there.

His arms banded around her back and he rested his cheek on her head. Her hands slid up his arms to his broad shoulders. She inhaled his scent, this morning more Rory than horses, hay, and spring breezes. She rose up on tiptoe and wrapped her arms around his neck. "Not enough. Hold on to me, Rory."

"Always." His arms contracted around her into a tight bear hug, just the way she liked it.

She held him tighter, turned her head, and kissed his neck. She buried her face in his warm skin and savored this moment, both of them with their barriers down, completely connected.

His big hands rubbed up and down her back, settling on her hips. He gently set her away. "I've got work to do, but I hate to leave things between us so . . ."

"We're fine, Rory." She put her hand over his heart and smiled softly up at him. "Everything is going to be fine."

"As long as I have you, I have everything."

Surprised by his sweet words, she stood stunned, staring up at him. "Rory, I . . ."

He kissed her softly, cutting off the words she'd held inside her far too long. She loved him. She wanted to tell him dozens of times, but it never seemed right. Until now, when in his quiet way he told her he loved her without actually saying it. Maybe that's all this was between them. He needed to hear the words from her. He needed some kind of reassurance that she cared as much as him.

Rory ended the soft kiss far too soon for her liking. He traced one finger over her forehead and down her cheek. "You take it easy today. When you get home, how about we take a walk down by the creek and talk."

She held the words of love lodged in her throat, thinking that tonight, when they were alone at sunset by the water, would be a perfect time to tell him. "I'd like that."

"Do you mind if we keep this"—he cocked his head toward her belly—"to ourselves for a little while?"

"It's best to keep it to ourselves for the first trimester. The chances of losing the baby are greatest in the first couple months."

"How do you know that?"

"I got a book last week. I've been reading it in my truck on my lunch break."

"You've known for a week and didn't say anything."

"I wasn't hiding it from you. I wanted to be sure."

He took two steps away, then turned back to her. "If you're not feeling well and need me to come get you, call me. I've always got my cell with me. If you can't reach me, call the ranch. Granddad can reach me on one of the radios."

"I'm fine, honey. Really."

"I need you to know if you need me . . ."

"I already know, Rory. I'll see you tonight when I get home. Pack us a sunset picnic to take on our walk."

She almost hesitated to suggest another picnic after the way the last one turned out, but Rory gave her a soft, indulgent smile and nodded, making her glad she'd said it, giving them a chance to put the past to rest and start new tonight. He turned and left to catch up with his brothers and start his work day, especially since he'd slept in with her again.

Sadie turned back to the desk for her tea. She took a sip and stared down at the huge photo of the ranch from above. Quite a spread. The creek ran down one side. A river snaked through the top portion. Grassland, clumps of trees, dirt roads, and cows spread over thousands of acres. Something caught her attention, but she wasn't quite sure what she saw. It looked like a misty cloud over a rocky hill, but the helicopter couldn't have been up that high to hover over a cloud. It hit her all at once. Not a cloud. Smoke from a stove or fire venting out of the hill through a natural or manmade hole. A cave. The perfect place to hide an illegal meth lab and a bunch of wanted criminals.

Rory's words came back to her. *I'm trying to keep you safe.* As much as she'd like to save her brother from jail, she had to face the truth. She couldn't save him from anything anymore. He'd crossed the line. Rory wanted to protect her. She wanted to protect their child and their life together. She wanted to move forward. Tell Rory she loved him. Marry him. Raise this child and more with him.

She turned the pad of paper on the desk around, found a pen under the stack of photos and wrote Rory a note.

Rory, you smoked Connor out. I've given him until sunset to turn himself in. If he doesn't, I'll call Agent Cooke myself. I can't wait to see you tonight. Love, Sadie.

Sadie set the note on the picture and went into the kitchen to drop her mug in the dishwasher and pull her phone out of her purse. She found the last number Connor used to contact her and texted him.

SADIE: Connor, this is your last chance. Turn yourself in by sunset and I will pay for a lawyer to represent you against the MANY charges against you. If not, you're on your own.

"Hey, pretty girl. On your way to work?" Grandpa Sammy asked.

"Heading out now. When you see Rory, would you tell him I left him a note in the office."

"Sure thing, pretty girl. You have a good day."

"You too." She kissed Sammy on the cheek, smiling when he grinned at her. She loved the old guy. He nagged his grandsons unmercifully about settling down and giving him a grandbaby. She couldn't wait to tell him that Rory was finally going to give him one.

CHAPTER 26

Connor stared in disbelief at his phone and the text his sister sent him. He'd kept this burner and turned it on once a day hoping to hear from Sadie. Hoping she changed her mind and came through for him. He threw the phone against the cave wall, splintering it into several pieces on the jagged rocks. He stomped on several pieces on the floor, freaking out and trying to think what this really meant.

"Fuck." If she made good on her threat, he was screwed. He'd spend the next ten-plus years of his life in a cell. If Torres's people didn't kill him first to keep him from talking.

"What the hell is wrong with you now?" Derek asked, dropping the duffel bag filled with cold medicine on the floor.

Frustrated, pissed, he spoke without thinking. "We're fucked."

Derek's gaze locked on him. His eyes narrowed to menacing slits. "What do you mean?"

Sadie's cryptic message could mean only one thing. "She's going to rat me out to the cops."

"Did you fucking tell your sister where we are?"

"No."

"Then how does she know?"

Connor didn't really know, but his paranoia about recent events led him to one conclusion. "You heard the damn helicopter."

"Enough about the damn helicopter. I told you a dozen times, it's nothing but the forestry service or news copters."

"And you say I'm stupid. It's the cops hunting us down." The hairs on the back of his neck stood on end.

"Then why aren't they surrounding this place demanding we come out with our hands up?"

"They will be soon."

"You should have let me fucking kill her."

Connor scratched at his arm, drawing blood from the wound that never healed because he couldn't leave it alone for all the creepy crawlies under his skin. The anger rose up inside him, turning into a fury he couldn't control.

"You don't have to. I'm going to fucking teach her a lesson."

If she'd just helped him out when he needed the money to get out of this mess, he'd be out of this damn cave and living somewhere with a shower, a refrigerator, some fucking decent heat.

"She can't fucking tell me what to do anymore. I'm a grown man, not some kid for her to order around and bend to her will. I'll make her see. She can't take everything and leave me to fend for myself. She owes me. Half that fucking ranch is mine, and she's going to pay up or fucking shut up for good."

Connor grabbed his backpack and headed for the cave entrance.

"Go get her, man. Fuck that bitch up." Derek answered his ringing phone. "Trigger, man, too bad you're not here. Connor is worked up and after his fucking bitch of a sister. It's hilarious."

Only Derek would get off on Connor's need for revenge.

Connor didn't often regret anything in his life, but as he stepped out of the hole he'd been living in far too long, he wished things hadn't gone so far or so wrong. He wished he lived back on the ranch, in his room and the home he'd always known. He'd like a shower, a hot meal, to watch TV and kick back with a few beers. He hadn't had any of that in a long time. He'd likely never have it again. Not here. Not with the cops after him. Not with his sister about to rat him out. That fucking Kendrick cowboy stole her away and turned her against him.

Everybody walked all over him. Derek. His sister. He was tired of going along. He wanted to be in charge. He'd show his sister that she couldn't threaten him and get away with it. If Derek ever pulled that knife on him again, he'd bury it in the guy's chest.

Fuck his sister and her do-the-right-thing bitching. He'd show her. She'd pay up his half of the ranch, or else. Yeah. She'd give him what she owed, so he could get out of here before he ended up dead or in a cell. He'd find a new place to live where no one knew him, no one told him what to do, and his own sister didn't fuck him over.

CHAPTER 27

Rory walked into the kitchen after coming back to the house early to shower and pack the picnic dinner Sadie requested. At first, all he could think about was what happened last time they went on a picnic. A split second after that, he thought of this picnic and the chance she gave him to make things right. To celebrate the baby on the way. To tell her how much he loved her and couldn't wait for them to be a real family. In fact, he'd snuck away three days ago to buy her a ring. He didn't even tell his brothers. He'd kept it from his grandfather. He could add up the time he'd been with Sadie and come up with the fact she was late and they were having a baby. He didn't need the wake-up call this morning to confirm it. He'd been waiting on her to tell him for sure so he could gauge how she felt about it.

If he read her right, she'd only given him a small glimpse of how truly happy and excited she was about the baby. He owed her the same, because she'd read him all wrong. She saw his worry and concern, but she hadn't looked deeper to see that he wanted her, this baby, and any more she'd gift him. The weeks they'd shared together proved his life before had been so much less than complete. Now, if he lost her, he'd know what he was missing and life wouldn't be worth living.

His grandfather walked in and slapped him on the shoulder to get his attention. "Hey, son, your girl left you a note in the office."

"What's it say?"

"How should I know, it's your note."

"Didn't you work in there today?"

"No, I went into town most of the day to get supplies and have my checkup with my sweet thing."

His granddad loved Dr. Bell, or Dr. Bowden as she went by now that she'd married Dane. She'd always be his granddad's sweet thing and just Bell to Rory and his brothers. They'd gotten close these last months since she and his buddy Dane got together. Dane was the complete opposite of him. Dane played the field and left every blonde for a hundred miles in his wake, but he'd fallen for Bell, and they shared something special. Rory had seen it every time they got together, and he'd wanted the same for himself. He never thought he'd have it, because while Dane had run wild, Rory had somehow turned into a hermit on his ranch. Not by choice, but by circumstance. Now, he'd give up everything to spend his life with Sadie and their baby.

"Everything okay?" Rory's concern for his aging grandfather rose up.

"Fit as a fiddle. Blood pressure is down, so she adjusted my medication. What's going on with you and my pretty girl?"

"Nothing."

"Don't look likc nothing. You keep staring at her like she holds the key to some secret."

"She's the key, Granddad. She unlocked everything good in my life."

"Is that right?"

"Yeah. Don't gloat. I get that you're happy I found someone, but I really don't need you pressuring me right now."

"Oh, why is that if everything is so great with you two?"

"It is great, but we've got something we need to talk about and some plans to make. Let us do it in our own way and in our own time."

"Things have moved pretty fast. It seems to be working for you, so why slow things down now?"

"I'm not slowing things down." In fact, he planned to take a huge leap forward. Forget all the getting to know you better, living with each other to see if things worked out. No, he planned to marry her and love her and do anything and everything to make her happy the rest of her life.

"Okay then."

"That's it. After all the pushing, that's all you have to say?"

"I wanted you to open yourself up to letting a woman into your life and experiencing a real and true partnership that is based on love. You've done that. You know what it is now. It is the better part of life. It is what makes us live and live well."

"You don't have to convince me that Sadie is the best thing in my life. Everything will work out. It has to."

"Rory, if something is wrong . . ."

"It's not. It's good. Really great. I need her to know that I feel that way."

His grandfather pushed him toward the office. "Go see what she left you."

Rory walked into the office thinking of all he needed to do for his picnic, but mostly he tried to think of an imaginative way to ask her to marry him. It needed to be special. Especially after the underwhelming way he'd reacted to the pregnancy news.

The note sat atop the large photos he'd left on the desk. He thought he might frame the one that showed the house, barns, and pastures. With his mind on picture frames, he turned the note and absently read the words.

"Fuck." Rory read the note again, trying to understand what she meant about him smoking out Connor. "Damnit, Sadie, why didn't you just tell me where to find him?"

Rory pulled his cell from his pocket and dialed her phone. The nerves in his belly tightened his gut. It twisted painfully when her phone went to voice mail. He waited out her sweet voice telling him to leave a message. "Sadie, sweetheart, call me the minute you get this."

Something about the note niggled at his mind. He stared down at the photo again and back at the note and back again, wondering what she'd seen that he missed. Her words didn't make sense.

Smoking. Smoke.

His eyes locked on the spot he'd picked up the letter from and stared at the hills and the puff of smoke that looked more like a wispy cloud. He'd missed it the other times he studied the pictures. He'd been looking for a trailer, shed, or some other makeshift building hidden in the trees or out on some remote spot on the property. He'd never thought to look in the caves.

"Fuck." Frustrated she'd seen what he missed, and might have put herself and their child in jeopardy by tipping off Connor that she knew where to find him, he tried her cell again. Nothing. Voice mail. It could be nothing but that she'd gotten busy on her shift at the diner and couldn't answer. She might have left her phone in her purse, despite the fact he'd told her to keep it close just in case.

His mind spun one dark thought after another; all of them ended badly.

He jumped when his phone rang. He swiped the screen to accept the call and put it to his ear without looking to see who called and desperate to hear Sadie's voice. "Sadie, where are you?"

"It's Agent Cooke."

"What now?"

"Something is going down right now. I'm not sure what, but I got a cryptic message from Beck about Connor going off on some drug-induced tirade. I take it Sadie isn't with you."

"No. She found the hole Connor's been hiding in. She gave him an ultimatum to turn himself in today or she'd turn him in."

"Where should she be?"

"At work."

"Hold on. I just got something."

Rory held the line, with his patience straining against the precarious grip he tried to hold on to for Sadie's sake. She needed him calm and thinking clearly, not going off half-cocked and out for murder if her brother put her in harm's way. Again.

Sadie cleared the dirty dishes from a table and loaded them into the plastic tub. She pulled the wet rag from her apron and wiped down the table. Tired after her shift and ready to go home to Rory, she picked up the heavy tub and carried it back to the kitchen and set it next to the sink.

"Here you go, Ronnie."

"Thanks a lot." The sarcasm in the young guy's words made Sadie smile. He worked hard, but didn't really like cleaning up at the diner. Still, he made decent money for a high school senior.

"You headed home to that smokin' hot man of yours?" Luna stared at her from the other side of the counter. She stuffed her order ticket into the carousel and spun it toward the cook.

"I am. We've planned a sunset picnic."

Luna gave her a saucy smile and a wink. "Going to have something hot and sweet for dessert under the stars?"

The smile bloomed easily on Sadie's face and in her heart. "I hope so." Sadie worried about her friend working the late shift and getting off in the wee hours of the morning. "Careful driving home tonight. It's awful dark on those back roads."

"I will. We need a girls' night soon."

"Definitely." Sadie wanted to share her news with her best friend, but first she needed to clear the air with Rory so they could celebrate.

The bell over the door jingled. "Hey there, Wayne. How's my favorite customer." Luna and Wayne had a regular Tuesday and Thursday night dinner date. Wayne ate here each week. Same days. Same time. Always in Luna's section. He ate, but he really came for her company.

"I'll leave you to your hunky cowboy." Sadie winked at her friend.

"He's my guy," Luna said with such affection, Sadie believed she really did have a soft spot for the silver-haired man.

"Have fun. I'm outta here." Sadie stopped off in the small office to collect her purse and sweatshirt. She pushed her arms through the sleeves and zipped up the front over her white T-shirt and black denim skirt. Her feet ached in her black boots. She couldn't wait to get home and take them off. Well, after her dinner with Rory. They had some things to talk about, but she knew it would all work out. It had to. For their sakes and the baby's. Life couldn't be so cruel to take her mother and father so young, then bring Rory into her life to show her real and true happiness, only to take it away before they'd really had a chance to live the life they both wanted. Yes, things hadn't happened the usual way for them, but they loved each other. They deserved a chance to be happy.

She had Rory and the baby, and all she needed now was to end this business with her brother. Stop him from stealing Rory blind, and get him to accept that he needed to take responsibility and pay the consequences of his actions. When faced with jail or death, most rational people would choose a life behind bars to no life at all. Her brother hadn't acted rationally in a long time. She hoped he found a clear moment to realize she was trying to save his life.

Sadie walked back through the kitchen area, waved goodbye to Ronnie, and stepped out the back door, breathing in the cold evening air. She dug her keys out of her purse and headed for her truck. Halfway across the parking lot, she stopped midstride, pivoted, and headed back to the diner to grab two thick slices of apple pie to take on her picnic. She'd smelled the sweet, cinnamon scent all afternoon and craved a slice. She hadn't eaten in hours. Her stomach grumbled even at the thought of food.

Shoes scuffed across the blacktop behind her, rushing and drawing close. She turned to look over her shoulder just as someone grabbed her around the chest, his hands locked in front of her. She couldn't move her arms, but struggled to get free.

"Let me go."

"You're coming with me." Connor's deep voice held a hysterical edge. High, he'd probably been binging on meth for days. He smelled like stale cigarette smoke, beer, and body odor. His bony chest pressed against her shoulder blades. After she'd been held in Rory's strong arms, against all his tight muscles, the difference in her brother's scrawny frame startled her. His choices were sucking the life right out of him.

"Connor, let me go." She struggled to break his hold, but he didn't release her. Stronger than he looked, he managed to haul her back several feet to a waiting car with the trunk open.

"Don't you dare."

He didn't heed her warning and shoved her backward, so she fell into the gaping hole. Her shoulders hit a tire iron. Connor pulled her feet up over the lip and they thudded on the spare tire. She reached for Connor, but he swatted her hands back, grabbed her purse strap, and yanked it away from her. He pulled a gun from behind his back and pointed it right at her chest. She immediately covered her belly with both hands.

"Stay put. Don't move."

Sadie narrowed her eyes, fury spreading through her body in a wave of anger she couldn't contain. "This is the second time you've pointed a gun at me. You truly have lost your mind, you know that? I get my hands on you, I'll teach you a lesson about empty threats and doing stupid things."

"It's no threat. You move, and I'll shoot you."

She almost believed him, but then his hand shook and a trace of fear filled his eyes. He couldn't quite make himself do it. Instead, he slammed the trunk, sending her into darkness. She sighed out her relief, knowing next time she might not be so lucky. Her brother was slowly losing his mind.

"Fucking bitch. You think you can just turn me in to the cops. Your flesh and blood. No fucking way."

She slammed the flats of her hands up against the trunk lid and pounded them against the rough metal over and over again. "Let me out. We can talk about this."

"I'm done talking. All you do is tell me what to do. He left you everything. Half that ranch is mine." She heard the deep hurt and anguish in his voice. He missed their father and grieved for him as hard as Sadie did. They'd done it alone, because he'd chosen his life and she'd chosen hers and they no longer shared the bonds they'd once had as children.

"Connor, please, let me out. We'll talk this through. I'll pay for a lawyer."

"I don't need a fucking lawyer. I need money. With you out of the way, it'll all be mine."

Stupid idiot. He couldn't possibly believe that he'd see a dime from their father's estate when the cops were after him. Irrational, delusional. Sadie slammed her hand against the trunk lid again.

The returned hard thud made her jump. He must have slammed his fist on top of the trunk. That didn't disturb her as much as the warning and ominous tone in his words. He'd gone to the dark side, drawn in by the drugs and the evil men he hung out with until he believed the only way to handle a problem was to eliminate it.

"Connor." No answer. "Connor!"

The driver's door creaked open. She didn't even know where he'd gotten the car. The door slammed and the engine roared to life. He hit the gas and the tires spun in the dirt and gravel parking lot.

They hit the blacktop and raced away from the diner. Away from her only chance to get help. She hoped someone discovered her missing before it was too late. How long would Rory wait before looking for her? She didn't know where Connor planned to take her. She hoped to his hideaway in the hills. If so, she hoped Rory got her note. She hoped he figured out where to find her and got to her in time.

CHAPTER 28

Rory was ready to punch something when Agent Cooke came back on the line. "What's happened?"

"Connor apparently made delivery to get him out of the trouble he was in weeks ago, but he and the others got hijacked. DEA took down the rivals and confiscated the drugs, but Connor's in debt to Torres now and promised an even bigger shipment . . ."

"And he's about to choke on it if he doesn't come through with the product."

"Connor's been on a three-day binge. When he got Sadie's text, he went off the rails."

"What does that mean?"

"He stole some guy's car out of a gas station."

"Great, he's compounding the charges against him."

"There's more."

"Of course there is." Rory didn't hide the sarcasm in his voice, but his gut twisted painfully, thinking that Connor acting out resulted in only one thing: Sadie paying the price.

"The guy he stole the car from keeps a loaded .45 under the seat. The details are sketchy at best, but when

Connor took off, he went looking for his sister. Beck is trying to find them now."

Rory slid his hand over the back of his neck and squeezed his tight muscles. He tried to think what Connor would do. Would he hurt his sister? He'd never done so in the past. Not physically, but if he was tweaking hard on drugs, out of his mind, and looking for retribution, he just might be capable of anything.

"We need to find Sadie. She's not picking up her cell."

"I've got someone checking her work," Agent Cooke assured him.

"Not good enough. We need agents on my property."

"We've searched everywhere and found nothing."

"Yeah, well, we should have had Sadie look at the pictures with us. She found him. That's why he's after her. She threatened to turn him in unless he did so himself."

"Why didn't she call me? If she's giving him time to escape—"

"It's nothing like that," Rory cut him off. "She wanted him to do the right thing. To see he's got no way out of this and if he keeps going down the path he's chosen, he'll only end up dead."

"Fine. I'll give her the benefit of the doubt."

"Trust me. As much as she doesn't want to see her brother behind bars, it's a better option than burying another member of her family."

"You got that right. I'm headed your way. We'll land the chopper on your property like we did last time. You can point out the location we need to check and we'll see if we can't end this thing before dark."

Rory stared out the window at the sun sinking fast.

They had only a couple of hours before nightfall. He wouldn't get his picnic with Sadie.

"I need to know where Sadie is. I'll call the diner, see if I can find her."

"Too late," Agent Cooke said with a distinct note of inevitability and regret in his voice. "I just received word. Our agent checked the diner. She left thirty minutes ago at the end of her shift according to staff, but her truck is still in the lot. The agent found her purse tossed in the truck bed."

"Which means she doesn't have her phone. You're sure?"

"The agent found some distinct tire treads in the lot. Someone peeled out of there in a hurry."

"Connor grabbed her."

"It looks that way."

"But what does he plan to do with her?" Rory didn't want to think about it. "Get here as fast as you can. I'll be ready." Rory hung up and went to the gun cabinet. He pulled out three rifles and the shells and loaded each and every one of them.

The car bumped over ruts and skidded around corners, the back end swinging out around a curve in the dirt road her brother drove down way too fast. Sadie rolled toward the backseat, hit her shoulder on the top of the car, and threw her hands in front of her to stop her momentum as the car came to a jarring halt.

She rolled to her back and held her breath when the car door opened, then slammed. She put her hands up in front of her, ready to ward off an attack. If her brother brought her to Derek with the devil tattoo and evil intentions, she'd need all her wits about her to either talk her way out of this situation or fight him off before he hurt her. She tried not to let her mind go to the baby, but the worry for her child had grown into a living thing inside her that made her heart race and her insides grow cold with fear.

"Connor, please, let me out of here." The suffocating stale oil- and gas-tinged air threatened to choke her and send her into a panic attack. She tried to remain calm, but the too warm, cramped compartment closed in on her. Her whole body broke out in a sweat in the stifling interior. She desperately needed some fresh air and water.

Metal scratched metal and a snick sounded a second before the trunk popped open. Dim light filtered in. She blinked away the temporary blindness and scrambled out of the trunk. She launched herself at Connor, smacking him on the shoulder.

"What the hell? You can't just dump me in there and drive off with me."

"I guess I can and I did."

A black Mustang pulled in behind her brother, skidding to a stop and sending up a cloud of dust. Trigger jumped out, his eyes narrowed, his lips pulled back in a tight line. "What the fuck did you do?"

"Where the hell did you come from? You can't be here. If Derek finds you here, I'm dead."

"You're already dead, dumbshit. That fucking cowboy comes for her, he'll kill you."

Sadie fisted her brother's shirt in her hands and shook him. "It's over, Connor. Rory knows about this place." She hoped she wasn't bluffing. She hoped he got her note and read its meaning. She kicked herself for not being explicit and putting a big damn X-marks-the-spot on the photograph. She should have done what her father expected and done the hard thing. "I should have turned you in the second I discovered this place. If there's a bad choice and worse choice, you choose to make things worse every damn time."

Connor exploded, grabbing her shirt and hauling her up to her toes. "Not this time. This time, I'm in control."

"Bullshit. You can't even control yourself. You're high. You haven't slept in days by the looks of you. You have absolutely no plan. You think getting rid of me will solve all your problems, but that's not you, Connor."

"You get everything you ever want. This time, it's mine." Connor's eyes glassed over with mania, brought on by the drugs he cooked up and sent out into the world. Those drugs ruined lives. They'd ruined Connor's.

She planted both hands on Connor and shoved him back, breaking his hold on her. "Why are you doing this? You don't want to hurt me. You're angry and hurting because Dad died. You don't know what to do with all that grief, so you're trying to take it out on me. The thing is, I'm done, Connor. I can't do this anymore. I won't be the person you blame, the one you hurt to make yourself feel better, the one you take and take and take from without giving anything back. I won't be your scapegoat for all that's wrong in your life. I can't watch you waste away, those drugs stealing your dreams, your future, your life. I can't. I won't."

"It's about time you got back," Derek called, walking out of the cave behind Connor and dropping two large duffel bags at his feet.

Sadie hadn't paid much attention since leaping out of the back of the trunk and confronting her whacked-out brother. The hum of a generator nearby droned on and added to the whooshing gusts of wind whipping through the gully between the rocky hills on both sides of them. The dark hole in the side of the hill wasn't much more than a wide jagged slit with a large over-hang that shadowed the entrance. Large trees grew nearby; their canopy overhung the gap between the hills that came together not far from where the dirt road ended at this secluded hideaway.

The shack concealed by large bushes with fans in the windows could only be the place Connor cooked up death.

Derek stopped midstride when his gaze collided with hers. The vile smile died quickly when Trigger shifted behind her, drawing Derek's attention.

"Are you stupid or suicidal? Why would you bring him here? This place is off-limits to everyone but us," Derek said.

"I didn't bring him here. I took her, but he came out of nowhere."

"You took her?" Derek strode forward, making Sadie's gut tighten with nerves. Adrenaline surged through her veins. Her heart thrashed against her ribs so hard she could barely breathe. She wanted to run, but froze in place, knowing better than to play the scared fawn to Derek's wolf. She plastered on a bored expression, hoping to cover the fear building inside her.

Connor puffed out his bony chest and sneered at her. "Yeah. She won't fuck this up for me. If she can't turn me in, I can deliver. I'll finally be set."

Trigger swore and shook his head. "Torres will

never let you out from under his thumb. You're living on borrowed time. If the drugs don't kill you, Torres will when you fuck up again and put his operation in jeopardy like you did when those guys hijacked the shipment and the cops showed up."

Sadie turned and stepped back, putting all three men in front of her.

Connor tried to keep up his bravado, but the sweat trailing down his face and the way his gaze shifted back and forth showed how out of control he felt. "If Torres doesn't want to work with us, we'll go with the deal Guzman offered."

Trigger swore. Connor's gaze fell to the dirt. Derek's eyes filled with fury. Sadie had no idea what was really going on here, but it all felt wrong.

Derek pulled his knife and pointed it at Connor. "Why can't you keep your fucking mouth shut?"

"Me? You're the one who blabbed at that bar that we had a huge score moving through Missoula. You nearly got Trigger killed. He barely escaped getting shot and arrested."

Sadie's gaze flew to Trigger. The man gave nothing away in his eyes or expression. He kept his unyielding attention locked on Derek and the knife.

"Something else went down that night." The suspicion in Derek's voice matched the gleam of distrust in his narrowed gaze.

Trigger reminded her of a lion ready to pounce. "People get caught for one simple reason. They can't shut up."

"Still, how'd those cops get there so fast? I might have tipped off the other side, but someone else ratted us out to the cops."

"You're already playing both sides with Torres and Guzman, maybe the reason you think you can get away with it is because you're the rat squeaking to the cops," Trigger shot back.

"Fuck you. I'm no snitch."

"You're not loyal either, except to the almighty dollar you keep chasing with no regard for the threat Torres and Guzman pose if they find out you're playing both of them."

Connor stepped forward, confusion lighting his eyes. He tilted his head, eyes narrowed on Derek. "Is it true? Did you tell the cops? Are you the reason that batch got fucked up? Are you the reason I've got Torres breathing down my neck for the hundred grand?"

"Connor, no. You can't possibly owe that much money," Sadie said.

Connor turned to her and in a moment of clarity discovered the truth. "This is what they do; they suck you in and make it impossible to get out. I can't get out."

"Connor, you can get out. Turn yourself in, and I will help you."

"There's no help for him now. He goes to the cops and Torres will have him killed. Don't you get it, bitch, they own him now." Derek turned back to Trigger. "But they don't own you. You've stayed on the outside of things. You push to get in, but never quite get your hands dirty. You tipped off the cops." Derek pointed the knife straight at Trigger's chest. "You're a fucking cop, aren't you?"

"Shifting the blame? Covering up what you did by accusing me?" Trigger shook his head, his lips drawn back in a tight line. "If anyone fucked up, it's you and him." Trigger cocked his head toward Connor. "You two are bumbling your way through this shit instead of keeping your heads clear and sticking to business. You should be cooking up the next batch," he said to Connor. "Instead, you've stolen a car and kidnapped your sister. What the fuck were you thinking?"

Connor grew even more agitated, scratching at his arm and making it bleed. "I did what I had to do."

"The only thing you had to do was deliver," Trigger snapped. "And you, you stupid fuck. Who the hell goes into a bar and brags about a drug shipment and a big score? It's no wonder Torres is trying to cut you out and replace you with someone who knows their shit."

Derek remained calm while Connor fidgeted and paced back and forth. Sadie stood absolutely still, trying not to draw anyone's attention.

"Let me guess, you want to be the one Torres puts in my place. That's why you've been working me to introduce you to him," Derek said, going utterly still. The ominous vibe rolling off him frightened Sadie. One spark could ignite a fire and start a fight that no one would win.

Trigger planted his hands on his hips. "Which is it, asshole? I'm a snitch out to take you down, or I'm the one who wants to take your place?"

"Either one puts you in line to work with Torres."

"I don't know why I fucking try to keep you two in line and focused on the business. We're supposed to be making money, instead we spend all our time cleaning up one mess after the next." Trigger glared at Connor. "There's no getting out of this fuckup. You're going down for kidnapping."

"No, I won't."

Trigger raised his hands and let them fall and slap

his thighs. "What are you going to do? Go for broke and kill her? You really want to spend the rest of your life in jail? Face it, you couldn't live with yourself if something happened to her."

"Maybe all we need to do is get rid of her and make it look like you did it," Derek suggested, crouching, ready to strike, the knife held out in front of him.

Trigger pointed his finger at Derek. "You better put me down first, because there's no fucking way I let you put a hand on her again."

"Is that right?"

"Try it and find out," Trigger taunted.

An engine rumbled in the distance drawing closer.

"Looks like you get to meet the big boss man himself."

Trigger locked eyes with Derek. "You invited Torres here?"

"He wants to see what we've got going. He wants to pick up what we've got. Connor made up a really clean and pure batch. This will appease Torres and set things right."

Trigger frowned. "You're lying to yourself if you think Torres will ever trust you."

The car drove in behind Trigger. Armed men poured out of the SUV ahead of a man in khaki pants and a denim shirt, his black hair slicked back, his dark brown eyes locked on them.

Sadie didn't need any introductions. The man had power and death in his eyes. He commanded the space around him. One look made his men fan out as they approached.

Connor tilted his head to the side. "Do you hear that?

It's another helicopter," Connor blurted out. "I told you. It's the cops."

Trigger slanted his gaze toward her, then cast it over to the trees. The whap, whap, whap of helicopter blades drew closer. Rory had gotten her message. That, or Trigger had contacted his brother. Either way, help was coming.

Torres's gaze narrowed on Derek and her brother. "You set me up."

His men drew their weapons. Everyone, including Sadie, ducked for cover. Torres ran back to his vehicle, jumping in even as it backed out. His men shot at them to cover Torres's retreat as they ran to the car and climbed on the running boards and dove into the back.

The chopper crested the hill, gliding in fast.

Derek went after Trigger. "You fucking sold us out." Derek lunged for Trigger, swiping the knife through the air at Trigger's gut. He jumped back out of the way, then swung his huge fist straight into Derek's jaw, sending him to the ground.

The helicopter hovered overhead, whipping up dirt and leaves in the downwash. Sadie backed up, blocking her face with her hands to keep from getting anything in her eyes. Trigger walked toward her. In the commotion, she lost track of Connor, but spotted him when Trigger reached for his head, fell to his knees, and face-planted in the dirt. Her brother stood behind him, a rock in his hand. He raised it to smash it into Trigger's skull again. Rory ran out from the trees and tackled him to the ground as a shot rang out from above. Connor grabbed his bleeding leg and howled in pain, then went berserk, trying to fight off Rory to get away. Rory held him down and shook him to get him to stop.

Sadie ran to Trigger and rolled him over. His eyes fluttered and squinted against the chopper's downwash. She leaned over him and brushed her fingers over his long hair at the base of his head. Her fingers came away sticky with blood. His eyes went wide, his gaze locked on something behind her. She glanced over her shoulder too late to move out of the way. Derek plunged the knife in his hands down toward Trigger's chest. She gasped, lying herself over Trigger's body, hoping the inevitable didn't happen. Trigger tried to push her away, but not in time. DEA agents ran out from every direction. Another shot rang out and a heavy weight landed on her back, the knife slicing through her shoulder. Fire exploded down her arm and up her neck. She stared across the dirt and grass at Rory with his knee planted on her brother's back, a DEA bulletproof vest covering his chest and a small gun in his hand pointed in her direction. Shocked, her vision tunneled in and winked out.

CHAPTER 29

Rory dropped the gun and lunged for Sadie the second her eyes fell closed. The blood running down the top of her shoulder and over Trigger frightened him more than the fact he'd shot Derek and dropped him right on top of the woman he loved. Rory shoved Derek off her. One of the DEA agents dragged him several feet away, dumped him in the dirt, then checked his pulse. Trigger grabbed Sadie by the shoulders and rolled her off him, gently laying her next to him. The bloody knife fell away.

Rory dropped to his knees beside her, thankful the knife wasn't sticking in her, but still scared out of his mind that she'd passed out. "Sadie. Sadie, sweetheart, please wake up. Please be okay," he begged.

The helicopter finally moved away and disappeared over the treetops. Rory thought he'd be able to think again without all the noise, but all he did was think one thought. He couldn't lose her.

"Please be okay." He ran his shaking hand over her pale face and laid it on her soft cheek.

Trigger pulled her sweatshirt away from the wound. "Look, man, it's not that bad."

"She's bleeding."

"He didn't stab her, just cut her deep on the top of her shoulder. She'll need stitches, but it's not that bad. See." The relieved sigh Trigger let out eased Rory's worry, but not enough to slow his racing heart.

Rory took his eyes off Sadie's too pale face and studied the open gash seeping blood that oozed from the wound. Trigger was right. It wasn't that bad. It could have been a hell of a lot worse.

"Rory," Sadie mumbled, her eyes fluttering open.

"Sadie." Her name came out on a relieved exhale. "Are you okay?"

"My shoulder hurts."

Trigger took the gauze one of the DEA agents handed him and pressed it to the bleeding wound.

"Ow!" Sadie tried to move away from Trigger and the pressure he put on the wound. "Stop."

Rory brushed his fingers over her forehead and into her hair. "Shh, you're okay. It's okay. You're bleeding. He cut you."

"He likes to watch me bleed."

"He's dead, sweetheart. He'll never hurt you again."

Sadie let out a ragged sigh. "You saved Connor." She rolled her head and stared over at her wailing brother. Another agent wrapped a bandage around his leg. He tried to shove the agent away with his handcuffed hands. "The shooter in the helicopter would have killed him to save Trigger."

"Beck," Trigger corrected her. "Thank you for keeping my secret. You saved my life."

She placed her hand over Rory's heart. "Rory saved us."

An SUV skidded to a halt at the edge of the clearing. Agent Cooke jumped out, went to the back of the vehicle, and pulled Torres out of the backseat and stared at them.

Sadie smiled. "Beck, turn around."

Beck turned and sighed, hanging his head, his eyes closed.

"It's over," Sadie whispered. "You're out."

Rory loved her so damn much for keeping Beck's secret and understanding all the man couldn't say to her but needed her to understand. Beck had reached out to her in a silent plea to let his brother know he needed to get out. She saw that need inside him. Recognized it because she'd been looking for a way out of this futile situation with her brother. The depth of emotion hidden behind the wall Rory felt around Beck and all he kept hidden behind his closed eyes told him how much Beck needed this to be over. The look he leveled on Sadie conveyed a depth of emotion Rory didn't understand.

Sadie did. She reached out and took Beck's hand in hers and held it tight. "You can go home now, Beck. Caden is waiting for you."

"I'll never forget what you did, laying yourself over me like that. If he'd managed to plunge that knife into my—"

"Stop. It's over, Beck. Go home."

Caden walked up behind Beck and planted his hand on Beck's shoulder. "She's right, little brother, it's done. We got him."

Sadie pressed her good arm on the grass and leaned forward. Rory helped her to sit up. She immediately touched her hand to her too pale face, rolled to her side, and heaved, gagging, but nothing came up. She curled in on herself and held her stomach. "Rory," she begged. "Something's wrong."

Rory reached for her, but she went limp in his hands. "No. No. We need an ambulance."

"Chopper is just past the trees in the field," Caden said, kneeling beside Sadie. "What's wrong?"

"She's pregnant."

The shocked and distraught look that crossed Beck's face matched the worry engulfing Rory's system that she might have saved Trigger, but Rory might have lost her and their baby.

The helicopter ride to the hospital nearly sent Rory into a tailspin. Sadie remained groggy, but not truly conscious. He didn't want to think the worst.

The minute the chopper touched down on the hospital helipad, doctors and nurses whisked Sadie away. He'd been relegated to sitting in the waiting room answering questions for the DEA agent Caden sent to take his statement. He'd put the agent off long enough to call Bell and beg her to haul ass down here to check on Sadie. He didn't trust anyone else.

"Mr. Kendrick, Dr. Bowden asked me to come get you. Your girlfriend is waiting for you down here." The nurse held out her arm to indicate the hallway that led into the emergency room. Rory stood and followed her, his stomach tied in knots, his heart barely beating. The closer he got to her, the less he was able to breathe through the one thought that refused to leave his mind. If they lost the baby, he'd lose her. She'd never forgive him for not protecting her and their child.

"Right in here." The nurse slid the glass door open.

Rory stepped into the room and pushed the curtain aside. Sadie sat up in the bed in front of him, an IV line running into her arm. She didn't smile, just stared at him, tears gathering in her eyes and spilling down her cheeks. The sadness he saw in her wrenched his gut, sucked the breath right out of him, and stopped his heart.

"No," he whispered, shaking his head, not wanting to believe that he'd lost everything.

The anguish and despair that flooded his eyes and filled his whole face broke Sadie's heart. Tears glistened in his eyes. She'd been so happy to see him, but still so overwhelmed at all that happened. "Honey, no, I'm fine. The baby is fine."

The relief that swept over him and rocked his big body told her how much he wanted this baby. Their baby.

He pressed his hand to his forehead above his eye and sighed so heavily she felt it all the way across the room.

"The baby is fine," Bell assured him.

Rory startled like he hadn't even seen Bell standing by the counters, writing in her chart.

Sadie held out her arms. Rory rushed her and hugged her close. He kissed her half a dozen times and held her face, staring into her eyes.

"You're okay? You're sure?"

"I'm fine." She held his wrists, her grip tight. She needed to hold on to him.

"But when I came in, the look in your eyes."

"I'm sorry. I should have told you where my brother was hiding. I should have called the cops immediately. You told me to let him go, but I wanted him to . . ."

"Shh, sweetheart, it's okay. I understand."

The overwhelming guilt swamped her again. She'd put his life in jeopardy. All their lives, and for what, a brother who had little if any regard for her or anyone else.

"If something happened to you . . ." She gripped his wrists tighter.

"Me? You're the one who almost got stabbed."

"You threw yourself in front of my brother when you knew that agent meant to kill him. You saved him for me."

"I knew you couldn't live with yourself if something happened to him."

She placed her palm on his rough jaw. "I can't live without you. Do you hear me? Don't ever do something like that again."

He managed to find a halfhearted smile for her. "I promise."

"Where did you get the handgun you used to shoot Derek?"

"Trigger had it stashed in an ankle holster. You laid yourself out on him, but he reached down to get the gun. He couldn't get to it in time, so I grabbed it and killed that bastard."

She pressed her hand to his face and looked into his eyes. "Are you okay? That can't have been easy."

"I'm not sorry I did it. Caden refused to let me bring my rifles. He wanted to keep me out of it, but I couldn't sit back and let your brother get hurt or let that asshole hurt you again. I'd do it all over just to keep you safe." He pressed his hand to her belly. "Both of you."

Sadie slid her hand around Rory's head and pulled him in for a soft kiss. She held it, letting him feel how much she appreciated everything he'd done and how much she loved him.

"Hey you two, remember me?"

Rory pressed one last kiss to her lips, leaned back, and sat on the edge of the bed. He kept his intense gaze on her but asked Bell, "What's the damage, Doc?"

"Twenty-two stitches in her shoulder. Severe dehydration. She's just about done with that IV line and the vitamin drip we added. You can take her home in an hour. Her blood pressure and heart rate are back to normal. It's still very early in the pregnancy. Stress is not good for hcr. She needs to get some sleep and take it easy the next few days. No strenuous activity. Limit the questions and rehashing of events until she's feeling better."

Tears gathered in Sadie's eyes. He understood them all too well. "I'll take you over to see Connor before we leave. He's out of surgery. He'll be fine. They'll keep him here a few days, then transfer him to the infirmary at the jail."

"I don't want to see him right now."

"Are you sure?"

"I want to go home with you."

"Whatever you want, sweetheart."

She couldn't do it. She couldn't listen to Connor spout off the same crap and lies. It might be too late, but about time she let him suffer the consequences of his actions and live her own life. She had so much to live for and Connor almost took that away from her. Rory saved him. He'd saved her in so many ways He'd shown her a life and happiness she wanted more than anything. He'd shown her love so infinite it filled her up and made her believe dreams really do come true. Now all she had to do was live them.

CHAPTER 30

Sadie sat bolt upright in the dark, gasping. Her heart pounded in her chest so hard her ribs ached. She shook off the nightmare and all thoughts of Rory slamming into her brother as the shot rang out. In the nightmare, the bullet hit him instead of her brother. The thought of losing him sent a chill up her spine.

Rory slid his big arm around her waist, planted his hand on her hip, spreading warmth through her system and calming her down.

"What's wrong, sweetheart?"

She slid her hands over his warm skin and held tight. "Nothing. I'm headed for the bathroom again." The IV and vitamin refill she got at the hospital definitely made her feel better, but it went right through her the last few hours.

Rory brought her home, put her into the shower to wash up, then tucked her into bed. He joined her for both, always touching her softly, sweetly, letting her know he was there. He couldn't seem to let her out of his sight. She appreciated the attention, but worried about him, too. He'd gone quiet on her again. She hoped shooting Derek didn't leave a permanent mark on him.

She understood it disturbed him, but hoped he'd find a way to live with it. He'd done it to save her life.

She stared down at him beside her. Golden whiskers darkened his jaw. His hair fell over his forehead in soft waves. She brushed her fingers through it, pushing it off his face. The silky strands glided through her fingers. Rory pressed a kiss to her side, then fell back onto his pillow.

"Hurry up. I want you here with me." He hugged her close, then removed his arm so she could slip from the bed and run into the bathroom.

On her way out, she stared at the big man in the bed, his arm stretched out to her empty spot, his face half buried in the pillow.

So handsome. The man she loved. The man she wanted to spend the rest of her life with. The man who'd nearly dropped to his knees and cried because he thought she'd lost their child. A man who cared deeply for his family, her, their baby.

"I'm so lucky," she whispered to her father in heaven. She missed him and wanted him to know she was okay.

For the first time since she left her shift at the diner, she felt okay. She had Rory.

The thing with Connor weighed on her. Rory tried to get her to go see him in the hospital before they left, but she couldn't bring herself to do it. He'd nearly gotten her and Rory killed. If he wanted to make things right with her, he'd have to come to her. She wasn't going to make things easy for him anymore. Instead, she'd focus on herself, Rory, their baby, and the future she wanted more than anything.

She pressed her hand to her grumbling stomach and bypassed the bed and headed for the stairs. Bell might have filled her up with fluids, but Sadie needed something to fill her belly. She padded down the stairs and walked into the dim kitchen. With the lights out, she opened the fridge and pulled one of the apples out of the vegetable bin. She closed the fridge and set the apple on the cutting board and sliced it up. She took a bite of the crisp, sweet fruit and chewed thoughtfully, wondering what else she could have with it. She opened one cupboard after the next, looking for anything that sounded good. She found the peanut butter and pulled it down, knocking over a can of peas. It thumped on the counter, rolled off, and thwacked the floor. She bent over to pick it up, stood straight, and caught herself on the counter when the dizziness hit again. Afraid she'd pass out and hit the floor, she quickly sat, leaned back against the cabinet, and put her head down, waiting for her stomach to settle and her head to stop spinning.

The lights flicked on and Grandpa Sammy stood in the doorway staring down at her, sitting on the floor in her nightgown. "Are you all right?" He rushed to her side and squatted next to her, his big hand on her shoulder.

She blinked away the spots in her eyes from the bright light. "Sorry I woke you. I seem to be a bit off balance."

Grandpa Sammy narrowed his eyes on her, stood, went back to the kitchen doorway, and yelled, "Rory, get down here."

"I'm fine. You don't need to wake him, too." Sadie pressed her hands to the floor to push herself up.

Grandpa Sammy pointed a finger at her. "You stay put."

She sank back to her butt and stared up at him and the anger simmering in his eyes.

"Um, I'm really okay."

Rory pounded down the stairs and rushed into the kitchen, wearing nothing but his jeans, zipped and barely hanging on to his hips. He spotted her on the floor and pushed past his grandfather. He knelt beside her and brushed his hand over her hair. "Sweetheart, what happened? Are you okay?"

"She's pregnant, isn't she?"

Rory's eyes went wide, then filled with resignation. He kept his back to his grandfather and stared at her. He cupped her face and brushed his thumbs over her cheeks. "Dizzy again?"

"A little bit. I'm hungry."

"Bell said you might be when I got you home and the stress and trauma wore off. I should have fed you before I put you to bed."

"It's okay. I came down to make a snack."

Rory tucked his hands under her arms and lifted her up and right off the floor. He set her on the counter and handed her a slice of apple. "Eat."

She took the apple and bit off a huge bite.

"I want an answer," Grandpa Sammy demanded.

Rory sighed and spun around to face his grandfather. "Yes, she's pregnant."

"Holy shit," Colt said, stepping into the room behind Grandpa Sammy.

Ford followed with an "Oh my God."

Sadie wasn't sure any of them was happy for them, or upset by the news. She grabbed a spoon from the strainer by the sink and dipped it into the peanut butter, stuffing it in her mouth and licking off the creamy peanut goodness. She'd let them work it out. She was too tired and hungry to participate.

"We talked about this. I told you to make sure you did things right," Grandpa Sammy scolded.

"I'm pretty sure he did it right," Colt said, a silly grin on his face. "She's pregnant."

Sadie covered the laugh that bubbled up from her gut and licked peanut butter off the spoon again, hiding the smile on her lips. Rory glared at her over his shoulder.

"What? That was funny."

"None of this is funny," Grandpa Sammy said. "You were supposed to act responsibly. Do right by her."

"I was responsible."

"He definitely did it right," Colt added.

Ford smacked Colt in the shoulder.

Grandpa Sammy's face darkened with anger. "It's your responsibility to take care of her."

Rory squared off with his grandfather. "I did take care of her. I planned to take things slow, do things in the right order. What I didn't plan for was the condom to break. It was an accident. I didn't mean for it to happen, but it did, and now we're expecting a baby we both want and can't wait to meet."

Grandpa Sammy glanced past Rory at her.

She pulled the spoon from her mouth, leaving a huge lump of peanut butter behind. She spoke around it, pointing the spoon at Rory. "What he said."

Grandpa Sammy pointed a finger at Rory. "You better do right by her."

"Are you kidding me right now? Do right by her. Of course I'll take care of her. I nearly lost her and my child today. I killed someone to protect them. Not just to save them, but to save myself. I can't live a second without her. She is everything to me. I love her. I'm going to marry her." Rory went to the cupboard, pulled down the mug he'd made for his mother in grade school, and dumped out the black velvet box. He held it up to his grandfather. "I bought her a ring days ago, but I need more time. I need to know she loves me, not because of the baby, but because it's how she truly feels. I need time to convince her to marry me and make a life with me and our child here on the ranch."

"Yes." She didn't have to think, she just blurted it out. She sat there watching Rory lose himself in defending his actions and what happened to his grandfather and completely forget she was sitting right behind him. The stress and trauma they'd been through these last weeks and especially today weighed on him. He wanted everything to be perfect, to go the right way, to be everything she deserved and he wanted for her.

That was all well and good, but all she needed to know, all she needed to hear, was the plain and simple truth. He loved her. That was all she needed.

Ford and Colt gasped, staring at her. Grandpa Sammy smiled like he'd won the lottery. Rory spun around, his eyes wide when he realized he'd forgotten about her, lost in the moment.

"Why do we need more time? Either you love me or you don't. Either you want me or you don't. If I do and you do and you want it and I want it, then why can't we have it? Why can't we just make it be? I'm tired of waiting for everything I want in my life."

She looked him right in the eye and gave him everything he needed and deserved. "Yes. Yes, I love you. With everything I am, every breath I take, every beat of my heart, I love you. I have wanted to tell you that for so long, but held it back because of one stupid thing or another, but I can't do it anymore. I won't do it anymore. I loved you before we made this baby. I will love you every day for the rest of my life.

"I look at you and see only one thing. You're my everything. You're the one I want to be with always.

"So yes, I will marry you. I will be the best mother I can be to our child, but more than anything, I want to be your wife."

"You do? Just like that?"

"Why not? I fell in love with you just like that."

Rory slid his hand around her neck and drew her in for a soft kiss. He pressed his forehead to hers and gazed into her eyes. "I love you more than I can possibly say."

"I know."

He stepped back, flipped open the lid on the velvet box, and pulled out the diamond engagement ring. He held the ring up for her to see. Two pear-shaped diamonds sparkled in the light, their round sides touching in the center, the points out to the sides. Beautiful. Unique. Perfect.

She held Rory's intense gaze.

"I can't live a single second without you by my side." He glanced at the two-stone ring, then back at her. "You and me?"

"You and me."

He slid the ring on her finger. Tears spilled down her cheeks, but she smiled so big her face ached. He kissed her softly, wiping away her happy tears. He leaned back and repeated, "You and me."

Rory picked up the sliced apples and stuffed them inside the peanut butter jar. He handed it to her and picked her up right off the countertop. She locked her legs around his waist and wrapped her arms around his shoulders and held on. He spun around and walked straight past his brothers and grandfather.

"Night, sis," Colt called.

"See you in the morning, pretty girl," Grandpa Sammy added.

"We're going to be uncles," Ford said, making all the men laugh. The joy she heard in their voices made her smile.

"Uh, Rory, what are you doing?"

"Taking my fiancée to bed."

"Okay."

"I hope you're this easygoing for the next sixty years."

"We'll see."

Rory slammed the door to their room, walked to the bed, laid her out on top of the already rumpled sheets, and leaned down and kissed her softly. "Yes, we will."

EPILOGUE

Sadie stood in the living room of her old house and stared at the transformation. A coat of paint, new carpet, the old wood furniture polished and rearranged, a brand-new dark brown leather sofa to set off the neutral cream walls. She'd finally finished working her way through the house, cleaning out the clutter, discarding what needed to be trashed, moving the things she wanted to keep to Rory's, now their, house. She'd removed all the personal items and redone the bedrooms and living spaces with only the best pieces of furniture and decorations to make the place feel spacious, but still lived in. Comfortable.

She walked down the hall and stopped outside Connor's old room. It stood empty. The walls had been patched and painted the same cream as the rest of the house. Rory had repaired the door and the cracked window. All of Connor's furniture needed to be tossed, too damaged, dinged, or destroyed by his many tirades. His personal items she'd packed into boxes and stored in the garage, including the picture album she'd found filled with photos of him and her as kids with their mom and dad. She kept several of the pictures of her alone with her mother and father to go with the photo she kept in her and Rory's room of her with Connor on the steps when they were young and she'd held on to him. It hurt to let him go. She hoped to one day mend that relationship, but right now, she needed to find her way with Rory and their baby to the life she'd always wanted.

Luna walked out of what used to be Sadie's bedroom. The pretty navy and white quilt lay over her bed. Oversize antique keys hung on the walls on opposite sides of the bed above her old nightstands they'd repainted white to match the dresser. "Hey, you ready to go?"

They'd spent several hours putting the finishing touches on the house and organizing the kitchen. "All set."

They walked down the hall to the kitchen to grab her purse off the counter. Luna stood between the kitchen and living space, looking around like she hadn't just spent the last few hours rearranging things so they were just so.

"I wish I had the money to rent this place from you. Whoever gets it is very lucky. It turned out great."

"Thanks for all your help. You've got a great eye for knowing what's worth keeping and how to set it up so it's functional and pleasing to the eye."

"Whatever family rents it, they'll love it."

"It's not for a family. It's for Ford."

"Really? You never said he wanted to move out of the Kendrick place."

"He doesn't know about this yet. Rory and I want to

surprise him later. We think he'd like his own place, his own ranch."

"It's the perfect setup. I assume you'd earn part of the profits from the ranch since it's your land now."

Sadie nodded. "Plus I'd like to put a little something away for Connor."

"For when he gets released?"

"Money for a fresh start—if he wants one." Sadie glanced around the house again. It didn't feel like home anymore. That had been the point of making the changes. A fresh start for Ford—and her. "Do you think I'm crazy to hope that Connor will be different, even better when he comes out of jail?"

Luna hugged her close. "No. I think you're sweet and kind and generous. I think if he wants even half of what you want for him, he'll have a good life." Luna leaned back and stared her in the eye. "Ready to go?"

They were supposed to go to town and catch a movie. After four days home with Rory after the whole DEA drug raid and him hovering, she needed a night out with her best friend.

"Let's go."

"Are you sad to leave this place?"

She thought of Rory and the life they were just beginning but that felt so right and comfortable and so full at the Kendrick ranch. "I'll carry my memories with me, because that's all that's left here. I'm ready to go. I want to be with Rory and start a new life with him."

"He adores you. The kiss he laid on you before we came over here, man, you'd have thought I was taking you away from him forever."

Sadie smiled. "After all we've been through, he wants to hold on. He loves me."

"We need to stop by there before we go to town. I left my purse in their kitchen."

"Oh, uh, okay. I can pay for the move and dinner and bring you your purse tomorrow."

"I kind of need it. It won't take long."

They walked out and locked up the house. Sadie went down the new porch steps Rory put in yesterday. She turned back and smiled at the pretty bushes and flowers she'd planted along the porch.

"It's a really great house."

Luna draped her arm over Sadie's shoulders and stared back at the freshly painted house with her. "Yes it is. Sure you wouldn't rather live here with Rory?"

"No. His place is the home he's worked his whole life to hold on to. Mine is with him."

"Fair enough. Let's go."

They chatted about school, diner gossip, and Sadie's plans to reveal her surprise to Ford. They pulled into the driveway behind several cars and trucks she didn't recognize, except for Dane's.

"What is going on here?" Sadie glanced at Luna, who valiantly held back a smile. "Luna, what is going on?"

"Just come with me."

"Who's here?"

"You'll see. No more questions, just come on."

They hopped out of Luna's Jeep and walked through all the cars and trucks to the front porch. Luna led her inside, through the house, and out to the open back door. Luna whistled to get everyone's attention. The crowd gathered on the back patio turned as Sadie stood in the doorway, staring out at everyone, the pretty lights strung over the patio, casting a soft glow as the sun set, the barbecues lined up along the back, the picnic tables set with pitchers of wildflowers, lemonade, beer, and champagne among the pretty white and yellow dishes. A huge sign hung at the back of the patio. The crowd was filled with familiar faces from the diner, the entire Bowden family, including Rory's buddies Gabe, Blake, and Dane with their wives and children. Everyone yelled what the sign said, "Congratulations!"

Sadie pressed her hand over her racing heart. Rory stood with Dane and Bell, Kaley sitting on his arm against his chest, her arm hooked around his neck. He spotted Sadie and handed Kaley off to Bell and made his way through the crowd and up the steps to take her hand and pull her close. "Surprised?"

"Rory, honey, what is this?"

"Our engagement party."

"You did all of this for me?"

"I had some help." Rory tipped his glass of beer in the direction of his brothers and grandfather, and Luna standing as far away on the opposite side as Colt.

Luna rushed forward with a glass of champagne for her.

"Um . . ." Sadie didn't take it. She opened her mouth to say something but closed it, not knowing if she should say anything about the baby in front of all their friends.

Colt moved in, holding out a glass of lemonade.

Luna narrowed her gaze on Colt. "A celebration calls for champagne."

"She can't have that," Colt whispered, handing Sadie the glass of lemonade and withdrawing back to Ford and Grandpa Sammy.

Luna's eyes swept over her and landed on Sadie's belly. Sadie stared up at Rory. He smiled like a lunatic.

"Oh my God, you're pregnant." Luna slapped her hand over her mouth after blurting that out. A hush went over the crowd. Everyone stared at her, waiting for her to confirm Luna's words.

Rory took over. "Thank you everyone for coming tonight to celebrate this very special occasion. Yes, Sadie and I are getting married. That's reason enough to celebrate. I mean, she said yes. To me." That earned a laugh from everyone. "That alone made me the happiest man alive." He bent and kissed her softly, then pulled back, smiling like she'd never seen. So bright. So open. So filled with love. "So you can imagine how I felt when we found out we were expecting a baby, too. I mean, a guy like me doesn't get that lucky. But with a woman like Sadie in my life, man, I've got happiness, the blessing of a child on the way, a long and happy life to look forward to, and love like I never thought possible." Rory stared her in the eye. "I love you so much." He kissed her again, and they lost themselves in the moment.

Everyone cheered and sipped their drinks. Luna mouthed a silent apology for outing her about the baby. Sadie only smiled. After all Rory said to her, she didn't care that everyone found out about the baby before she had a chance to announce it herself. After all, these were their friends, the people who shared their lives and were the happiest for them.

Rory hugged her close and she whispered in his ear, "Thank you for this. I love you."

"You and the baby are the best part of my life. I

wanted everyone to know and see how happy you make me. How happy we are together."

Before the barbecue got under way and she greeted all their guests, Grandpa Sammy stepped forward, held up his glass, and toasted them. "Welcome to the family, pretty girl. Welcome home."

**Need more of bestselling author
Jennifer Ryan's Montana Men?
Get ready for the next thrilling installment
in her acclaimed series!**

Colt Kendrick knows one thing about a small town, you can't avoid anyone for long—especially a girl he crossed the line with and who just happens to be best friends with his brother's fiancée. Luna could have been the one if he hadn't done her wrong. Now, Colt's intentions are nothing but honorable, but his thoughts about Luna sure aren't. Can he convince the one who got away that he wants her forever?

Luna Hill thought she lost her shot with the sexy cowboy, but with one scorching kiss, she's convinced that lightning just may strike twice. When she's offered the opportunity of a lifetime, but one that could have terrible consequences, Luna must decide what her heart desires most.

Colt will do anything to keep Luna safe, including put his life on the line, because nothing is more important than the woman who showed Colt he has a heart—and it belongs to her.

Coming October 2016

REL 0316

At Avon Books, we know your passion for romance—once you finish one of our novels, you find yourself wanting more.

May we tempt you with . . .

- **Excerpts** from our upcoming releases.

- Entertaining **extras**, including authors' personal photo albums and book lists.

- Behind-the-scenes **scoop** on your favorite characters and series.

- **Sweepstakes** for the chance to win free books, romantic getaways, and other fun prizes.

- Writing **tips** from our authors and editors.

- **Blog** with our authors and find out why they love to write romance.

- **Exclusive content** that's not contained within the pages of our novels.

Join us at
www.avonbooks.com

AVON

An Imprint of HarperCollins*Publishers*
www.avonromance.com

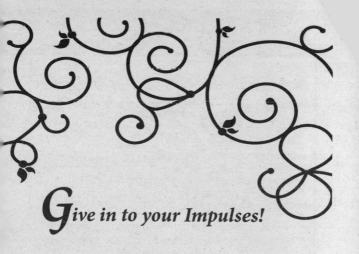